Everything Will Swallow You

ALSO AVAILABLE BY TOM COX

Fiction
1983
Villager
Help the Witch

Non-fiction
Notebook
Ring the Hill
21st-Century Yokel
Close Encounters of the Furred Kind
The Good, the Bad and the Furry
Talk to the Tail
Under the Paw
Bring Me the Head of Sergio Garcia
Nice Jumper

Everything Will Swallow You

Tom Cox

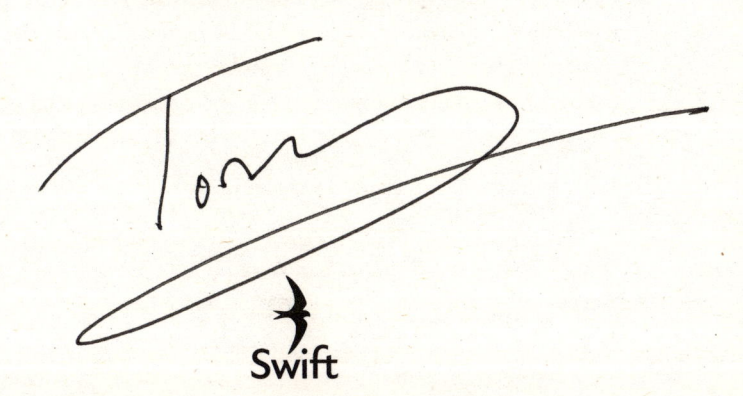

[signature: Tom]

Swift

SWIFT PRESS

First published in Great Britain by Swift Press 2025

1 3 5 7 9 8 6 4 2

All rights reserved

Copyright © Tom Cox, 2025
Chapter illustrations © Jo Cox, 2025

Text Design by Jouve (UK), Milton Keynes

The right of Tom Cox to be identified as the Author of this Work has been asserted in accordance with the Copyright, Designs and Patents Act 1988.

Printed and bound in Great Britain by CPI Group (UK) Ltd, Croydon CR0 4YY

A CIP catalogue record for this book is available from the British Library

We make every effort to make sure our products are safe for the purpose for which they are intended. Our authorised representative in the EU for product safety is Easy Access System Europe, Mustamäe tee 50, 10621 Tallinn, Estonia gpsr.requests@easproject.com

ISBN: 9781800755918
eISBN: 9781800755925

For Ellie

With special thanks to Alasdair Cross, Amanda Peters and Dave & Jan Thomas

The Reason Your Shampoo Wants You to Use More Shampoo is Because That Means You Will Buy More of Your Shampoo

The deer had been kicking the shit out of the hedgerows again. You could see their trail of destruction, curiously evenly spaced, all along the high ridge. 'Bambi and the vegan diet are a clever bluff where deer are concerned,' thought Eric. 'They lull everyone into thinking they're delicate peacenik flower children when in truth they're punk anarchist mystics.' This lot, here in west Dorset, would nut down fence-posts as if it were booting-out time on Friday night and the fence-posts had just called their sister a slag, sail through barbed wire like it was the mesh curtain over their gran's back door and trash your delphiniums, never once pausing to tot up their fucks along the way. Over in the big field where the farmer particularly didn't want them to go and a triangle of spidery dying elms looked like the marker posts of some oncoming dark ritual, they'd pop up from their hiding places in the cabbage in threes, gallop silently away, then freeze and stare back with a synchronicity that appeared choreographed.

'They're checking you out, pal,' Eric told Carl. 'Fellow oracles. Intimidated by your power.'

'I was thinking we could try that new Indian in Axminster tonight,' said Carl. 'I fancy a break from cooking. I think I'm leaning towards a dhansak.'

'Iggy Pop has deer energy, I reckon. Like one of those whatdcharmacall them, the little ones. Muntjac. The way he used to run around the stage. Or maybe he's more like a bantam rooster, darting up to everyone with his chest puffed out, always legging it about in those little circles. Did I tell you about the one my neighbours had when I lived in Wales? Right little hooligan, he was. There was no hedge between the gardens so he'd be around a lot. The prick would come at me, claws flying all over the shop, every time I turned away from him. I'd be always walking about with all these cuts on the back of my legs.'

'Dhansak is a curious one. The takeaways never seem to come to an agreement on the spice level. I've had some with quite a kick to them – nothing that I couldn't handle, obviously, but the kind that would have someone of your inferior constitution blowing your nose every six seconds – but I've had some pitifully weedy ones, too. I see Iggy more as a centaur, myself. The bare chest and that feeling you get that he might have a couple of possible extra legs that he could whip out in moments of crisis. Hold on. Did you hear that? Over there. Was that a dog? It sounded a lot like a dog.'

The day, bracingly cold, chasing away weeks of pissant winds and concerningly lukewarm rain blasts, was one of those where a sun halfway up the sky will hold the landscape frozen in perfection for a number of hours, offering a bittersweet illusion of permanence. Dorset was a painting, balanced in the admiring hands of Horus. Where the busy little rivers had leaked, the ice, splintered by bootsteps, resembled the kind of glass you might find on the floor of an abandoned pub, but under the vandalised hedgerows it remained shadowed and solid. Soon it would begin to spread again and the Marshwood Vale would be drained of comfort, burping and groaning with the part-explicable sounds of the greedy January night. The transition was something Carl could already sniff on the ground directly in front of his nose. Looking at his only timepiece, which was now falling fast over the cliffs three miles to the south, it struck him that, as usual, they were going to be late. Eric had agreed to call at the Meat Tree's house – which was around half an hour's drive from where Eric had parked the van – to pick up the keys to the manor at five. The Meat Tree had emphasised that he had to go out by six at the absolute latest. It was now at least a quarter past four, and where was the van parked? Two miles away? More?

'Here,' Carl thought, 'is one of the drawbacks of going out on walks with a collector.' The impulse that made Eric feel the need to own nineteen Linda Ronstadt albums, including several from after the mid-seventies, when she began to go off the boil, was that same one which, half an hour before, had made him insist on following a footpath purely because it was one of the dwindling number in the Vale that he and Carl had not previously ticked off their list. It certainly could not be described as a *bad* footpath. Whether it was a *necessary* footpath, however, was highly debatable. And now here they were, a mile on from its source, ducking away from a potential Border Collie Situation through a hole in the hedge made by insurrectionary deer, onto an unmarked path beneath the steep brim of an Iron Age hill fort, in the direction of who knew what.

'I've got a lot of trust in deer, me,' said Eric. 'What you've got to remember is that every place you walk, every one of these routes that some guy in an office decided to stick a sign on saying 'Bridleway' or 'Public Footpath', was originally made by deer, long ago. They know where they're going and they know the best way to get there.'

'I do completely see that,' said Carl. 'But at the same time we have no way of knowing where the particular pre-Christian deer who originally made this path *were* going. My guess is that it probably wasn't a Victorian terrace on the outskirts of Sidmouth owned by a book dealer, nor a haphazardly parked van waiting to take them to it.'

'Cheeky fucker. That was some top parking.'

'You left it sticking half out into the lane, looking like a stolen vehicle somebody abandoned before fleeing into dense woodland to evade the police. I'll be impressed if it's even still drivable by the time we get back.'

What would you have thought, if you'd been relaxing in the grass behind a hedge – a dense one, as yet unwrecked by a nihilistic buck or doe – and heard the conversation of Eric and Carl, from their unseen position on the other side of the brown-green divide? Would you have pictured, in your mind's eye, a long-married homosexual couple? Two rivalrous professors of philosophy or zoology out for a stroll: one unlikely, a rough and ready maverick motormouth, the other more housebroken and genteel? A man still assimilating after arriving from the extensive and unknowable lands of the north, and his well-spoken friend from . . . another country, somewhere that you couldn't quite pinpoint? Had there been a space in the bottom of the hedge, and had you spied, through it, two booted feet accompanied by four furry ones, you might have wondered where along the path the missing biped was speaking from, or perhaps just thought, 'Oh, that's sweet: the talkative man and his erudite migrant lover have a pet whippet.' Whatever the case, it is extremely unlikely that you would have correctly guessed what was there, hidden from you by the tightly knotted twigs and branches.

The union of Eric and Carl Inskip was one that would not have been easily anticipated by society but, like any couple who'd been cohabiting for close to two decades, they were not unprone to sarcastic bickering. If somebody had witnessed this bickering – which Eric and Carl took careful measures to ensure almost nobody ever did – they might have observed that, more often than not, it was Eric who played the role of bickeree. The ways in which Eric had infuriated Carl, in the almost nineteen years they had known each other, were so numerous as to be unlistable but, even at his most exasperated – even at the height of his infuriation with Eric's tardiness, his forgetfulness, his sticky-handedness, his repeated failure to close the door while urinating in the downstairs toilet, his general way of progressing through life like a boulder pinballing down a tiered forest chasm – Carl repeatedly found disarmament in Eric's endearing way of never speaking to him as someone outside his realm of being, never as a lesser or something *other*, but in the casual manner that you would speak to a close, trusted long-time friend. In short – and, as he thought this, he suspected that at least one ex-lover might refute it – if you ever happened to be mad at the guy, he somehow made it impossible for you to stay that way for a length of time that would significantly erode your relationship.

As they rounded the base of the hill fort, an abrasive choir of voices could be heard directly below them: a quacking conference, with no space for one authoritative voice to raise above the din and call for order. Through the gaps in the trees could be seen a sloping field where, on a large patch of ice, 200 or more ducks had gathered, apparently for no reason other than to discuss what was most pressingly on their minds.

'Ah, man, I do *not* enjoy that,' said Eric. 'Why are all those ducks there, like that? There's no reason for them to be there. There's not even a pond or river. It's just a field. I'm telling you, pal, I'm not happy about it. That's far too many ducks.'

'I love you,' thought Carl. 'You are a ridiculous human being, and I love you.'

As the path followed the curve of the earthworks, it pitchforked into two fading prongs then died away to lethargic winter-bramble mess and decomposing tree-trunk muddle. Above the two friends, the Iron Age fortification steepened. Did the deer who had originally formed this path – Norman? Roman? – lose heart and decide to throw in the towel at this point? Thinking about the dog, and the falling sun, Carl pressed on, thorns tearing at his flanks, with Eric a few steps behind. Every time he dropped a gear, allowing his companion to catch up, he could hear a small whistling noise coming from Eric's chest: like, but in a slightly different register to, the other small whistling noise he had recently witnessed on car journeys when Eric became visibly troubled by congested traffic or the senseless actions of his fellow drivers. Carl leapt a fallen tree and, seeing no easy way through directly ahead, began to scale the steep prelapsarian wall to his left. For this exercise, being quite sure there was no other human in sight besides Eric, he took his weight off all fours and rose to his full height, which was his preferred state, particularly where severe gradients were concerned.

Behind him, accommodating the change of direction less easily, Eric remonstrated with piked branches and vines.

'Ey, do one, you divvy.'

'Lay off, soft lad, or you'll get what's coming.'

'I paid thirty quid for these here keks, you fuckin' binhead, and I'm not having the likes of you ruining them.'

'Everything ok, back there?' asked Carl.

'Sound, pal. Don't you worry about me.'

Those who know Dorset well – those who, like Eric and Carl, have spent many hours deep within its creases, slits and folds – know it is the most deceptive of the West Country counties. It is the taller-than-average broad-shouldered gentleman you meet and think 'Oh my, look at his freshly cut, neatly parted hair and tailored clothes, he must be enormously civilised – maybe I will accept his invitation to dinner', whose house you then go to, only to find it is a hole in the ground containing half a chair, a corn dolly and the remnants of an old fire. Driving the top roads, eyes directly ahead, you'd never suspect a place like the one Eric and Carl found themselves in right now existed. Unfarmed, uncoppiced, unmanicured, unpollarded, unconserved, unmaintained, it was as toothy as it was halcyon. It was the place foliage came to live its best unfettered off-grid life, unafraid to be a cunt: a dark spunking of undergrowth where trees did their most clandestine bidding and badgers and foxes and rabbits hid from every soul in Christendom who'd ever wished them ill. Eric found the steep barrier of earth that faced them tough going. Knots of old brambles grabbed and tore at him. Unseen tree trunks punched at his shins. He felt that a spirit not far from the surface of where they trod had been awakened and its one mission was to vanquish him. 'Will this be the venue, then? The one where I will finally expire?' he thought, looking up into the latticework of the trees on the rim of the ancient tribal defence point from his position, on his back, on the rapidly crisping damp earth, where he'd been knocked for the third time in as many minutes. 'Here, in soft southern Tory Wessex? I, who have made my bed in the L8 postcode of Liverpool, and behind a tin mine in the Cornish interior, and in the bit of Nottingham people from Nottingham warned you not to live in, and under the frowning brow of a Welsh mountain, and, for four whole months, opposite a bookies in one of the more antagonistic towns in south Derbyshire?

'But – hold your horses, pal – what is this miracle, that is now saving me? Why am I now floating above the ground, free of the tawdry attentions of underbrush and sharp bristles? Is this my final ascent to the Good Place? And what will be the verdict when I am there? What will count against me, when all is added up: how many of my blunders and infractions?'

But it was just Carl, hoisting him from his damp place of despair towards the waiting sky.

They were an hour and three minutes late arriving at the Meat Tree's place, a tall redbrick house, built to last, where barely an inch of interior wall was not covered by fabric, art or bookshelves. This was what the clock on the van's dashboard informed Carl, who, once night had fallen, relied on devices less romantic than the skies for his timekeeping. Fortunately the Meat Tree, having known Eric for over a decade, had made allowance, substituting 'six' for 'seven' when emphasising to Eric his deadline for leaving the building. A few acquaintances of Eric's had distanced themselves from Eric over the years as a result of his apparent antipathy for all notions of punctuality – one even going so far as to arrange an official summit to discuss the problem – but the Meat Tree wasn't one of them. Possibly the central fact to know about Eric was that Eric was Eric and was always going to be Eric and that was just something you had to accept if you wished to regularly continue to spend time in Eric's company. In a more general sense, the Meat Tree was also aware how pointless it was to campaign to alter the core ingrained behavioural habits of any man of sixty-seven, being almost one himself. He opened the door to his friend with a grin and a fraternal pat on the shoulder which, once he saw the state of Eric's trousers and footwear, evolved into a restraining arm.

'You know the rule, Inskip,' said the Meat Tree. 'Shoes off before you come in. Why not give yourself a good old shake while you're at it.'

'For fuck's sake,' said Eric, complying on both fronts. 'I feel like a naughty horse. Why don't you get me to do a little dance while I'm at it? I'm pretty nifty at the Watusi, but it's been a while.'

From the window of the van, with a subtle smile spreading across his face, Carl watched this scenario, which bore sturdy resemblance to one he'd hypothesised on the way here. He enjoyed visiting the Meat Tree's house, loved its maximalist ambience of learning and needlepoint warmth, but, not having the luxury of footwear of his own to remove, had decided to stay put, being worried about shitting up Meat's nice Turkish rugs. He also had a Rosamond Lehmann novel he was keen to get back to, even if that meant clambering over the seats for half a dozen hastily devoured pages in the back of the van.

'That new?' asked a now marginally less-soiled Eric, stepping into the Meat Tree's hallway and pointing to a painting above him at the head of the bare wooden staircase, depicting a lugubrious woman in a hooded black cowl, whose warning eyes appeared to track his every step as he ventured deeper into the building.

'Fairly new,' said the Meat Tree. 'I got it in Bridport, off Salford Ricky.'

'Ricky! Bloody hell. You don't want to get anything from that tottering fiasco. You should have come to see me. I've got a ton of depressing shit like this in the lock-up.'

'Ah, he's not a bad sort, Rick.'

'I've known shadier Mancunians, I will admit. Shite jackets, though. Don't know how he manages to find so many quite that shite. He must go to Shite Jacket Warehouse or something. So who is she, the bird?'

'Well, the title on it says "Welsh Woman" so I'm deducing from that that she may have been a Welsh woman. Mid-seventeen hundreds, I'd guess, from the Palladian frame. There's a signature but it's almost completely faded. Carl not with you today? Tea?'

'He's in the van, sleeping. We did a long walk. I knackered him out. Don't think I've ever seen him panting that much. Nah, pal. You're all right. I won't keep you. I know you've got to leg it. So what's the deal with this place tomorrow?'

'The Meat Tree' was of course not *quite* what it had said on the Meat Tree's birth certificate, in 1957, when it had been presented to his soon-to-emigrate parents in Astakos, Greece. The name derived from a misunderstanding by Eric and Carl's friend Mel, back when Mel and Eric had briefly been a couple. 'Who's Dimitri?' Mel had asked, the first time Eric had referred to his bibliophile acquaintance in a text message to her. 'Are you going mental?' asked Eric, who, while aware of Mel's occasional feathermindedness, was unnerved by this blank spot, since she'd already met Dimitri twice and heard Eric talk about him on dozens of occasions. Later that day, in person, they straightened it out. 'Oh, *DIMITRI*!' said Mel. 'So *that's* what he's called. I always thought you were saying 'the Meat Tree'. I had assumed there was some kind of story behind it but didn't like to ask. If I'm honest, I did think it was a bit weird.' By assuming the story, Mel – in a thoroughly Mel act of Melness – had made the story, become the story. From that point on, to the weary forbearance of the Meat Tree himself, the name had stuck.

In truth, the Meat Tree didn't look much at all like a meat tree. What nobody could think, upon scrutinising him for the first time, was 'Giant Redwood made of ham'. He weighed a little less than a child's go-kart and stood fractionally over five and a half feet high, with wiry grey hair, a neat beard and clean hands with long fingers and smooth fingernails. Ideal fingers for gently examining and evaluating rare books, which was how, for the last couple of decades, since being made redundant from his post at a small municipal library on the Somerset Levels, the Meat Tree had earned a living.

What the Meat Tree and Eric had in common was that their jobs involved picking through the clutter and dust of lives, relieving others of what they had realised they couldn't take with them or what, if those same others were too late in coming to that epiphany, sisters and brothers and children and nephews and nieces and grandchildren did not have the time or inclination to selectively put up for auction. They were the ones who placed it back into circulation, finding a slot for it on the ever-spinning carousel of Lovingly Made Hard-To-Find Old Things That Get Better As They Age. Neither had chosen their profession for its anthropological perks but they enjoyed them almost every day. They heard so many small, intertwining stories, they couldn't help but become storytellers themselves. They hung around along the seams of life, regularly experiencing truths about its shape and weight that most people rarely did. But that was where their similarities ended. While the Meat Tree's specialisation was books, Eric dealt in used records, 'plus a few other bits and bobs' as he would put it, although the 'few other bits and bobs' part had begun to dwindle more recently. The people who bought what the Meat Tree had to offer spoke quietly and with great care, as if wiping every word with a soft cloth before it left their mouth. They complimented one another on their expensive scarves. They circled awkwardly beneath bookshelves in a dance of exemplary manners until finally one of them gave in and reached the shelf first and picked up the exact first edition hardback the other one had been trying to hunt down for years and had travelled here, several hundred miles, specifically to find. 'Are you sure you don't mind?' they asked. 'No, please, really, be my guest,' they said. 'Exquisite endpapers on that,' they said.

Eric's clientele, by contrast, wore politeness like a thin summer cardigan. Upon entering the building and seeing a box marked *Rare cosmic jazz: 1/2 price!*, they relieved themselves of this impractical garment by absentmindedly letting it fall to the floor, where it was soon trampled by shoes discreetly stained with street vomit, piss and last night's spilled ale. The money that many of them might have been better advised to spend on toiletries they splurged on freakbeat 45s and scarce Afrofunk and post-punk test pressings. Any concept of acceptable elbow room that society had taught them became a distant memory, in sight of their prey. Devoid of daintiness, the dance they performed was that of haggling goats. You could almost hear the clack of locked horns as an agreement was reached. When it wasn't, the time lag and physical distance between saying 'Ok, I'll leave it in that case, mate' and mumbling 'Stingy wanker – he'll be lucky to be get half that much for something in that condition' was expertly judged, just as it had been so many times before. A few of them were just casually looking for a bit of recorded music to listen to in its most authentic form, but most were lost in a descending mist, striving to fulfil some atavistic hunter-gatherer need, as urgently and single-mindedly as if the survival of their nearest and dearest depended on it. What they generally discovered when they got out of the mist and back to their front rooms was that they owned some more records to add to some shelves that already contained a large number of records.

The beauty of Eric and the Meat Tree existing in independent universes within the same universe was that they could help one another out every now and again with no peril of treading on one another's toes, no danger of crossing the streams from their proton packs while rounding up their ghosts. Eric read books but felt scant physical attachment to them. When he'd finished them – and, no less frequently, when he hadn't – he left them, usually much stickier and more dog-eared than when he'd found them, in friends' bathrooms, hotel rooms, on trains, buses, benches, on walls above blacktop estuary footpaths. The Meat Tree was a person only lightly shaped by the musical revolutions he'd lived through, not tied to any genre or era, a marginally more than passive consumer of other people's recommended noise, which is to say he had a Spotify account he sometimes remembered to use, a couple of Beatles LPs and a copy of Simon & Garfunkel's *Bookends* in the loft and just about knew who PJ

Harvey was – mainly because, nine years ago, she'd ventured into the Meat Tree's short-lived physical book shop in Lyme Regis and purchased a hardback about pagan iconography in the churches of Wessex.

The key that the Meat Tree now placed into Eric's hand, entrusting him with its safekeeping, would tomorrow open the door to a building more than three times the size of any that either man had ever resided in: an eighteenth-century manor house containing one of the most flabbergastingly excessive book collections in southern England. The Meat Tree had already done his work in Batbridge Manor, over the course of three intense and exhausting visits, separating what he would offer the family of Batbridge's late owner a non-insulting fee for from what would soon be removed by a less-highly-regarded book dealer and a house clearance company. During the course of his investigations, he had lifted a stray horsehair blanket and spotted two split cardboard boxes, both half-filled with long-playing vinyl.

'Of course, I can't vouch for its condition,' he told Eric. 'The place is riddled with damp and probably hosts at least three warring colonies of rats. And what's in there might just be worthless crap. But maybe there's some more that I missed. And you *really* need to see this place – as an experience alone it's worth the price of the petrol. I swear to you that it's not quite of this planet. Whatever the case, it's probably worth a look.' It was *always* worth a look. That was more than an attitude or piece of advice. For Eric, it was a philosophy to live by. What kind of purveyor of vintage items would he be without it? Probably the kind who no longer purveyed vintage items at all but was living a far less varied and interesting sixty-something life after retiring from a significantly more beige job.

Carl, now back in the passenger seat after finding himself regretfully unable to focus on Rosamond Lehmann's 1932 novel *Invitation to the Waltz*, watched his best friend emerge from the

Meat Tree's front garden under the glow of a street light, neglect to reclose the gate, then cross the road back towards the van, a spring in his half-limping step. Between his index finger and thumb he held a piece of knotted string attached to a dark brown metal key of comically large dimensions which he dangled theatrically at Carl in the manner of a man who, thanks to his conversational swagger and influence, had secured the use of the honeymoon suite of an exclusive medieval castle hotel for the weekend. 'Ok good,' thought Carl, 'it looks as if he isn't going to die just yet.'

Ninety minutes earlier, scaling the hard-packed former defence pinnacle of the Durotriges tribe, feeling 76 kilograms of wheezing, thorn-damaged record dealer on his back, he had felt less confident about that.

'Can you just give me a minute or two, pal?' Eric had croaked in a stale scrap of his normal voice, when Carl, having negotiated the worst the hill had to offer, had deposited him on a ledge just under the summit's shaggy, overhanging rim. Returning to all fours for the final part of the ascent – though it was dusk on a weekday, there was no guarantee that fellow walkers would not be milling around the summit of the hill fort – Carl had sought out a soft spongy patch of grass to stretch out on while he waited, with a good view of the last of the sun dropping over the distant cliffs, and, feeling the cooling grass under his tail and hands, permitted himself to indulge in a brief analysis of the destination he and Eric had reached in life.

It *does* feel like a destination, he had thought. And not a bad one, at that. Just over the last green shoulder on the left, less than four miles distant, in the narrow cleft of a salt-blasted valley, could be found the cottage they shared: an overstuffed, rented cottage, certainly, but an attractive rented cottage, significantly more idyllic than the majority of places they'd lived together in the past, with a spacious garden, and where they felt reasonably confident in being permitted to stay – and being able to afford to stay – for the foreseeable future. After a little wobble during the nadir of the pandemic, Eric's business had bounced back to rude health, and beyond. No doubt aided by the sea air, Carl's coat had never looked in better condition. Clients Eric talked to about the gigs he'd been to in his youth often closed one uncomprehending eye when he cited dates, having mistaken him for a man a decade younger than he was, partly due to his skin and posture but also due to his uncontainable entrepreneurial energy, which Carl had never seen him spark and fizz with more of. Any restrictions regarding their diet were imposed by health concerns, not financial ones. Their domestic environment – although never quite as clean and tidy as Carl would have preferred it to be – was quietly earthy and stylish, filled with the chairs and tables and cookware Carl (and, to a more distracted, less aesthetically particular extent, Eric) wanted, rather than cheaper stand-in versions of it. They owned six charismatic chickens, none of which attacked their legs when their backs were turned. Their local swimming pool, though a bit chilly for ten months of the year, was pleasingly uncramped, measuring a total of 139 million square miles, and, with a little light trespassing, could be reached on foot in less than eleven minutes. Their life was dominated by Eric's work but left Carl ample time to follow his passions: needlecraft, reading, Dolly Parton, husbandry, obscure historical facts, snorkelling. They went on holiday, sometimes, but – since there was so little to escape from – didn't especially feel the need to.

'Have I cursed us, in a moment of absentmindedness?' Carl had asked himself, as he stretched out on that rapidly cooling grass. Did I break the golden rule of never saying 'Things are going really well right now!' because it's always when you say 'Things are going really well right now!' that everything bursts into a giant rolling ball of fire, or at least begins to splinter and crack? If so, at which point must it have been that I let my guard down? Six, seven weeks ago? That was when he'd first noticed the noise: the one that leaked from Eric's body in the front of the van when he was dealing with anything even marginally stressful in front of him on the road, the one that Carl tried not to worry about but instinctively wanted to reach over and repair, like a plumber poised with a putty knife in front of a damaged pipe. Then there'd been the forgetting of things that had never previously been forgotten: names of oft-visited places and favourite records and songs and even bands. A map incorrectly read. The year of a record's pressing, in perhaps the most shockingly uncharacteristic error of all, incorrectly identified. Just little incidents, but enough of them for Carl to take notice. And then a moment of larger significance. From his bedroom window Carl had seen an old man in their garden, with an old man's late autumn posture, taking two packages from the postman at the gate, then dropping the packages, then bending to pick the packages up, failing, then having another go, then, finally, on the third attempt, finding success. 'Who is that old man, stealing our mail?' Carl had thought, before releasing that he was looking at his housemate: looking at him from an angle he'd never looked at him from before; not his usual Carl angle, but perhaps the angle from which others now saw Eric. And then just a few minutes ago, in that wild place below him, this vulnerability that might have been predominantly comic, even a year ago, but which now, bewilderingly, unbalancingly, wasn't.

There was a lot Carl knew about himself and a lot he didn't know. In fact, Carl sometimes wondered if there was any other creature on the whole planet who simultaneously knew so gargantuanly much and little about themselves as Carl knew about Carl. Carl knew that Carl was fundamentally kind and had never intentionally done anything to hurt another living being. Carl knew that Carl had an immense tolerance for spicy food, more immense probably than that of any human, even more immense than Eric's friend Reg Monk who, it was said, had once eaten all of the hottest curry in the spiciest restaurant in Newcastle upon Tyne – a curry so hot that the manager's official policy was that he'd waive the bill on it if anybody was superhuman enough to eat all of it – then ordered it again, polished off every last morsel, then had gone home and stunk his house up so much that his wife Jill had moved into her sister's place for the following four days, taking the kids with her. Carl knew that Carl possessed a capacity to be a more sociable being than he was, and that a whole other strand of happiness would spread from the fulfilment of that capacity, but that circumstances rendered it almost completely unexplorable, and that was fine, because in the grand scheme of life, things could be much worse, and indeed had been. Carl knew that Carl was more intelligent than Eric but knew that did not make him better or more important than Eric. Carl, though deeply in love with Wikipedia, also knew some of the minus points of living in an age where something like Wikipedia existed. Carl knew that Carl was sensitive and that life would be less painful if he wasn't so sensitive but also that he didn't want to be less sensitive, no way, not in a million trillion years, not for all the spicy food in Thailand. Carl knew that he would like to stand proud and upright in public and walk around on his two stronger back legs and converse with more people than just Eric and his friend Mel and knew that his self-esteem would be greater if he did and knew all the problems this would cause and why it was utterly prohibited by Eric, and by himself. But Carl didn't know where and when or to whom he'd been born. Carl didn't know why he was covered from head to toe in fur or why he had a tail or why he had four hands – exceptionally clever, dexterous hands, each equipped with two opposable thumbs – or why those hands had a total of twenty-four fingers and why they were hidden in the folds of what looked like fluffy paws. Carl didn't know what the official name was for what he was, or if there was one. Carl didn't know why he was here, right now, only that it was right, or as right as anything ever could be, in this big cosmic accident people called 'the galaxy', with its knock-on effect, 'consciousness'.

But within the enigma that Carl was to Carl, there were narrow triangles of knowing: they came to him in slivers of phosphorescent light, in a language his brain didn't speak, but – because that brain was a sophisticated and empathetic one – could roughly translate into noises splashed and rutted with meaning. The triangles frightened him on occasion, especially as he wasn't totally sure whether they were in his head or in the world or both. Some of them contained images he knew he'd already seen, without knowing where or when. These images made him feel like time didn't exist, which also unnerved him, because he loved time; loved the way it shaped the landscape, loved the way the sun abided by it, loved what it did to faces and to music and to objects crafted with passion and honesty by hands.

The triangles had slowly become larger and more frequent in recent years. And something about that frequency gave him another knowing that he felt physically, coursing innately through him, felt in his face and legs and arms and tail and torso and eyes and all eight of his thumbs: the knowing that he was not destined to be here very long. But he didn't talk about that or worry about it. It grounded him, in fact, framed his relationship with Eric. It allowed him to find an extra solace, every day, as he observed Eric. The solace that Eric would always be completely Eric – both right now and after Carl was no longer around. It was a given: one of the facts of life. This new, potentially diminished, more vulnerable Eric – furthermore, this new, potentially diminished, more vulnerable Eric in some not too distant future, without Carl there to look out for him – was not part of the plan. Carl had never expected it, pictured it, or allowed for it, and it knocked him sideways. It was a cold thought, colder than the ground he was stretched out on had become since being deserted by the day's strong, pragmatic sun.

But now they had a vegetable dhansak, a chicken jalfrezi, four onion bhajis and two portions of pilau rice and everything was going to be ok.

On the track leading down to the cottage, the puddles were zipping themselves back into their translucent sleeping bags in preparation for another cold clear night. Eric edged the van carefully down the track leading to the cottage, the aroma of the double-bagged food, cooling in the footwell beneath Carl, a song whose temptress of a chorus seemed to beg, 'Touch that accelerator a little bit harder, big boy.' Had they arrived here any later they'd probably have had to leave the van at the top of the hill, near the main road, due to the ice, and stagger down on foot: a zigzagging gravelly stumble of well over a mile in the dark. Not far inland, houses spilled down hillsides like dice shaken from a velvet bag and formed villages and hamlets, but here, in the space between the main arterial road and the sea, which was much bigger than it appeared from that road, the buildings were arranged misanthropically. There had been a community in this spot, with its own chapel, but not for more than 200 years. The chapel was now missing a couple of walls and attracted mostly four-legged worshippers: rabbits, stoned-looking cattle and sometimes – when he needed a quiet place to read, away from the late 1960s proto heavy metal albums Eric liked to play – Carl. Six hundred yards up the hill, at diagonal points north of the cottage, situated more or less the same distance away from each other, were three farms: one vacant and for sale at a price deemed by Eric to be 'a colossal piss-take', another owned by Dan and Anne Fentonbrook, a well-spoken couple from the South East who were still perceived as fresh-faced incomers to the area (they'd moved here twenty-five years ago, in 1998) and a third occupied by a Dorset native called Russell Loosemore, now well into his eighties, who, if you talked to him for long enough, and he hadn't told you before, and probably also if he had, would recall the time when the old World War II radar station at the top of the hill tumbled down the hill in a landslip.

'I'm fucking starving,' said Eric when they'd parked. 'I think my hair is looking better today. Don't you?'

'It's hard to pass judgement, considering that we're stood in almost complete darkness right now,' said Carl.

'I've been using that shampoo, the one I got from that place where all the staff won't leave you alone. It says on the tub hat I should grab a generous amount and that I'll see the best results if I wash daily.'

'Natural oils are important, though. I suspect the reason your shampoo wants you to use more shampoo is because that means you will buy more of your shampoo.'

'Did you leave the living-room light on?'

'No. I'm guessing that will be Mel. She probably parked around the back.'

'Oh! Should we have got her some food? I feel bad now.'

'She'll probably have already cooked for herself. You know what she's like. There'll be nothing but some chilli flakes and half a packet of Maltesers in the kitchen and somehow she'll turn it into the best risotto you've ever eaten.'

Carl, who had sampled Mel's cooking on several occasions and found it too bland for his tastes, tactfully refrained from comment. 'Hi, Mel!' he said cheerfully, rising onto his back legs as he opened the kitchen door and planting a kiss on Mel's cheek that, though delicately administered, was all nose and tongue. 'We've been to get a takeaway. We only got two portions but Eric says he's not feeling very hungry, so he's happy to give you about three quarters of his.'

'Oh don't worry about me,' said Mel, who stood above the sink, holding a glass of red wine in one hand and in the other a scrubbing pad, with which she was non-committally removing some streaks of melted cheese from a plate. 'I've just eaten. Pasta. I hope you don't mind. There wasn't much here but I found a courgette in the food waste and it looked fine. Maybe someone put it in there by mistake when they were tired? What I always say is, "Ask not what your pantry can do for you. Ask what you can do for your pantry."'

'Good day?' said Eric.

'Ohmygod I don't even know where to start. How about you?'

'Sound,' said Eric. 'Went for a walk. Almost had to call out an air ambulance rescue team. Popped into the Meat Tree's place afterwards. He sends his love.' The Meat Tree, who in Mel's presence always had the look of a man standing on a brittle porch eyeing a patch of extreme incoming weather, had sent no such thing.

'So,' Mel began, 'you wouldn't believe what happened to me this afternoon. I met this bloke ca—'

'Now,' interrupted Eric, grabbing some cutlery from a drawer just beyond Mel, then heading to the living room. 'Sorry but if you'll both excuse me I'm not going to speak to any fucker until I've shoved every last bit of this lot down my neck. You don't want to make me hangry, do you. You wouldn't like me when I'm hangry.'

As Eric settled down into what in all but name was his own exclusive personal armchair, jalfrezi on lap, and searched for a TV channel showing some form of news, Mel and Carl huddled on the two-seater sofa, careful not to disturb a teetering pile of singles that Eric had purchased last week from the widow of a former northern soul DJ. Mel minded this arrangement less than many others might, since she always enjoyed breathing in the aroma of Carl: a mixture of salt, nutmeg and downy warmth, plus an extra spicy something she couldn't quite pinpoint. Dismissing her refusals, Carl forced a bhaji on her, unaware that Eric had already scoffed every last flake and crumb of the other three. Carl decided he'd give the dhansak about a 7/10 for taste but only a 5/10 for heat. Twice he bit into it and tasted something springy and dry that defied logic, only to discover he was in fact biting into Mel, via a long nomadic corkscrew of her hair. With great delicacy, he twanged the offending coils back into place, to the obliviousness of their owner, who, no longer being able to contain herself, was defying Eric's prandial wish and running him through her day.

'So Deborah and Tony asked me if I could do an afternoon at The Loft today and I was sure they'd said get there at 11.30 but it turned out they'd said 12.30 so I decided to walk to the top of that hill, the one with three trees on it that makes it look like it's wearing a wig, because I never had . . .'

In its rampant indecision, its dogged mission to use its time to cover an area as large and divergent as possible, Mel's hair always appeared an entirely apt extension of Mel. At fifty-seven, she was a care-flaying inspiration to anyone in middle age worrying that they still hadn't decided what they wanted to do when they grew up, that their life hadn't locked onto the one set of rails that would carry them redoubtably into the future. During the time that Carl and Eric had known her she had announced the beginning of at least twenty-six different careers, few of them easily anticipated, most of them quickly, painlessly forgotten. At present, her income came from the sale of vintage clothes and fabric and sporadic part-time shifts at The Loft, a large warehouse twenty minutes' drive inland which was devoted to the secondhand wares of over forty traders, including Eric. As a working life, this would have sounded, to those who hadn't experienced the weather system that was Mel in person, more tranquil than it was. Mel nipped around the borderlands of

Dorset, Somerset and Devon between shops and landmarks of intense national beauty in her small, obnoxiously coloured car with a way of making everything appear to be part of a schedule, even if it wasn't. Something of note had invariably just happened to her or, if not, was soon about to. If there was someone in her catchment of flitting that she didn't know, it was highly likely she would imminently know them, or at least know *of* them. Carl was aware that, at one point, for a period of several months, she and Eric had regularly touched one another's naked bodies, and that this arrangement had long since drawn to a close, without tears or recriminations or possibly even discussion. Both were people who operated at 45 rpm, their 33 rpm settings long since abandoned. He didn't know quite why it hadn't worked out between them but wondered if it might have been a question of space: there was only so much room for words in any one relationship and if neither party was able to turn down the waterfall, where did that leave you? These days, depending on who she happened to be dating or not dating at the time and several other less explicable factors, Mel came in and out of Carl and Eric's lives with the capricious bustle of a travelling carnival. As far as Carl and Eric were concerned, that was fine. She knew which rock the spare door key was hidden under in the garden, and she often brought cake.

'. . . I mean that's ridiculous, right? I must have driven past that tree a thousand times in the last thirty years, and I've never been to the top of it. Have you ever been? It's ever so nice. The trees don't seem so much like a wig when you're up there. And then I'm on the way down and this woman who's holding this dog, it's got a muzzle on it, says to me, "If you don't mind, would you just say hello to him? We're training him – he's an XL Bully," so I did, I said hello to it, this dog, which looked a bit scary, and I was wondering why this woman didn't tell me its breed or its name and just insulted it instead. I mean, why would you say that about your own dog as soon as you met someone, especially while asking them to say hello to it? I didn't even think it looked that big.'

'That's the breed,' said Eric. 'They're called XL American Bullies. A lot of people aren't happy about them. A bloke threw one off one of the cliffs near Lulworth last month. Reg Monk told me.'

'*What?* That's terrible. How could anyone do that? It's not the dog's fault if some stupid humans are breeding it to be a bully.'

'Would anyone like some tea?' asked Carl, who was feeling less than comfortable at the turn the conversation had taken. He picked his iPad up off the coffee table and located the page he'd saved that morning on its browser. 'Did you know that female hyenas have non-ejaculating penises?'

'Anyway,' continued Mel, 'that wasn't what I was really trying to say. So after that I went to The Loft. Oh my days it was cold. I wish Paul would put the heating on in there. It's still January, for heaven's sake. I'm not kidding, I had to go outside at one point and stand by the river, just to warm up. Ooh, don't let me forget, Eric. A girl came in asking after you. Very nice eyes. She left her name and number. I wrote it down on a postcard of Golitha Falls. I couldn't find anything else. It's in my coat. I only realised afterwards that it was one of the vintage ones Paul was selling. £1.20, so don't tell him. I thought for a minute that she was one of your old floozies from your rock-star days but she looked a bit young. I'm guessing she wants to sell you her great-granddad's records or something. Anyway, about an hour later I'm going over to the back room, to see if I could find an electric heater underneath all Paul's junk, and on the way I pass this bloke, and he says, in this nice deep voice that's a bit like chocolate, "Excuse me, I'm ever so sorry, but I'm wondering if you might be able to help. I seem to have got myself into something of a predicament." So what it is, right, you know that carved woman with the serpent's head, sort of African, the one that Leslie Hobhouse has been trying to sell for ages and keeps reducing, he's got his coat trapped in its mouth. God knows how he'd done it! It's a really lovely coat, too, tweed, with this beautiful embroidered silk lining, so there's the two of us, trying to get it out of this serpent's narrow mouth, and it didn't take too long, really, but long enough, especially as I worried about damaging the coat. And afterwards we get talking and he gives me his business card and he tells me his name is Cliff, and he lives on the edge of Eype and he used to live in London and edit books.'

'Every time I go to Eype or see a sign to it, I can't help making an "eeep eeep" noise in my head, like a little mouse,' said Eric.

'I do that too,' thought Carl, but didn't say it. He wanted to find out what happened at the end of Mel's story.

'Doesn't everyone?' continued Mel. 'Anyway, it's not until later, when I'm back at the car, that I look at what it says on his business card: Cliff Falls. He lives in Eype, right over on the far edge of it, nearest the sea, where they had that massive landslip last year, and he's called Cliff Falls! You couldn't make it up.'

'I could,' said Eric. 'I can make all sorts up. I've got all the top skills, when it comes to making stuff up.'

'Cliff Falls! It's brilliant. I haven't stopped chuckling to myself about it all afternoon. I'm going for a drink with him next Wednesday. Sometimes I think I'd quite like a non-ejaculating penis myself, but only for some of the week.'

That night Carl flipped and flapped about in a rigid tray a few inches beneath sleep, never quite finding the leverage or grip to reach the softer shelf above. What Eric had told Mel about the dog being murdered had got him replaying an incident from many years ago that he'd done his best to forget: a regrettable altercation with an Alsatian, at a similarly cold and barren time of year, on some godforsaken Cornish headland, back when Eric had been renting a house in that part of the country. It lived on in the memory as a generally depressing day: cold, rheumatically damp, full of wind and inarticulate anger, the sky a collection of grey shades of pain. Eric had later received a parking fine in a vast beachside car park he hadn't realised he needed to pay for, where his van had been, comically, the only vehicle parked. Carl had never looked at the sea and been more afraid of all the ulterior motives it had for being the sea. For several yards along the coast path, the Alsatian had nipped at his heels, its dripping teeth either uncomfortably close to his haunches or his bumhole. He was used to this, from dogs – it was why he avoided them, when he could – but this one was a monumentally persistent fuckwit of a brand he'd never previously dealt with. 'Piss off, you binhead, or I'll drop you like an egg from a tall chicken,' said Eric, waving a stick at it, to no avail. He had been nervous around big dogs since being bitten by one in Knotty Ash as a seven-year-old. Where was the owner? They'd seen him earlier, but he must have fallen well back. Under one big black cloud that felt like a big Satanic hat Eric, Carl and the Alsatian were collectively wearing, they approached a lichen-coated Napoleonic watch house where the headland turned back on itself, and it was here that the Alsatian chose to make its strike, so quick and clinical and deep that Carl could feel a chunk of his flank leaving the rest of the body. All he knew is that a second later he was in the air, and the Alsatian ahead of him was higher in the air, screaming – screaming a scream that sounded like a song inspired by that Satanic cloud above them – then returning to earth in a deep frost hollow, a cricket pitch's distance to their left. 'I do not know quite what I've done but I know I have done it in a way that ensures that Alsatian is not dead and will go on to live a full, if considerably less fearless, life,' Carl had thought.

'I am sure of that.' Nonetheless, the thought did not stop him and Eric making a hasty escape, nor did Carl's memory of the thought, right now in present-day Dorset, prevent him from replaying the incident in his mind, over and over again, and imagining the Alsatian, in pain, at the bottom of that crevice. And in that hard tray of messy undersleep he was in, in its cold sauce of nonsensical anxiety, the Cornish crevice conflated itself with the Wessex crevice from earlier today, and the Alsatian became Eric, on his back at the bottom of it: not the Eric of today, but a Carl-less Eric, an Eric of the not-too-distant future.

'What am I?' Carl asked himself. 'My own Ghost of Christmas Future, putting extra hours in during the off-season?'

At first light he rose, crept downstairs and gently opened the back door of the cottage, careful to not wake Mel, who had bedded down for the night on the sofa under an old towncoat Eric kept promising himself he'd wear again but never did. Her cat Bathsheba, who had emerged from an eleven-hour sleep in the airing cupboard on the house's most expensive towel, observed him high-handedly from the sofa's arm. The forecast was for another bright icy day and the sun was only just beginning to airbrush the back of the cliffs orange. The Golden Cap was what people called the tallest of them: the highest point, at 191 metres, on the entire south coast of the UK. At its summit a person – which Carl did often view himself as – always got the sense of having been granted access to a secret mezzanine far above England's living room. You looked down at the plateaus below with the understanding that they were cliffs and you were on something else. Whenever Carl scaled it, he was always struck anew by its scope, of how massively, if it ever collapsed, it would swallow everything beneath it, and, in turn, how massively everything beneath it would swallow it.

Everything was always crumbling along these few miles of coastline, falling away, turning itself inside out and upside down, as if the particular earth, soil and sand of the region was easily bored, leading to a propensity to reimagine itself from new angles. Talking to people who were visiting the house for the first time, Eric would often describe it as 'the little white cottage at the bottom of the hill' but that was not strictly accurate. A building being pelted so regularly from above with this much debris could never quite raise itself beyond off-white, no matter how hard it tried. 'Where is it all coming from?' Carl would wonder, on the wildest nights. The next morning he'd half expect to open the door and find the cliffs gone but there they were, looking much as they always had done. They were like those celebrities who've been subject to widespread deathwatch for years, the ones whose self-abuse has become public legend, who you then see a new photo of in a newspaper and are surprised to discover they still have two eyes, a nose, a mouth, a protective head of hair, upwards of six teeth. The kind of people whose death, when it finally comes, is met with a flurry of clacking keys as a large proportion of people who felt certain they'd died years ago verify the facts on a nearby device.

But today Carl headed in the opposite direction, past the Fentonbrooks' farm, past the 'Hens On Path!' sign that always made him sad – he suspected it had been put there because something bad had happened to the hens on the path – and up the hill, where the footpaths criss-crossed one another through the gorse and cattle chewed on steaming piles of ex-grass. He saw nobody. Carl had walked untold hundreds of miles with Eric but he also liked to walk alone. There were of course many persuasive arguments for him not to go for walks unaccompanied, but he did not wish to hem himself into the box of Individuals Who Don't Go For Walks Unaccompanied, the subtle cage of Those Who Wait For Permission From The Head Of The Household Or At Least A More Assertive Map-Reading Friend Before Experiencing The Freedom Of The Breeze In Their Hair. He usually did not go upright as, in the event of a problem, it would complicate matters twofold, but sometimes found the novelty of doing so impossible to resist. He chose his times carefully, preferring the untrustworthy half-light that bookended the coastal days. Today he opted for a conservative two and a half miles: up to the radar station – not the one that old Russell Loosemore had seen fall down the cliff in 1942, but a later, sturdier replacement – then back along the low ground where, under the cover of a hedge, he rose briefly to his full height. It was around here that, a few weeks ago, in one of those confusing triangles that invaded his vision from time to time, he had, for just a minute, before the image disappeared, watched a weeping male figure, dressed in drenched raggy clothes, holding an inert woman in his arms on the beach.

Today, however, the near-inaccessible foreshore remained deserted. Behind it, the greensand rock of the Cap was now thoroughly burnished by the sun. In these moments, its similarity in colour to the churches of the region was unignorable. And who was to say it *wasn't* a church, just because human hands had not built it? After all, it did what churches were supposed to do: it reached for the sky and filled those in its vicinity with awe and fear and, perhaps, a curious kind of reassurance.

Eric had almost purchased a real church not all that long ago. Which is to say Eric had seen a church advertised for auction at a starting price with tenuous connection to reality, then had gone, with Carl, to view the church, then talked about all the things that were going to happen after he bought the church (gig venue, arts centre, rehearsal studio, tent erected allowing Eric and Carl to live in the church's epicentre during renovations) then watched as the church was bought by someone far wealthier and less idealistic than him for several hundred thousand pounds above the price on the advert. Carl had done his best to disguise his relief. The church was in a village twenty miles inland and nothing ever seemed to work out as well for them when they were further from the sea. Also, during his researching of the village, the first thing he'd found was a story about an overweight, locally adored pig which had escaped from its meadow then fallen down a steep bank into a river and drowned, and he feared that, if they lived there, he'd be haunted by mental images of the enormous pig's demise, or to be exact haunted even more by it than he still was now, which was already quite a lot. And not buying the church had led Eric and him here, and here, he thought, was *obviously* much better. Just look at it!

When Carl got back to the cottage Eric was unloading the van ready for the day's trip. A couple of coffee tables he hadn't quite worked out what to do with yet. A lamp he'd found in Honiton which he felt confident he could flip for twice the price he'd got the dealer down to. A bell.

'Is that a bell?'

'It is.'

'You didn't tell me you'd got a bell.'

'I didn't tell you when I brushed my teeth this morning, either. Some things are a gentleman's own business.'

'Are you not forgetting something quite significant here?'

'Look, it's *fine*. Art deco. Not even a century old. Not even in the same universe as that other one, as far as bells are concerned. It came from Reg Monk. He was clearing out a 1930s place over in Budleigh Salterton. It was for the servants, I think. Can you believe she brought her cat with her?'

'I actually can. We are talking about Mel here.'

'I just went to dry my hair with my towel. It's covered in all this brown fur. Can you see any on my hair now? I feel like I've got brown fur on my head. She said she was worried about it getting lonely. Did you know that she feeds her earwax to it? She just stuck her blummin' finger in her ear and gave it some, a few minutes ago, in the kitchen. I saw her.'

'I'm ready!' said Mel, who, not having anything else planned for the day, had decided to join them. She was well wrapped up in a duffle coat and a red Fair Isle sweater she'd appropriated from a high-altitude window cleaner she'd briefly dated in 2014.

Before they left, Carl went inside for his customary pre-trip check-around. He moved the kettle and a couple of Eric's muddy socks from yesterday off the Rayburn, but decided not to turn off the radio, concluding that Bathsheba would appreciate the company. He noticed a couple of new black handprints on the wall and made a mental note to see to them this evening. When he got back out to the van, Eric was still talking about the earwax. What he told Mel he was most curious about was how she'd first discovered that Bathsheba had a taste for it. Had it been a total accident, or was it her habit to try out all her bodily fluids on pets until they hit on one that really did it for them? 'And what about this Cliff Avalanche bloke? Are you going to tell him about it when you go on your hot date?' he added.

'I woke up with her tongue in my ear one night and it sort of progressed from there,' replied Mel. 'It's not my fault my cat's weird.' Carl was thinking about the time he'd eaten some of his own by mistake and been surprised to find it was nowhere near as saltily bearable as he'd predicted, instead tasting like something that, if manufactured in the right quantities, could probably be useful in biological warfare. All the same, he refused to pass judgement.

Some Older, Even More Tasteful Wallpaper

If Penny Carlton-Muxloe was ever asked to name the summer that had been the happiest of her life – which, to her disappointment, she almost never was – what she would have said, without need for cogitation or measurement of the evidence, and probably before the question was even entirely out of the mouth of the person asking it, was 1968. She'd had other summers since then which had glued themselves to her mind: 1977, when she met David and swam for the first time with dolphins. 1999, when she defied the odds, as a rank outsider, to become mayor of a small town in north Wales. But nothing quite compared to 1968: the summer she milked her first goat; the summer she turned seventeen; the summer when she first truly floated above it all; the summer when, most significantly of all, her uncle opened his large old house up to allcomers. It was not uncommon for people to think of orange when they remembered the middle part of 1968: the orange of rice fields on fire in the Mekong Delta or ammunition lorries exploding as Russian tanks entered Prague. But when Penny remembered that period, she thought of a different orange: the hazy untarnished orange found in the unhurried gardens of dreams.

The goat she'd milked had been called Sandy. She always remembered that because it shared the name with the Keats-obsessed young man she'd milked it with. The two of them – Penny and Sandy the poet, that is, not Penny and Sandy the goat, although how thoroughly fucking excellent would that be and, in the vicinity of the manor, in 1968, perhaps not so far-fetched – had been on their way to find a swimming spot they'd heard about from some of the other people staying at Batbridge Manor when they'd spotted the goat and paused to bid it good morning. 'Might yah like to come in an' arve a propah intraduction?' the goat's owner, hidden from them by branches and the happy orb of dazzling pain that was that morning's sun, had asked. And moments afterwards there they'd been, two people who'd been acquainted for less than twenty-four hours, taking turns tentatively, and eventually more assertively, to squeeze a teat where it met the bulge of an udder. Where was he now, Sandy? Did that day still glow as orangely and pleasurably in his mind as it did in hers? Did he too remember the particular way that, later, the sun – also quite orangely – appeared to single out the deepest part of the river beyond the lip of the humpback bridge and warm it just for them so the water was transformed from a place of shrieks and masochism to a protective cauldron of swirling addiction that neither of them wanted to leave?

You couldn't control the lint that stuck to the Velcro pad of other people's memories, Penny was well aware of this, but that awareness didn't stop her lack of agency in this regard being an enormous source of frustration to her. No two people retold a mutually experienced day in precisely the same way, and herein you found much of the reason why every great individual work of art Penny had ever enjoyed *was* great. Yet finding that other people either rewrote the moments of her life that defined her, or didn't remember them at all, never failed to cause her dismay. It had been, she reflected, part of what had eroded her as a person. It had happened so often that now, cynically, in her head, she found herself having a hypothetical argument with the twenty-first-century Sandy the poet – wherever he was, *whoever* he was, if he still existed – just as she had once argued with David about events they'd both experienced which he saw drastically differently or had chopped and binned in his ongoing rewrite of personal history.

'You don't remember the goat?'

'Nope, no goat. The animal *I* milked that day was a sheep. I'm positive.'

'What about the swimming? Surely you remember that? That bridge we jumped off.'

'I definitely *went* swimming that summer. But not with you. That was with another girl, in a better river. She was taller, and French.'

Giving her hypothetical Bad Faith Sandy – whose real-life incarnation had, after all, most probably done nothing to deserve this in the fifty-four and a half years since she'd last seen or spoken to him – a break, she had a little word with herself and returned her attention to the other ghosts of Batbridge Manor. Ghosts could cause you plenty of trouble. They could emerge unexpected in 1962 from an olive-green bath with water dripping from their rotted limbs and frighten your little sister half to death. They could sing their haunting verse at you through the old pipes of a building. Their beseeching eyes could stare at you from a framed military portrait balanced on a pre-war dresser and plead with you not to let property developers buy their house, even though they knew that, to an extent, your hands were tied in that regard. But what ghosts didn't generally do was tell you that you were wrong about the defining memories of your life.

In the four and a half weeks since her uncle's death, Penny had spent considerable time following the manor's ghosts through its fourteen rooms, spinning and twisting, in a delicious leisurely way, through the long-gone orange days when she'd bonded most thickly with the place. As the primary beneficiary of her uncle's will, it was she whom the heavy responsibility of the destiny of the building and its contents fell to: a destiny that — despite her awareness of her uncle's childless widower status and his abiding fondness for her — she'd given little, if any, consideration to until late last month.

Nobody had ever counted her uncle's book collection but the house clearance company who'd come to survey the place put the total somewhere upwards of 50,000. No surface in the house remained free of books. In her uncle's bedroom, on an old mattress, could still be discerned an indentation in the shape of his frail compact body, which, walled in on either side by forgotten foxed memoirs of small rural lives and 1940s guides to beekeeping and xenophobic adventure stories for boys, had the look of a sort of trench, accessible only by the narrowest of human tunnels. Elsewhere, books blocked the entrance to rooms entirely or had somehow intertwined and overlapped with the house's long-neglected stuffing. In the far east corner of the ground floor, beside the old servant's entrance, piles of books, precisely ceiling high, appeared to have taken upon themselves the very task of saving the building from falling to rubble. In a couple of days the house clearance firm would be back to take it all away, aside from the parts that couldn't be taken away for safety reasons. That would not be a quick job, even for five men: six days, they estimated, and they said even that was being highly optimistic.

Staring at the chaos induced an overwhelming inertia: it presented no starting point, no route in. Then there was the sale of the house itself. It was a lot of work, requiring Penny to spend many hours there, although not, it might be argued, quite as many as she *had* been spending.

One floor below her she could hear the floorboards creak with the tentative foraging of the man Dimitri had sent, the one who owned the unusually beautiful dog and never stopped talking. Where was he from? Liverpool, perhaps? Chester? He'd come here with a woman, younger by a decade or so, possibly his wife or partner, although Penny didn't detect that sort of chemistry. When the woman spoke it sounded like glass shattering into thousands of fragments, but in a strangely alluring way. Both visitors seemed wholesome enough. She knew she could trust Dimitri, a friend since her days working on literacy programmes in Caernarfonshire in the nineties, which was why she'd given him the spare key. It might have been said that, today, she didn't need to be here at all. Yet here she was. Again.

'*You're living in the past, man.*' That had been an oft-used insult amongst her social circle, in her late teens and twenties. But there were different ways of living in the past that didn't always mean the same thing. There was the way that obstinately refused to see the good in change, revered a version of what had been and twisted it into simplified shapes while forgetting the essence of all you'd been while you'd lived through it; a way that, on principle, feared all that was nipping at its heels, without ever pausing to turn and examine it. But there was also the way that, merely in becoming a person with more road behind them than ahead, a psychic landscape of the past naturally grew inside you, enterable through doors in a present that it could coexist harmoniously with and even complement. It enriched you, enriched the experience of a storied old building like this, on the site of a much older one, where your own memories led you to the imagined ones of long-deceased former residents, where you pulled back a peeling strip of the orange wallpaper your uncle had inadvisably added in the 1960s and saw the infinitely more tasteful wallpaper underneath – estimated date of arrival, 1903 – and wondered, 'Was there some even older, *even more tasteful wallpaper* under that?' There, right in front of you, just a short leap back, almost touchable from here in 2023, was 1923, 1823, 1723. (Hadn't her mum once said that her great-grandma had spoken to a man who remembered the Great Fire of London? Or was it her great-grandma's great-grandma? Whatever the case: what a series of short hops, skips and jumps it all was.)

But Penny knew there was a little more to her presence here than that. Her many recent visits to Batbridge Manor had come to also represent a defence of her uncle and his lifestyle. It had begun with the mistake she'd made in talking to the journalist from the regional newspaper, a woman who'd no doubt been tipped off by the estate agents as soon as they'd been commissioned to act on behalf of the family. 'HOUSE OF INFAMOUS WEST COUNTRY HOARDER TO BE PUT UP FOR AUCTION,' said the headline the next day. What was left of the descriptions Penny had given of her uncle's life and character had been truncated almost beyond recognition, all meaning and nuance bent and shaken from them. The main photograph showed the crumbling attic ceiling, the books wedged beneath it and the floor, loft insulation strewn around them, the caption telling readers that they were seeing 'Just some of the conditions of devastation and domestic neglect that surrounded Charles Muxloe, 93, at the time of his death.' Then the dreaded below-the-line comments: 'THIS IS AN ILLNESS. People like this are not well and need therapy.' 'Why didn't his family help him? Selfish wankers.' Penny had not felt so helplessly furious for years, not since the darkest throes of her divorce from David. Who were these screen-addled judgement-packed vomitbags to say who Charles had been or what he'd 'needed'? While making their pronouncements on the pictures, they neglected to see or paint the bigger one. They never imagined the young man who, alongside his new wife, restored a crumbling house then had the pleasure of living in it, enjoying its atmosphere, and inviting countless others to join him, for many years. Had they ever known the joy of surrounding yourself with love and knowledge and learning? What exactly was the more socially acceptable way to live out your final years that they would commend: the one where a person does everything cleanly and neatly and correctly in the eyes of society, right until their final breath? And did it make anyone who achieves it better, or happier, in their last years on the planet?

In the days since then, Penny had been unable to stop herself working on her defence, even though she was aware that the people she was aiming the defence at probably didn't have a whole lot of feeling or opinion about what she was defending or, for the most part, even know what it was. As dealers and tradesmen arrived at the house, the stories she told them emphasised precisely what a healthy social life Charles had maintained right up until the end – his trips to the farmer's market and to Truro to see his girlfriend (Gladys, a mere stripling at eighty-three) and the village book group he attended and his work as a church warden and his never-less-than-immaculate appearance. For nonplussed electricians and scaffolders she intricately painted the fireside garden singalongs of that particularly special summer of almost fifty-five years ago: the outfits, the smells, the scraggy tents, the 'waifs and strays' who – through her uncle and aunt's generosity and sheer word of mouth – descended on this walled space in a remote part of Devon and created their own small, unlikely, off-kilter idea of society.

'Sounds like whatdoyermacallit, the one in America, where everyone took their clothes off and rolled around in the mud,' said a man called Derek with a thick Black Country accent who had come to reattach a door last Tuesday.

'Woodstock?' said Penny. 'You know what? For some of us, I suppose it was.'

It had been Penny's mother who had put forward the idea of Penny, fresh from her GCE Advanced Levels at the time and mentally only half committing to the idea of studying Art History at Durham that autumn, travelling down from Wiltshire to spend the summer at her uncle Charles and aunt Annika's place to help Charles 'organise his book collection, which had got a little out of control'. She grinned in recollection of this comment. How many books had Charles kept in the house, back then? No more than a couple of thousand, surely. Whatever the case, it had seemed a lot to Penny at the time and at seventeen she had already begun to think of her uncle's decision to line the walls of Batbridge Manor with them as a vital warding off of evil. *Okay*, so there had been that one guy who turned up at the house during Penny's second summer there, nobody quite knew how or why, who called himself the Warlock: the one whose grubby presence had always made Penny want to brush something invisible off herself and who a couple of the girls sleeping in the living room had woken in the early hours to find standing over their beds, staring down at them with his pedestrian underpass eyes. But his tenure was brief. After exploiting the gentle atmosphere of tolerance created by Charles and Annika, he'd eventually run his thin creepy fingers along the thighs of the wrong guy's girlfriend. Robin? Ruben! That was it. Huge arms. Useful for the physical ejection of shitbags. He'd literally picked the Warlock up and thrown him through the porch, sending him tumbling down the front steps, the Warlock's form flying past Penny and a couple of other bystanders like a lumpy slow-motion bullet. Impregnable wall of a chap, Ruben had been. Built like an American fridge from the future. Viking helmet of hair the colour of margarine. Where was he now? Hard to imagine him not being twenty-two, forever. He'd done the ejection job coolly and unsensationally, as if it was just another of the list of chores he performed for Charles and Annika, no more fuss than mending a dodgy fascia or replacing a broken slab. He had been another good find for Charles, who – sometimes to Annika's despair – was a collector of people as well as books, although never in a self-serving or ruthless way. How many bodies had passed through the place during that period? 150? More? Out of all of those, one rotten apple wasn't such a bad ratio.

For all its spectres – even that one her sister had seen in the bathtub when she was six, and really, in the end, what was so spooky about getting clean? – and the dark exterior look of its windows, the house had always been a warm and light place. How had the man from the Wildlife Trust who'd come to assess the breed and rareness of the bats in the loft last week put it? 'Like a sepulchre filled with honey.' Penny had tasted the honey prior to 1968 but that was the summer she bathed in it.

Precisely how often had the past jumped up and annihilated her in the last month? How many times had it sprung from closets and cupboards and boxes and drawers, landing on her with all its compelling woozy heft? The first time had been on the first day she'd come to look at the house in its uninhabited state, when she'd opened the wardrobe in the main bedroom – that ostensible bibliographic bombsite – after negotiating the paper foothills and seen his pressed trousers and tweed jackets on the hangers and the pristine line of polished shoes below them. It was a wonder she was even still standing after that, still walking around, like a human woman, at a height of comfortably above five feet. Then that other small rapturous death, just yesterday, when she had somehow crawled around two pyramids of 1930s Great Western Railway guides in bedroom six – a part of the house that had been always something of an enigma to her – without sending either of them toppling, and peeked behind the brown elasticated curtain covering a recess below the window and found what was perhaps the real legacy of Charles's generosity, the proof of his acquaintances' true feelings towards his years as the Landlord of the People. How many letters? Seventy? And, to go alongside many of them: records, paintings, self-published poetry collections, pottery, long-since-emptied jars of – yes – honey, complete with handprinted labels.

'To Charles. Remembering summer 1970, for all time, and on, into whatever comes after.'

'I can't quite believe I'm saying this but we finally made the album. ONLY three f-ing years later! See if you recognise the guy on track one, side two.'

'Dearest Charles. James and I were wondering who should be the first friend to sample this and of course we instantly thought of you. The business is still a bit of a work in progress but we're having a lot of fun working it all out, and most importantly of all, the bees seem happy!'

'I will never forget the generosity you and Annika showed me. I was so deeply sorry to hear about what happened to her. I hope this doesn't sound too strange to you but I sometimes feel like you are both there beside me, as I paint and sew.'

'So what would those below-the-line commenters have thought of all this,' Penny wondered. 'Would they have then still talked about the "loner", the man isolated from other people amidst the illness of his books, the antisocial hermit whose weird life touched nobody else's, whose welfare nobody thought of?' Immediately after asking these questions she reprimanded herself for giving the matter even a moment's energy. If her uncle had taught her anything it was that there were always people out there skimming the surface of you who would think ill of you and, in most instances, it needn't have a shred of impact on your well-being, if you didn't permit it to. Instead you simply went about your quiet way, surrounding yourself with all that was positive and curious and erudite, and trying, if at all possible, at all times, to be thoroughly decent to everyone you met.

It hit home to Penny, seeing those letters, and those accompanying creative works – some of them inauspicious, some of them beautiful, some of them as yet uninvestigated – that she had probably never inspired quite that level of fondness from anyone. 'My immediate thought is wasp,' her father had said, after dinner one night, when the whole family were around the table discussing which animal they saw each other as and Penny's turn had arrived. He'd been teasing, but the associations had stuck and left their unintended mark on her. Her self-perception remained of a small, colourful creature, abrasively loud, fond of sugary drinks, lazily profane, quick to anger, grouchy when woken from boozy naps. But that was unfair of Penny to Penny. It turned a blind eye to the part of her that – particularly as she'd got older – shared her uncle's sweetness, his enjoyment of quietly bestowing on others what he'd accumulated, opening up his space to them. It manifested itself differently to the way it had with him – her domestic set-up was ascetic, fuss-free; she often thought she'd offload her own dead cells to a registered charity if she could – but it was there. She was not the person who, as soon as she saw you, said, 'I've got something special for you!' then proceeded to give you something part-special. She was the person who appeared perennially preoccupied, barely seemed to notice you, then, just as you were leaving, casually handed you the thing which was infinitely more special than the thing that the person who hyped up special things ever gave anyone; handed it to you superficially because the special thing was of no use to her but technically because of the joy she knew she'd see on your face when you received it, which had become one of her life's central pleasures.

It was because of this that when the talkative Liverpudlian man had arrived, forty-five minutes earlier, with his splinter-voiced Medusa-haired friend and their attractive feminine dog, she had chosen not to lead him directly to the small pile of records she had located behind that knee-high elasticated curtain, even though – despite her own particular musical areas of expertise being baroque, renaissance and pre-1955 jazz – she had a strong instinct that they were going to be much more pertinent to his cultural – and possibly commercial – interests than the more accessible couple of boxes downstairs already pinpointed and isolated by Dimitri. She would wait a while longer, tell him a little more about the history of the house. She wanted, anyhow, to find out more about him and his aurally intriguing friend. She had accepted the dispersal of her uncle's possessions – even the more valuable ones – but was always keen to be reassured of the wholesomeness of their destination, the potential for their satisfying rebirth. Plus she was keen to find out what breed the dog was. Those *eyelashes*. Stunning. She had a feeling she'd seen one before, but not for a very long time, and the official name was, like so much nowadays, proving a little synaptically elusive.

Downstairs, Eric still couldn't bring himself to quite let the topic of the earwax go. By sheer badgering, he'd somehow managed to extract from Mel that, two years ago, struggling with her hearing – or, to be more exact, having been *told* she was struggling with her hearing by the hypercritical and hectoring tennis coach she'd been seeing – she'd gone to get her ears syringed and persuaded the ear doctor to save the contents to take home to Bathsheba. 'That wasn't a medical procedure, pal; that was a fucking takeaway!' said Eric. 'How did he give it to you? Did he bag it up with some prawn crackers?' Mel, for her part, was less bothered by Eric's taunting owing to being on a high, the result of locating a trunk full of exquisitely tailored 1950s clothes and being told by the nice lady whose family owned the house that they were 'yours if you want them, to do what you wish with'. Everyone was in a relaxed mood apart from Carl, who Eric, via the window of the third bedroom, could now see stretched out on the upper tier of the manor's garden on an intricate wrought-iron bench, with his chin on his paws, where he'd been, without moving, for at least the past half hour. Eric suspected that he was having 'one of his moments'. On the way here in the van he'd been his usual self, telling Eric and Mel facts he'd read recently on the internet, such as that you weren't allowed to go to Antarctica until you'd had your appendix removed (apparently it all dated from this one time a guy had gone there and been required to remove his own, using surgical retractors and some mirrors). But as soon as they'd walked through the front door, Eric had seen Carl's eyes trying their hardest not to be eyes any more and become a mouth that could speak sentences at Eric. Eric would find out what was bothering him soon enough. In the meantime, he reappraised that bench. The ironwork really was a bit tasty. Victorian, he guessed. He made a mental note to bring it up when brokering the deal. The paintings in here, on the wall behind him, too. Claustrophobic families of multicolour blobs. Must have taken all of eight minutes to splash on there. Not his thing, personally, but they'd sell. If not, Reg Monk would know somebody.

He'd found little of interest in the two boxes of LPs downstairs, save for three surprises, each so heavily scratched it seemed entirely possible that at some point during the last half-century they'd been repurposed as miniature ice-skating rinks: the third West Coast Pop Art Experimental Band album, 1973's *Afrodisiac* from the legendary Nigerian bandleader Fela Kuti and the lamentable but bafflingly highly valued debut 'In Transit' by pub rockers Showdogs, a record that to Eric's mind had always had more than a whiff of 'recently divorced dad wanders drunk into the leisure centre disco and disgraces himself' about it. Other than that: mostly landfill, save for a couple of lateish pressings from the more artistically fruitful halves of the careers of Led

Zeppelin and Bonnie Raitt. Not that it would help it achieve its £100-plus price tag but Eric in fact suspected the West Coast Pop Art LP would play free of ticks, pops, sticks or clicks, despite the deep scratch covering all of 'Suppose They Give a War and No One Comes', the album having been manufactured in the legendarily indestructible period for vinyl prior to the oil crisis and ensuing PVC shortage that led record companies to cut corners in production methods. Then, when they didn't need to cut corners any more, they carried on cutting corners because they discovered cutting corners hadn't stopped them selling just as many records and would, in the long run, lead to more profits.

It was hard to hurt a record made in 1967 but that hadn't stopped a lot of people giving it a damn good go. Looking at the state of a lot of those that passed through his hands, Eric wondered if he'd been going to the right parties in his youth. When it came to the most rare and acclaimed East African output of the 1960s and 1970s, the phenomenon was threefold. Not that Eric had ever had the opportunity to visit that region of the planet, but he had, on his musical travels, developed a strong mental picture of it as an uninhibited and hedonistic place where, after exhausting their original purpose, records were often deployed as frisbees and breadboards.

Nope, he doubted he would – even if he could buy that bench and move it on – justify his time and fuel costs today. But that didn't bother him overly much. He and Carl had scored big on a couple of other private collections recently. Not feeling as creaky as he'd expected to after his travails on yesterday's walk, he was looking forward to the one planned for today and enjoying soaking up the atmosphere of the location the latest point his life as a hunter-gatherer had brought him to. Foreboding from the exterior, where it looked out at the surrounding valley like a disapproving hollow-eyed affiliate of the zombie clergy,

Batbridge Manor had surprised him as he'd wandered its rooms. In its deeper personality it reminded him of nothing so much as a happy old teddy bear politely asking to be patched up. Eric, in his entrepreneurial way, especially upon hearing from Dimitri about its bohemian past, had immediately thought 'couple of walls down, gallery, arts café, Friday-night gigs'. He'd fantasised about such a venture for years, although always with the understanding that part of the pleasure was the fact that it hadn't happened and therefore hadn't had the opportunity to fail. Lurking behind the disappointment of losing out on that derelict church he'd bid for a couple of years ago, there'd been an element of relief. Even if he overlooked the physical limitations imposed on him by age, he had doubts about his ability as a renovator: his attention span was too migratory, his love of dereliction too lingering and ardent.

On walks in the countryside, and sometimes not in the countryside, he and Carl clambered over rubble mountains, hurdled 'KEEP OUT' signs, flouted the crooked warnings of condemned doorways and Flat Stanleyed themselves through slits in doors, all in the name of one of their favourite pastimes: exploring abandoned buildings. Had they chanced across the manor on one of their rambles and spotted a gap in its framework, they'd have been through it in a jiffy. It had been like that at the start of yesterday's walk when Eric had spotted a bungalow hidden below a ledge just off the B3165 on the stretch between Marshwood and Raymond's Hill. Essentially just two and a bit walls and some of a roof. As he and Carl had stood in its former living room, they enjoyed the spectacular picture-frame view east over the Marshwood Vale, Carl pointing out a spot at the far side of the valley when Eric had once run away from a shaggy-faced ram ('Who wouldn't have? It was bigger than a fucking pony!'). Eric, who'd become adept at this kind of guesswork, suspected the building had last served as a home some time in 2010 or 2011. Small, not a family space. Dozens of bottles on the floor: old bottles, not bottles redolent of a recent teenage break-in. Medium-dry sherry, mostly. Positioned in their centre, like a totem, the jewel case of a Shirley Bassey 'Best Of' CD. There was a doorbell and an attractive circular feature window, still intact. Carl, examining the render on the northern wall and that window, said he suspected 1958 as the year of construction. Eric owned a pair of shoes that were six years old which he thought of as the shoes he bought 'last year'. That made 1958 approximately eleven years ago. Which meant eleven years ago someone opened the door of this building and thought, 'Here is my smart, newly constructed home, where I can get plastered on bottles of fortified wine and bellow along to showtunes!' A whole life, or something quite close to it, was probably lived here. Meanwhile, time would have always been there, lurking outside, making its own music, tapping the gradual merciless beat of it out on the walls.

'You're interested in *that*?' clients had sometimes asked Eric, as he singled out a curious trinket while sifting through their relatives' possessions. 'I'm only interested in everything, me,' Eric might reply. That, however, was not strictly true. There were a lot of things Eric wasn't interested in. Eric wasn't interested in domestic albino hedgehogs or hair dye or the new iPhone or artificial lawns or David Walliams or toasters or vape fluid or embossed wallets or breeding pugs. Eric wasn't interested in bathroom showrooms or plastic surgery or greetings cards or hair-replacement surgery that they said would make people think of you as the guy with the hair but actually made people think of you as the guy who'd had hair-replacement surgery. Eric wasn't interested in going into space or going online to find a Russian wife or investing in Bitcoin or meeting the overly proud sister of a professional boxing promoter on a cruise and moving to one of the cleaner parts of Kent solely to be with her or bagel cutters or long-term misanthropic solitude or consolidating his assets or purchasing a pointlessly large new clock for his living-room wall. But doing the job he did, seeing the lives he saw, rooting around the houses he visited, being the naturally curious person he was, led to a breeding of interests that only increased with every passing year and, as it did, so did the realisation that this breeding left less time to be an expert on anything. Records? Well, yes, to an extent. But one thing you could always be sure of in the used vinyl business was that no matter how much knowledge you accumulated about music there was always someone out there who had accumulated more.

If Eric did have an area of expertise, it was the craftsmanship of time: the lulls and crescendos of that song it played on buildings, on objects, on art. A point had been reached where he could almost anticipate the key changes before they happened. His radar was, of course, stronger in the area of old records than anywhere else. He had become uniquely sensitive to the complex shifts amidst the latticework of culture and opinion which suddenly decreed that a £75 album of many years' standing was poised to become a £300 album. He had refined and developed an extra-sensory perception for impending collectibility. He was alive to the possibility of records almost everywhere he went, but sometimes he just *knew*. It was like he could see through walls, through fabric. So when he spotted the custodian of Batbridge Manor descending the stairs carrying a tote bag filled with what could have been a dozen unopened calendars or twelve-inch-high pictures but were more likely to be a similar number of albums and heard her announce, 'Erm, I found a few more – I'm not sure whether they'll be of interest,' he felt a finely honed gland twitching familiarly, somewhere he could never quite pinpoint but that he thought might possibly be in his neck.

'Ooh lovely,' said Eric, keeping it nice and cool. 'I'm always more than happy to take a look. Bit of all right, this place, isn't it. You don't fancy keeping it for yourself, then?'

'Good gracious no,' said Penny. 'Far too big for little old me. And the work that needs doing is truly formidable. I must say I *do* like your dog. So pretty, and so *quiet*. What breed is she?'

'He's a Longtail Cast-On. He's having an off day today. Lots on his mind.'

'Not at all like my old spaniel, Edward, then. The only thing ever on his mind was "dinner" or maybe "rabbit".'

Several rooms away, they could hear Mel sneezing. More out of long-ingrained habit than anything, Eric flinched, like a man who'd heard a glass smash on the pub table behind him. Penny thought, 'I've heard people who sneeze like there is dynamite in their abdomen and people who sneeze like their sneeze is a tiny secret they're going to selfishly only part-tell you. I once knew a man who sneezed like Mick Jagger sings and a woman who sneezed like she was cartwheeling into a room where people were pleased to see her. But I have never heard a person sneeze like this.'

'Sounds like this was quite the party house at one point.' His voice betrayed none of the excitement rising in his chest. He'd allowed himself just the smallest peek inside the tote bag now. Was that *Amethyst Deceiver* by the Meredith Stackpole Mushroom Band? Mono UK first pressing, with original inner? Surely not.

'We did have some times, it has to be said. Lots of people coming and going. It was mostly my uncle's doing. My aunt . . . she didn't exactly *dislike* it, but I suspect she might have preferred a quieter life. She had a tendency to feel overpeopled quite easily – a lot like me, really. But he loved it and never asked for anything in return. Charles loved the feeling that the house was alive with voices and ideas. Word got around and there were always at least a couple of tents planted out there in the orchard. People were forever falling flat on their face after tripping over guy ropes in the dark. Quite a lot of Americans came, musicians, and told their friends, which made the place a bit of a stop-off on the gig circuit back then. Evidently when they went on to whatever they did next they remembered Charles. I hope there's something in there you find worthwhile. It's amazing how people still want these things, isn't it? I doubt anybody would have suspected it at the time. I asked my grandson, he's twenty-two, what he wanted for Christmas and the first thing he said, without a moment's pause for thought, was a turntable.'

'We call it the Time Machine Problem.' *Holy crap was that Kak's self-titled 1969 debut LP, featuring Gary Lee Yoder from The Oxford Circle? Blummin' eck, it was.* 'Every record dealer you talk to will mention a version of it at some point. The wish that you could go back to a time when some LP that everyone's wetting their knickers about nowadays, excuse my French, was something they couldn't give away, so you could buy up every copy of it you could get your hands on. In a way that's what we're all doing now, trying to be the person from the future, right now, who's come here in that time machine. But none of us really know what's coming next. We're all making it up as we go along. Of course, the thing is, and what most people don't realise, is that very few things are valuable. People hear about the "vinyl revival" and think that means vinyl in general. It doesn't. Most records are worth next to nothing. Then you have the internet, confusing everything even more. People see the prices on Discogs or eBay and get confused, not realising they're looking at the price some chancer is asking for a record, instead of what it would realistically sell for, or they don't realise they have a different pressing of it which is a lot less valuable. Ha, speaking of time machines, I wouldn't mind one so I could go back and be at the studio while this lot were making this.' He held up the 1971 album *Bilious Attack* by Acid Reflux. 'Such a solid record, full on ten-out-of-ten spacey sludge-rock weirdness, and then they ruin it with three shite ragtime novelty tracks taking up most of side two. Once I got there I'd be sneaking in and setting off the fire alarm every time they tried to record them.'

'Oh dear, is he boring you with tedious record-bloke talk?' said Mel, who had now joined them in the hallway. She was holding a couple of coats made of Welsh wool and a lilac boatneck blouse. 'He does that. Give it a rest, Eric. I'm sure the lady has no wish for a complete breakdown of exactly why the fourth LP by The John Spacefrog Collective didn't fulfil its commercial potential.'

'Not at all,' replied Penny. 'I'm finding it all quite fascinating. I may be wrong but I don't *believe* any of the gentlemen from Acid Reflux stayed here. I know people sent their records and books to my uncle but things got left around the place and forgotten, too, when people were passing through. There was a large man called Chickpea. I'm not sure why I remember him. I know he worked as a sound recordist at one point. So I suppose he might well have arrived with records. When he vanished one day he left everything, literally including the shirt off his back. It's really quite hard to pinpoint the provenance of most things, amidst the chaos. As for the records, I don't know that Charles ever actually played any of them. Much as he liked hearing people playing their guitars in the garden, folk and rock and soul weren't exactly his tipple. He was more of an Elgar man.'

'Well, there's some quality stuff in here,' said Eric. 'I'd definitely be happy to take it off your hands.'

'I found a few more bits,' said Mel, holding up one of the coats. 'Are you absolutely *sure* it's ok to take them?'

'Really, please be my guest,' said Penny. 'You're doing me a favour. They're performing no useful function here. My aunt died more than thirty years ago and rather sweetly my uncle held onto most of her clothes. But in the end one gets to a point where one just has to let it all go and all you can hope is that somebody else gets some pleasure out of wearing them.'

'There was one more trunk in one of the far bedrooms but it was a bit awkward trying to reach it and I didn't want to damage anything.'

'Oh well, yes, that can be a problem. I could always give you a call if I find anything else when the house clearance people come back.'

'Ah that would be lovely.'

Draping the dead woman's clothes over one of the smaller book islands in the hallway, Mel rummaged around in her handbag, pulled out a business card and handed it to Penny. Penny examined it, seeing the silhouette of a small donkey with the words 'Mel Sherwood: Media Mogul' below it.

'Oh bugger, no, that's from ages ago. I was doing some subediting at an equine magazine for a while, but it folded. Let me give you a better one.'

'A new career every week, this one,' said Eric. 'Isn't that what they're supposed to do, though, magazines? Fold? Otherwise they'd be just a sheet.'

'The other thing that stopped me trying to get to that other trunk was that I think I saw a wasp's nest up above it,' said Mel, ignoring Eric.

'Ah yes, we have a few of those here,' said Penny. 'I'd rather not disturb them, if it can be helped.'

'They're very underrated, wasps, I think,' said Mel.

Penny smiled. 'Yes, I have been coming more around to that point of view lately.'

Everyone Was Called Ken Back Then

What people never suspected when they heard Eric talking to and at them, jamming and folding and elbowing words into every available space, was that what they were hearing was a correction of a previous version of himself: a small quiet Eric who, although absent for half a century, never stopped being reachable to present-day Eric, never ceased to exist as an adjunct to himself that he pulled along dutifully with him. When Eric spoke now, he was speaking for himself, but speaking no less so for six-year-old Eric, and seven-year-old Eric, and Eric of every age up until seventeen, the Eric who wished he could say the sentences that other people said that encouraged other people to respect them and nod and laugh and sometimes maybe even later join them in a private conjugal place and consensually engage in a form of brief bewildering rapture. Words had not come easy to the Eric of half of the 1950s and all of the 1960s and a tiny bit of the 1970s that was still the 1960s in all but name. He felt them catch heavily in his chest or scramble up his throat and get wedged tight against one another. He looked at his friends – most of whom were, to be fair to Eric, older than him – and marvelled at their ability to respond to the universe with wit and insight, marvelled most of all at the speed with which they did it, the way they apparently never had to root and rummage for it.

He had been a twig of a lad, blowing up and down the streets of the northernish cities where he grew up, often in pursuit of his tall and heedless elder brother Mike. A scaler of fences, a thrower of stones, an explorer of bombsites, a ducker through holes in crumbling walls, a loser of shopping lists, an avoider of consequences. Out after dark. In before the shit hit the fan. F in maths, E in geography, D in English, C in history, but the quickest runner in school. It was as if his legs contained all the speed that legs could but additionally had borrowed the speed words should have had as they emerged from his mouth. He didn't just run quickly; he walked quickly, too, a little camp dance to his step as he climbed to the top of Everton Park or, later, one of the seven hills that give Sheffield its pleasingly spreadeagled shape. His peers were not bashful in coming forward with reviews. 'Nancy Legs' was added to the more commonly endured taunt of his school days: a prolonged consonant noise, both hesitant and Neanderthal, chorused by the cruellest boys in the class every time he opened his mouth to drown out what he was attempting to say, which of course made him even more afraid to open it. But he fought impressively, considering his size, fought fights he probably had to fight and fights he was nudged into which he felt bad about winning.

A group of older boys – greasy-haired smokers in bollock-choking flared jeans, drummers, guitarists, synchronised after-school pissers against saplings – noticed. Friends of Mike. He ran up Broomhill every Friday afternoon to fetch them Red Barrel from the offie, the one with the myopic gap-toothed lady on the till. Never had any bother getting served. None of them could believe how quickly he was gone and back. Then: the party of his young life. Mike off at the pictures with some girl, Karen from the Men's Department at C&A, working on her with the assistance of his inventive puns – 'Worse things happen at C&A' was one – or perhaps it was her sister Trisha whom he went out with just after. Eric was the youngest in the building by more than a year. And by no means a small year, that year you live from fifteen. Wandering the house, feeling like a diminution. Picking up the guitar and plonking himself down on a grazed Ercol rocking chair. Casually knocking out the chords to 'Strange Brew' by Cream. Alun Bannister, who Mike had told Eric was in a band, coming out of the bog just in time to hear it. 'ERE, YOU LOT, FUCKIN' HELL LISTEN TO THIS.' Wiped his hands on his flares, not quite thoroughly enough. Used one to shake one of Eric's. Three rungs of the social ladder skipped in one night.

It had been their dad who'd taken the three of them – Eric, Mike and their mum – from Liverpool to Sheffield. Or, more accurately, it had been their dad taking himself off fuck knows elsewhere that had taken them there. 'I can't stand it any longer,' Mary Inskip – formerly Woodcock – had said to her three sisters, Pauline, Joan and Theresa. 'I see him outside every boozer. Any time some lanky black-haired bloke is crossing the street or I hear some scally giving it some gob on the bus I'm convinced it's Prestwich Harry.' Eric, by contrast, barely encountered his dad in his own mind, let alone on the street or public transport. It wasn't as if he'd been around much when he'd *been* around. Prestwich Harry Inskip lingered in his head now, if at all, as a long wisp of smoke smelling of false promises or, on more vivid occasions, a contorting shadow obscured by a light mist of beer. The public story was that he'd gone out for a bag of chips and a sausage – saveloy, it was generally alleged – and had never come back. At least it was more original than a pack of cigarettes.

The sausage element of the story had the loudest ring of truth to it. There had been rumours: a floozy in Philadelphia he'd met on shore leave in his navy days, a dancer in Leeds, an actress in Paris, a parking attendant in Wigan. Eric had been eleven when it happened, Mike fourteen. Six months later Mary had taken the boys across the ankles of the Pennines in a van that looked more like a small truck. A toothpick of a man called Stan who worked with her at the Football Pools office in Aintree and had been sweet on her for years drove the van on her behalf. Eric and Mike sat on a stack of their nan's old cushions in the back with the tailgate half down and watched the hills recede into a halo of drizzle. Their guitars – the Gibson formerly belonging to Mike that Mike had been teaching Eric to play on and the fancier Rickenbacker that Mike had recently bought from RP Dalglish Pawnbrokers on Great Homer Street – sat on either side of them like treasured dogs frozen upright in death. 'What's that?' asked Eric, a mile past Glossop, pointing at a drenched grey pelt pressed into the road. 'Badger,' said Mike. 'Oh, I've never seen one before: I always thought they were brown and spotty,' said Eric. Mike, lighting a cigarette, looked at him with the bemused fondness with which you might assess a garden gnome who'd recently gained sentience.

Sheffield was nearly as rainy as Liverpool but wore a heavier jacket that inhibited its ability to dance and strut in quite the same way. The city's layout reminded Eric of a group of people standing around staring at a hole in the ground but not in a bad way. Both boys started a new school and became as popular and unpopular as they'd been at their last one. Mary got a job on reception at a public swimming pool. 'I used to work at the Pools and now I work at the pool!' she announced to anyone who'd listen, and anyone, including Eric, who wouldn't. At the end of the day she fished blood-stained plasters out of the pool on behalf of two lifeguards who went by the names Big Ken and

Small Ken and who, without words, somehow managed to convey that they were far too busy preventing the population of South Yorkshire from drowning to be concerned with so menial a task. On the same day in November 1969 that a tan unchaperoned dog ran into the leisure centre, before being chased out by Mary's colleague Norma, a dog of similar mongrelistic description and colour was seen racing along the corridors of the science block of the school where Eric was now a somewhat befuddling and moderately respected fourth year. There was some speculation that it was the same dog but nobody was able to confirm it.

By seventeen, Eric had moved to an unheated flat in Nottingham and had been playing guitar in Alun Bannister's band, Witch Fuzz Magic, for over a year. Wowed by Eric's prowess, Alun had magnanimously transferred to bass and vocals but remained the band's principal songwriter. 'If it's all right for Paul McCartney, it's all right for me,' said Alun.

'Me nan served McCartney in the sweet shop where she worked in Anfield,' said Eric. 'All the Beatles wuz there apart from Ringo. George Harrison turned up with this massive shopping list. He wuz walking about saying, "Creme tangerine and Montélimar, a ginger sling with a pineapple heart, a coffee dessert, cool cherry cream, coconut fudge." My nan told him to sling his hook 'cause they didn't have any of it. John Lennon wuz behind him looking glum. "What's the matter with yer, John?" me nan asked. "Cat got yer tongue?" John told her he just wuzn't feeling great about the future, generally. "Chin up, son," me nan said. "Tomorrow never knows." Knowing what happened after that, she still feels a bit cheated.'

The previous summer, in the back of a Comma van parked at a motorway service station midway between Long Buckby and Ashby St Ledgers, Eric had lost his virginity to an East Anglian shoe-shop assistant named Janet Fish who told him he reminded her of Steve Winwood from the band Traffic, in the process instantly clearing a lifelong log-jam beneath Eric's larynx. Since then words had sprung from Eric with even more torrential force than the ejaculation Janet had triggered with a few carefully timed observations whispered in his left ear. These included clean words, mucky words, true words, false words, words he didn't know he knew, funny words and words he'd been wanting to say since 1958. For those who'd known his muted former self, this explosion was disorientating at best, exhausting at worst.

Prior to a gig Witch Fuzz Magic had been due to play in the West Midlands, Eric popped over to his mum's new terrace in Wolverhampton, not far from the venue, for tea, but after forty-five minutes of reports on the events of his life in the two months since he'd last seen her, she had to excuse herself and find a pillow to support her head, which had abruptly and mysteriously acquired a new weight. 'Perhaps it's the drugs?' Mary Inskip thought. She'd heard there was one some of the rock musicians took that turned them into manic raving lunatics. She really wasn't sure at all about this whole musician business. It didn't seem like Eric at all. And what future was there in it? Giving thanks for small mercies, she thought what a good thing it was that she no longer lived in one of Eric's childhood homes. She remembered hearing about all manner of lost young things who'd turned up at Elsie Starkey's place in Dingle, getting Elsie to make them sandwiches and going up to Ringo's old bed and doing all sorts: stretching out on it and making moaning noises like I shouldn't wonder.

'Do get yer hair cut, love,' she told Eric, as he kissed her on the cheek and left for his soundcheck at JBs in Dudley. 'It makes yer look soft the way it is now.' As for Janet Fish, Eric had never seen a lovelier, more tender vision in his life. However, in trying to keep track of the twirl and tumble of his post-coital free jazz scattershot enthusiasms on every topic from Tranmere Rovers to Granny Smith apples to the third Led Zeppelin album and realising her belief that she'd snagged the mysterious silent type had been a misjudgement, her ardour cooled. Later, while Eric used the Gents, she slipped away to the car park and rejoined her friends Wendy 'Pom-Pom' Taylor and Mandy Aveyard, who'd been her accomplices in sneaking away from their parental homes and hitch-hiking across to the Blue Boar Services from Mildenhall, Suffolk. Wendy said she'd got talking to a Norwegian medical supplies salesman who'd casually mentioned that he'd heard Traffic were playing a secret gig in Bradford tonight and could give them a lift in his Saab at least as far as Derby, although it would be a squeeze as he had samples on the back seats. The search for the real Steve Winwood resumed.

In the band, too, Eric's words could bring problems. Containing so many of them and being in danger of sloshing over his own rim, he inevitably felt the impulse to start emptying some into his art. Alun's respect for Eric as a guitarist knew no limits but as the founder and leader of Witch Fuzz Magic he jealously played security guard and nightwatchman to the band's lyrics. In Alun's view it was high time the band took a darker, more serious turn. 'The sixties are over,' he announced. 'People wanted to look a bit more deeply into their souls, get behind the mirror and through the wall.' What that meant, as far as Eric could see from Alun's new writing, was elongated, swampy, jammed-out midsections with a little bit of certifiable tune either side where words such as 'elf', 'dragon', 'sabbath' and 'sorcerer' were deployed as frequently as possible. Alun had never been much of a fan of Eric's puns, even the really good ones Mike had come up with that Eric passed off as his own. Eric accepted that but he missed the more restrained fantasy imagery of the power trio's debut single 'Jennifer's Orchard', its more direct romantic energy. He was less keen on wading through the boggy topography of the new songs. He'd read *The Lord of the*

Rings and its most notable aggregate effect had been to make him want to drop-kick a hobbit. He felt a little alone: a team of one against Alun and Witch Fuzz Magic's drummer, Noel, who – though never opinionated on anything – was certainly not complaining about the new scope the jammier songs gave him to step into the limelight as a soloist. Witch Fuzz Magic had had their deal for a year now – a long time in music, in 1972 – and Duff Pickering in A&R was starting to emit crabby noises regarding how long the album had been in the oven. Both he and Eric felt Alun was stalling, looking too hard at what was around him, always with a beadier eye on the new album by Zeppelin or Rooster or Purple or Widow or Sabbath than he had on his own fretboard. Eric suspected, too, that Alun's nervous trend-watching perfectionism might be a dishonest articulation of something else: an admission that this 'being in a band' business was just a phase for him.

Alun talked like a largely undiluted North East Midlander of the struggling classes but his dad Ken owned a bookbinding factory, a big obstinate block of architectural hurt, almost completely devoid of natural light, down amongst the burgeoning wastescape on the edge of the city near Bobbers Mill. It churned out catalogues, calendars, dull trade magazines. 'Almost everyone was called Ken back then,' Eric would later remember, when discussing this period of his life. 'Even quite a few of the women.' Bookbinder Ken and his wife Doris had a mini bar at home. When Eric visited their house and exclaimed in wonder at it, Ken, with a wink, said, 'That's the thing about catalogues, Eric my son: people will never stop wanting them.' He said they were thinking about having a swimming pool dug out the back next year. Eric's eyes saucered. In the winter of Eric's seventeenth year, Ken gave him some temporary work helping operate one of the guillotines, pairing him with a man everyone called Steppo who leaned everywhere he went like a galeblown tree and carried with him an odour of a rotting sweetness, not unlike engine oil. Eric couldn't pick up the basic operating method, no matter how he tried, and was no more useful at the two other tasks he was subsequently demoted to. He suspected he would have been sacked, not to mention lamped by the impatient Steppo, if he had not been a friend of the boss's son, but instead they had him 'organising cardboard' in one of the skips out back. 'Eyup, Inskip's in t'skip!' he heard a distant football-terrace voice trill.

As six varieties of box rained down on his head, he could see, via a letterbox-shaped window, the hunched lamp-lit form of Alun in one of the offices on the upper floor, where the bandleader was learning to do the company accounts.

Eric believed in nothing more fervently than the power of love at first sight. His ardent conviction was that faces, postures, vibes, eyes told the whole multilayered story, if we could only make ourselves look. He'd even alluded to it in 'Thermodynamic Equilibrium', a song he'd written which he viewed as his best (dismissed as 'maybe a B-side at some point' by a frowning Alun). Admittedly there was scope for error in the process, but that only added to its magic. Contrary to his thoughts while reclining on Noel's rain-damp Afghan coat with Janet Fish, she had not been The One after all. He was able, in time, to forgive himself for that: the Blue Boar's car park had not been well-lit. His X-raying of the soul of Maureen Adams, by contrast, was carried out in the bright light of morning. That is to say: what little of it filtered through the smeared windows of the cafe on Barker Gate where she worked and where, for six days in succession, Eric had gone, even though it was on the opposite side of town, to eat eggs, chips, bacon and bread so thick with grease that his final sensation at night before falling asleep was of his unbidden tongue tasting its semi-permanent coating on the runway to his throat. After a two-day break for a gig in Preston, during which he worried constantly about the potential for Maureen's mystical evaporation, he returned, this time adding mushrooms to his order and, after forty-five minutes of pretending to read a recent issue of *Goal* magazine with Tottenham Hotspur striker Martin Chivers as its cover star, found the nerve to speak to her.

'D'yer mind if I ask yer a question?' said Eric, as Maureen set his third cup of strong tea of the morning down on the table beside him.

'You just 'ave, 'aven't you?' replied Maureen.

'Yeah. But I mean another.'

'Can't say as I'll answer it but you can try.'

Eric held the photo of Chivers up for Maureen to examine. 'Do yer reckon he looks like me?'

'Nah, he's uglier.'

'Ah, that's good. Because some people reckon he does. Others reckon I look like Steve Winwood.'

'I don't know who that is.'

'Ah, he's sodding brilliant, he is. He were in a dead good band, Spencer Davis. *Keep on runnin'*. Now he's in Traffic.'

'Well *I* 'aven't 'eard of him.'

Eric looked at her again, more closely, smiling. Something about the way she delivered the phrase – which was, it would turn out, one he would hear delivered the same way dozens of times over the coming years – pushed a lever in his chest, took what was beating in there up a gear, maybe two.

'Is that what you do, then?' She pointed to the magazine. 'Play footie?'

'Yeah, I'm a right sportsman, me. Fighting unfit. Nah, I'm in a band.'

She let out a muffled something that was not quite a giggle. 'Oh yeah? Have you been on telly, then?'

'Nah, but we will be. We got a record deal 'n' all.'

'Is that the way you sing in your band, that way you did just then when you went *Keep on runnin*'?'

'Nah, I just play guitar. I leave the singing to another feller.'

'Probably best if you keep it that way, I'd say.'

When her shift was ended they walked up Mansfield Road to a green rectangle called The Forest, which wasn't like a forest at all, then back towards town via the Arboretum. She said her name was Maureen: a redundant disclosure, since Eric had committed it ferociously to memory the first time he heard one of her co-workers yell it across the cafe. She said she sometimes watched the football but music did nothing for her; she didn't really get on with any of it. 'Yer 'avin' me on,' said Eric. 'None of it at all?' Pressed, she admitted to having once danced drunkenly to a Tom Jones song. On Arboretum Street a man in overalls leaning on a wall pressed a nostril, easing the ejection of a stream of green slime from its twin. The slime bounced across the concrete and festooned one of the prized winklepickers Eric had inherited when Mike had outgrown them. 'Filthy fuckin' nobhead,' Eric said, but walked on, raised above retaliation by love.

Wiping off the winklepicker on the long grass, Eric told Maureen the grey squirrels in the Arboretum would eat peanuts straight out of your hand. 'Look, come 'ere, I'll show you!' he said, pulling a packet from his jacket pocket, and holding a handful out. Sure enough, seconds later, three eager squirrels arrived, one biting enthusiastically into Eric's left thumb. Maureen said the wound looked nasty and that she supposed he should probably come back to her house, which wasn't far away on Portland Street, and get it cleaned up, plus looking at the sky it was getting a bit black over Bill's mother's. 'Don't worry, me mum's out at work,' she said. But Eric wasn't worried. He was keen to meet everyone who'd had even the most marginal hand in the creation of this undeniable brusque fact of a woman.

The following day, he brought over a bunch of pink roses and a toy squirrel, both purchased at Woolworths on Lister Gate. She said she didn't like fluffy toys and never had but went to find a vase for the roses. By then, he'd remembered the rehearsal and been dismissed from the band. Invariably late to band meetings, he knew he'd let everyone down more significantly this time but in a way he'd done Alun a favour, giving the singer a solid excuse to do something he'd been wanting to do for months.

Later, when Eric and Maureen were married, friends and acquaintances would occasionally ask them about Eric's musician days, about what it had been like for Maureen being asked out by the guitarist from a band whose debut single, after being described by none other than DJ Kenny Everett, on his BBC Radio Solent show, as 'a fuzz-laden freak anthem', made it all the way to number 38 in the charts.

'Well *I* 'adn't 'eard of him,' Maureen would say.

All the time, Mike was at least two steps ahead of Eric. By the point Eric had joined Witch Fuzz Magic, Mike had left rock music behind and started listening exclusively to jazz. Two weeks before Eric moved to Nottingham, Mike, who'd been working as a train conductor while living just outside the city in Beeston, quit out of nowhere and moved 150 miles south to Bath, where he picked up part-time work in a bookshop and sporadic jobs reviewing LPs for *Melody Maker* and *Jazz Journal*. He hitch-hiked to Paris and Berlin, had his toe stood on by Charles Mingus in a club in the former, got introduced to Lou Reed in a dive bar in the latter but was unimpressed by his manners, even taking into account the fact that manners were one of the last three or four things you'd expect from Lou Reed. Just as Eric was catching up, waking up from a sluggish and monotonous period in his life, contemplating an escape of his own, he received a postcard from Mike of a dramatic clifftop awash with wildflowers, informing him that Mike had moved to the strange and often misunderstood sea county of Cornwall and was once again receiving a steady monthly pay cheque from British Rail. Eric, who for some reason had previously retained a picture of that part of the UK in his head as a moderately sloping field made of knitting material, was spellbound: he'd never seen a more beautiful place in his life. When, five months later, in November 1979, as a fresh de facto divorcee, he hitched down to Exeter then took a train along the bridge of the United Kingdom's right foot to meet Mike at Redruth train station, he could not have been more excited.

'Don't tell me Uncle Ray persuaded you to enlist!' said Mike, assessing Eric's closely cropped hair as they hugged tentatively on the rain-slandered platform. 'Or did our mam finally get to you?' Mike's own hair, after a protracted neat phase, was back to its length and shape of ten years ago but with a fringe to go with it: Jett meets Jagger. He was wearing a dust-flecked black coat that seemed in grave danger of swallowing him and rendered him beyond what a person generally expects from their sibling in terms of mystery. A limp, which Eric noticed as they descended the steps from the platform to the road, enhanced the Byronic effect. A fellow British Rail employee passed them on the steps and he and Mike nodded to each other in an 'isn't everything damp and shit' sort of way. 'Fell off the sodding roof,' he said when Eric asked about the limp. 'Went up there to sort the aerial so I could watch the Reds lose to Forest. It's better than it was. But I got myself lamped in the pub last week too, which has set me back a bit to be completely frank.'

'Nah, don't be completely Frank: I've seen too much of him recently and he's a right divvy,' said Eric, wishing that, just once, just for five fucking minutes, he could make himself shut up.

What Eric saw on the walk to the narrow terrace where Mike now lived managed to decisively debunk both of his two previous mental images of Cornwall. The streets were all tipped-over newsstands, dogshit and day-old re-squashed chips. A man of indeterminate age with a face like a crumpled invoice staggered out of the bookies and up the hill ahead of them, discarding a beer can in a front garden with the special insouciance that comes with hallucinating an everyday non-explosive object as a hand grenade. On the hills above town, where Eric had expected to see trees he saw giant old circular chimneys instead, crumbling walls protecting quadrangles of pale green nothing. It wasn't the ugliest place Eric had visited by a long way, but, what with the intensively mined landscape and the rain and the pebbledash and the vinegary animal fat smell in the air, there was something familiar about it, something almost like . . . home.

'It gets much nicer in summer,' said Mike. 'Usually for at least one full weekend.'

He shouldered open a damp-warped front door and led Eric directly into the cultural solace of the house's one nearly spacious room. It could have been a small bookshop: the kind owned by someone who opens a bookshop to be around books and crosses their fingers hard that nobody will come in to buy anything. Piles of birdwatching guides and Penguin Classics on the floor: Koestler, Kafka, Woolf. Eric spotted cornflakes and cigarette ash ground into the carpet: a surprise, as Mike had always been much more dirt-conscious than him. Mike's little black-and-white TV – now containing a full signal – had been left on with the volume muted. On it, Eric saw Michael Heseltine's face. 'Minister for the Environment,' tutted Mike. 'While they're at it they might as well make him Minister for Little Girls in Red Coats On Their Way to See Their Grandmas. He does know his ornithology, though. I'll give him that. Chippy down the road do you tonight? Not had time to get anything else in. Well, actually, I had, but I didn't.' Eric, who was trying to remember what hornithology was and whether it was something to do with goats, said that was more than fine by him.

For much of the following three days they walked, first climbing past derelict engine houses and other relics of the eighteenth-century copper and tin industry to a monument on a hill above town. 'Francis Basset,' said Mike, staring up the ninety feet of stone to the Celtic cross at the top. 'He's who it's all about. I'm a bit split on him to be honest. He was anti-slavery but he also stopped a food riot and he was a baron, so I imagine all in all he was probably a right twat. Fuck I'm cold. Let's walk faster. I feel like my knackers are about to fall off. A lot of blood spilt on this hillside, that's for sure. Goes back millennia. They're finding flint arrowheads, even now.' Eric wondered how Mike could not only know so many things but stop them leaking out of his head and getting lost.

There'd always been a sadness about his brother in the colder months of the year. It was almost as if he expanded in unison with it, as if it became part of his stature. It seemed more looming here than ever, inextricably intertwined with a sorrow that blew relentlessly across the denuded landscape, catching everything in its vortex. But each time their walks reached the five- or six-mile mark he brightened, like a man who'd climbed out of a fetid trench and run for the horizon after hearing a word carried on the breeze that sounded like 'armistice'. He talked about the pub in Penzance where he went to play jazz guitar once a month and about the sound of trains, which had become a strange form of addiction for him, to the extent that hearing them for most of every working day wasn't enough and he'd recently gone further, buying an LP of railway field recordings to fall asleep to at night. They compared the times that they'd been thumped in the face since they'd last seen each other: Mike by his neighbour in the pub after complaining about the neighbour's Great Dane crapping in his front garden, and Eric by Maureen after talking too much in a B&B just outside Pontefract.

Mike asked Eric if that was why it had ended. 'Nah, it were because of strawberries, mostly,' Eric said. 'She reckoned she had a phobia of them and I kept forgetting and bringing them into the house. She told me I was being cruel and torturing her. We worked on it. I thought jam would be ok but it turned out to be almost as bad.' More seriously, he told Mike what a relief it was when they'd finally called it a day, cut the ailing juxtaposition off at the roots. The way he'd remembered what it was like to wake up one day and not feel you were disappointing someone just by wanting to go out and do one of the things you were passionate about. He'd been to his first gigs for years: Siouxsie and the Banshees, Squeeze, The Buzzcocks. 'Just a suggestion, pal,' said Mike, as, on the final day of Eric's visit, they skimmed stones into a winter-blackened sea that, beyond being wet, bore no resemblance to the one in the postcard he'd sent Eric. 'But have you thought of marrying someone you have something in common with next time?' Eric mutteringly agreed that it might be an idea. He was thinking about a girl in a Blondie t-shirt he'd momentarily seen through the train window on the platform at St Austell, in whose short spiky black hair and strong purposeful nose he'd seen a beckoning epicurean future. He was also thinking about how a lot of Cornwall reminded him of the callously shaved spine of a giant naturally hairy creature, and about how that creature, quite understandably, never wanted to give you a hug, and about how he'd rather like a hug, actually, and would quite like to go home, even though he wasn't totally sure where that was any more.

They had always been a family of movers, Mary's rabble. Spain, Dublin, Ireland's rugged West Coast, Belfast, Liverpool. Then, in the time of Mike and Eric: Sheffield, Nottingham, Derby, that part of the West Midlands where the towns all rub against each other like fat businessmen in the atrium of a conference hall, a few less picturesque settlements lining the M4 corridor, Bath, Cornwall. Mary, by now, had moved to a 1930s block of flats in Bristol where she lived with a bored Pomeranian who found its one joy in life via the impartial shredding of documents. The pair of them had been led there, with brief stops in Reading and Malmesbury, under a mixture of pretences false and true, by a resurgent carpet warehouse manager called John, now long out of the picture and, in Mary's cryptic words, 'onto more glamorous things'. For four weeks during his separation from Maureen, Eric lodged with his mum and the Pomeranian and generally found the experience less claustrophobic and more agreeable than he'd imagined, the one exception being the afternoon when he discovered that the Pomeranian, who had initially been called Emlyn Hughes but was now generally simply referred to as 'Mo', had eaten his paperback of Peter Benchley's *Jaws*. This was particularly galling since Eric had only had thirty pages left to read at the time, although he'd seen the film, and assumed the ending would have a not-dissimilar anti-shark thrust to it. A letter from Maureen, explaining that she was willing to consider a trial reunion on certain conditions relating to Eric's behaviour and domestic hygiene, also had a narrow escape, as did a further letter from Maureen that arrived on the doormat three days later, advising Eric to disregard the reconciliatory sentiments expressed in her previous correspondence.

Later, what he'd remember most about the flat was the mollifying smell of its carpets, their reassuring thickness. He came back from walks through the steep city aching and pressed his face against their rich fibres, catching only a slight whiff of Pomeranian. Permitting himself to milk the benefits offered by this temporary return to the planet of maternal sympathy, he complained melodramatically to Mary about the unfamiliar pain that vibrated from his knees to his ankles. 'Don't worry, luv, you've just got Bristol Shin,' she reassured him. During the course of his walks, he'd fallen in love at first sight with a total of seventeen people which, unless he'd remembered incorrectly, beat his all-time monthly record of sixteen in the unforgettable Nottingham summer of 1971. Being in a new place shook him up and he could feel the nomad Woodcock blood bubbling in him.

Over the previous few years he'd been living off the money he got from cleaning buses at the back of Nottingham's new Broadmarsh Centre and playing guitar in a wedding covers band: a musical vocation that served to rub salt into the wound of his current predicament. After his spell in Bristol, he found a bedsit to rent in a bellicose town called Ilkeston, half an hour's bus ride from Nottingham. He had drifted from many of his childhood friends but had been reunited with Noel, the drummer from the now long-defunct Witch Fuzz Magic, after bumping into him, quite literally, in the doorway of the bogs in the Crystal Palace pub on Clumber Street at a point in the night of such intoxication that both men were clinging to the last soaked threads of the power of speech. They'd never been close, despite their single mums once knocking about with one another most Friday nights at Walkers Bingo in Somercotes, but the following day they ran into each other again, hungover, in the jazz section of Selectadisc on Market Street, and, after Noel had purchased *Liberation Music Orchestra* by Charlie Haden, decided to go up to a pub the Lace Market and seek out the hair of the dog that bit them. Eric had lost his cheque book somewhere near Friar Lane so Noel spotted him a couple of lagers.

Noel asked Eric if he'd seen much of Alun.

'Not a dickie bird. Not for blummin' yonks,' said Eric.

'He lives in this massive get-fucked house near Wollaton Park now and looks like a jacket potato,' said Noel.

Noel, by contrast, had lost close to two stone in the years since he and Eric had last been hanging out. A tight black corduroy suit with pink silk lining clung to his slight frame, tapering at the ankles above matching white socks and trainers. Eric noticed a red tick on the sides of the trainers which gave the impression they were congratulating themselves on being trainers. Noel's painstakingly sculpted quiff and hairless face gave no clue to his progressive sludge-rock heritage. He said he was only in town for the weekend to see his mum and actually living in North London these days, engineering records for Polydor, mostly electro stuff. 'To be frank, Eric youth, I'm not that into much of it but the pay's good and the women in the office are fit as owt, especially the ones in PR,' he said. He asked how Eric's mum was. 'She's in Bristol now, right? Living with that Romanian bloke,' he said. 'Nah, she's on her own,' said Eric. 'I don't know where you got the Romanian thing from. The last guy was from Lutterworth. Worked in carpets.' Noel said he should come down and stay in Kentish Town some time, that he could probably get him some session work, if Eric could bear to leave the fuzz pedal behind.

It was only on the bus back to the bedsit that the penny dropped for Eric. 'Fuckin' hell,' he thought, with an audible guffaw that woke the snoozing grandmother in the seat beside him. 'He meant the Pomeranian!'

Cars Were Never Supposed to Be This Big

Once they were walking, Carl felt better. The day had pivoted, letting mild sagging clouds through a narrow window in its rear wall. The unforeseen melt of the glistening varnish on everything reminded him just how much of the lower parts of the landscapes remained underwater. A couple of floods necessitated a detour from the planned route, a steep climb through woods where black earth sucked impartially at their legs. The rain felt less like rain and more like a purifying mood they just happened to be walking through. He relished the feel of his hands as they splashed through the little pools that were slowly draining into the spongy acid turf. The triangle of knowledge that had hit him as soon as he'd walked into Batbridge Manor had been one of the vastest he'd ever experienced. It made him feel like he was falling backwards through a series of unlocked exits. 'Help me,' he wanted to say to his two companions who, as they engaged in the customary pleasantries of a previously unvisited porch, suddenly felt so far away. That not being an option, he padded quietly off, found a door leading to the garden, let the weight of what was hitting him – all the images informing him that he knew this place, more than knew it, that it was somehow part of him – knock him over, because there was nothing else he could do. When he did give in and permit it to do that, he was relieved to discover that most of the pictures he saw were not negative. As they gradually slowed, he analysed the garden: the secret upper tier, through the attractive gap in the granite wall, which – maybe because of something he was seeing in those flickering images coming through the triangle or maybe something in the atmosphere he felt in wandering through it – made him think 'monks'. There was a rambling rose behind him, swallowed by 2022's brambles, and 2021's, and possibly even 2020's. He was aching to get in behind it, chop the bastards off at the ankles, give the big red goddess a chance to breathe. He'd probably leave the moss on the steps leading up to the peeling conservatory to do its thing. It gave them character. But the steps begged for extra definition. Something stately on either side of them. Cordyline, perhaps, or trachycarpus. Trachycarpus would perhaps be the obvious choice but cordyline should never be underestimated. At the beginning of winter, on another record hunt not far from here, he and Eric had driven past a moorland house where they'd once lived and seen the little one he'd planted in the garden there in 2016. It had really gone to work in the intervening years and now reached the roof gutter.

A couple of years ago at a desultory record fair in Taunton, where one of the other dealers had put on the second Crosby, Stills & Nash album in an attempt to pump some life into the morning, Carl, from his elongated meditative position under the table, had heard Eric drift into a discussion of the concept of déjà vu with Reg Monk. Reg said he believed it was the universe opening up little windows to the other lives we had lived, past, future and parallel. Eric, being Eric, the man who saw death as a black wall protecting nothing but the void, immediately pooh-poohed Monk's romanticism. 'Nah. Faulty wiring in the brain, that's all it is, pal, nothing more. Dust on the needle. An old biscuit crumb stuck in the groove. Blow it away and it's business as usual. I've never been here before and I'm not coming back again and that's probably for the best.'

Considering the manner of their first meeting and his unquestioning acceptance of all his housemate was, it never ceased to baffle Carl how little credence Eric was willing to give to ideas of the unexplainable or supernatural. It was frustrating to have to wait to tell Eric precisely what he'd seen through those triangles in the manor, a wait that would be even longer now that the small industrious lady responsible for the building had unexpectedly accepted Mel's invite to join them for the walk, but what was there to be so impatient about? He could predict what Eric's reaction would be. Eric would no doubt tell Carl that Carl was 'probably just sleep-deprived', turn it into a joke or deftly reroute the conversation to a quasi-related topic. It would be doubtful that he'd be up for a lengthy investigation into Carl's growing theory that recently he'd been experiencing something a little like what Reg Monk had been talking about, albeit a bigger, more engulfing version. Carl *adored* that Eric took him so nonchalantly for whatever he was, without feeling the need for analysis, but sometimes he wished he'd just turn off the irreverence for a minute or two and indulge him in serious conversation where everyone looked the details squarely in the face. 'Ah well,' he reasoned to himself, philosophically, but not satisfactorily. 'Rough with the smooth. Maybe I just have to accept that it is part of the emotional avoidance that so often comes with being a man of the generation that he belongs to.'

Like a giant oil beetle, they made their way up the valley, Carl as the head, Eric as the thorax and Mel and Penny as the abdomen, the whole body never less than connected. Carl loved the ritual of these walks, which had become a traditional feature of any foraging expedition in an unfamiliar place – and in many familiar ones – for him and Eric. He had recorded and numbered all of them in his notebook. Mel had joined them for several. Not often did the trio add new members to their party but when they did, on days like today, Carl always welcomed it, despite the fact that it limited the potential for self-expression. He liked the young old lady from the tumultuous house, with her sharpened edges and lack of accent, and not simply because of the way she repeatedly flattered him about his appearance and instinctively knew the precise point behind his ears where he preferred to be touched. She had a bullshit-free aura about her, a lack of self-dramatisation and a nice colourful shoulder-bag. He was struck by the certain knowledge that her own house was a smoothly functioning one, that she kept her sofas clean, always remembered to put the food waste out and prevent invasion by fruit flies. 'Why can't Eric find a woman like this to be with?' Carl wondered. 'Is it me? Have I been in some way responsible, without ever meaning to, for preventing him finding such a woman?'

There was no need for Eric to consult the map, since Penny knew the best paths – including unofficial ones – to their destination: a collection of three stones at the head of the valley that were sometimes referred to as The Siren and Her Daughters. Penny said the legend was that on every full moon, the Daughters, and sometimes the Siren, if she happened to be feeling expansive, got up and danced, but Penny had been up there during several full moons over the years and had never personally witnessed it.

'Maybe people just haven't been playing the right songs,' said Eric.

Four strangers, edging their way downhill, passed them as they climbed to the summit. Three of these strangers had a version of the same thought: 'What I am seeing passing me is the New Older People, so different to the Older People of thirty or forty years ago. They are the ones who flow with technology's alterations without shrieking or resigning, who stay busy, who have not reserved their retirement bungalow in advance, who progress tidily up gradients in lively-minded trios, barely catching their breath on the way.' The fourth stranger had no thoughts at all, but that was because he was a man called Damian who had just leased a car with a showy, outlandishly manufactured steering wheel and he was lost in a reverie about how nice it would be to soon touch this steering wheel once again, a small near-erotic frenzy building inside him as, with every step, the prospect became more real. At the top of the hill, Carl was relieved to see that Eric only looked partially ragged. 'Maybe,' Carl thought, 'that visibly frail person I saw upended below the hill fort yesterday, and outside our front gate a few weeks before, was an aberration.'

Eric took the Siren and Mel and Penny took a Daughter each, everyone with their own stone to lean on save for Carl, who preferred the grass. There was something different about the earth here to the earth at home, something at once strange and familiar. Carl wanted to sink his hands into it. Maybe the desire indicated something more profound than he could yet fully parse. Or alternatively he just hadn't done enough gardening recently, was feeling the urges that the true botanist feels as winter passes into its final stages.

'I know sirens are fond of rocks but aren't they supposed to live closer to the sea than this?' asked Mel.

'I think the implication is perhaps that at the point when she was around this *was* the sea,' said Penny.

'It probably will be again, before long, the way everything is going,' said Mel. 'Ooh, don't these puddles look oily.'

'Hey,' said Eric. 'Did you know that it wasn't until 1975 that olive oil was available to buy anywhere in the UK except chemists?'

'Thief!' thought Carl, furrowing his brow. The olive oil fact had been one he'd told Eric yesterday after reading it on a blog about the history of cooking.

'Gosh, in my mind it was much earlier,' said Penny. 'But I know that for a long time it was only used for unblocking ears. He's extraordinarily well-behaved off the lead, isn't he. Does he never bark *at all*?'

'Nah,' said Eric. 'It's not his thing. He's a philosopher, this one.'

'You should count yourself lucky I don't bark right now, you rank fucking plagiarist,' thought Carl.

Mel and Eric, followed by Carl, walked to the far end of the plateau and tried to locate a nineteenth-century shipping tower on the coast, five miles distant. A low black chain of cloud was worrying its way towards them from the headland and Mel talked about the summer when she was small and her mum coated herself almost permanently in olive oil and vinegar, having heard from a neighbour it was the best sun protection. 'She smelled appalling and got skin cancer numerous times in her sixties. On the other hand, she had the best tan in Wolverhampton.'

Upon hearing a low moaning, the three of them spun abruptly around.

'Oh, er, oh, oh, er . . . oh-h-h.'

The moaning carried implications of distress but had a diffident quality to it, as if it were equal parts apology and cry for help. Penny was nowhere to be seen and their first impulse was to look with panic towards the steep gorse-decorated drop to their left where sharp rocks and forgotten half-trees jigsawed their way down to a blackly flooded chasm. It was Carl's idea to look directly above their heads instead and, as he did, Eric and Mel's gaze followed, where they were greeted, with a small timid wave, by a horizontal Penny from six feet above them, where, supported by nothing but air, she offered the awkward appearance of a woman who'd reluctantly agreed to recline on an invisible chaise longue.

'Please don't be alarmed,' she said. 'I'll be down in a minute, no doubt. I'm sure it will all be fine.'

'Shit,' said Eric.

'Oh gosh, shit,' said Mel.

'I am intrigued to know what happens next,' thought Carl.

Eric and Mel instinctively searched the barren hilltop for an unlikely soft object – a fully inflated lilo, or a thick blanket, or perhaps a parachute – but, finding nothing, all they could do was place faith in the reassurances offered by the now familiar voice speaking to them from this shallow heaven while, to its rear, the clouds rolled heinously in.

'I'm dreadfully sorry to have worried you,' Penny said, around an hour later, when they were back on low ground, close to rejoining the lane that led back to the manor. 'It used to happen not infrequently, but hasn't for a long time. I'd almost forgotten about it, to be honest. Quite unexpected.'

'Well, I can tell you this: I'm cancelling all my holidays and returning all my gig tickets for the foreseeable,' said Mel. 'The year might be young but it's already peaked, as far as I'm concerned. I've never met somebody who can levitate before. I'm mostly just glad you're ok. I was a bit scared for a moment. You came down much more . . . softly than I expected you to.'

'I reckon it was the Siren's doing,' said Eric. 'Or one of her Daughters.'

'You joke, mate,' thought Carl. 'But what do you really think about this? Is it altering your outlook, even a little? Is it inviting analysis and open discussion? Has it put a chink in something stubborn and old and fortified?'

'It's a little embarrassing to admit but the first time it happened was on the night I relinquished my virginity,' said Penny.

'I remember thinking, almost calmly, "Oh ok, what is this now? Perhaps it's just another part of growing up nobody told me about." Unfortunately the young man I'd led up to my room did *not* handle the sight of me pressed against the ceiling with equanimity. I believe he'd been more than a little terrified of me, even before that. But on the whole I've been fortunate enough to only experience the phenomenon in private, or amongst sympathetic and discreet company.' She smiled at Mel and Eric. The incident in Wales at the reopening ceremony for the botanical gardens in 2001 flashed across her mind, and the chain of events that followed, concluding with her failed re-election campaign, but she decided it was best omitted, largely because she liked accuracy, and accuracy in this instance would necessitate a long and nuanced description of the gossip and the politics of the whole saga. 'All of it would no doubt be rather useful if I had any control over it and it was accompanied by some actual propulsion. I'd love to just whisk myself off to Cyprus for a weekend without the bother of airfare and I imagine it would be the most invaluable asset when cornered by a total bore at a party but for the most part the onset of these episodes, and what triggers them, remains one of life's infuriating mysteries. Their primary redeeming feature is that they are always brief.'

'But why *now*?' Penny wondered. Recalling similar past incidents, she decided that, quite simply, the explanation was that it had been an exciting and emotional day. Probably the most exciting and emotional she'd had for some time. And it was far from over yet.

'I like your shoulder-bag,' said Mel.

'Oh, this?' said Penny. 'Thank you.' She was noticing within herself a strange urge to tell these people stories about herself. For example, to tell Mel that the bag and its seventeen different colours had been embroidered by her friend from Dorset, Elizabeth Kettlebridge, in July 1971, and that in the winter of 2022, when Elizabeth flew over from her home on Australia's Gold Coast to see Penny for the first time in more than a decade and the two women went out for an Italian meal in Bristol, Penny made a point of bringing the bag, and in the taxi on the way to the restaurant, Elizabeth saw that Penny was wearing the bag, and instantly burst into tears of happiness. But Penny restrained herself and settled for merely telling Mel that the bag was quite old.

The rain marauded in and the bottom of the valley became a part-blocked plug hole. The slurping riot of it made it only just possible for each of them to catch what the others were saying. An SUV hurtled down the lane behind them, far too fast, and, hearing it only just in time, they performed a synchronised triple leap halfway up a wet bank of grass and ferns. Mel slipped, sliding back down to the neglected tarmac on one muddy leg.

'You fuckin' plantpot!' shouted Eric, into the downpour.

'Sometimes I think we're living in some kind of afterworld that was never intended to happen,' said Penny. 'Cars were never supposed to be this big.'

When they'd rounded another bend they became increasingly aware, despite the redoubling gloom, of a figure ahead of them, sprawled at the side of the lane with a huge backpack beside him. As they drew closer, something told Eric that the sprawling might not be entirely voluntary, and he picked up speed. He identified a man, probably not yet out of his twenties, clutching his left side, with streaks of mud decorating his trousers, jacket, face and a head of hair that, under less dishevelling circumstances, might have been described as 'golden'.

'You ok, pal?' said Eric. 'Did the bastard clip you?'

'Erm, I think it can be safely said that he did,' said the young man. 'I leapt out the way but not quickly enough. I'm pretty sure he knew he'd hit me, too. But he didn't stop. I mean . . . Who the hell drives that fast?'

Eric helped him to his feet. 'The planet is full of shitbags. Probably over seventy per cent. That's the problem. Ok, let's have a look at you. I'm guessing you didn't get his number? Can you walk?'

'No. Erm, I think so.' He lifted his shirt to reveal a blossoming, scraped bruise, a little reminiscent of a large aubergine, rising up the left side of his torso from his hip.

'Looks like you're going to live.'

The foliage had died back to its most recessed annual point, hence behind them, along the raised bank of dead brambles and bracken, it was possible to see clues to the inner life that the comely deep countryside normally bustled and hustled to keep hidden. The front left hubcap of the oft-anthropomorphised Peugeot that once carried four teenagers through a summer which throbbed with misdemeanour. A pair of pillar taps from a twice-remodelled bathroom. Drink bottles long-drained of fizzy childish liquid the colour of fluey discharge. A rusted can of 1990s engine oil, its blackened top congealed shut, leaving the contents jailed for eternity. A stained, saturated cushion from a two-seat sofa half-interred in swampy ground, alone, rather than beside its partner, as had been subconsciously anticipated by all who'd farted on it. A trio of bin bags full of who knew what, the weighty look and shape of them a threat, a riddle. Mel and Penny, with Carl, who was thinking about Eric's strange convivial way of drawing in light chaos wherever he travelled, had caught up by now and Mel and Penny introduced themselves to the well-spoken young man, who told them his name was Billy, and introduced Billy to Carl, who said hello to Billy as best he could with his eyes.

Billy said he'd walked here from the station, more than ten miles, and was going car-free for a year, seeing how it worked out. There was something smart and benign about him, a little self-importantly so perhaps, but, beside it, a space he left generously unbolted for strangers to step into. Not one of his new acquaintances here on the lane looked at him and thought, 'This man is likely to betray me if I offer him help.' One by one everyone in possession of a phone checked it and discovered they had no reception so it was soon decided that Eric would briskly walk the mile or so back to the manor then return to pick them up in the van. They'd then drop Penny off and head home, stopping on the way at the Accident & Emergency department of the Royal Devon and Exeter Hospital so Billy could get his ribs and leg looked at. Eric pointed to a derelict barn behind a leaning gate on the opposite side of the lane, its corrugated iron roof blasted half to the ground, and suggested that it might be a useful place to shelter while they waited.

'Not likely,' replied Mel. 'It looks like the kind of place where you'd meet the ghost of a suicidal donkey.'

He was back with them in less than half an hour. Mel and Penny joined him on the front seats. Carl sat in the back on the Victorian bench with Billy, who, perking up noticeably on being asked by Mel what had brought him to the neighbourhood, shouted forward that he was working on a research project, for a book. He said his last one had led him to Antarctica, so he thought it was time for something a little less physically and emotionally taxing – that had been the plan, at least, until today.

'I am sitting beside a man without an appendix,' thought Carl.

The bench started to slide a little as the van met a steep hill, so Carl and Billy moved off it and onto the floor. Penny reached beneath the stereo and examined the beginnings of the turtle-neck Carl had been knitting for Reg Monk's wife Jill and, assuming it was Mel's, asked Mel what she was working on. Mel, who had no grandparents remaining in the arena of the living, said it was a scarf for her nan.

'Big scarf!' said Penny.

'Big nan,' said Mel.

'Ooh, vinyls, niiiice,' said Billy, reaching for one of the two bags containing the records Eric had procured from the manor. 'Is that *Clear Spot* by Beefheart? My dad used to have that.' This reminded Eric that he'd yet to remunerate Penny and he asked Mel to reach into the glove compartment and hand Penny the envelope containing the £700 in cash that he'd drawn from a bank in Lyme Regis the previous morning. Penny thanked him but didn't count the contents so would not find out until that evening that he'd paid her £150 more than the price they'd agreed on.

'I've been thinking of trying my luck on the comedy circuit,' Mel said. 'Just pubs, for starters. Wait and see if that works out before moving on to the bigger stuff. Festivals. Stadiums, maybe. I've been doing a bit of writing in my downtime. I really think it might be what everything has been leading up to, in a way, for me.'

Eric moved the van forward through the big bowl of rain, breathing little tattered breaths and grimacing at the too-bright headlights of too-big cars, just as he had at Billy's superfluous pluralisation of the word 'vinyl'. Carl dozed, but only until Mel detonated another sneeze. Listening, Penny was unable to stop herself mentally reviewing the sneeze's unique strength and quality. 'Outstanding!' she just about managed to stop herself from commenting.

'Mermaids, Merpersons and Other Unexplained
Creatures of the Jurassic Coast'
by Colette Dobson
International Folklore Society Journal,
Spring 2108

'I first took a mermaid as a lover in September 2071,' writes James Difford, in his quasi-pornographic memoir *The Salt Wench*. 'I met her on a quiet morning near Durdle Door, where I reprimanded her for placing her full weight on the limestone arch and potentially hastening its erosion. With gratifying haste she was locked completely under my authority, patently gaining a thrill from the harsh tone I took with her when she stepped out of line. There was one particular hardy crooked tree in a declivity on the cliffs above Chapman's Pool which she especially enjoyed being tied to while I whipped her, the saline moans from deep in her chest syncopating with the weather.'

One of the most curious fads to come out of the post-gadget darkness of the 2070s was 'Piscine Erotica', of which some claim

Difford's book is a generic early example, with others (though definitely not this writer) arguing for its status as an important text whose personal and unexpurgated nature in fact gives it more right to belong in the folkloric canon. Whatever the case, the eighth and ninth decades of the twenty-first century mark a notable rise in the intimacy of relationships between humans on land and part-human creatures of the ocean, with numerous eyewitness accounts put down in letters, plus such books and pamphlets as *The Seahorse As Big As an Actual Horse*, *The Merfolk of Eype (and Other Stories)*, *The Crustacean Who Cherished Me*, *The Talking Sprat of Weymouth Pleasure Beach*, *The Brinewolf and the Captain's Bell* and *The New Oxford Encyclopaedia of Fish Fairies*, all of it inevitably forcing one to ask, 'What precisely happened? Was it something in the water?'

The boom in UK mermaid stories in the aftermath of the Big Shutdown was countrywide but it's impossible to turn a blind eye to the emphasis on the seventy-mile stretch from Poole to just beyond Budleigh Salterton often referred to as the Jurassic Coast. In fact, stories of merpeople in this region have been told for hundreds, if not thousands, of years. The 1970 song 'The Mermaid and the Barquentine' by the folk-rock supergroup Equinox retells the seventeenth-century story of a lady with a flipper instead of legs who pulls a sinking vessel and its crew to safety just east of Lyme Regis then weds its captain on the Undercliff. Not far away, a couple of miles inland, on the River Axe, it was said that in 1812 a long black-bearded 'fishman', covered head to toe in oil, was dragged onto the bank by a trio of local children who then kept him in a cage and charged locals a shilling to look at him, although it was soon revealed that he was merely an unusually large eel.

Many sightings of fishmen and fishwomen were reported on Chesil Beach in the mid-nineteenth century, in the gap between the sea and the lagoon known as The Fleet. From a similar time comes the legend of the 'Mermaid House' on the east coast of the Isle of Portland, where six fishwomen resided, making their living by charging sailors for sexual favours but also inviting neighbouring human women over for lavish highbrow afternoons, where the art and theatre of the day were discussed and tea was served from expensive bone china. It has been rumoured that the topless mermaid featured in 'Ship in a Bottle', a 1974 episode of the children's TV show *Bagpuss*, and subsequently described by the conservative activist Mary Whitehouse as 'filth', was inspired by a holiday taken by *Bagpuss*'s creator Oliver Postgate when, at fifteen, he skinny-dipped with an eighteen-year-old trainee midwife from Milborne St Andrew.

The cataclysmic data loss that occurred in the Big Shutdown means the majority of reports of merpeople and merbeasts from the late 1990s to the mid-2060s have fallen into a historical black hole. We will never know how many texts or emails were excitedly sent about the mermaids of the Jurassic Coast, nor how many digital photographs of them were taken. Instead, we must refer to the surviving physical literature of the era for our evidence. In *630 Mile Breaststroke*, his amusing but often lazy and erratic 2017 memoir about swimming parallel to the entire South West Coastal Path, Colin Claxton-Murray recalls noticing a seal bobbing about in the waves beside him near Charmouth, then doing a double take after he saw 'it had the serene face of a conventional man in early retirement being introduced to the merits of peyote'. However, he proceeds to infuriatingly gloss over the incident, preferring to move on to his obsession with a proud old tree mysteriously decorated with lost car registration plates, and – apropos of nothing – a tedious anecdote about the time he thought he saw Michael Phelps on a London bus but was too scared to talk to him. In his 2055 autobiography *Mountains and Molehills* William James Stackpole claims that when first residing in Dorset as a youngish man he gained the acquaintance of a semi-aquatic speaking dog which had been reincarnated as itself, over and over again, every twenty-one years, stretching back to time immemorial. Back in the late 2080s I remember my own school friend Sadie Woolcott talking about her gran's sea-obsessed elderly dog and claiming that it used to walk around on two legs for hours at a time. However, it is worth bearing in mind the possible unreliability of both of these sources. Among the pupils of Puddlebury Comprehensive, Sadie – known behind her back by the nickname 'Doris Bullshit' – had, by year nine, developed a reputation as a teller of tall tales. Meanwhile Stackpole, who in the 2020s had been considered very much the poster boy of UK nature-writing, was widely known as a volatile and unreliable juicehead in old age, given to extended periods of writer's block and outlandish claims, such as the famously debunked, career-trashing one that he had once hiked from the base of the 978-metre Scafell Pike to its summit in under two hours then slid down it on an old kitchen tray.

Are merpeople real? And, if not, what psychological truths sit fermenting behind our invention of them? After another West Country-based connoisseur of merdogs, Tiffany Pearson, wrote her 2031 children's book *The Sea Spaniel*, she confessed the idea had come to her, as a passionate coastal swimmer, upon being frustrated by her Springer puppy's fear of the waves in the area around Dartmouth ('He just barks at them, as if he thinks they're going to kill me!').

The feminist folklorist Sharon Tatchall has suggested that mermen are often created out of a fantasy of 'the elusive ideal of a strong-armed trustworthy man, outdoorsy and somewhat feral, yet easy to keep track of on dry land and free of iniquitous motives rooted below the waistline'.

Difford, author of *The Salt Wench*, was alleged by one of his three ex-wives to be 'sex-mad, but with no real interest in anything going on with a woman's physique below the hips'. As the confessional narrative of his mostly terrible book goes on, a surprising turnaround occurs. Tilly, the mermaid that Difford has entered into the allegedly consensual S&M affair with, unties herself from the whipping tree, and begins to lash him with a belt. 'I didn't even know you had a belt,' Difford tells her. 'No, well, it performs no useful function,' Tilly replies, 'but I appreciate its decorative aspects.' To Difford's surprise, he enjoys feeling her violent licks, as the welts spread across his back and, while he luxuriates in the sensation, he begins to re-evaluate some – but perhaps not enough – of his life's transgressions. Meanwhile, a couple of hundred feet below, the waves crash onto the shore. Difford isn't a skilled enough writer to add this, but, as she read this section, yours truly imagined those waves going in and out in time with Tilly's blows, as if they were the steady breaths a vast, eminent monster makes itself breathe in front of a captive audience in prelude to the delivery of yet another revelation.

People's Notebooks

BILLY

Dorset. Safety. Serenity. Security. Or maybe not? Tried the nocturnal approach to writing. Wondered if a change of schedule might help. No luck. Strange noises outside at around 2 a.m. Scuffling, somewhere near the back door. The clang of an old galvanised steel watering can being knocked down the steps. When I checked, there was nobody there. Probably just badgers. Attempted and failed to refind sleep. Perhaps it's the sugar in the booze keeping me awake? I should stop. I think it might also be the cause of the fears. Irrational. Horror-film images, effortlessly banished by daylight. Tried to count breeds of sheep, as suggested to me by Eric, but it wasn't as effective as I'd hoped. In the end I just got up, walked up the cliff and down to the foreshore, waited for the sun to rise from the wet place where it somehow rests without melting. There are worse problems to have.

MEL

At this time of year I will often drive to a place and while I do, as many times as not I will notice a flying insect knocking itself senseless against my car's windows, again and again, never once taking a moment to pause and learn from the mistakes that have hurt it. Not dying in a traffic accident will remain my priority on such occasions but competing with that will be my dogged dedication to releasing the insect back into the great outdoors. When I finally succeed, however, a melancholic mood will set in. What if the insect is scared and misses home? What if, in trying to find a place for itself, both spiritually and physically, in this unfamiliar region, it mistakes another insect for its uncle, then, in a moment of excruciating awkwardness for the two of them and any insect bystanders who happen to be around at the time, realises this other insect is just an insect who has similar facial features to its uncle but an entirely unfamiliar voice and a vastly more unkind personality? A lot of people might argue that I probably shouldn't spend so much time dwelling on these things. I have, after all, reached the point in life when some people might be planning their wedding. But like so many women of my class I wish not to marry until I've experienced Europe.

CARL

My favourite grasshopper fact is this:

Grasshoppers first appeared on the planet 250 million years ago
Grass did not appear on the planet until 40 million years ago
Imagine it: 210 million years, just hopping around on whatever surface you can find, feeling incomplete, waiting for the grass that will make you truly yourself.

ERIC

I used to know this fella, Tipsy Bishop. I'm not great at remembering names but I always remember his because I used to think 'Tipsy Bishop – if that was the name of a band I'd probably buy their album, but I'd have to listen to a couple of tracks on YouTube first.' He was always at the record fairs. Hair like rotting kale in a rain shower. Couldn't stop flicking it around. Never seen a man over fifty enjoy his own hair so much. He must have thought it looked completely different to the way it did, but fair play to him, if that's what helped him through the day. Anyway, he sold me this record at a fair in Frome: *The Love Age* by Daisy and Peter Loveage. 1969. Recorded during the week of the Manson Family murders. Brilliant, brilliant, *brilliant* album. I gave him £90 for it then put it out on the stall for £140. Two weeks later, there's another fair, in Exeter this time. Tipsy is there again. Picks up a pile of stuff off the stall, mostly from the 'New In' and 'Progressive' sections, and hands it over to me. 'Would you take £400 for this lot?' I look through the pile and do my sums: he's asking for nearly £50 discount on the best prices at the fair but he's a regular, he's caught me in a good mood, and I know he needs money for shampoo.

'Go on then,' I tell him. 'But only because I fancy you.' I can't help notice that one of the records in there is *The Love Age*. Exact same first US pressing of it I had off him in Frome: original insert, flipback gatefold sleeve. 'Didn't you only just sell me that?' I ask.

'Did I?' says Tipsy. 'Maybe I did. Oh well. I just couldn't leave it sitting there, all lonely. It looked too nice. And I thought I'd give it another chance.' I take the money and he looks chuffed to bits as he wanders off but, after a few paces, he turns around.

'Do you ever wonder what it's all for, Eric?' he asks. 'You know – why we do what we do?'

'Not often,' I reply, 'but I can't pretend the question hasn't crossed my mind, on my more introspective days.'

'I suppose it's better than just waiting around to die, right?' says Tipsy, then he's gone, without waiting for my answer.

When somebody asks me what the record selling business is like, that's the story I tell them.

BILLY

Victim-blaming: that's what they call it and it's not good. I'm the victim and I blame me, and I shouldn't. I just met some odd people, trusted them a little more than I should have, and regretted it. I am trying to remember that I did nothing wrong, unless being open to experience and assuming the best about people is wrong. If a chicken arranges its feathers in a way that it believes is best but which also proves to be most alluring to a hungry fox, then gets eaten by the fox, who is the cause of the problem? The chicken or the fox? On the other hand, what am I whining about, really? Nobody tied me to a bed and broke my ankles with a sledgehammer. I am still here, fully intact, although I think I found a few more grey hairs yesterday (that's a bonus of being a blonde: nobody really notices). I suspect they've probably lost interest in me by now, both of them. Suspect, and hope.

You never get a cold at the same time as another cold. You never break your leg on the same day that your hand gets run over by a combine harvester. That's what life tells you. But if you do? What happens then? What happens when, just as you get stalker number one, it turns out there's been a double-booking? I will tell you: you try to convince yourself that neither of them are really stalkers because they haven't done the things that films tell you stalkers do. They haven't locked you in a room or talked about your fictional love affair with them and future wedding or broken into your house and stolen your photo albums and underwear. So, with your guard down, you are a little too free and easy with personal details, and a gradual accumulation of small disturbances – all of which you tell yourself aren't disturbances – build up. The way she stares at you like you are a small woodland animal. The way he turns up at four events in a row and shows you the same twenty pictures on his phone of his two St Bernards. The way, when you are on the high street, she jumps out from behind a pillar, three times in the same month. The email she sends, after the piece you wrote in the newspaper about swimming the Tiber, which tells you how good you look in your trunks and congratulates you on 'losing your little tummy'. The letter he sends, to your home address, which you did not realise he knew, going into graphic detail about his sex life, and complaining about the ways you have let him down in your new book.

They actually turned up to the same launch event once. Windsor, was it? Or Woking? Some place beginning with 'W' and too close to the M25 motorway to possess a personality. Seems a long time ago now, long enough to forget a lot of the other details about the night. But what does stick with me is the side-eye as they instinctively identified each other as rivals and checked out each other's gifts. He'd bought dog treats and some terrible book with a corgi on the cover that I politely accepted but would not have read for a thousand quid. Told me he'd been all the way to Ipswich to get it signed by the author, just for me. She'd gone a step further, with the framed painting she'd done of Ossenfeffer. He was nine months dead by then. No dogs in the new book. But that didn't bother her. It was so big, the bookshop manager had to help her up the stairs with it, gold frame and all. I wondered how the hell I would get the thing home on the train.

I do feel safe here, most of the time. Why would they come all this way, for a start, and how would they know? I've been careful. It's been years now. Obsessives move on to new obsessions. But at night, I still get the fear sometimes. And when that car clipped me on the lane, I did not initially think, 'You utter twat!', although I did, of course, think that shortly afterwards. What I initially thought was, 'I wonder if that was Gary or Marge.'

CARL

Eric brought a book home from the library for me once. The title escapes me now, something aimed at seven-to-ten-year-olds, all about the evolution of animals and humans. Eric intended it as a joke – I was in a big nineteenth-century Russian literature phase at the time – but I read it anyway, just like I always read everything he gets for me. What I remember most about the book is a drawing of a line of fish creatures, crawling up a beach with the legs they had newly grown, ready to eventually become all kinds of land-beings, leaving the vast puddle of amniotic fluid to their rear once and for all. Like that was how it happened. Like they all just grew legs one day and decided to properly check out the shore. Like it didn't take millions of years of minuscule increments of evolution. They all had this wide-eyed, thrilled look about them, as if every one of them couldn't wait to become a human, go to the shops, get a posh tie and a nice jacket. It always makes me smile when I think about it. The artist probably found it hilarious when he drew it. Which is how I know that, at the precise time he did so, he couldn't have been standing directly in front of the sea.

Sometimes in the early mornings, I hike up the crumbly golden edges and imagine the sea throughout the ages, looking not unlike it does now. It can feel like standing in front of the world's biggest 'Be Quiet' sign. The sea is the teacher who enters the room and quietens the unruly class. It's a one-minute silence, coming in and reprimanding you for your frivolity, except it can last as long as the sea wants it to.

When you're alone in front of what the sea truly is, it's never funny.

MEL
I have never understood the big deal about vampires needing to be 'invited in' before they can enter a house. That's not 'being a vampire'. That's just being polite.

PENNY
Lunch with Mel. Second time this week. Me in a floral gilet and a shirt I picked up on my last trip to Nepal, she in jeans and an old t-shirt that says 'Satan Is Real' on it. Later she showed me the stall where she sells her clothes. She strikes me as a sartorial chameleon. Her mind is a rolodex of twentieth-century outfits: sixties pea coats, Edwardian hats and walking skirts, seventies bell-bottoms, shoulder-padded eighties business suits, fifties pedal pushers and boat-neck blouses, dropped-waist twenties flapper dresses. Paul, who owns the warehouse where she works, talked about a hornet problem near the back entrance. 'You be nice to those hornets,' said Mel. 'They're not out to get anyone; they're just being hornets.' I told her the story about my dad and the wasp.

'Is there anything anybody said to you when you were young that has had a lasting effect on your self-image?' I asked.

'Well,' she told me. 'Let me think . . . My second boyfriend described me as "a quagmire in a headscarf" and I'd be lying if I said that hadn't proved to be fairly timeless and definitive.'

MEL
I met an extremely old lady who told me my tomato plants would grow more successfully if I tickled their leaves with a rabbit's foot. I did give it a go but the rabbit, who I'd barely met at the time, asked me to stop.

PENNY

<u>Seagulls: A Poem</u>
They're just gulls, really
The 'sea' bit is superfluous
I found that out
When I was speaking
To an esteemed nature writer
And called them 'seagulls'
He seemed rather angry
Though not as angry
As my ex-lover
Was
The time one of them
Stole a fresh pasty
Directly
From his eager hands
For the second time
In a week
His first week
In the South West
He had decided he loved pasties
But not yet learned the rules:
KEEP YOUR PASTIES COVERED
At all times
When outdoors
And within five miles of the coast
Don't give your pasties
To (sea)gulls
Give them your old microwave ovens
Clocks
And kettles
Instead

They will take them away
And recycle them
Because while they might be hooligans
And thieves
They are always thinking
Ultimately
About the planet
And its health

CARL
Walk 598:
The Killerton Estate from near the railway line at Hele, skirting Bradninch, kissing the edge of Broadclyst with the ceaseless moronic roar of the motorway in the background. 'Why this particular route?' I asked Eric. 'No reason,' he replied. 'Just fancied it. Somewhere new.' I soon saw through the subterfuge: Antique Village at the start, only 200 yards from where we parked. '65+ individual units selling antiques, vintage and retro items on an epic scale!' boasted the promotional literature. It's like a disease with him, the shaping of the whole of life around secondhand goods. He parted with not so much as a two-penny piece, just walked around the place tutting at prices. His incorrigibility only grows with age. 'Do you ever get any old vinyl washing up here, by any chance?' he asked the elderly, half-deaf volunteer in the National Trust bookshop at Killerton, later. 'The washing-up?' she replied. 'No, they have other people employed specially to do that, over in the kitchen. I do enough of it at home.' In the woods, finally, we looked for the ghost of an unfinished building: the much bigger, never-completed mansion that the remaining Killerton – a garishly pink dreamhouse in whose bedrooms you half-expect to find a dozen or so real-life Georgian Barbies running badger-bristle hairbrushes through their long margarine tresses – replaced in 1778. No

triangles opened up before me allowing any greater insight than a general 'atmosphere' still apparent in the depression in the earth that (allegedly) marks the earlier building's foundations, but at the hilltop, in what they call The Clump, I wondered why a fellow visitor was dressed in a wool tunic barely covering his otherwise exposed genitals then realised I was being given the briefest glimpse into a much earlier time: possibly an occupant of the Iron Age earthwork that once stood here. It was gone as soon as it arrived and we walked on.

In the hermitage of a folly dating from the opening year of Queen Victoria's reign, knuckle-bones of deer formed part of the floor. A chapel, built a year later, featured a bird carving to commemorate a swallow whose nesting schedule builders chose to work thoughtfully around. 'Kind people have existed throughout history,' I thought, before seeing three squirrels, ground into the tarmac by speeding tyres, in the space of 200 yards on the lane leading to Danes Wood. As the mist descended behind us, I was left with the bittersweet sensation of someone leaving a small protected island for the danger of a nation.

MEL

It is claimed that over 100 spiders per year will crawl into a person's mouth while that person sleeps. The exception to this is my most civil house spider, Ian, who would never force himself on anyone.

We're Probably Not Going to Hear the End of This From London Supporters

On a day of desolate blues and greys in the fourth year of the twenty-first century, reflected unhappily in a sea that thrashed about as anxiously as a duvet wrapped around a man chastising himself for a tactless comment, four people witnessed Eric meeting Carl for the first time: Eric, Carl, an art student called Jackie Murchington and a trainee bus driver called Joe Bester.

Before that, however, Eric had a couple more lives to live. Maybe even three or four, depending on how you looked at it. It was still only 1981.

Now began what Eric's mum Mary would call Eric's 'fancy pants' period. The tailoring on the pants, however, due to being fancy, took a while. Eric hired a stall at a Sunday market in Calverton to sell half of his record collection, used the proceeds to buy a beat-up Mini Clubman from a shady-looking turf farmer in Papplewick as dismayed ponies gazed on from behind a bent fence, chucked the remaining ninety-two LPs onto the back seat with his guitar and a few clothes, rattled down the M1 to the Kentish Town flat where Noel from Witch Fuzz Magic lived, crashed beside Noel's bowing mattress on the floor in a room of trapped farts for a few days then, upon Noel's ungentle urging, moved to the floorboards of the adjacent kitchen, floorboards always coated with a topsoil of thickest Borough of Camden dust, Eric pretending to sleep while Noel brewed the morning coffee that would help propel Noel to the studio on time to record the work of slim, aesthetically fastidious young men and women in eyeliner called Sadie and Ali and Paul and Glen and Toyah and Richard and Felicity and Gregg and Boy and Ruby Tunesmith and Darren.

Despite what felt like an encouraging rehearsal, arranged by Noel and witnessed by a couple of Polydor execs, the session work was not quick in arriving for Eric. He was brought in to play with a synth duo called Nefertiti and Peter Climax. 'You'll love this pair,' said Noel. 'One sings in this deep baritone and the other sounds like he's having a full-on nervous breakdown.' But in the studio Eric once again found love an elusive concept. The music struck him as something fit only to emerge from the orifice of a modestly priced children's toy. He felt awkward and fidgety in his association with it. The singing, meanwhile, was what might be heard in the depths of a 3 a.m. fever dream at the nadir of a bout of influenza. The album bombed, commercially and critically. Eric's bank statement informed him his total worth, at the dawn of 1982, was £23.12, although he did find a freshly laundered and still potentially useable pound note in his jeans the following day while daydreaming on the Northern Line. He woke himself up each morning snoring dust in a way that suggested he was siphoning the contents of Noel's kitchen floor to a toad that lived in his lungs who was not bashful in coming forward with its appreciation at being fed. He lost his Tube ticket for the fourth time in a fortnight, and as he fumbled for it in his pockets and bag, a woman in a mohair jumper that matched her cherry-red lipstick passed through the barrier ahead of him at Chalk Farm station and Eric planned his lost future with her as she faded from sight down the escalator. 'What compels me to repeatedly hide paper and cardboard from myself?' he wondered. 'Why must cardboard and paper even exist? What drives its mission to repeatedly hurt me?'

On that subject: something had been nagging at Eric lately, something that happened years ago and had, oddly, scarcely nagged at him at all when he'd first discovered it. 'Letter here for you,' Maureen, who'd been sorting through a wicker basket full of old magazines and bills in their box room, had told him one day in the summer of 1976, handing him an envelope with a three-year-old London postmark on it. 'Looks like it's from fuckin' yonks ago. Didn't yer see it? I wonder what goes on in that 'ead of yourn sometimes.' Eric spotted the familiar sign-off before he read the text above: 'Duff Pickering, Witch Fuzz Magic's old A&R man'. Pickering's two paragraphs were brief and to the point. He said he had been sorry to hear of Eric's dismissal from the band but wanted to know that he was very much all ears if Eric ever wanted to talk about future projects, something beyond the macintosh-wearing, trainee-maths-teacher crowd. Progressive sounds were fine, and they had their audience, but their shelf life was going to be limited. More polished and dynamic times were coming and Pickering could see a place for Eric in them.

'Polished' was a word that held little appeal for Eric, especially in a musical sense. Plus, three years had elapsed since then. There was nothing to suggest that the offer in the letter was open-ended. Opportunities in music generally weren't. Additionally, Eric had been a married man by that point, with responsibilities, as Maureen kept reminding him. The time to go swanning off down south on a fool's errand had long passed. But more recently, in idle moments, of which there were currently many, a parallel unlived life had begun to parade itself in front of Eric, tauntingly. The sensitive acoustic debut album described by *Rolling Stone* magazine as 'an urbane confessional masterpiece' and its accompanying sell-out tour. The move to LA. The tempestuous love affair with Cher wrecked by Linda Ronstadt's constant spying on the couple's Topanga Canyon mansion. The blossoming transatlantic accent. The begging letter from Jackson Browne's management team bullet-pointing the advantages of inviting Jackson to be the support act for the 1980 world tour. Eric telephoned the offices of Witch Fuzz Magic's old label Dark Circle but was informed that it had been subsumed by a multinational called Vital Music, folding entirely not long after, and that Pickering no longer worked in the building.

With the session work coming in at a rate somewhere short of a dribble, he'd secured a job on the counter in Merries, a sweet shop near the Archway Road. 'Just like your nan!' said his mum, when he told her. 'Ooh, she'd be so ruddy proud if she were still here.' The shop, all dark wood and Harold Macmillan-era enterprise, was owned by a jolly bespectacled hedgehog of a lady called Maude who had inherited it from a century-long line of women blessed with a similar prickly optimism. Eric could never work out if Maude was forty-eight or seventy, and would never in a billion years have dreamt of asking her, but was sure the answer was one or the other and nothing in between. At his interview, which was really more of a friendly chat over a bowl of aniseed balls, he brought out the big guns, for the first time in over a decade reviving his joke about The Beatles trying to buy confectionery from his nan. He suspected the lyrical references were a little lost on Maude but she chuckled and seemed extremely taken with the photo he'd brought along of Ada grinning above a dozen neatly stacked bars of Fruit & Nut in the sweet shop in Anfield where she had never really met any famous musicians.

'All right, Ringo,' Maude said, as he left. 'I'll see you on Monday, 9 a.m. on the dot.' He'd have preferred George, if it had been up to him, but he raised no complaint.

Maude was relaxed about holiday time at Merries, so when, that October, Eric received a last-minute call to ask if he could head down to a studio in Dorset for ten days to fill in for a highly regarded session guitarist who'd checked himself into a substance-dependence clinic, she told him to make a fortnight of it. The city air had been doing nothing for his eczema and, for the three nights before packing the Mini and heading down to Lyme Regis, he drifted off to sleep so vividly imagining the spray of crashing autumn waves hitting his cheeks that he almost stopped tasting the thick dust on his tongue. A West Country break in a comfy bed proved to be precisely what he needed: not just as a much-required hiatus from a sherbet lemons habit that was teetering on harmful but as an opportunity to breathe clearly for once and to see Mike for the first time in almost three years. The band, who were essentially just putting the finishing touches to their debut, were vastly better than he'd imagined: stripped-down and sinuous and irregularly futuristic, sort of second Silver Apples album meets Alan Vega. He found himself guiltily wishing the famous guitarist had checked himself into the clinic earlier. At the end of two final long days of recording, a dazed Eric allowed himself to be assertively taken to bed, twice, by the daughter of the studio's owner, an Elizabeth Taylor lookalike who, in all interactions, without quite being mean about it, made him feel a little like a rest stop on a journey to somewhere more important.

Mike, who was now renting the lower floor of a barn in a part of Cornwall a little less cut off from the main body of the United Kingdom than the part of Cornwall he'd been in before, drove up to meet Eric for a walk near Abbotsbury, where the Fleet lagoon tracks the sea towards the Isle of Portland like a precocious lanky apprentice. Mike told him a story about a heifer blocking a level crossing near Liskeard, how it had required the strength of him and three other men to shove it off the tracks. He could detect a bit of 'Winter Mike' coming on but he was pleased to hear his brother had found love, with June, a typist for a solicitor in Launceston. Mike said June and her daughter would probably move in with him next month. They'd already acquired a ginger kitten, which was living with Mike. For the time being they were calling the kitten Bodmin, after the town just over the hill in the direction the kitten appeared to have come from when it jumped a wall and wandered unexpectedly into Mike's kitchen.

The walk ended in the pub at a village called Puncknowle, sheltering under a circular hill 600 feet above the sea, where Mike asked the landlady if the etymology was associated in any way with Puck. Eric wondered whether he was talking about hockey until Mike said Puck was the first creature to walk the shores of England: a mischievous nature sprite, with curiously domesticated tendencies, who reappears throughout history, including in Shakespeare's *Midsummer Night's Dream*. 'I shouldn't know about that, my dear, but my old grandma swore blind she saw some of the little people dancing on the hill when she was a girl,' said the landlady. 'You mean fairy folk?' asked Mike. 'You can call them that if it suits you,' said the landlady. Afterwards, the purples and blues of the sky's natural autumn dyes ran and swirled and marbled above Puck's Knoll and Mike drove Eric to a dingy record shop on a side street in Weymouth and Eric rescued, from a bargain rack, at 50p a piece, just before closing time, the third and fourth Scott Walker solo albums, *Chamber Music* by Hetty Pegler's Tump from 1969 and an apparently unplayed copy of Kaleidoscope's *Faintly Blowing* from the same year. 'You mark my words pal, these are going to be worth a bomb one day,' said Eric. 'You're a grade one fuckin' lunatic,' said Mike, fondling the judiciously compiled Alice Coltrane anthology *Reflection on Creation and Space*.

A few months later, via a conversation in a pub in Camden with Noel's pot dealer, Eric finally tracked down Duff Pickering, who had graduated from A&R to a more corporate role in the London office of Vanishing Point, a new label funded by a couple of guitar-collecting city bankers and specialising in bands who sounded like Dexy's Midnight Runners might sound like if they didn't sound at all like Dexy's Midnight Runners. The two men agreed to meet in the Royal Festival Hall café on the South Bank the following Friday after Pickering had finished work.

'Sorry I'm late,' said Eric to a balding man in a window seat he hoped he'd identified correctly as the shined residue of 1972 Pickering. 'I lost my Tube ticket somewhere in Waterloo East. Took me yonks to persuade the guard to let me through.'

It sometimes seemed voices changed in Eric's head when he hadn't heard them for a while, took on a stealth evolution of their own. Pickering's Knutsford accent had existed in his mind for some time as the conciliatory sound a wolf might make when giving you a charitable few minutes to get away before biting indiscriminately into your organs. But today the sounds that came from his mouth were barely regional, lighter and more avian. Pickering said it wasn't a good time for guitars. Eric wondered what guitars might have to say about that. He'd seen at least seven of them having a fucking great time lately. Eric found himself retelling Pickering, at length, Mike's story about the heifer on the level crossing which led Pickering to interrupt him with an abrupt thought, which Eric thought was going to work its way back around to heifers in some unexpected and ingenious way but just turned out to be about the time, prior to a gig, he'd had to urgently find Martin Fry from the band ABC a fresh gold lamé suit after Fry had spilled gravy on his regular one. Pickering said he thought Clapton's latest album was the best of his career. Eric said he thought it sounded like a robot standing over Robert Johnson's grave, pissing battery acid. 'If it's just work you're after, and you're not too bothered what it is, I can look into it for you,' said Pickering. Eric thought about how Pickering's head reminded him of some of the hills he'd seen in Dorset where a small crown of depleted trees clung resolutely to the top, despite the prevailing wind.

'The old ball-and-chain's birthday tomorrow,' said Pickering, nodding towards two full shopping bags, as they got up to leave. 'Don't want to get myself a telling-off.' Eric wondered why married men – married people, in fact – were always doing this: publicly characterising their spouse as some kind of unforgiving sitcom prison guard. Eric, who in fact *had* been legally tied to someone who sometimes resembled an unforgiving sitcom prison guard, had never done that during his marriage and certainly didn't do it now, retrospectively. He'd always spoken loyally and positively of Maureen to friends, even on days when she'd recently called him a dismal waste of space for failing to mend a broken shelf or dug her fingernails painfully into the helix of his ear as punishment for forgetting to buy bleach for the third day in succession. Yet on the Tube ride home he was ambushed by a niggling envy for Pickering, for his home life of exchanged gifts, mutually planned evening meals, attractively boxed wine glasses and kitchen knives.

At least Eric had a place of his own now. Well, a cupboard, really, over in Tufnell Park, twenty minutes' walk from Merries. He'd not brought anyone back to the cupboard yet to sit on or near one of its two shelves but the mere knowledge that he could was a big improvement on the kitchen floor that Noel refused to vacuum and refused to let Eric vacuum. He'd begun to look fresher, less griddled by city living. It was his belief that the sheer unlikeliness of a man of his age and genre working in a shop specialising in boiled glucose made him temporarily more attractive than he was, so when customers flirted with him he took it less seriously than he otherwise might have. 'We seem to be getting more young, single mothers in here recently,' said Maude. 'I can't think for the life of me why.'

To anyone closely observing Eric in these years, the blind spot he'd developed for the romantic merits of good-natured humans who were drawn to his personality and looks would have been blatant, but in this regard Eric was still over a decade away from achieving self-awareness. Perhaps because life itself had often been tough, and had often seemed to have most value directly after the times it had been toughest, there was a conviction inside Eric – silent, but working away in a backroom of the mind, all the time, driving his decision-making – that finding and winning over a girlfriend needed to be tough too and much of its value derived directly from that toughness. It was less that he turned down the advances of the chatty, open-faced women who shared his interests and more that he didn't see them at all. Didn't notice when they ignored more convenient seats on the train and sat beside him instead, didn't see the feather boas they accidentally-on-purpose trailed over his shoulder as they waltzed past him onto nightclub dance floors, didn't fully hear them when they said that they, too, hoped to one day live on a farm with three pigs and two sheep and permit them to be pigs and sheep without asking anything else of them.

A new girl, Melanie, had started working in the sweet shop in late 1984. He sometimes talked to her about the hypothetical unfettered pigs and sheep, too. On the rare days they shared a shift the shop was a river where a trapped log had been dislodged by an irrefutable current. They pelted each other with enthusiasms – favourite songs and snacks and films and beaches and rivers and animals and Tube lines – and then wondered whether the clock was playing tricks on them by informing them it was 5 p.m. Parents purchasing bonfire toffee and Parma Violets for their offspring closed the tinkling door on their way out with the lingering discomfort of the intruder. But he assumed his new colleague to be around five years his junior (he was in fact out, on the low side, by a further five), too young to be considered in any amorous sense by the twenty-nine-year-old Eric, whose median age of desire when it came to the opposite sex was averaging out at around thirty-seven. Also she burped even more loudly and sybaritically than his mates back in the Midlands and had a shaved head, which scared him a bit. Meanwhile he entered an on-off situation with Leonora Arbuthnot, the privately educated daughter of the couple behind a high-profile public relations firm, who was having terrible difficulty deciding whether or not to break up with her long-term professional middleweight boxer boyfriend. The highly sensitive taps operating the spigot of this arrangement – their 'On' and 'Off' and 'Hot' and 'Cold' functions – could, for some reason Eric couldn't quite grasp, be solely accessed by Leonora. She told Eric that although her family were doing well now, her dad had, just like Eric's mum, had to pull himself up into the world from 'a struggling working-class background'. In time, Eric would realise that what she meant by this was that the six-bedroom Georgian house just outside of Harrogate where Benjamin Arbuthnot had grown up with his coal mine-owning relatives had suffered the disadvantageous condition of being located in Yorkshire rather than, say, Chichester or Royal Tunbridge Wells. Dodging the issue of visiting Eric's lodgings, having learned the details of its square yardage, she usually met him at the pub or her place, where he listened eagerly while, in a confusing accent she seemed to have leased for eighteen sentences a day from a Dagenham fish-seller, she outlined ways in which Eric could improve his outfits and posture and told him what 'potential' he had – he wasn't quite sure for what but found the prospect no less stirring for that – before sending him off with kisses from the softest lips he'd ever known.

'She's banned me from saying "I'm going to the bog" when I go off for a piss,' he told Mike on the phone. 'But then I said "I'm going to the toilet" and she said that was wrong too. She said it's got to be "loo" or nothing else. I don't get it. Why is "loo" better than "toilet"?' Mike expressed reservations, especially about the boxer ex. 'If you really want to get yourself knocked out by someone twice the size of you, you could just come down here and go out drinking in Wadebridge with me. At least you could blow the cobwebs away the next day in some proper country air.'

In August 1985, Eric was surprised to receive a telephone call from Duff Pickering. 'Sorry not to have been in touch,' he explained. '*Life*, you know how it is. Went into hospital to have my gall bladder removed. Then there was the whole Live Aid thing. Yawn yawn, et cetera. Anyway, there's an opening here if you want it. PR department. Thought it would suit someone like you, with the gift of the gab. That is, if you've not hit the big time since we last spoke. I assumed you hadn't, as I haven't spotted you on *Top of the Pops* or *The Tube*, but I'm not jumping to any conclusions. Some singer-songwriters are quite low profile here, but do well for themselves solely as a result their fanbase in the Far East.'

When, in a further discussion, a prospective salary was mentioned, Eric was struck by the rousing vision of being able to move out of the cupboard, rent a bigger place he could invite Leonora to, with its own bathroom, a little courtyard, maybe. Oddly, however, he found himself torn regarding the sweet shop and the vision of no longer being swept through it and fed cheese-and-tomato sandwiches for lunch by a bustling Maude. Merries had confounded his expectations by becoming the best and fairest place of employment of his three decades on the planet so far.

Watched from the walls by solemn painted cattle, he tearfully admitted as much to Maude while sipping pale southern tea in her spacious flat above the shop. It would, as it turned out, be the final time that century that the water of emotion rolled over his cheekbones. Maude suggested he stay on, just for Saturdays. 'We need the extra help, now Melanie's left,' she said. 'She's left?' asked Eric. 'Yes, sir,' said Maude. 'Went off travelling last week, to Africa I think. Or was it Brazil? There will be no stopping that one, that's for sure.' Eric instinctively scratched at his chest then, only once having done so, realised that it hadn't been itching.

On 14 November 1988, the twentieth anniversary of Conservative Party Leader Ted Heath appointing Margaret Thatcher as Shadow Transport Secretary, Mike was killed by a high-speed train on its way from Bodmin Parkway to Lostwithiel. Eric did not feel himself fall to the living-room carpet of his flat while he was being given the news by Parkway's veteran station master but when the voice – a chapped and shingly voice, containing all the melancholy and mud of winter in the Cornish interior, all its roadkill and rain and piles of agricultural refuse – had said all it had to say, he realised his chin was pressed to the carpet's well-trodden orange fibres. The fine grain of a wooden chair leg filled his field of vision. He pressed the button to make the line cease moaning unkindly at him and listened to the hopeful hum of the dial tone, then when it returned to the monotonous unkind moan pressed it again and, as a natural part of the centring repetition of this action, took his rest there for what might have been ten minutes or two hours. He noticed the carpet didn't smell anywhere near as nice as his mum's in Bristol.

On the application Mike had made for his position repairing tracks for Great Western Railway a decade earlier he'd listed Eric, unexpectedly, as his next of kin, so it was down to Eric to deliver the news to Mary and June. The first phone call turned out to be the hardest of his life. During the course of the second, which was barely any easier, he learned to his surprise that June and Mike had ceased to be a couple four months earlier.

'Oh but the cat!' June cry-coughed. 'He'll be all alone, in the barn. Bodmin misses Mike terribly when he's not there. Will you take him? Please. I can't. I've got a Bearded Collie now and I live next to a horrible road. And he can't go to the RSPCA. He just *can't*. He's not that kind of cat.' Afterwards, Eric still did not cry. He drank a reprehensible glass of London tap water and stared at the small park across the road. An old woman in a black raincoat was trying to coax a dog away from a bench. He thought it might have been some kind of Collie although perhaps not a bearded one because the fur around its face just looked like fur, not like a beard. He discovered that he missed the dial tone painfully so after another unspecifiable aperture in time he swam back down to the floor and listened to it for a while longer.

Looking back at the days that followed, later, it would seem to Eric that a temporary moveable structure had been built. The structure had three walls, each of which was made of a person: Eric's aunt Pauline, Eric's aunt Joan and Eric's aunt Theresa. The structure had no roof so it let the rain in. But rain was just rain and, working unassisted, it rarely destroyed people. Inside the three-sided structure were Eric and Mary who, due to the way they were wedged and cushioned tight inside it by the three other Woodcock sisters, didn't have to look outside the structure and face anything that was there. The wedging and cushioning also meant that the structure could move them around: just short distances that the small tasks necessary for remaining alive dictated, but without their feet ever having to touch the ground. The structure couldn't last for long, but it lasted just long enough to yield the result that, when it gently dismantled, everyone who was part of it had survived.

Eric realised that, whatever he did for the rest of his life, he could never be as strong and kind as these three women. Who had invented aunts? And why wasn't that person famous like Isaac Newton or Thomas Edison or other people who'd invented important things in history? He thought with great sympathy about people with only one or two aunts or no aunts at all. How on earth did they cope when something horrific happened to them?

When it was all over – although he suspected it would never be over, not fully – Eric performed some actions and said some words that managed to simultaneously be important and trance-like and instantly forgettable, then woke up to find himself in a small car, which with some surprise he recalled as belonging to him, holding the steering wheel and pointing himself and a small – by human standards, anyway – passenger through a concrete gap between a megalithic sun monument and some bald-looking fields. 'Winterbourne Gunner Vegetable Tournament' announced a brittle weather-washed sign. 'Andover 28. London 91,' announced a more solid sign, impervious to the elements. 'Fuckinell, Andover are going to need a lot of goals to catch up,' thought Eric. 'As it stands, it's an absolute drubbing. We're probably not going to hear the end of this from London supporters.' On the back seat was a guitar, two boxes of books, a bag of clothes and a box of jazz records. On the seat beside him was his passenger: the largest ginger cat he had ever encountered. It sat placidly with its eyes pointing in the same direction as his, as it had since making its undramatic escape from an inexpertly sealed cardboard box not long after the Mini rattled across the Cornwall-Devon border. 'Disastrous building plans,' a voice on the radio managed to blurt out as Eric reached for the off switch. He looked again at the cat, which continued to placidly watch the horizon. There was something about its strong jaw and thoughtful eyes that, if it hadn't been quite so simplistically accepting of its predicament, you might have called disturbingly human.

'*What?*' he wanted to say uncharitably to it, but, halted by a reticent burgeoning admiration, an innocent new hurt finding space to open up against the odds, he said nothing and continued to steer the car through the narrow slit in the future in front of them.

The following January, Mary suggested to Eric, Pauline, Theresa and Joan that it might soon be time for her to go to Paignton. She said the name of the town like it was a euphemism, a universally available exigency people the world over preferred to skirt around. But she was living eight hours' drive from the euphemism at that point, with Theresa, on a fat shin of land between the River Mersey and the Dee Estuary. People in that area of the country who knew her and people she met in her next home would sometimes say she never recovered from losing her favourite son. How true that statement was came down to definition. If recovery is completely rebecoming something you once were, Mary didn't recover, just like nobody ever does from anything. But if recovery is turning away from the alternative and living on to an age beyond those likely to prompt the phrase 'before her time' and once again experiencing intermittent moments when the earth's organic pleasures succeed in distracting you from the heaviness now forever within you, that is what Mary did. The Pomeranian, by contrast, barely lasted the winter.

This Is a Story by a Writer

As the century's final curtain began to close, Eric veiled himself deep in its folds, out of sight. In a new home, under the handsome brow of a Welsh mountain, he hid from many things, including Britpop, dentists, the police and metropolitan cocaine culture. He wasn't in trouble with the police; he was just a little concerned about them pulling him over as a result of his bald tyres and the mud-obscured registration plates that he always half-intended to wash but never did. It was a time when the enthusiasm he used to reserve for new music had transferred to new rewilded bottle dumps and quarries. He woke every day and walked immediately to the kitchen and drank, directly from a tap with a pressure many small waterfalls would have envied, the coldest clearest water he'd ever drunk. He imagined it rushing into every alcove of him, putting right all the wrongs the capital had done to his insides. He breakfasted on wild strawberries. He stared at a pagan face carved at some indeterminate but alluring point in history into the sedimentary rock at the rear of his garden and it stared back. He let his hair and beard grow, wore walking boots and one of the same two big charity-shop jumpers every day, dressed to impress the aloof smoky peaks and nobody else. He improved his skin. He ignored his potential. He watched, on bright windy summer and autumn days when no meteorological event seemed fully off-limits, shadows sweep across the land like gargantuan cinema curtains. He grunted respectfully at men called Bryn mending walls who looked up lazily and grunted not quite as respectfully back. He circled mountains with a hiking guide named Harri who lived three stone cottages away and politely declined Harri's invitation to put on a helmet and crawl a mile down a tiny hole to reach a cave the size of a parish church. He cheated the rules and switched seasons, sometimes as often as four times per day, just by walking up and down massive hills.

It was a time of brows: the green one that, in clearer weather, Eric could see looming above his bedroom window; the high cerebral one evoked by the titles on the shelves of the little dusty bookshop at the foot of the mountain which Eric kept telling himself he'd read and sometimes did; and the distinctively lush grey ones directly above the eyes of his friend and employer Reg Monk. Eric had first met Monk in 1971 when Witch Fuzz Magic had supported Monk's gaseous and variegated second band, Prestigious Woodland Village. In July 1968 his significantly more magical first band, Pudding Lane, had retreated to a cottage overlooking the River Wye and made what remained one of Eric's all-time favourite examples of pastoral British psychedelia with their still largely neglected *Plague Prevention Committee* LP. Monk, whose fuzz guitar drew perfect shapes around leader Simon Wyatt's lyrical evocations of Restoration-era Bacchanalia and mysticism, had been the most visually quiet member of the band but, as he approached fifty, could turn heads as he walked into a salvage yard or Radnorshire beer festival. So impressively luxuriant were his eyebrows, there were probably numerous ways he could have successfully styled them, not omitting plaits, had the desire taken him, but he'd settled on the straight fringe. Classic. Striking. Dependable. The brow bangs plus a badger stripe of rigid white hair on top of his head and the pectoral results of two decades of lugging heavy furniture into and out of vans had transformed him into a creature whole physical galaxies away from his twenty-something self, but his wife and business partner Jill was patently no less besotted with him than she'd been on first meeting him, way back in December 1969. This encounter – which, when quizzed by Eric, Reg and Jill dismissed as 'less love at first sight than lust at first sight' – had taken place backstage at the German music show Beat Club, where Jill was contributing backing vocals to the newly formed Fairfield Parlour, and Reg and the rest of Pudding Lane – in what turned out to be the band's strained swansong – had been performing their songs 'Londinium Confidential', 'Acid Bakery' and 'The Garden of John Dee'. Unlike Reg, Jill still looked almost exactly as she had at the close of the sixties, when she had been briefly touted as 'the Welsh Lulu' and legendarily dismissed a condescending Joanna Lumley to her face as 'a stuck-up giraffe'. Her squeaky-smoky voice – which on record always sounded more Barry St John or PP Arnold than Lulu to Eric – had only grown richer with age. Eric was at least half in love with her, and his chance meeting in the summer of 1996 with her at Portobello Road Market, where they had been running their hands over opposite ends of the same finely woven Turkish rug, could not have come at a better time. That is to say: a time when Eric had reached the point where he would more or less have preferred to set fire to his own thorax than spend another month working in PR in the capital.

When Eric thought of the preceding decade, he had a tendency to group much of it under the encompassing term 'The Delayed Inevitable' (coincidentally also the name of one of the better minimalist Talking Heads-esque outfits he had been paid to tout the virtues of in his early duties as an underling of Duff Pickering at Vanishing Point Records). The expiration of his and Leonora Arbuthnot's ability to exist amicably in the same small building. The final heat death of the Mini Clubman on the verge of a minor arterial road. His identical twin root canal surgeries. The end of his patience for lying to journalists and DJs about music he was increasingly indifferent to. With hindsight everything looked strung out and frayed, although at the time he'd often gone to great lengths to kid himself it wasn't. 'Perhaps this is just a phase, this business where she just looks at me and sighs, instead of saying hello, when she arrives home?' he asked himself, regarding Leonora. Michelangelo said he saw the angel in the marble, and carved and set him free. Eric wasn't sure what Leonora had seen in him – it most assuredly wasn't an angel – but after years of carving, and quite a bit of sanding, she was visibly dismayed with what remained, despite the effort the marble had gone to, against its nature, to conform to her wishes. The diminished chunk of marble tried when it could to avoid some of the 'northernisms' that made its chiseller wince, always used the word 'loo' when excusing itself in its chiseller's presence, reluctantly severed contact with the female friends its chiseller informed it were only spending time with it because they had the hots for it, learned not to protest (despite not holding the same view) when its chiseller traduced his accent or, at a dinner party, in the manner of a whistleblower delivering a secret truth about the universe, told some of its fellow university-educated friends in the public relations industry that it 'didn't actually like any Irish people, to be honest'. But one day the chiseller went a cut too far, describing – on the way home to the South East, after having tea and cake with the chunk of marble's original architect and the chunk of marble in a café in Widnes – the chunk of marble's original architect as 'uncouth', and implying that the chunk of marble's original architect didn't have the chunk of marble's best interests at heart. The chunk of marble – somewhat taken aback at its own powers of individual propulsion – walked out into the freshish Home Counties air, got a hotel room, made a plan. But as that plan progressed, the chunk always – in part as an attempt not to resemble its chiseller's bad points – made an unchiselled point of remembering its chiseller's good points: some of the early chiselling the chiseller did that wasn't so harmful and was maybe even beneficial, the two occasions on which he'd witnessed the chiseller give copper-coloured coins to the homeless, the chiseller's wit and imagination and lofty sharp intelligence and spasmodic loyalty and undeniable love of animals, for example.

When Eric's and Jill Monk's appreciative exploratory hands almost touched, in the middle of that Turkish rug, a mountainous salvation began for Eric. One accepted invite to the converted church where she and Reg lived on the northern edge of the Brecon Beacons was all it took to be set in motion. Eric quit Vanishing Point – now referred to by many of its employees as 'Varnishing Point' since a change of direction brought about by the success of Blur's 'Parklife' and the ensuing signing of half a dozen bands who sang big echoey overproduced songs about swaggering around in the culvert of what they had hurriedly caricatured as English life – sold the Clubman, said goodbye to Maude (she'd retired and closed Merries four years earlier but still lived in the same flat, above what was now a struggling juice bar) and Noel and nobody else, bought a used van with 73,000 on the clock off one lady owner, loaded it with records and books and clothes and an inquisitive but typically sanguine Bodmin, drove it back to Jill and Reg's place, found a cottage to rent within a week, comprehensively hosed himself outside and in with upland water, and breathed unselfconsciously for the first time in a decade.

His teeth hurt and he mentally wandered back in time to the middle of Thatcher's Britain and decisively closed the lid on a jar of sherbet lemons. For all its magic, Wales couldn't save his molars, but it irrigated his soul, transformed it from a formally acceptable lawn to an uncultivated meadow, spilling out at the edges, into thickets, leaping mountain streams. Meanwhile, Bodmin went to work, doing his assiduous best to clear the same thickets of rodent life. Eric marvelled at the two poles of the cat's character: the murderer and the creature of soft innocent warmth who let out a gently revving noise of surprised pleasure every time Eric touched him, a small ribbon of neo-meow that always had a hint of purr wrapped up inside it.

Eric idolised Reg and Jill. They were, in his eyes, the people who'd done everything right. Despite Reg being described by Brian Eno in 1974 as 'the one person I'm sonically in awe of right now', the following year they'd quit the music business entirely and moved, with a new baby, to Reg's native North East. They'd never made their dead-eyed late-period cocaine albums or checked into rehab or gone to Rick Wakeman's summer barbecue or bet their future on perms and keytars. Instead, they'd bought and sold cabinets, lamps, rugs, paintings; first from a shop in Gateshead and then from the front half of the sprawling lower floor of their current home, a converted Methodist church in one of the valleys of Jill's childhood. Eric joined them, manning the till three days a week, helping Reg lug wardrobes and tables and ottomans into a building that smelled to customers of archival carpentry and the incense that is perennially the incense of the stranger who has better incense than your own. On the remaining four days, he took trips that were gratifying in their lack of ambition: went to Hereford to see Britain's largest ducking stool, took solitary excursions to small cinemas and National Trust gardens, reversed into a garage sale in Aberystwyth and haggled over a Sardinian floor pot. It was a period when Eric was trying to remember what he was good at. Having concluded the answer was nothing worth bragging about, he tried to remember what he enjoyed.

When he did try that, what he usually ended up working his way back to was that day on the market in 1981, a few miles outside Nottingham, when he'd sold 100 or so of his records: the pleasure he'd felt at seeing the excitement in people's eyes as they pounced on them, at being able to so exhaustively answer their questions about the ones that intrigued them. A few collections formerly belonging to old heads who'd rebought their music libraries on CD were beginning to wash up in some of the artier towns of mid-Wales. Reg gave him his own little space in a corner of the church to sell from. But Eric, feeling open, in a way he hadn't for years, kept his options that way too. He learned to scythe his back lawn, helped Reg refit a 1963 1.5 litre Sunbeam Alpine, took a creative writing course in Hay-on-Wye shaped by a thoughtful waistcoated scarecrow called David Bush. Bush told Eric and his fellow pupils to 'write about what keeps you awake at night' so Eric thought hard about what kept him awake at night then wrote about the noise of Bodmin crunching mouse bones a few inches from his face and skilfully separating toxic gall bladders from other interfunctioning innards. 'Ok, *good*,' said Bush.

Bush said Eric had a tendency to overuse the imagery of trains in his prose. Eric's most well-received story was about a forty-three-year-old man who, searching quite literally in the landscape for his accent, which he had lost, found his accent hiding under some mountain heather. An awareness grew in him of a difference between him and his fellow students: their steeped entanglement with the written word; the fact that, unlike him, in the preceding years they had prioritised it over other activities – watching gigs, say, or catching that week's episode of *Lovejoy* on the BBC. If Eric could have just settled for writing the best sentences that he spoke exactly as he spoke them, his prose would have flowed more effortlessly, but something about having a pen in his hand made him freeze up, made him feel the need to stiffly announce, somewhere in the rhythm of his delivery, 'THIS IS A STORY BY A WRITER.' He concluded the pastime wasn't for him.

Every night before he slept, the last words he said were 'I love you'. That he said them to a giant orange cat, loudly purring a few inches from his face, rather than a full-size human woman making the equivalently contented noises of her species and gender in approximately the same location, did not trouble him at all, did not make him feel lonely or sorry for himself. On the contrary, it made him feel calm, completely in the place he wanted to be and like he wished he'd experienced the pleasure of living with a cat earlier in his life and not believed the hype when people dismissively said cats were 'aloof' or 'arsey' or 'only motivated by food'. Bodmin, despite the healthy appetite that sustained his bulk, was in fact minimally motivated by food in comparison to the way in which he was motivated by chest rubs and roaring log fires and any potential opening to sleep on Eric's neck. 'Aloof' was not a word anyone who'd spent more than ten minutes with him would rush to in an attempt to describe him. 'Needy' was closer to the mark. 'Slobbery' would not have been inaccurate. As for 'arsey', the only times Bodmin neared such an outlook were the occasions after Eric had been so unfeeling and cruel as to leave the house for a few hours and attempt to have a life. In short: with his nose-kisses, his uninterrogative acceptance of his life, his absolute trust in Eric's care and love, his long kind face, this animal smashed Eric into a million pieces every day. The idea of life without him was something he prohibited his mind to stare at: a car accident he found the discipline, again and again, to drive on directly past without craning his neck in its direction.

In Wales, Eric did not seek love, first sight or otherwise. He did not look for a person with a superior or arrogant or sneering aspect to their walk or conversation or opinions. And, if he saw one, he did not gravitate towards them in the hope he could be elevated by them from his low beginnings in life. He existed. He relearned what Eric was. He did not look for an onerous romantic challenge, nor did he find one. As it happened, however, he *did* find some of the lost parts of his accent – the parts that, unintentionally, had been smoothed off in his time in the South East – out there in the landscape. The northern edge of the Brecon Beacons was close enough to the part of Wales that sounds like a bracken-invaded version of Liverpool for some of those noises to drift down over the mountains and have their loosening effect on Eric. Merseyside was also just close enough for him to drive there and back to see his mum in a day. There was some talk for a while of her moving into a retirement facility in Barmouth but in the end she stuck with her first choice: Paignton – or 'Pain Town', as Eric was already calling it – which, being the location of her favourite childhood holiday, seemed to Mary a poetic and apt location to live out her days. At this point a useful confluence of events occurred: Reg and Jill, their two children now having left home, were in the later stages of a long-term plan to move the business. Reg had heard a rumour from a Cornish antiques connection about an old boy down in Bodmin, less than two hours' drive from Pain Town, who was retiring, which meant that the lease on his small record shop was up for grabs.

'But Bodmin can't live in Bodmin!' Eric instantly thought. 'That would be ridiculous.'

There was, too, another aspect to the idea, related to Mike, that he didn't want to confront and that gave him an extra little shivering hesitation. Nonetheless, he asked Reg if Reg might be able to confirm the rumour and put Eric in touch with the appropriate party. Reg confirmed the rumour and put Eric in touch with the appropriate party.

On their last sociable night before relocating, Jill and Reg filled the church with people. The old rug section was cleared, creating a small dancefloor. As the evening's appointed disc jockey, Eric put together the most watertight song list of his life: funky, but varied, each tune blessed with some intrinsic Regness or Jillness. Guests included a ninety-two-year-old vicar, two former international rugby union players, six farmers, three thatchers, two mountain guides, a woman nobody had ever met but who was having a well-known affair with a stonemason (the stonemason, suffering with gastroenteritis, sent his regrets) and five unappreciated legends of prototype heavy metal. Perhaps the most unexpected guest of all was Eric's NHS dentist, whom Eric, being copiously under the sway of Midazolam, did not remember that he had extended an invite to in the hazy euphoric moments following his double root canal surgery. The dentist, to Reg and Jill's delight, turned out not only to be a big Pudding Lane fan but to own the now nearly impossible-to-find single Jill had released in 1970 via the Motown subsidiary Rare Earth on whose A-side she'd covered Otis Redding's 'Respect', with an unexpectedly funkified version of 'Rain' by The Beatles as the stealth flip.

But such dizzying high points in life owe much of their intoxicating pleasure and meaning to the deep dank troughs that surround them, and several more of those were impending.

The next few years can be summarised as follows:

1999: Eric and Bodmin move to Bodmin. Eric opens a record shop. He calls it Pudding Lane. More than 50 per cent of people who come in ask him why he called it that when it's technically on Crockwell Street. Eric explains. 'Uh,' say the people. The record shop has a slow start. Eric frames the original gig poster Reg gave him for Pudding Lane's 1968 gig supporting The Byrds at The Roundhouse, featuring Graham Sutherland's transcendental and otherworldly 1955 abstract painting of the Great Fire of London. Eric misses the deific renewing properties of the Welsh rain, laments its mid-Cornish equivalent; the way it resembles a malady, a calamitous truth, a regrettable decorative decision. He pants through malefic moors, stalked by floods of mist, falls over a lot, sees Jill and Reg less than he'd like to. His aunts Theresa and Pauline die within a fortnight of one another. The Red Hot Chilli Peppers release their *Californication* album. Eric exits a small antiques shop in St Austell in protest at being subjected to a song from it. Bodmin the cat turns seventeen, looking not a day over ten. Bodmin the town turns 913, looking every bit its age. In one of its three newsagents, where he has been buying sherbet Dip Dabs in an attempt to alleviate sorrow, Eric drops an envelope containing a letter he'd been about to post to his aunt Joan containing some of his concerns about his mother's health. The envelope is handed back to Eric by Rebecca Westerfield, a thirty-four-year-old admin assistant for a medical firm specialising in artificial limbs. After recognising each other again at a gin festival in Truro, Eric and Rebecca regularly begin to spend time together. She tells him she is 100 per cent certain that having children must be part of her future. Eric tells her that he is 99.5 per cent certain that having them won't be part of his, although flails, waffles and flaps in his attempts to explain why, both to Rebecca and to himself. The day before Millennium Eve, he introduces her to Bodmin. 'A lot of people had their doubts when I decided to adopt a full-size horse and let it live inside my house,' Eric tells her. 'But it's worked out ok so far.'

2000: Rebecca moves in with Eric. Pudding Lane Records registers a profit of £7,126.25 for its first year of trading. Wheezing chronically and failing to sleep, Rebecca admits she is allergic to cats. Rebecca moves out. Primal Scream release their *XTRM-NTR* album. Reading an excitable review of it in the *Guardian* newspaper by their obnoxiously young music critic Tom Cox, Eric pops the album on in the shop but finds Cox has been a bit hasty with his enthusiasm, as is so often his foible. He and Rebecca visit a car boot sale in Bude where Eric buys her a wide-brimmed felt hat, brand-new, and a hotdog, also brand-new. They stop a mile outside Camelford on the journey home to allow Rebecca to regurgitate the hotdog without despoiling the van's interior. After eight months of knowing her Eric realises he is in something with Rebecca and, though it's entirely new to him, wonders if it could be love. Eric learns, by letter, from Maude's daughter Sarah, that Maude is in hospital recovering from surgery for lung cancer. A man in a polo shirt, possibly high on at least one illegal substance, comes into Pudding Lane and, bobbing around its racks like a bad actor playing a boxer in a film, aggressively asks Eric why he has so many records and doesn't stock more CDs. Eric answers the question the same way he always does, by saying, 'Because I don't want to, pal.' The man leaves, muttering to himself about aliens. Bodmin begins to sleep on Eric's neck every night, as opposed to every other night.

2001: Bodmin, possibly due to hearing problems, begins working on a change of sonic direction: almost what is, for the first time in his life, a meow, but not quite. Rebecca gets a new job working for a different medical supplies company, sixty-eight miles away in Exeter. They decide to make the distance work. Eric often visits his mum before heading to Rebecca's. One day, as they walk along the seafront in Paignton in a gazpacho of rain, Mary asks him if she remembers the day she and he got married and tells him he should never have left her for those slags in Wigan and Clayton-le-Woods. Maude dies. After his last visit to see her in London in hospital, Eric wanders the streets like a ghost from a deceased unsuspecting century, hits up some of his old favourite record shops, finds many of them gone. On the way back from one of those that remain, he is mugged in a pedestrian underpass in Wandsworth by a young man wearing a hooded top and holding a knife who, going purely on his accent, appears to share Eric's regional roots. Obeying the man's instructions, Eric dances until change jumps out of his pockets and onto the ground. 'Now stand on yer 'ead,' instructs the man. Eric refuses. The man takes Eric's wallet. 'Yer ridiculous, you are,' says the man, leaving, with a final wave of his knife. On the way home, Eric looks for reasons not to agree with the assessment, doesn't find as many as he'd hoped to. Mariah Carey releases her *Glitter* album. Eric doesn't notice. On the same day the Twin Towers fall, Eric's garden shed collapses in what can only be described as a moderate breeze. He tells a neighbour that its collapse is 'weird' and 'impossible to explain', but no terrorist activity is suspected.

2002: Coldplay release their second album, *A Rush of Blood to the Head*. Mary suffers a massive stroke – also her second – and dies, followed into eternity a week later by her sister Joan. Helping Eric through his grief, Rebecca shelves the conversation she'd been hoping to have about the children issue. Bodmin is diagnosed with kidney failure and an overactive thyroid. Eric continues to tell him he loves him every night. Bodmin continues to purr, only now more loudly. Eric notices Bodmin has lost weight. Eric notices Eric has put on weight. Eric asks Rebecca if Rebecca minds. 'No, it just makes you more cuddly,' says Rebecca, pinching his stomach. Witch Fuzz Magic reunite for a gig at the wedding of Alun Bannister's daughter Jane in Matlock, where Eric plays guitar for the first time in seven years. Everyone looks loosely the way they always have done, when the lights dim. Ken Bannister is there, still going strong and banging on about the merits of catalogues at seventy-six. On the drive home Eric takes a detour to Upton-upon-Severn to the arts and crafts house of a nervous art history professor to relieve him of an extensive collection of 1960s jazz, mostly released via the Blue Note label.

2003: Dido performs at the MTV Europe Video Awards. Rebecca and Eric break up, after finally having the children conversation in a more serious way. Rebecca says to Eric she still loves him as much as ever, and he says the same about her, but they agree that there's no compromise to be made and, because of that, no viable future apart from the further delaying of the inevitable. For the rest of the day, after Rebecca uses this phrase, Eric has 'Berlin Letter', the debut single by The Delayed Inevitable, as an earworm. 'You can't have half a child, can you?' Eric says on the phone to a commiserating Jill Monk. Awake in the early hours of the following morning, he decides that perhaps he could have kids after all, perhaps he'd surprise himself and enjoy it, but he doesn't call Rebecca. Three months later, Rebecca calls Eric to tell him she is pregnant by Craig Foster, an experienced and respected BMW salesman on Exeter's thriving Marsh Barton industrial estate. Rebecca tells him she wanted Eric to hear it from her before he heard it from anyone else. The following morning – a bright one in August, with what was left of summer feeling wrung out and fractious – Bodmin walks into the living room, where Eric is watching a VHS recording of the previous night's episode of *Match of the Day*, meows at Eric, has a seizure, then expires in Eric's arms before Eric has a chance to get him into his wicker basket and take him to the vet's. Eric, in explaining to people how amazingly long the cat he inherited from his brother had lived, would later, but definitely not now, joke that Bodmin had been cruelly snatched from the world just as he'd reached the age where he could legally drink in America. In September, Eric, barely functioning, constantly marooned in archipelagos of thought, pops out of the shop to get a cheese and tomato cob and forgets he's left the kettle boiling on the small stove behind the counter. He takes longer than usual, owing to dawdling in two charity shops and having to explain to Tina, the lady in the bakery, who has little experience in the area of northern bread terminology, what a cob is. Firemen arrive in time to save half of Pudding Lane's stock but the Blue Note jazz is a casualty. Eric regrets not researching a better insurance policy. Jill and Reg drive over from the Dorset-Devon border and kindly provide Eric with new racks for the remaining vinyl and a spare till, help him begin the interminable clean-up. That night they take him out for a balti in Launceston. He goes home to a house that has never seemed emptier, tries to meditate himself to sleep but can't sleep because he can hear a fly letting out a helpless garbled death scream somewhere in the room. He tries to locate the fly but fails and it continues the death scream. 'So perhaps it is this,' he wonders. 'Perhaps after all it is not birdsong or Pudding Lane or Rebecca's laugh or Bodmin's meow-purr. Perhaps it is this that is the real sound of what we are.'

For the second time in fifteen years, Eric found himself waking up from a survivable open-eyed form of sleep on a southern road tracking the nibbled coast in a north-easterly direction. This time there was no cat in the passenger seat, no cars or clothes or guitar in the back. Behind him: the shop half-charred, the fly finally silenced by the Great Beyond. He wasn't sure where he was going but by the time the earth had graduated from blacky-brown to browny blood-red, by the time the South West Peninsula was branching off in the rearview mirror in vain pursuit of a fleeing France, it became apparent. First, though, he went to Weymouth: low-hanging coastal town of plague, funfairs and bored goth teenagers. He looked for the record shop he'd been to with Mike in 1982, couldn't even find the side street the shop had been on, let alone the shop, presumably long-defunct.

He stared at a thrashing grey sea, thought about loneliness, thought, unusually, about Prestwich Harry Inskip and his naval service and about the inconceivable solitude to be found somewhere out beyond the horizon. Eric had never been lonely before, not properly. He decided he'd done pretty well, managing forty-eight years before finding out what it was like. He went to an antique shop, bought a big old ship's bell from its top floor from a man with a stutter. It hit him, as he did, that it had been a long time since he'd heard a stutter. Perhaps they had become less fashionable in the twenty-first century. In his tongue-knotted childhood, Eric had never stuttered but that could have been an alternative path for him, he supposed: one of his growing collection of unlived lives. He returned to the car and retraced his steps twenty miles east, parked in a lay-by above a chapel overlooking the sea. He walked further up the hill to a fire basket, swung back west, dropped down to a shoulder of beach protecting a lagoon after passing a blue scarecrow on a bench that hadn't been here in 1982 when he'd done the route with Mike, stared numbly at a World War II pillbox which had, let himself fall onto the shingle, and slept.

Directly above him, on the knob of land where St Catherine's Chapel had stood since being built by Benedictine monks seven centuries earlier, the art student Jackie Murchington and the trainee bus driver Joe Bester were squabbling. A year ago, they'd been star-aligned sweethearts, meeting in Beaminster churchyard after dinner, climbing to the summit of Gerrard's Hill, overlooking the town, leaning on the trig point and watching the sunset, carving their names into one of those fucking mental trees you found up there. But now they were all crossed wires and snagging worldviews. Jackie wanted to talk about the sixteenth-century dissolution of the monasteries – or had, before Joe had pissed her off. Joe, who resented having been dragged up this pointless hill in the middle of nowhere, wanted to talk about taking the mufflers off his Subaru. Jackie was still miffed with him for throwing a Starbucks drinks cup out the window of the Subaru that morning in Dorchester and braking at only the final second to allow a woman with an hourglass figure to cross a zebra crossing, then, as the woman's hourglass figure passed the windscreen, doing the universal symbol for 'boobs' with his hands, as if Jackie was one of his idiot mates, as if she wasn't the person he'd said he'd maybe like to marry one day, once he'd paid off some loans and saved some money instead of spending it on his car. He was a carelessly discarded receptacle away from being dumped from a great height, a carelessly discarded receptacle away from *being* a discarded receptacle. She was on thin ice too: if she kept on having a go at him like this, she could *forget* getting that soggy quarter of a KitKat he'd saved her from yesterday in his jacket pocket. But even amidst their rancour, as they descended the hill, they both noticed the long brown dog emerge from the waves below them and settle down beside the solitary man on the shingle, saw the way it walked upright from the water, feeling around in front of it like a recently blinded man.

'Fucking hell, did you see that?'

'Mmmm,' said Jackie, thinking, 'Ok, so he wants to talk about dogs now, as if nothing's happened.'

'No, I mean did you really see that. That's no normal dog, man. It was walking like a bloke.'

'I don't know. It's hard to see from here. I should think it was probably just standing all the way up to shake something off itself, a big bit of seaweed or something.'

'Nah, man. I'm telling you, we just saw the Creature from the Black Lagoon. I can't wait to tell Christ and Dean about it down the Red Lion tonight. They're going to absolutely shit themselves.'

Eric, for his part, even in his present unsurprisable state, was a little nonplussed to wake up to find he had been joined for his lunchtime nap by a member of four-legged society. 'All right, pal,' he said, mistaking his companion initially for an unusually shrivelled Borzoi, or perhaps a Lurcher who'd had a particularly hard start in life. 'Where's your owner, then?'

The creature said nothing in reply but Eric got the sense that, had it been able to, it definitely would have, despite the fact that its heavy-lidded eyes had still not opened. His own eyes, which had been sleep-sagged and not functioning at optimum capacity during the first moments of his assessment of the animal, now began to take in more aspects of its appearance and energy (or lack of it). Despite the dog's completely saturated look, its fur somehow managed to simultaneously give a dried-out bleached impression which, in addition to its closed eyes, put Eric in mind of vinegar. He was able to discern some terrible yearning in its long bones. Was it extremely poorly? Or blind? Or both?

'What next?' was a thought Eric had had several times in the last few awful days and, thinking it again, he was glad to for once have an answer of sorts. 'We'd better find your people quick-sharp, soft lad,' he told the creature, rising and brushing clinging beach pebbles off his salted corduroys. 'Or get you to the vet's.' The creature attempted to blink one closed eye, as if in response. Eric was a little dubious about its ability to stand, let alone to walk, but soon, with scant encouragement, it was padding quietly alongside him up the hill in the direction of the van. 'It's amazing how much they can do purely by smell,' Eric thought. The 'they' in the observation, which would have meant 'creatures in the canine family' five minutes earlier, now had a question mark hanging over it but, perhaps partly due to his current state of mind, Eric kind of embraced the question mark, let himself move with it. However, when they arrived at the van and he opened the passenger side door and, without encouragement, the animal leapt up onto the seat and got itself into a comfortable if melancholic position with its front paws under its chin, its more hound-like qualities were once again apparent.

By this time, Jackie Murchington and Joe Bester were back on the road too. Jackie, a rationalist, had already put what they'd seen on the coast in her past, although she did secretly admit to herself it had been a little anomalous. Joe, however, would not bloody stop going on about it. He told her he reckoned there was all sorts out there, if you really looked. Ghosts were real, for a start. He knew because he'd done a Ouija board with Dean and Christ at Christ's mum's house last summer. Everyone knew there was hard photographic evidence about the existence of Bigfoot. Joe would so love to get baked with that massive furry blurry motherfucker. And then there was that one time when he was looking for his Adidas Sambas amidst the empty food wrappers and other crap in the boot of the Subaru and he'd found not only his Sambas but one extra lone Samba that he'd never bought or put there and which had different laces and who could explain that, in any scientific way? But as life went on for Joe, after Jackie left him, as it flaked and diminished, of all his supernatural experiences it was that day above Chesil Beach which clung hardest to his mind, became the one he'd most frequently bore people with over meals and pints of strong lager, the one that – along with Jackie and two or three other things – could be numbered among the episodes of his life that he never really got over, until the day he died.

Rats Will Run Up Your Leg But Nothing Will Matter

Early days of May. That momentous initial spaffing. Everything striding brightly forward, once and for all, fulfilling February's little clump of hasty promises, showing March what a month can be if it replaces its muddy socks and gets its act together, coming good on April's rain-damaged pledge. Car Boot Season, 2023. People in roped fields admiring one another's Alaskan Malamutes and trying to barter twenty-five pence off the price of an old bucket. Eric exuberant, Carl pulled along in the slipstream of it, not without reservations. Banks taking their customary holidays but, as ever, deciding to save money by not going anywhere fancy. Everyone else on their way somewhere or other. Throbbing sense of life as nonsensical race. Service stations crammed with the anxiously micturating masses. Roadside verges stencilled by balancing quotas of death and life: cowslips, mushed badgers, forget-me-nots, truncated rabbits, bluebells, annihilated homeward-bound fox cubs.

The day had set its tone not long after sunrise, Carl striding out under the sheltering motherly lies of a perfect blue sky to water his broccoli and courgettes and finding a rat floating in the food waste container: unfortunately not a one-off experience for him. Half a dozen times or more he'd reminded Eric not to leave the container to soak with the lid off. The rats dived in impetuously at night for shreds of potato and orange peel then invariably perished, unable to scramble up the steep black walls back to safety. Undecided on what might be an appropriate funeral, he carried this one by its cordy tail to the far end of the chicken run, where a scrum of hens ran frantically for it then recoiled, as if from a wounding remark. Not more than ten minutes later, when he came out again to continue the watering, the corpse had vanished. He suspected it had been carried off by Frank, the bolshy crow who regularly visited the garden, eating almost everything in it that wasn't rooted or nailed to the ground and hurling himself into the conservatory window in protest any time supplies looked in danger of running out.

As Eric drove to the first of the two boot fairs they'd planned to hit, Carl kept his eyes on his knitting, his industrious hands under the line of the window. They passed a spot on the dual carriageway where, a month earlier, they'd seen a cat sprawled out on its side, motionless, in the slow lane. At the time they'd discussed the idea of Eric coming off at the next junction, turning around, going back for the cat, stopping, dashing out into the road to move it. It *had* been dead, hadn't it? Carl was almost sure, wanted to be sure, wanted to think that the light he'd seen reflected in its pupils was that of the headlights of busy bank holiday traffic rather than some last beseeching life in the poor creature. He couldn't help thinking about it now, just as he couldn't help thinking about every ex-badger, every denied rabbit, every forlorn fox, every thwarted squirrel, on the road.

That was at least half the reason for the knitting. It was a way of training his brain not to look.

Years ago, Eric had attempted to teach Carl to play guitar. Carl hadn't pursued it and concluded that was probably for the best. If he wrote songs, they'd no doubt be terribly dispiriting: wretched ballads of little lost lives, cracked howls of protest, laments for the better carless planet that never happened. By comparison, the bleakest Townes Van Zandt lyricism would be a family picnic, the late life recordings of Johnny Cash a high-energy megamix of spring-break beach anthems. That was one of the many plus sides of jumpers: you couldn't knit a depressing one, no matter how hard you tried.

Roadkill floated past Carl in nightmares, where roads were often rivers. Badgers popped up a lot, windscreen-splattered owls had none of the infrequency he would have preferred. In the most concerning dream of all he rolled an unidentified corpse off the coast road near home onto the grass verge only to discover he was looking into the hollow eye sockets of a magpie-pecked, desiccated doppelganger of himself. Despite his horror, he held on, waiting for the nightmare to finish, waiting for a dreamland scientist or zoologist to identify his discovery – identify *him* – but the nightmare was like a three-and-a-half-hour film recorded on a three-hour VHS tape: it always cut off just before the denouement. He woke from it feeling fittingly hollow-eyed and withered. Over the ensuing days he avoided roads when he could and, when he couldn't, watched more anxiously as death's shapes scrolled past on the tarmac.

As soon as he and Eric arrived at the boot sale Carl spotted a table boasting a combination of vintage garden tools and taxidermy: a wonky barn owl, two inflexible courting blackbirds and a squirrel up on its hind legs in a state of high alert that suggested it had seen something potentially concerning in the direction of Yeovil. He'd witnessed some macabre objects during his visits to car boots with Eric over the years: a coffee table with a pinewood top anchored to the front trotters of a deer, a book bound in dog skin, even a human skeleton, once. What grisly nutcase wanted this stuff in their house? Carl was thankful Eric's taste for the old and dustily strange didn't run to this particular twisted corner of hobbyism. Ok, so in 2012 he'd once sold a stool made from the vertebrae of a sperm whale but he'd bought it sort of accidentally, as part of such a big job lot of furniture that he'd not initially noticed its presence, and he was quick to offload it.

No, when Eric came to a car boot sale, what he was looking for was rare cultural artefacts, rugs, fabric, books, pottery, programmes, posters . . . and, of course, records. Now was spring's crucial pocket of gold: the time when the accumulated bestrewings of winter spilled out from garages and lofts into the open air. Who had died last Christmas? Had they once been a person of refined taste and niche interests? Or were they just another foot soldier of popular culture with three Bay City Rollers singles and half a Hornsea tea set? There was always an uneasiness that went with visiting a car boot, however fruitful it proved to be. From April through to early June much of the best fossicking was accompanied by the precarious sense that what you were in the business of was the exploitation of death. You were Frank, swooping down and snapping up the corpse of the rat before anyone else could get to it. You were the magpies from Carl's dream, pecking at the eyes of the creature that could have been Carl.

From late July to September, on the other hand, you were, for the most part, looking at the last boiled-down residue of the corpse's stock: a selection of dregs swilled around and poured from one smeary receptacle to another. The same old stuff going back and forth between the same old men and women called Norman and Doris and Keith and Tony Cracknell and Babs and

Sloping Pete and Michelle and Mary Peffleton-Slowhawk. There was a cogent argument to be made that Eric and Carl should not be bothering with any of it, since Eric had no shortage of stock coming in from elsewhere and it was a long time since a purchase from a car boot had justified the time or travel expenses devoted. But Eric's Fear Of Missing Out – 'FOMO' as some fellow young folk Carl talked to in his online group chat called it – was never stronger than in these feverish early weeks of car boot season. And Carl suspected there was even more to it than that for Eric: the people-watching aspect, its tumble of life. What they heard predominantly at boot sales was a working-class West Country voice: a voice they didn't hear so much in the high-end tourist towns, the second-home meccas, the Totneses, the Bridports, the Causley Mopchurches, the Salcombes, the Chagfords, the Padstows. Its accent was nothing at all like Eric's but it felt more relatable and familiar to him than many of the sentences he'd heard spoken in hipster coffee shops and farmer's markets. He liked getting in amongst it, in amongst people – people of course being ultimately what Eric – and his livelihood, for that matter – was all about.

Conversations danced and evaporated around Carl as, following Eric, he weaved around tracksuited and denimed legs. A man carrying a watercolour of an Edwardian horse race began to explain to a woman why he was responsible for the rise of the artist Tracey Emin and Carl was frustrated not to catch the full story. ''Ere, Paul,' said a greasy-haired wizardly man, who Carl put as somewhere between the ages of 60 and 160, picking up a World War II gas mask. 'Look at this! Shall I get it?' Paul, who was sitting on the back of a 1980s Land Rover, answered with an authoritative nod and the gas-mask seller agreed to a price of £12. 'I wore that in the supermarket the other week,' said the seller. 'Nah, I'm lying. They'd never get a mask on *me*, THE BASTARDS, *not while I'm alive*.' As well as residual post-pandemic chat, popular conversation themes included other upcoming car boot sales and the various methods people had put into practice to survive the winter.

Carl was aware, like so often before, of something that had been noticeably less common in his early years as a resident of the British Isles, prior to the election of the current government: the regularity of discussions and visible manifestations of poor health in public places. It predated Covid, went far beyond it, branched out from its perimeters. People talked about surgeries and follow-up surgeries and waiting lists, other hardships they'd undergone. There was a fatalism to it, but a sanguine Britishness too, a palpable attitude of 'Ok yes it's shit and there's probably not much hope but at least the sun is out and there's a Denby coffee pot and an antique salmon spear to be haggled over'.

Eric made a beeline for a stall advertising its wares with a chewed-looking cardboard sign that said 'PrE-lOVed RECORDS!' in red marker pen, Carl padding along behind him. The phrase didn't quite piss Eric off as much as people saying 'vinyls' but he wasn't a fan of it. How did they know for sure they *were* all pre-loved? Perhaps they were pre-hated, pre-ignored, pre-judged, pre-used as a coaster or ashtray. What was wrong with plain old 'secondhand'? It struck him as another part of the needless upgrading of everything. Nobody was just excited any more; they were 'super buzzed'. Nothing was 'good'; it was 'ideal' or 'perfect'. 'Awesome' used to refer to the Grand Canyon or the Pyramids. Now it meant 'Thanks for emailing me that PDF document'. Albums weren't 'released' any more, they were 'dropped', a phrase no doubt supposed to conjure a swaggering image – a microphone nonchalantly discarded after an incisive quip, for example – but which tended to put Eric most in mind of a globule or squirt of excrement falling in a careless workaday fashion from the rear of a goose or pigeon flying overhead to nowhere special. Nobody was an office dogsbody any more; they were a 'Junior Account Executive' or 'Assistant Director of Visitor Experience'. This wasn't just the natural evolution of language. Words were being demoted, fired without severance pay, except they didn't call it being fired any more; they called it being made redundant. What did you say when you were genuinely amazed by something in a world where every second, somewhere, the banal necessities of life, from a mediocre Caesar salad wrap to a packet of screws someone had sold you to mend the wonky leg on your work desk, were being ranked as 'amazing'?

Eric moved over to the stall, with low hopes, shook his head internally, but not physically, at a mid-sixties Rolling Stones LP that, at one of the area's better record shops, in the same pressing and better condition, was being sold with a £14 lower sticker price. Somewhere in the last decade everything had turned inside out and upside down. The 'vinyls as lifestyle statement' crowd had come in, pushed up the prices with their 'dope tunes', 'dropped' new releases and 'amazing' coffee. Record shops – the good ones – and small vinyl sections in antique warehouses had become the last remaining places a record buyer might still find an honest bargain. The charity shops had been sucked dry. The bigger boot sales, like this one, were hotbeds of dealers in or on the cusp of middle age, often just scraggier versions of the new hipster record shark: the one whose trade relies on the ignorance of the nineteen-year-old who has just got a turntable and doesn't yet realise they don't need to pay £40 for *Dark Side of the Moon* or *McCartney II*. Eric fucking hated that shit. But his strength was playing against it, fostering loyalty in the buyers on his mailing list and the regulars at The Loft and at record fairs by never trying to squeeze them dry, not preying on the unenlightenment of youth (even if the youth did say 'vinyls' when they meant 'vinyl'). Sometimes, Carl felt, he was *too* generous. But, as Eric pointed out: 'What is it costing me, really, pal?'

Eric had now picked up a copy of *Astral Weeks* by Van Morrison from the dealer's 'NEW ARRIVALS' box. Carl didn't have to look twice to sense the kind of mood he was in and knew what was coming.

'So this here pressing, pal?' said Eric to the man behind the pre-loved sign: a pointy-faced individual with eyes that looked like they were trying to remember the last time they had seen joy and resolutely failing. 'You say it's a UK first?'

'Yep,' said pointy face. 'One hundred per cent. The very first one.'

'Fifty quid. That's a pretty good price, even with the big scratch on side two. I imagine it plays through that fine?'

'Sweet as a nut. All of these are play-tested by me at home.'

'You see, it's funny though, because what jumps out at me here straight away is that it's got the green insert, which, on a closer look, I can see is the UK pressing that came out in 1972. The UK first is orange. You don't see it much now. Often goes for two hundred or more. My pal Reg, he really knows his stuff when it comes to this kind of thing, he sold a mint one for two hundred and seventy last year. He generally puts this pressing out for about eighteen quid, though, being a straight and fair sort of guy.'

'Let me have a look.' The dealer rumbled to himself for a few seconds as he pretended to examine the record. 'Ah, hmm, so it is.'

'I'd change the price accordingly on that if I were you, pal. You don't want any angry customers.'

Eric moved away from the stall, which also gave Carl the welcome chance to escape two women in headscarves who were making kissy noises at him and speaking in a language he didn't understand. People and their dogs were always wanting to touch Carl at boot fairs. Eric was forever being asked what breed Carl was, what the shampooing regime was that made his coat so luxurious ('I generally just plonk him in the sea three times a week'). Eric, knowing how little Carl enjoyed this rigmarole, had developed a special purposeful boot sale walk, giving the two of them the look of being on a mission, even when they weren't. But Eric couldn't help getting sidetracked. He talked to people. The people he talked to often knew other people. The other people knew other people who were sometimes selling record collections. Mostly it was a sustainable and functional system, a route into the otherwise inaccessible places where valuable records were sleeping, unloved, misunderstood, misappraised.

It had led to adventures, too, not all of them pleasant. In 2019, following up on a connection he'd made at a boot sale in north Cornwall, Eric had agreed to meet a man called Derek Thrush in the car park of one of Devon's more coveted crematoriums. Mel and Carl warned against it, speculating that it was Thrush's plan to chop Eric's body into numerous morsels and dispose of them deep in the swampy foundations of a building site on the east side of Exeter, but Eric waved off such concerns, pointing out that, if murder was on Thrush's mind, it would make no sense to meet him at a crematorium then move him away from it. After following Thrush in convoy down a warren of narrow country lanes, he had arrived at an empty bungalow nonsensically distant from their meeting point, which, as if weighting the information with special meaning, Thrush assured him 'belonged to Ian Blackstock' before unlocking a nearby barn, stacked floor-to-ceiling with records. Watched by Indian Runner ducks from the threshold, Eric, wondering who the fuck Ian Blackstock was, had done his best to root through a few boxes of mostly disappointing 1960s pop and rockabilly albums while Thrush – a man brimming with even more words than Eric but none of Eric's improbable skill as a listener – impinged further and further on his turning circle, spoke angrily about his forthcoming court case centred around his alleged racial abusing of a careworker, attempted – on the basis of nothing but Eric's panicking bewilderment – to recruit Eric for an infamous political party specialising in Far Right ideology, then, as a send-off, opened up his shirt and showed Eric his colostomy bag. Later, enduring the 'What did we tell you' taunts of Carl and Mel, Eric would confess it had been a lot of bother to go to just to purchase two Nancy Sinatra albums for approximately half their market value.

The day was rapidly warming up and, as Carl did too in conjunction with it, he began to regret wearing his harness. The unusual, pouched harness had been purchased for him in autumn 2018 by Eric as a combined fifteenth anniversary and birthday present. What strangers generally thought upon seeing it was, 'Ah, what a useful method of enabling that dog to transport its own plastically sealed faeces through the countryside,' none of them for a second suspecting the strictly hygienic selection of wool, needles, yarn, crochet hooks, tape measures and miniature cutting implements it often contained. As it happened, prior to arriving at that day's second boot sale, it did occur to Carl that he needed to empty his bowels, but, being wholly self-sufficient in that area and craving a little alone time after the claustrophobic overstimulation of the first part of the day, he excused himself and told Eric he would find a quiet spot where he could sit this particular low-budget pageant out.

Fair number two was a new one – or rather a regularly frequented fair in a new location – only ten miles east of home, on a hillside overlooking the long-defunct Seaton Junction railway station. He and Eric had walked through the quiet woodland around here on numerous occasions and Carl was confident he could find a spot in it where he could knit without danger of being seen or accidentally rescued by a well-meaning stranger. He was glad to be in the shade and to be able to remove the harness. There was a sore circle on the back of his neck in the place where a satsuma-faced woman called Daphne selling teapots had been roughly massaging him earlier. He could still feel the heat of her clumsy touch, and it made him crave the gentle, intuitive ear strokes of Mel and Penny.

After tidily burying the former contents of his stomach behind a conifer, he stretched out on a carpet of moss and leaves and breathed properly for the first time that day. No sooner than he'd done so he found himself looking into a prism of the past, seeing, in the valley below, the station as it had been long before its 1966 closure. A passenger train was pulling in, carrying pigs, sheep, chicks and Guernsey calves, as well as humans and that day's mail. He suspected it was a farm removal in process, train being the popular method for such a thing in the early years of the last century. The stationmaster bustled along the platform, a kink to his walk the one visible sign of the pint of strong ale he'd used to kickstart his morning. Weighing the evidence, and appraising the outfits on offer, Carl put the period as somewhere halfway through the 1920s.

In 2004, Carl's first year as an avid reader, one of the 234 books he'd enjoyed had been *The House on the Strand*, an unlikely time-slip acid fantasy written, early in her seventh decade, by the bestselling Cornish novelist Daphne du Maurier. The book had been published at the height of the hippie era, in 1969, and concerned the journeys of a man called Dick Young to the fourteenth century after Young had agreed to be the guinea pig for a new drug concocted by his biophysicist best friend. Carl had recommended the book to Eric, who had got about halfway with it before abandoning it on a deckchair in the small greenhouse in Mel's back garden. When Young travels back in time in the book, he is unable to interact with the characters he encounters, who remain unaware of his presence. Carl's experience, when faced with his polygonal glimpses into the past, was not dissimilar. He was there but he was not there, had no material impact on what he saw transpiring. Unlike a time traveller in a novel or film, though, Carl did not flit between significant events and famous occasions. When his window into the past pointed his gaze at the Dorset section of the Monarch's Way footpath, named for its tracing of Charles II's getaway route from the Battle of Worcester in 1651, Carl did not see the harried twenty-one-year-old future king bustling along the path, pursued by Cromwellian forces. He mostly saw some grass and mud that looked a lot like the grass and mud there today and some sheep that were not massively different from 2020s sheep, aside from having noticeably less wool on their back (a recently acquired fact that Carl had enjoyed telling Eric was that hundreds of years ago, prior to mass profit-driven breeding, the average sheep had only produced a fraction of the wool of its twenty-first-century equivalent). He often saw people, too, going about their business, as with today's scene at the disused station, but the most significant and dramatic aspect of Carl's historical visions was that during every one of them he got a strong sense that he had once been a part of them, in at least some small way. He never saw *himself* in his visions, not like he saw himself – or another version of himself – inside that recurring nightmare about the cadaver on the coast road, but that didn't stop him searching. He couldn't help it: it was an organic by-product of his ever-increasing yearning to understand what he was, who he was, why he was so alone in being what he was, here on the Devon-Dorset border, here on planet earth.

'Going granular' was a favourite term of Mel's. It was her code-phrase for a surreptitious way of leaving a social gathering, without the folderol of saying goodbye to everyone you felt you should say goodbye to, a tactful fading into the night. The phrase could also be applied to the way Carl's visions tended to disperse. When the scene at the station in front of him had gone granular, he returned to his knitting. As it stood, he'd not got as far as he would have liked to: half a sleeve, maybe, if that. The brief from his client had not been the most precise he'd ever received but he'd committed the details of it to memory as soon as he'd heard them barked drunkenly into the dark saline air behind the Golden Cap last month.

'This sounds really weird but I've never had a big sloppy cardigan and I wish I did,' William had said, not to anyone in particular, just to the night itself. 'Just something you can throw on, at a time like this. Maybe in a nice earthy green, a bit *mossy*.'

They'd been sitting around William's giant hand-forged firebowl at the time: Eric, Carl, Mel, Eric's friend Roy from Clocktower Records in Bridport, the two eldest Fentonbrook children from Holly Farm, a thirty-something couple called Chuck and Sofia who looked like they'd walked straight out of a clothing advert in a 1960s issue of *Vogue*, and William. He still referred to himself as 'Billy' but Carl couldn't help also thinking of him by his full name, since that was what it said on his books: William Stackpole, and subsequently, on the more recent work, as if to add gravitas and emphasise the weightier turn his career was taking, William James Stackpole. Back in winter, in the rear of Eric's van on the way from the dripping depths of the south Devon countryside to Exeter hospital, Carl had increasingly got the feeling that he recognised the man sitting beside him and, later, as his freshly bandaged companion began to reveal more about his background, he'd made the connection between the disarranged individual to his left and the author photo on Stackpole's 2010 debut *Will the Stone Circle Be Unbroken: A Journey Around Britain Through Deep Time*. Carl had read the book in 2013, during a particularly enjoyable summer binge of knowledge centred around the British landscape's early shaping of itself. He'd found the prose a little academic at times, but been impressed by Stackpole's precocious topographical knowledge and the easy, if at times arrogant, sociability that, as if by magic, opened up access to druids, alternative historians, dowsers and other mystical figures around the British Isles. The dog that accompanied Stackpole on his adventures – a Patterdale named Ossenfeffer – also leased it extra character and charm. Another reason Carl recalled the book was that it had been the impetus for him bounding into the kitchen and asking Eric, 'Did you know that Stonehenge sold for £6,600 to a private buyer in 1915?' (Eric didn't.)

Billy had looked preposterously, collegiately young on the jacket of that book and now, at forty-two, looked no older than the age he'd been then. Did he even shave his jaw? It seemed doubtful. He'd camped in their garden that night. In the morning, they'd found the tent still there and Billy gone. He'd returned in the dying embers of the afternoon, staggering down the track like an angel of dusk with a rucksack full of beer and canine treats. Billy told Eric it was his thank you for the kindness Eric had showed him since finding him dazed and horizontal in the wet grass, at the laneside. He added that, somewhat embarrassingly, he'd been asked for ID in Axminster Co-op when buying the beer and, realising he'd left his driving licence in his tent, had resorted to proving his age by going online on his smartphone and showing the cashier a national newspaper story about the prestigious travel-writing award he'd won last year for *Cruel Summer*, the book about his period in Antarctica: the one in which he'd experimented, for the first time, with writing memoir in half-prose half-poetry form. 'Ok but what I still need to know,' Carl wanted to ask, 'is did you have to have your appendix out before you went?'

With Eric's encouragement, Billy continued to camp in the garden for the rest of the week. On the fourth night, Mel popped round, and over a curry that made Billy's nose and eyes gush like a double-tiered Lake District waterfall – Eric took the credit although Carl had in fact cobbled it together from one of his own private recipes while Billy was out hiking the coast path again – they all watched a documentary about rabbits. Billy asked if anyone knew that the average erect human penis contained more blood than the average wild rabbit. Eric and Mel, who'd heard the same fact from Carl five months earlier after he'd read it in the same scientific journal that Billy had, pretended to act astonished. There was a pause while Billy, Eric and Mel did their best to eat more of Carl's madras without crying and Carl thought about how much he was looking forward to getting to sample it himself, later, when Billy had gone outside to bed, and then Mel said: 'That's all very well. But what about the *above*-average erect penis?' This led her onto a recounting of the details of her disastrous date with Cliff Falls from Eype the previous night which had been killed, stone dead, when Falls had attempted to initiate sex by crawling in slo-mo from the doorway of his living room to the sofa where she sat and making what could perhaps best be described as 'strange leopard sex noises'. Eric asked if anyone needed any water and everyone said yes and Billy talked to Mel about the time he'd fed a leopard a chicken drumstick in a wild cat rehabilitation facility on the Arabian Peninsula.

'It was a big chicken drumstick, but I don't think the leopard mistook it for a come-on,' said Billy. 'There was no seductive prowling or disturbing sex noises. It just kind of pissed off back into the trees at the back of its enclosure.'

In witnessing Eric's interactions with Billy, Carl saw something new in Eric he'd not quite seen before. Was it almost . . . fatherly? Eric showed Billy the old smuggling hot spots over near Beer where the brandy boats would come in from Roscoff and Cherbourg in the early 1800s. Billy pored over Eric's collection of vintage maps, marvelling at his rare misprint of the 1970 Lake District Ordnance Survey Tourist Map with the reverse image illustration of Ashness Bridge in Derwent Water on the cover. Without ever going into the subject in depth, Eric had mentioned to Carl that he'd never wanted children; he had also rarely talked about his time as the teenage guitarist in a band signed to a proper record label during the early 1970s. But now here he was, fetching a long-neglected acoustic guitar from the spare room and talking Billy through a few chords on it, putting Witch Fuzz Magic's 'Jennifer's Orchard' single on the turntable and loaning Billy his walking guides and wetsuit. Billy talked about his geographical separation from his own parents who had moved to Oregon eleven years ago, about the money he'd inherited from his aunt which had funded some of the far-flung research trips for his books, how hurt he'd felt by the mean comments about it made by some of his contemporaries on or close to the nature-writing scene. On a couple of occasions he alluded to some 'rather frightening incidents' involving a couple of his fans but, when gently pressed by Eric, declined to elaborate. He woke repeatedly at dawn, walked across the cliffs, sometimes alone, sometimes with Carl and Eric, made picnics for himself, fed the leftovers to the chickens and Frank the crow. He said he'd fallen in love with the Jurassic Coast, could feel the setting and thrust of the new book mutating day by day.

'It's kind of embarrassing but . . .' was one of his favourite ways to begin a sentence, although he never seemed truly embarrassed about any of the things he cited as kind of embarrassing. 'It's kind of embarrassing but they'll pretty much let me do anything since the success of *Will the Stone Circle*. . .' he said of his publishers. 'As long as they've got a finished MS at the end, they're not too fussed about the smallprint. It's pretty much an open playing field.' By 'MS', Carl eventually discovered Billy meant 'manuscript'; a relief to Carl, since the idea of Billy's publishers demanding a finished Multiple Sclerosis was one that had confused and troubled him.

After a more meticulous rummage through the pile of records

Eric had bought from Penny, Billy let out a yelp upon finding the original pressing of *Amethyst Deceiver* by the Meredith Stackpole Mushroom Band and a louder yelp upon being informed by Eric that it was worth close to £2,000. Meredith, he informed Eric, had been a distant relative on his dad's side of the family, the American side. She'd cut the family off for reasons that remained cloudy to Billy and died tragically young, in a Brooklyn flophouse, from an overdose of alcohol and barbiturates, shortly before Billy had been born. Billy had heard the record once a long time ago but couldn't remember much about it, and now, upon rehearing it, lost himself in its marbled texture, in his late distant cousin's elongated Grace Slick wails and grunts. By now, he and Eric were deep into some weed Mel had scored from a fisherman in Exmouth. They explored the pile and what it led to more extensively: the lone album by RJ McKendree, a shy vagabond Penny thought might have stayed at the manor once, but couldn't say for sure; Hetty Pegler's Tump; The Great Uncomformity ('Not to be mixed up with the Great Unorthodoxy, who are equally great, also from Boston, and were making records at exactly the same time.'); The Beacon Street Union; the effervescing Elysian folk of Peter and Daisy Loveage; Joni Mitchell's underrated *Clouds* LP; Skip Spence's dark and desperate and otherplanetly *Oar*.

Records, as ever, led to more records. 'Are you sure you should even be holding this stuff?' asked Billy. 'It must feel like having gold dust on your fingers.' Eric introduced him to highlights from the West Coast Pop Art Experimental Band's output. Billy announced that he'd seen the light. Forget drover's roads, lichen and rare ground-nesting birds. He was writing books about psychedelic rock music from now on. 'Take my hand and run away with me through the forest until the leaves and trees slow us down, a vampire bat will suck blood from our hands, a dog with rabies will bite us, rats will run up your legs but nothing will matter,' sang the West Coast Pop Art Experimental Band. 'It's true!' said Billy to the band and Eric. 'Nothing *will* matter. They see into the meaning of everything. I'm having that as the title of my next book. All of it.'

He passed out with his head hanging off the armless end of Eric and Carl's sofa but was up at dawn again the next day, stalking the cliffs. He worked Clocktower Records in Bridport into the inland section of his route, hitch-hiked back with a rucksack full of vinyl, bought a Japanese direct-drive turntable half price off Eric, asked Eric to store it 'until he was no long living under canvas'.

Carl sometimes noticed Eric staring at Billy's hair a little longingly. But on these animated evenings Billy's eyes were often not focused on Eric, or on the records Eric played, but on Carl. It sometimes seemed as if he was staring deep into his forehead, trying to find something that he'd noticed there, for a flickering instant, then lost. Carl wasn't precisely *upset* by his gaze but there was something unnerving about it, something that made him want to move around and stay busy.

But then one morning he and the tent were gone. Not so much as a phone call or a text, for almost two months. 'He probably just got fed up with the cold,' suggested Mel. But Eric, and Carl, suspected that wasn't it. Carl had mixed feelings: he'd enjoyed Billy's company and enthusiasm – the different kind of energy he'd injected into the cottage – but it was an immense relief, after a fortnight of pretending and self-repression, to be able to stretch out and get upright at home again, to not be looked at so intensely, to catch up on his cleaning tasks and his backlog of fibre art projects, get to work on the garden ready for spring. Eric meanwhile became briefly withdrawn, less pun-orientated in his chat, stopped playing records in the house. The guitar was returned to the loft, the first pressing of *Amethyst Deceiver* sold to a retired barrister from Dusseldorf. 'How the fuck can a barista afford that?' a mishearing Mel asked Eric on Friday night in Frampton St Peter, where Eric, Mel, Penny and Carl had gathered for one of Dorset's most reliably difficult pub quizzes. 'They barely get minimum wage.' When Penny, who had been over in Dorset a lot lately, gently pointed out Mel's mistake to Mel, Eric barely chuckled. 'Oh dear, he really is a bit out of sorts,' thought Carl, knowing how much delight Eric normally took in laughing at Mel's expense.

The following week, Eric and Carl were walking along Cogden Beach through fresh sproutings of beach cabbage and Eric got talking to a young Belgian man called James who was washing his bloody feet in the sea. James told Eric he'd walked forty-four miles of the coast path in two days and wondered if he knew of anywhere cheap where he could pitch a tent. 'There's always our garden,' said Eric. 'Hold your horses,' thought Carl. 'He could be Antwerp's answer to Ted Bundy.' But he was glad to see his housemate perking up. On the beer terrace of the Anchor Inn, overlooking a sullen sea, James, somewhat delirious from his physical endeavours, enthused evangelically to a partially comprehending Eric about his abandoning of social media and embracing of outdoor life and the accompanying benefits to his mental health.

'I used to do Instagram but now I do . . . Outstagram!' announced James.

'Right on, pal!' replied Eric, whose total social media use still amounted to three thoroughly bemused weeks on Facebook back in 2011.

Having sent James off towards the eastern horizon with a cheddar cob and a spare cassette of James Taylor's *Sweet Baby James* album, Eric drove, revitalised, to replenish the stock in his racks at The Loft, where, as fortune would have it, he bumped into Mel and Penny, who were rearranging Mel's clothes racks and reorganising the colourful crocheted table mats she sometimes sold on Carl's behalf. 'I was thinking of opening up the cottage,' Eric told Penny. 'To travellers. Musicians. Artists. Writers. Like your uncle did with the manor. Maybe a gig or two. An open mic night, poetry readings. That sort of thing. I've become inspired. I was wondering if I could pick your brain sometime.' Penny said she'd be more than amenable to that but did express a few reservations about size limitations and location. Mel, using Penny for ballast as she hung a poncho on a partially eroded wall-hook, asked Eric if he'd ever called that girl back who'd been here looking for him a few weeks ago. 'Ah, gubbins,' said Eric. 'I didn't. I will, promise. Tonight. Pint later?' Mel and Penny declined, citing a new book group in Beaminster as their cover story.

The first knowledge Eric and Carl had about Billy purchasing Windy Gables, the farm directly behind Old Russell Loosemore's, was when, on an April morning sugared by accumulating birdsong, Eric found a purple envelope on the doormat with the words 'COME AND WARM MY HOUSE' written on it. Inside was an attractive woodcut of the Golden Cap with a gull soaring above it and an invite to Billy's inaugural party as a Dorset resident. It was addressed to Eric but Billy had added that Carl and Mel's attendance was also mandatory. Carl and Eric had only been to one soiree in the neighbourhood in the past, at the Fentonbrooks' place, a pleasant but oddly musicless affair at the end of last summer, now mostly memorable for the restraint Mel had displayed when Anne Fentonbrook had declared that the recent appointment of Liz Truss as Prime Minister was yet more evidence that the Conservatives had always been the only party who upheld the myriad advancement of women as one of their core values. This second party turned out to be significantly livelier, complete with homebrew provided by a professional forager friend of Billy's from Bristol and a flatcap-wearing DJ calling himself the Weymouth Unabomber who was installed in the old dairy on a podium constructed from discarded pallets and hay bales.

Eric talked to a pair of married headteachers from Whitchurch Canonicorum suffering from sleep deprivation due to the tenacious nocturnal escape missions of their rhododendron-obsessed pet goats into the verdant grounds of a neighbouring Georgian mansion, and to a body-shop technician from Ilminster who, when asked what genre of music he liked, replied 'mostly 80s, 90s, 70s . . . 60s, 50s . . . but also 2000s, 40s . . . and some 30s.' Eric's friend Roy from Clocktower Records, another Merseyside-born late-life entrepreneur who'd gravitated to the South West in middle age, talked to Eric about his ambition to one day own a football team and admitted to Mel that he'd only ever had three cups of coffee but could remember where and when all of them had taken place. By 10 p.m., the farm and its accompanying pastureland was filled with forty-seven humans, three dogs, Carl and one hand-reared ram which one of Russell Loosemore's sons, having heard the noise coming from further up the valley, had brought with him on an investigative walk, eventually saying he would take up Billy's offer to sample the punch bowl but declining politely on the ram's behalf.

Carl marvelled that, in such a short time exploring the area, Billy had amassed such a list of trusted acquaintances to invite to his spacious new abode. When the dairy's dance floor filled for Deee-Lite's 'Groove Is in the Heart', a floorboard snapped, almost in exact unison with the body-shop technician from Crewkerne shouting, 'And THIS is why nineties is my favourite genre!' Billy told everyone not to worry and, with the help of two old saw-horses found in one of the farm's several barns then pushed together, some hay bales and two hard-wearing extension cables, he moved the base of operations out under the stars.

'It took a big push to get the sale through and cart all my stuff over from London,' Billy said. 'But now I'm here and the future is beginning.'

Eric could not stop himself wondering just *how* substantial that latest advance from Billy's publisher, and the nest egg from his late aunt, had been.

Relieving the Weymouth Unabomber, Billy took to the decks himself, taking the mood down by playing what had, of late, become his favourite song by The Doors: 'I Can't See Your Face in My Mind'. Carl thought he looked worryingly chilly and scrawny, standing over there on top of a hay bale, singing portentously into a half-empty bottle of organic Pinot Noir. Russell Loosemore's son Brian slow-danced with the young ram, who Brian said was named Brian Clough. 'It gets confusing, having two Brians around the place,' said Brian the human, downing his fifth Stella Artois of the night. 'But neither of us would have it any other way.' Those who'd driven to the gathering began to go granular into the night. Eric and Mel discussed mid-twentieth-century fabric with Chuck and Sofia, the couple who looked like they were from the clothing advert in a 1960s issue of *Vogue*, and asked them how they knew Billy. 'We don't,' said Sofia. 'We're actually knackered. We did a twelve-mile walk today and parked just back there on the lane. We were on our way back to the car and heard the music and thought we'd have a nosey about what was going on.' Eric asked them if they always dressed so smart when they were out hiking. 'Of *course*,' said Chuck. 'Every hill is a special occasion.' Eric, while looking for some bushes to piss in having found the indoor toilet occupied, noticed a young woman in a two-decades-old Ford Fiesta parked in the track in front of the farm, who, before he got close enough to see anything defining about her face, started the engine and reversed the car away in a plume of dust, illuminated by the headlights. Carl, who was also looking for a place to wee, though not because the indoor toilet was occupied, was struck inexplicably but strongly by the suspicion that the woman knew Billy, had some romantic connection to him. *Was* Billy in a relationship? Had he even had one recently? Carl had never heard him talk about it and assumed not. He thought back, too, to those comments Billy had made to Eric about those 'extremely frightening incidents' involving his 'fans'.

'Intriguing,' Carl said quietly to Eric. 'Who do you think that might have been?' But Eric appeared to have temporarily zoned out and was staring intently at the night, his piss quest temporarily forgotten.

Back where the action was, later, Roy from Clocktower talked about aphantasia, the condition he had which rendered him unable to form mental pictures of memories. 'Great band, that,' said Eric. 'I prefer their early work before they went more prog rock and got the two keyboard players in.'

Roy said it had always been the same. He remembered being at school and hearing his male classmates talking about the boobs of girls they fancied, the way they'd imagine them later at home when they were in the solitude of their own bedrooms, but Roy, not being able to see anything in his mind, including boobs, could never relate.

'But you said you can remember the cups of coffee you drank,' said Mel.

'Yes,' said Roy. 'But I can't *picture* them.'

The remaining party guests all sat down beside the fire bowl. After trying unsuccessfully to persuade Carl to chase a stick, the Fentonbrooks' eldest daughter Rosie said there were a large number of dogs in her family but she'd never come across a Longtail Cast-On before. Eric said it was an obscure breed that originated in Uzbekistan in the 1940s. Billy, with an arm around Carl, spoke spontaneously and tumultuously about his profoundest knitwear desires. Carl made silent mental notes: size, texture, colour. On the walk home, down the hill, Eric drunkenly sang 'I caaaa-an't see your booo-obs in my mind' to Mel, who told him to shut up. It wasn't true, anyway. He *could* still see them in his mind, albeit vaguely, on the basis of the four times he'd witnessed them in the flesh during late 2017. Or was it five?

Doing something nice for somebody was about precisely that: doing something nice for somebody. It wasn't about the pat on the back – or, should it be your preference, the intuitive gentle tickle behind the ears – you received afterwards from the somebody you'd done something nice for. But that didn't stop Carl wanting to remember what it felt like to make an item of clothing for a new person from scratch then be the one to hand it to them. It had been a long time. He'd watched, a few weeks ago, in a state of some emotion, as Eric handed Jill Monk the turtleneck Carl had knitted for her then told her it had been made by Mel. He'd then continued to watch, over the following weeks, as Jill showered Mel, whose knitting skills were reserved to the area of ideas and people rather than wool, with homemade ginger nuts and compliments and tried, with little success, to steer her into conversations about early sockcraft in eleventh-century Egypt, Welsh blankets, the impact of the Black Death on fourteenth-century Monmouthshire weavers and other yarn-related topics that Carl would have loved to get his teeth into. When Billy's cardigan was finished, no doubt he'd have to go through a similar process. But the knowledge of that had no negative impact on his work rate. By the time he'd dropped off to sleep he'd finished nearly a whole sleeve. He woke, with the sense that a large amount of time had passed, to find Eric looming over him.

'Being a bit chancy, aren't you, pal? Thought you might be a bit deeper into the trees. We don't want another Sylvia Monkhouse incident.'

'I've not seen a soul. Unless you count the apparition of a few dozen long-deceased farm animals and a fractionally sozzled Stanley Baldwin-era stationmaster.'

'*Okay.* Whatever it takes to get you high, soft lad.'

Eric said he wanted to go back to the second boot fair because he'd seen an antique salmon spear he wanted which was £6.50 cheaper than the antique salmon spear he'd seen at the earlier fair, which he regretted not buying, plus he reckoned he could get the seller down by another two or three quid. Carl asked him why he wanted an antique salmon spear and Eric said they were quite 'in' at the moment and that Carl could ask Reg Monk if he didn't believe him ('But I can't, can I?' thought Carl) and, besides, it might be nice to have one around the place for a while. Eric also said, as if as an afterthought, that he'd bumped into Mel and Penny, who'd cobbled together a little stall where they were selling a few cut-price bits that had been hanging around too long at The Loft and some clothes Penny, who'd been making noises about moving down to Dorset from Wiltshire, had decided to clear out in readiness for a potential move. 'The pair of them are totally cleaning up down there,' said Eric. 'It's a bonanza.' Carl requested that he and Eric take a detour back to the fair so they could say hello to some sheep down in the valley that he'd enjoyed conversing with a couple of times in the past but a sign on the gate to the field informed them that the sheep, whose names were listed as Mavis, Edna, Buddy, Bella, Fatso and Fatso's Friend, had 'gone on holiday' and would be back soon, hopefully with lambs.

'Lambs!' said Carl, a bit louder than he'd intended to. But then he immediately thought about the heartless and terrible things that humans often did to lambs.

'To be honest, my thoughts are with Fatso's Friend,' said

Eric. 'Imagine that being how the world defined you: purely as the annexe of the person you hung around with. It's like in the old days when you'd get some bloke called Colin Smith and everyone would call his wife Mrs Colin Smith.'

'I'm not an annexe of you, and – although I do clean up after you and tend your garden – I'm thankful you've never tried to make me one,' thought Carl, who was still feeling brittle and sleepy. He came close to saying it out loud but there was a couple with a Yorkshire Terrier approaching from the other end of the lane.

By the time they reached the fair, everything was just about wrapping up. Carl immediately situated himself directly beneath Penny, in the hope of an ear scratch, which, as soon as she'd taken £3 for a red polka dot dress from an adolescent girl emerging rhapsodically from her doom-metal period, he duly received. Mel squeezed Penny's wrist and, because of the long Indian blanket draped over the table, nobody aside from Mel noticed Penny rise 2.4 inches above the ground. Eric went off to get the salmon spear but was scandalised to find it had sold, so spent the money on a large chips with mushy peas and an orange sausage from a nearby chip van instead, then, rummaging in a cardboard box a crewcutted man had already loaded back into his people carrier, was able to fractionally incinerate his own mind by finding, sandwiched between two worthless seventies *Top of the Pops* covers LPs, an original 1968 pressing of *Illusion's Bridge* by Illusion's Bridge, an album he hadn't seen in the wild since the 1970s punk era, when its critical reappraisal and journey to collectable cultdom had begun.

Suddenly panicked at potentially not having the two pounds required to purchase it, he rummaged in his bag for the padded lumberjack shirt he'd shed earlier that morning. In the shirt's inner pocket – one he rarely used – he found the necessary coins and a mulch of paper which, on further examination, could just about still be identified as a postcard depicting Golitha Falls in Cornwall as it was during the 1950s: the one Mel had handed him several months ago, with the name and number of a potential client scrawled on the back. Both had now been vanquished to illegibility by the washing machine. 'Oh well,' thought Eric. 'You win some, you lose some.' He put the mulchy postcard back in his bag, dug his phone out and typed out a quick message to a regular buyer who last year had mentioned his ongoing woes in attempting to find a copy of *Illusion's Bridge* for under £200.

'Hundred and ninety-seven squid profit,' he said to Mel and Penny later, as he folded up a wallpapering table for Penny and loaded it into her 1991 Volvo 940 Estate. 'Not bad for just walking around a field with your eyes fully open.'

'Great stuff,' said Mel. 'I'm really happy for you. It also means you can finally pay me back for that weed I gave you eleven weeks ago. You could take us all out to dinner too, if you like.'

'Yes,' said Penny. 'It would be a good way of celebrating.'

'Oh yeah?' said Eric. 'What's the occasion?'

'The sale on the manor went through,' said Mel.

'*And* the other much more exciting thing,' said Penny.

'Oh yeah, that too, I suppose,' said Mel.

'Yes, have you not heard?' said Penny. 'Young Melanie here is going to be famous. She's been booked for her first stand-up comedy gig.'

'Ah that's brilliant, pal,' said Eric. 'I'm made up for you.'

'*So* brilliant,' thought Carl.

'The White Lion in Broadwindsor, no less,' said Penny. 'Second on the bill out of four, if you can believe it!'

'I can,' thought Carl.

Ahead of them, they could see a train of black-clad adolescents moving towards the boot fair's exit. Penny said she thought it was sad, the way that children from rural low-income families could no longer afford to buy nice clothes from shops, nor afford the train fare to get to them. Mel offered the counterpoint that the choice to visit boot fairs by these fifteen- to twenty-year-olds, many of whom prioritised recycling much more than their predecessors, was potentially more ecologically than financially motivated. Eric said he felt out of touch and wondered aloud what you called kids like these now: Were they goths? Or did you call them emo kids? Or had that term died a death now?

'I think they're still happy to be called emo kids,' said Mel.

'I relate to that,' said Eric. 'I was a big Rod Hull fan as well when I was young.'

Like a fully grown child star who'd never known drudgery or hardship, the summer asked for patience from everyone as if that patience was its birthright. Its entrance was that of the magnetic bohemian who arrives confidently, calculatedly late to her own party. Strangers, picked up who knew where en route, clung to each of her arms. It was a summer you could never fully see, a summer always instigating a game of hide-and-seek. It strolled right into your bedroom, as nonchalantly as if it knew you, even though you'd barely met, then it swaggered away into the trees and beckoned you coquettishly to come and find it. There was always something hazy and inscrutable about its boundaries.

On otherwise bright days around the Dorset coast there was sometimes a new, extremely specific and localised mist, which wasn't quite like any mist you'd known, but wasn't quite like fog either. Sometimes when you were in the mist it seemed like someone was shining a spotlight on a tent wall from outside the tent and you were in the tent. If you were in the right place you could walk fully outside it in the space of one decisive step. On top of Gerrard's Hill, Carl and Eric did precisely that, walking out of the sparkly sunken cloud into a vivid clump of trees whose trunks preserved declarations of teenage love in time, carved memories of twenty- and thirty- and forty-year-old couplings that few people now remembered, sometimes not even the couples themselves.

Later, after the mist had sailed east to renovate the Isle of Portland as a fairy wonderland, Eric and Carl looked back at the clump of graffitied trees, from the low ground seven miles away, and thought, with satisfaction: 'There is progress, there is the ground we have covered, with these small legs of ours: it belongs to us now.' They enjoyed retracing routes they'd walked five, six years ago, observing what had changed, because something always had. States of emotion and seasons and weather took you by surprise with the angles they created. There was continuous fascination in the different ways a landscape could be seen as a newcomer or an oldcomer or an inbetweencomer, the way a valley you'd not seen for a few summers could sometimes say, 'Yes, you're quite right, I do believe we did meet before but I was in a weird place back then. My shirts are better now, I no longer hang around with Simon and I'm ready to talk.' Sometimes it was just a fresh coat of paint on the walls and ceiling, a modified accent, but that was fine. The best entertainment wasn't always flashy. Sometimes it was subtle, quiet. And entertainment was most assuredly what this was, even though much of the population wouldn't have entertained the possibility it was entertainment. In the closest cities and towns, people punched steering wheels in traffic jams and insulted each other in car parks. They waited for a quarter of an hour to order a sandwich then discovered it had sold out. But out here on and under the hills there was a feeling that, now the consumerist frenzy had received its legally approved restart, the fad that the pandemic had brought about for 'being out in nature' had faded. For the most part, as they walked, Carl and Eric, and the friends who sometimes accompanied them, passed few other humans on the paths.

Sometimes, early in the morning, when Eric was out on a home visit to assess a collection, Billy came over from the farm and took Carl walking. The broken, busted nature of the land, especially to the west of Carl and Eric's mud-pummelled cottage, fascinated the physically immaculate young writer. One day they hiked all the way to the Undercliff, over on the other side of Lyme Regis. Billy said he wanted to see the house where the famous author John Fowles had lived, and the teething pre-coastal earth where Fowles had based his novel *The French Lieutenant's Woman*. He also wanted to find the spot above Culverhole Beach where, on Christmas Day, 1839, the earth had torn apart and two cottages, an orchard and forty-five acres of farmland had smashed and crumbled down towards the sea, leaving a chasm three quarters of a mile long, 300 feet wide and 150 feet deep. He said he was thinking of writing a short story about it called 'The Day Santa Didn't Come'.

'If he comes up with a title that isn't so crap, I'll probably read that, but mostly for the potential atmosphere,' Carl thought.

Carl had in fact seen a past triangular vision of this place once, not in 1839, but a year earlier, before that most cataclysmic of all Devon-Dorset border landslips. It gave him a bigger sense of the scale of the geological devastation. Looking up at the still-standing cliffs, a mile inland, his knees buckled at the thought of all that had shifted and smashed apart here, the thundering bulk of it. They walked through this beautiful mess made by nature, this tumbled dripping hart's tongue fern paradise, marvelling at how long it stretched on for; how little sight it afforded of the two less topsy-turvy landscapes either side of it; how hard it was to enter and exit. Even when they were out and had moved a little inland, so much they saw was sinking into the earth: cars, sack-lifter barrow trolleys, cultivators and other old farm machinery, children's bikes, three morose-looking cows blocking a stile. Nature as swallower of shit. Nature as long-suffering parent, coming in and taking care of our nonsense. In Lyme, Billy popped into a bookshop where mannequins stared out from behind piles of old art posters and teetering stacks of hardbacks. 'This is kind of embarrassing, but the guy in there recognised me,' said Billy. 'No special discount, though, sadly.' Carl was well-versed in the way people spoke to dogs when they thought nobody else was around listening and thought dogs didn't understand them. They rummaged around in the blackest depths of their soul and, when they'd found something they thought worthy of examination, told it to dogs, confessed their sins like dogs were the trustworthiest of priests, made noises at dogs that they deemed too preposterous and undignified to make within hearing of a fellow human, told dogs who they secretly thought was a massive unredeemable beef whistle and why. But Billy didn't talk to Carl like that. Even when he was talking to Carl like Carl was a person, there was a restraint and, always with the restraint, a little smirk in his eye. Without being interrogated or physically prodded, Carl felt probed, examined, like someone on the end of the most surreptitious of MRI scans.

A few times, at the end of shorter morning walks, they swam at a little hidden beach under the disfigured tibia of the Golden Cap. Billy, a proficient swimmer, was visibly impressed by the serenity with which Carl moved through the water. There had been worries about sewage spills nearby lately, and the waves had none of the arresting transparency of the inlets on the Cornish coast where, when they were sure nobody was around, Carl and Eric used to snorkel in the early mornings. But being in the sea, as ever, felt like coming back to something fundamental for Carl. He stretched out, worked on his stomach muscles, began to rid his body of months of madras and vindaloo damage. Protected by a bubble of mist in that quietest of quiet places, he and Billy felt like two long lazy creatures in an untarnished dream, mindful solely of the earthly encasements that they were, liberated from extraneous desire. One time, after they'd swum, they climbed to the ruined chapel behind the cliff and Billy, producing some folded sheets of A4 from his rucksack, read some work-in-progress to Carl. 'I know you don't know what any of this means,' he said, 'but speaking it aloud helps with the process. It gives me the chance to spot mistakes I wouldn't if I was just looking at a typed page or screen. Please don't be afraid to say if you think any of it is shit, though.'

He was still shivery from the water and his voice trembled as he read, his purple fingertips struggling to turn the pages. Carl noticed there was more feeling present than in his earlier writings: the structure of the prose was less scholastic, less obviously keen to impress, less reliant on quotes from his predecessors for its underpinning. One line in particular caught Carl's attention: 'I feel safe from them here under the honeyed shoulders.' When Billy had reached the end he swaddled himself in the moss-green cardigan. 'It was so lovely of Mel to knit this for me,' he said. 'Unexpected, too. Are she and Penny some kind of couple now, I wonder.'

He reached into his bag and popped open the ring pull on a small can of overpriced craft lager. Carl could see from the tracking sun that it was not yet 10.30 am: a bit on the early side, even by his standards.

'I think you need to leave bigger gaps when you're planting your sweetcorn,' said Billy.

Buy Three Get One Free on Selected Haberdashery Supplies for the Next Three Days

Dreams are the dark alcove where guilt often goes to wring its hands. In Eric's fiftieth year, what he had dreamed most frequently about was Mike.

In Eric's dreams about Mike, it was Eric, not Mike, who had been left behind in the twentieth century, curtailed by death. Like an omniscient narrator in a film, speaking calmly from the astral realm, he took his audience – the audience which was himself but always *felt* larger – through the integrity-drenched high points of Mike's unlived life: the 1970s and 80s career as a reliably uncompromising and opinionated firebrand music journalist that he somehow managed to combine with a succession of low-key, fashion-rejecting folk-jazz solo albums composed for a future point when the world had caught up with him. 'When Mike opened the *Melody Maker* that day,' narrated Deceased Dream Eric, 'he saw that, once again, his editor – a public schoolboy, raised in the town of Winchester, well-educated but lacking imagination and spine – had altered some crucial sentences, withering the muscles of the points Mike had made in the lead review. Not having conversed with many people of ordinary backgrounds from the large part of the country located north of the M1's once surprisingly debauched and groovy Blue Boar Service Station, his editor had also clearly been confused by the phrase "mard-arse" and seen fit to amend it to "mad-arse". "But I wasn't *saying* the lead singer was a mad-arse," said Mike. "That would have been an entirely different observation. I was saying he was a *mard-arse*. You know, like mardy bum. It means cry baby. Because that's what the guy is." But he let it go. All such concerns would pale into insignificance as that summer Mike would be moving to Los Angeles to be with his new girlfriend, Belinda Carlisle, whose band The Go-Go's were riding high with their debut album and its unforgettable lead single "Our Lips Our Sealed", which as everyone knew would of course not have even existed had Mike not introduced the band to Terry Hall from The Specials and gently nudged both parties into a collaboration.'

On waking and reaching back into his mind for the dream's details, Alive Eric was surprised that Dream Eric had chosen Belinda Carlisle, rather than her fellow Go-Go Jane Wiedlin, as Dream Mike's fictional girlfriend. In one of the most exciting episodes of Eric's recent life as a record-seller, Wiedlin, via eBay, had purchased two records from Eric: the second Kathy Smith LP, from 1971, and – released in the same introspective year – *Ageism*, the little-known album of minimalist electro Americana recorded at Buffy Sainte-Marie's home studio by Daisy Loveage after Daisy's uneasy artistic split from her better-known twin brother Peter. Eric had been too politely British to ask if she definitely was *that* Jane Wiedlin but really how many people with that name and a connoisseur's appreciation of far-out underrated

Nixon-era singer-songwriters could there be living in the greater Los Angeles area?

While all this was taking place, Eric's new housemate, whose sleep patterns had yet to regulate into a sociable and convenient pattern, was typically awake, burning the midnight oil on the floor below. He had been quickly drawn to books, liked the feel of them when he grasped them in his twenty-four soft fingers, was seduced by a promise they seemed to make that, despite his own blinking newness and collateral unawareness of what words such as 'time' and 'old' and 'ratified' meant, he somehow knew was an old promise, a promise ratified by time. Once the words on the pages began to make sense, his hunger swiftly escalated. By his second week living with Eric, he'd already ripped through Stanley Booth's *The True Adventures of the Rolling Stones* twice, Daphne du Maurier's *Rebecca* and *Frenchman's Creek* three times each, and was halfway into a fourth reading of Walter Tevis's *The Man Who Fell To Earth*, a big favourite, despite the fact that Eric's threadbare 1964 paperback was missing pages 110–124. He would like, ultimately, to have lived in a house with more books. He did not complain, though, did not yet know how to complain, and would not have done so if he did. Although he did not know *why* he was in it, he was glad to be in this narrow warm dry building with hot and cold running water. It felt correct and calm, especially now it was long rid of that *thing*, that old metal maleficence (yet another good word that he'd learned recently) that had given his first few days here a distinctly less serene flavour.

What might people have thought, if they'd seen him that first day, stepping delicately down from the van, then limping into the house behind the first friend he had ever known? 'Ah, the alcoholic record-shop owner has got himself a rescue dog in an attempt to feel less lonely. Looks to be a weird Moldovan street hound or something. Maybe with some kind of dehydration-related illness. I applaud his kindness and optimism, but it could be quite a burden, not to mention a risk. What if it dies? Then he'll be even more sad and lonely and alcoholic. He'll probably end up killing himself. Especially if his unsuccessful record shop closes, as I have heard on the grapevine, from some other local small-business owners, that it probably will.' But, as it was, nobody did see. Not twenty-six-year-old Darren Firkins, who shared a wall with Eric, listened to the same appalling sports metal album every morning and every night, and, after he'd separated from his wife Lisa, went directly to the tattoo parlour down the road and had two of the letters of her name on his upper arm inexpertly altered, then told everyone who asked about it that it was a tribute to his sister, Tina (whom he was in fact currently at odds with since she'd begun dating a rival of his in the cavity wall insulation business). Not Darren's next-door neighbour, Sally Minton, whom Eric had only seen once, in half a decade of living within less than forty yards of her (and then only in twilit profile). Not Phyllis Brookfield, who shared Eric's other wall, and had once accused Eric, bafflingly, of daubing her front door with the contents of a tin of custard. Not a soul.

Over the two-and-a-half-hour journey south west from the Dorset coast, Eric's suspicion that his new rescue pet was not in fact of the *Canis familiaris* genus at all had been growing, but what clinched it was the moment when, as soon as Eric had closed the back door, the creature, with a relieved sigh, stood up on its hindlegs, staggered directly to the spare bed in the open room at the end of the hallway and, not entirely unlike a drunk teenager returning from a misspent nocturnal adventure, planted itself headfirst onto the mattress. This being after the creature had made a beeline for a huge empty plant pot Bodmin used to drink from and, in a slightly familiar but vastly more industrial and efficient manner, drained it entirely of rainwater, as Eric, who in that time hadn't even managed to get the front door unlocked, watched in wonder. But there the creature's activity ended, for a confusing, and eventually a little frightening, three days.

'Blummin' 'eck, does it not need to evacuate its bowels by now?' Eric wondered, as, during that period, he regularly poked his head into the spare room to check on the creature. It was, he was reassured to find, still breathing. He had left out some sheets of cheese and a couple of tins' worth of dog food, but all of it remained untouched. Some of the wrinkles in the creature's fur had stretched and smoothed, giving its face a pointier, more refined shape. When Eric went out to work, he left the radio on to provide it with some company: Classic FM, usually, or oldies stations, even though he couldn't stand the moronic ads and had misgivings about inflicting them on a being possibly not of this earth as an introduction to the belittlements of global capitalism. In the shop, still not reopened after the fire, he swept, vacuumed, painted, assessed lightly singed cardboard and wax for resaleability and binability. Ordering a cheese cob from the bakery or posting a record to Spain at the post office, he was aware of a new banality to the cashiers and his fellow customers: they were people now defined by not being in on the secret inside his house. The secret made him feel special, not unlike his first rehearsals with Witch Fuzz Magic, before he had told Mike or his mum that he had joined a band. Unlike that secret, this was one he felt a curious ability to go on keeping, go on living quietly with. Yet simultaneously, every day further that the creature did not wake up, he dreaded another looming secret, which – as a man who had lately had more than his fill of bereavement – he knew he would *not* live so easily with.

While those first three stupefied, nervous days were not without magic and wonder, the nights that chased them were a hellish vortex. This was many weeks before the dreams of Mike began.

Instead, Eric nightmared himself back to Chesil Beach and found it was a much more seething and ominous place. He let the surf cover his toes, only to find them bitten off by broken teeth. The teeth were an entity of their own, although appeared guided in their violent deeds by bulging disembodied jelly eyes. He drowned several times over, saw the laughing skulls of Victorian fishermen as he sunk to the sea bed, where rusty nails penetrated his back. When he awoke, the house was a seastorm, part tumultuous wave, part fulminating cloud. Each time it came around, 3 a.m. felt like an omen: something he wanted to run from but couldn't because trying to do so would be as impossible as trying to run underwater. From downstairs, he was sure he heard the creature cry out on a couple of occasions, but when he rushed to check on it, it remained asleep in the same position as before, making no noise aside from its wet hot breaths, which, unless he imagined it, had become a little heavier. It did occur to Eric, in these terrible hours, which felt finally as lonely as the most judgemental superior eyes believed people who lived alone to be, that he might have transported a dripping evil into the house. Yet what he saw on that bed looked nothing like evil, dripping or otherwise.

When he arrived home from the shop and unlocked the front door on the fourth evening, he instantly knew there was something altered about the house, even before he clocked the clean carpets and dustless skirting boards. The radio had been turned up, the station changed to one broadcasting the interrupting trapped-wind voices of politicians. He rushed, instantly, to the spare bedroom, and found it empty, the bed neatly remade. Smelling clean smells, he climbed the stairs and, hearing commotion from the bathroom, reached for the door handle, but he was a second too late: it was already being opened from the inside. There, in the doorway, stood his housemate. Eric looked at him and he looked at Eric. Eric could see, through the window, the ship's bell he had purchased in Weymouth, removed from the living room and now resting against the garden's rear wall, beside the wheelie bin. It seemed, for a moment, as though it was 50/50 who would speak first, but in the end it was the significantly furrier of the two who asked the opening question.

'Have you been in an accident at work that wasn't your fault?' said Carl. 'Because if you have you might be entitled to up to £10,000 compensation.'

Of course, he hadn't yet become Carl at that point. That didn't occur until the following Wednesday: their second day out together, the morning when it all began to feel official.

It started with what almost became their first argument. Eric arrived downstairs at 7 a.m., hungry as a country fox, looking forward to reheating last night's vindaloo but, after searching in the fridge, he realised the Tupperware he'd stored the leftovers in was now empty, spotlessly clean, on the draining board. He found the creature in the tiny room that had unofficially become its bedroom. Somehow it had managed to squeeze the ironing board into the narrow gap between the single bed and the wall that divided it from Darren Firkins and his idiot sports-metal CDs. Eric saw smooth clean bedcovers on the ironing board: his favourites, red with white stripes, what he thought of as his 'Sheffield United ones'.

'You don't need to do that, you know,' said Eric.

'Oh,' said the creature. 'Is crumpled bed not to be improved for the master?'

'Some posh people do it but it's not my thing. They only get crumpled again, after all. You wouldn't happen to know what happened to my vindaloo, by any chance?'

'Consumed. With high delectation. This being wrong and unhappy-making for the master too?'

'Oh my god,' thought Eric. 'Look at its thin face. *It looks so sad*. I don't know if my heart can take it.'

'I guess it doesn't matter. It's just . . . I especially like eating it the next day, when it's had chance to steep. Even more when I've had a few drinks the night before. People say breakfast is the most important meal of the day and that's even more true if breakfast is curry. Was that chicken sandwich I made for you not big enough?'

'Size was impressive. Fire level was . . . insufficient.' The creature pointed a paw to its stomach. 'High tolerance. Like the best Rolling Stone, Keith Richards.'

'You want it spicier, pal? Ah, no problem. I'll get you a curry too, next time.'

'Been reading. Again. *The Last English King* by Julian Rathbone. Best book since *The True Adventures of The Rolling Stones*. Stamped inside: "4.2.1999. To Kelly. Happy 31st Birthday to my favourite historian. Love from Dad." You are Kelly's dad?'

'Nah, I'm nobody's dad, pal. At least not that I know of. I got that one for free in a phone box in Padstow. I haven't read it yet. I thought you finished it on Monday.'

'Rereading. Better second time around. Dense plotting. Much detail. More matriarchal society, prior to Norman Conquest. Then bloodshed: Saxons hang in trees with sexual organs removed. Subsequently: the dividing of land amongst the wealthy dynasties, lots for the few, little for the many.'

'Ah, yeah. Not much has changed about that part. They're still at it now.'

'Learned also about housecarls of King Harold Godwinson, before his death from gruesome oozing eye wound. Bodyguards but non-servile. Nice to horses and kittens. Began to hypothesise and speculate. Am I a housecarl?'

'You can be if you want to, pal. Although I'm not sure I need much guarding, apart from maybe Phyllis next door. She doesn't like me much. Reckons I threw custard at her door but I never did. I've never bought any custard in my life. While we're on the subject, I wanted to say again: can you not call me the master? It makes me uncomfortable. Call me Eric. Would you like me to get you some more books? Why don't you make me a list of what you fancy?'

'Housecarl would rise to that challenge. Maybe housecarl can guard Eric's body after all, but with *a forcefield of knowledge.*'

The day was one of those particularly Cornish ones when the last gold of autumn is almost out the gate and the unresolved heavens dole out sun and rain and wind and knots of furious billowing grey in equal measure. Eric walked the creature through town up the hill towards Bodmin Beacon, expecting stares but receiving none, then tied him by his new lead to the curved metal divider of a double bicycle stand outside the library. As he zipped around the building, following the instructions on the lined piece of A5 in his hand as accurately and efficiently as possible, he returned periodically to the window to check on his companion, relieved each time to see him still there, sitting calmly at his station, further relieved to see that the billowing skies had not unloaded and saturated his fur. However, upon emerging from the double doors, books in hand, he immediately spotted an interloper: a lady of probably well beyond seventy years. Dimpled smiling face. Red coat. Helpful eyes. 'Leave him alone!' Eric wanted to say. 'He's only been on dry land just over a week, and he's still a little jumpy.' But instead he smiled, sauntered over, pretending to be unflappable, unfussable, part of quotidian small-town Cornish life: a dog owner.

'Oh is he yours?' asked the lady. 'A boy? Or a girl? He's a darling. What's his name?'

Back in Eric's musician days, he'd dreamed up titles for dozens of songs: more songs than Alun Bannister had permitted him to record, more songs than he'd written. The habit had never fully left him and, even now, he occasionally found himself coming up with fictional titles for the imaginary albums that the him of a parallel universe might have gone on to make. What he knew from the process was that when you were trying really hard to name something, the right name never came. Then one day, it would just be there in front of you, as if delivered to you directly from the kitchen of the universe.

'Carl,' he said now to the old lady. 'He's called Carl.'

Everything was miraculously better at night without the bell in the house. Carl told Eric that the reason he'd moved it was because it was haunted, a vessel of negative energy. 'Ooh, yeah, I've known a few of them in my time,' said Eric. 'Especially in the public relations industry. But seriously, pal, I don't know if I believe in that stuff.' Carl shook his head, frantically. 'Believe!' he said. 'Believe thunderously and with full heart!' The dramatic change in Eric's sleeping patterns since the bell's removal did seem a striking coincidence. A couple of weeks later, they discussed the matter further. Carl seemed happy outside, going on walks, but had been refusing to go out in the yard while the bell was still there. He told Eric that he had an immense sensitivity to the power of cursed objects and buildings. With all the books he was getting through, his vocabulary was coming on at such lightning pace that he was easily able to put together a sentence like 'I have an immense sensitivity to the power of cursed objects and buildings'. His accent was still unplaceable and ethereal but the early pidgin sentences, influenced by the radio broadcasts and limited literature initially available to him, were already part of his crude past. What had replaced them was so eloquent that Eric could not help being swayed by its counsel, even though his brain stalled and stuttered as it heard what it was hearing. So when Carl said that the best course of action with the bell was to drop it into the sea, he put up only the most vague and comic of protests – 'That cost me good money, that did!' – and agreed, the next evening, to drive out to the cliffs between Fowey and Readymoney Cove. Carl, knowing only too well that this was extremely close to the house of his new literary hero Daphne du Maurier, jumped up and down on the spot, with bulging eyes.

'I'm sorry to disappoint you, pal,' said Eric. 'But she's been dead fifteen years. Who knows, though, with your special powers – maybe we'll see her ghost.'

They didn't. Nor did they see any other human or shadow-human form out on the cliffs that night, although under a bright and full moon Eric felt exposed, glancing continually over both shoulders as Carl took the bell from him and used his greater strength to launch it over the precipice and into the waves below. 'That's better,' whispered Carl. 'It will rest now.'

'Fuck's sake, pal,' said Eric. 'That's some right Spidey Strength you've got there.'

In moments of self-doubt, Eric brewed theories: *Did I perish in a traffic accident on that drive to Dorset and am I in fact living in the dream state of my own afterlife? Or was I at some point transferred to an institution, and is the landscape I am travelling, with my new companion, the inner one I hide in, as I am remanded there, inert and empty-faced?* Pre-dawn Edgar Allen Poe thoughts that, when going about his business under the rising sun, Eric knew were nonsense. Mostly, he just felt like the chance recipient of a sweet deal. He'd never previously craved the companionship of a dog and – besides a general reluctance towards the complications it might bring, and a cringing antipathy towards the most babying kind of dog owners – he'd never dwelled for long on why not. But now he got it. 'The problem,' he thought, 'with most dogs, besides their expectation of others to be responsible for their cleanliness, is that they shirk housework and heavy lifting and have no interest in the life of the mind. Once you've lived alongside a dog you can explore Indonesian recipes with or have a proper conversation with about the formation of the Welfare State or Dolly

Parton's insurgent artistic breakaway from her early songwriting partner Porter Wagoner, what could conceivably compel you to return to seek out the company of a Cairn Terrier or Otterhound?'

More generally, however, Eric was moving ever further away from the last vestiges of his perception of Carl as canine. What dog had twenty-four fingers hidden in its paws and alluded shyly to a crochet hook when you asked it what it wanted for its first birthday? Where dogs went, wildlife scattered and hid. But Carl, with Eric, walked with dainty circumspection, as if permanently fingering the volume switch of his own pawsteps, sensitive to the needs of every blue tit and rabbit and heron. Carl didn't moronically chase crumbled branches recently discarded by dignified trees or bark or growl or audaciously shove his face in the arse of any being previously unknown or known to him. Carl did not harass or injure sheep; he greeted them politely, made enquiries about their health, and complimented each of them on their undervalued originality. For the most part, he did not appreciate the attentions of the dogs he and Eric encountered on their walks, the way they nipped at his heels, invaded his most personal areas, performed their tedious rowdy circle dances around him like he was a mobile Maypole at their uncouth village festival. There were, of course, solid, admirable dogs too: dogs with class and style, dogs who seemed to float along in a bubble of patrician restraint, assertively overseen by people who were well aware of the true nature of their responsibility, that they were the guardians of glorified wolves, people who did not mistake the mouldable sycophants who trotted at their sides for unusually meat-obsessed babies who, on the sheer basis of being *theirs*, were incapable of doing damage to a person, a farm animal, or another dog.

All the same, Eric began to choose their walking routes chiefly on the basis of potential sparseness of dog population which, in the end, was all to the good, because the places which were less likely to be foot freeways of dog walkers were invariably the most wild and beautiful places. They walked along wild garlic bridleways and woozy moss-anointed plateaus and footpaths temporarily disguised as small rivers. They walked to Tinker's Hill and Gillyflower Lane and Hobgoblin Knoll and Mortsafe Reach and Bonehouse Copse and Druid's Knob and Froglands and Stonerush Lakes and Little Fairycross and Death Corner and Hurtrocks Wood and East Taphouse and West Taphouse and, realising they'd somehow missed Middle Taphouse, walked there too. They walked to a solar farm and nine viaducts and thirty-seven quarries and fifty-four abandoned tin mines and a hydraulic ram ('Wait a minute, do I own an album by them?' said Eric). They walked to the cliffs and brushed against foxgloves and Eric told Carl not to lick himself after brushing against the foxgloves and Carl asked 'Why would I lick myself?' and told Eric the etymological roots of the word foxgloves. They walked down the cliffs and swam in the sea, and when they had finished their swimming and driven home, Eric bought Carl the hottest dish on the menu from the Bengal Palace takeaway plus saag aloo *and* onion bhajis and felt happier than he had for years. He had the realisation, as he watched Carl wolf down – no, not wolf down, Carl down – the hottest dish on the menu and the saag aloo and the onion bhajis, that one of the reasons he was happier than he had been for years is that when they'd been in the sea he'd been genuinely worried that Carl might slip away from him to wherever he had originally come from and that possibly nothing in recent memory had terrified him more.

An old gatepost was never just an old gatepost to Carl, a face on the cornice or bench end of a church never just a face, a standing stone never just a lump of granite. He saw every landmark as an arrow, a direct line into the fathoms of history. He had an instinctive feel for the grand folk threadwork of everything, rolling back through time, and the recent reading he'd been doing in the areas of topography and social history only heightened it. It was as if, to Carl, time was all happening at once, its events all potentially visible, like the moving lights you saw in the sky on a clear night that were in fact hundreds of years behind you. It was Carl who told Eric that the 'Lan' often appearing at the beginning of Cornish place names was a reference to ancient raised burial grounds predating the building of the churches now beside them. 'How many bodies would you guess are buried in the average rural churchyard in Britain?' he asked Eric, as they stalked the old horse-paths and mossy cemeteries of the Roseland Peninsula, glimpsing glinting creek water through the trees. He generously allowed three guesses in the end and, even with his final one, Eric didn't come close to the answer. 'At least 10,000,' said Carl. 'In Haworth, in West Yorkshire, where the Brontë sisters came from, it's thought to be more like 40,000.' They napped in fields and woke to find lines of sheep regarding them curiously from close at hand. 'Did you know that the meaning of the phrase "counting sheep" isn't just to count sheep but to count *breeds* of sheep?' said Carl. 'Try it sometime. Running through all those names – *Scottish Blackface, Jacob, Zwartbles, Manx Loaghtan, Barbados Black Belly, Florida Cracker* – is a much more effective method of sending yourself to sleep than just saying one number after another.'

'I suppose that's why,' mused Eric, 'you sometimes find shepherds who have loads of different sheep walking around with their arms stretched out in front of them and a faraway expression on their face. Me? I'm careful. If I see a shepherd in that kind of state, I keep my distance. Everyone knows the worst thing you can do is touch them.'

Not all of the historical debris that Carl stirred up on their walks stuck to Eric, as they rolled through the countryside, but a lot did. It coincided with his own increasing interest in the old, in what remained, and why, when the giant sieve of time had done its work. Every day was an education, a sequence of clarifying additions to his vocabulary. He noticed that the way he spoke was beginning to change, his accent softening, even at this less mouldable stage of life. There was a certain inevitability to it, he supposed. He had lived in the South West for approaching a decade now. But it was Carl, too, rubbing off on him, Carl and his big words, Carl and his love of the precision and poetry of language. When your accent tried out words for the first time, words it hadn't grown up with, it bended to their will, made allowances for their shape. But, as proud as he was of the places and dialects of his upbringing, he did not resent these small alterations. He was glad, as a man with little formal education, of his teacher, who always wore his knowledge lightly, and, unlike some of those who had taken it upon themselves to teach Eric in the past, was never self-righteous or arrogant when sharing knowledge.

Naturally, they were careful. Their ambulatory discussions occurred in the quiet places, when they were sure nobody was around. Walking through towns was frustrating, especially when Carl wanted to communicate something to Eric and had to use only his expressive damp eyes to do so. During these times, Eric delighted in winding Carl up, casting himself as Elizabeth Taylor in a Cornish version of a 1940s Lassie film and Carl as the heroic Long-Haired Collie hero.

'What are you trying to tell me, Lassie? Try harder! *There's a child trapped down the well and he's rapping on the walls to be let out?* Oh my god! No, sorry, I misheard. You'd just like me to replenish your stock of wool.'

'Have you seen something on the horizon, Lassie? A building, you say? What kind? Is it just the National Maritime Museum again?'

'What's that you say, Lassie? A new craft shop has opened in Exeter? And they are doing "buy three get one free" on selected haberdashery supplies for the next three days?'

They walked to Gibbet Hill and Thistle Ridge and Fox Tor and Patron's Wood and Giant's Mill and Piper's Pool and Lower Badger Farm and Upper Badger Farm and were downcast to discover there was no Middle Badger Farm, no provision in place for the silent central majority of the badger social hierarchy. They reduced the opening hours of the record shop to three days a week and walked to cairns and to plantations and to castles with no bricks and no turrets and no castles and to sunken lanes where the guts of the earth spilled up and out from its surface and a man made entirely of wire had been nailed abstrusely to a fence. They walked to Trebrownbridge, just because nobody was telling them they couldn't. They walked to Catchfrench and The Hurlers and The Cheesewring and Aunt Winnifred's Pinch. They walked to someone's garden with old sofas in it and an old black kettle nailed to a tree and didn't realise it was a garden. They walked to the half-derelict cottage at the end of the garden where a vegetarian ex-butcher lived with a bull and the ex-butcher invited Eric to stroke the bull and Eric invited the ex-butcher to stroke Carl and the ex-butcher told Eric the bull was called Scrunch and Eric told the ex-butcher Carl was called Carl and the bull sniffed Carl but not in a rude 'all up in your grill and your rectum' way and then the bull ate a packet of Rizlas and then everyone said goodbye, in their own individual ways, and Eric and Carl walked on. They walked to a big blue house in danger of being gobbled up by pink rhododendrons where a pruning woman in a light-blue sun hat asked him if he was looking for gardening work. They walked to a train station where you had to wave down the train to get it to stop and to a pub where a man sat at a table reading a newspaper next to a pig on a rope and a fat white cat seemed to be the only person interested in tending the bar. They walked to Skinner's Bottom, Jolly's Bottom, Greenbottom, Sandy Bottom and Happy Bottom. They walked so far that Eric arrived back at himself. Or at least arrived back at a version of himself that he'd last known in his early days in Wales, walking under the gruffly watchful brows of the mountains: lighter, in spirit and form, able once again to conceptualise attractive and eclectic futures for himself.

But it wasn't all fresh air and exercise. There were problems at hand, too. Principle amongst them was that it was 2006. The United Kingdom was in the grip of a populist mind-warp, an unbending new plasticity, an epidemic of reverse cultural snobbery cleverly designed to serve corporations and their rapacity. Formerly sane and discerning people pretended to like terrible songs and books and television shows for fear of being cast out of their social circles for the newly illegal hobby of appreciating art made with passion, individuality and integrity. Eric briefly joined a book group who were reading a novel called *The Da Vinci Code*. When he called it 'the worst load of bobbins I've ever read' and 'computer writing', he was virtually blackballed. 'They all thought it was brilliant. Am I going mad?' he said that night over the burritos he and Carl had made. 'You're definitely not going mad,' said Carl. 'It reminds me of Truman Capote's observation that Kerouac's *On the Road* was not writing but typing. Except *On the Road* is pretty much Barbara Kingsolver compared to *The Da Vinci Code*.'

The theme of the day in TV was the nastily gloating posing as the real: talent shows and reality series made so people could kid themselves they were glorying in the timeless appeal of low culture instead of doing what they were actually doing, which was looking down on poor people and working-class people and mentally unwell people and people deemed by TV producers to be unattractive. 'Look at this hideous old-looking woman!' said

TV. 'But don't worry: our experts can make her appear younger and more acceptable to society. Also stay tuned afterwards so you can drain your energy trying to choose a person to hate out of some random individuals thrown into a quasi-situation so we can sabotage their unimaginative dreams. Be sure to have some tissues to hand because we'll be playing those four shit songs that shows like ours always play in a lazy artificial attempt to create an emotional crescendo to our psychologically scarring false narrative.' Advertising chimed in: 'Also, while you're watching, we'll be explaining what's wrong with your life: that you want and need more of everything, even though you didn't realise you did and had been under the illusion you'd been getting on just fine with what you did have. Have you not heard? There are gadgets coming out *every week* and you need them all or you won't qualify as a person. Walking all the way to the living room to watch TV is just *so* dismally 1996. Why do that when you can buy a different TV for each room you happen to be in? But don't worry. If you have any doubts about the authenticity of what we are telling you, we'll be getting someone to do a voiceover in a northern accent, just so you know our pledges and sentiments are earthy and sincere.'

Cars, overhearing this and not wanting to be left out, joined the conversation: 'We were wondering if we could have more, too. What we'd primarily like more of is space.' The dual carriageway connecting Cornwall to the rest of the country was nearing completion. Two lanes heading east meant two edges of a sword: it would be easier for Eric to see his friends in Devon and Dorset. But a new kind of second-home culture was on its way, altering the character of the county forever, and, with it, a new kind of vehicle: higher, wider, designed to make its driver feel even more icily separate from their fellow humans, even more superior, even more removed from the remnants of what used to be called life.

Eric and Carl made the same mistake that countless otherwise enlightened individuals had been making for the best part of two centuries: they believed themselves to be people (and, yes, Carl *did* think of himself as a person, in a way) living at the scrag-end of history, a time when culture had bent as far as it could bend. Everything, they assumed, would stay more or less like this, now dystopia was finally here. But there was further to go. There always would be. Mindbogglingly, an era lurked only a few techno-capitalistic hills into the future where this time, when many people walked around with attention-vying rectangles in their hand but were not pressed by society to live entirely through them, this time of minimal digital surveillance and data harvesting, this time of only half-compromised privacy, this time of being able to get a doctor's appointment on the same week you asked for a doctor's appointment, this time when young people from ordinary backgrounds in ordinary jobs with an admirable amount of savings for their age and predicament could still expect to qualify to get mortgages on houses . . . this time would look like the essence of Edenic innocence.

Eric, who was not young but did come from an ordinary background, and Carl, who was but didn't, made no attempt to secure a mortgage on a house. That would not have been a wise or viable option, even in this era when mortgages were being handed out like cheap biscuits in a chain hotel. Eric's small pot of savings had dwindled to next to nothing and Pudding Lane Records was failing. It was more than the residual effects of the fire. Because here was another symptom of the new plasticity: it made for a terrible time in music, especially for people who made a living from music and were devoted to music in its purest forms. Although Eric loved psychedelia and jazz and raga and rock and folk and country and funk and soul and Afrobeat, he had always loved pop music too, including some of the kind of pop music people used to call 'manufactured'. But pop music had passed into a self-deluding mid-life crisis. It had the same shiny new face and trousers as ever but had never been more heavily supervised by the jowly and jaded. Not content with all those times it had been described as 'throwaway' when everyone really knew it wasn't, it decided to make itself exactly that, transform itself into the auditory version of single-use plastic. As soon as it was released from its manager's office, it hurled itself into the nearest wheelie bin, drove itself off forecourts, losing value as soon as it did, looking for a wall to smash into and transform itself into scrap metal, or would have done, if it had any metal in it. 'Indie', meanwhile, had become a term siphoned of all its original meaning: it was no longer an attitude or a position but a corporate mannequin of a former democratic hubbub of defiance. All the same, it was lapped up by many like cattle on the banks of a polluted river. 'There's no point fighting the current,' those doing the lapping seemed to convey, with much of their chatter. 'Resistance and insurrection is out of fashion. Also, why are you listening to The Doors? Haven't you heard? It's now a criminal offence to like their music. Don't get me wrong: I think "L.A. Woman" and "Peace Frog" are decent tunes, but my mate Simon, who has been giving *X Factor* a chance and finding it surprisingly enjoyable despite his intellect, told me in no uncertain terms that iconoclastic late-1960s boundary-pushing has been rebranded as overblown nonsense and I'm not one to rock the boat, especially now that rocking the boat is also a criminal offence.'

Obviously great records – even great pop records – were still being made. They always were. But they were harder to sift for, more muffled, more suppressed by the reverse snobbery of the zeitgeist and the general hostility in the direction of anything showing an inclination towards high art. And because vinyl albums – with their ambition to be beautiful all-round objects, to be more than just a functional part of a home's background – are always most prized at times when 'art' is not a dirty word, they were generally to be found on their knees, gasping for air, although not that hot kind being blown through the vents and apertures in technology by corporations. In fact, the time of vinyl – its best time, in fact, for half a century – was just around the corner, but nobody knew that. Irritatingly, as usual, nobody had a time machine. Record shops limped and scrabbled and grumbled. Especially those located in spurned towns towards the country's margins. Those who could hang on through these tough years would once again thrive. But many didn't hang on. They became tattoo parlours or nail salons or charity shops or something else the median member of the British public had much more use for than a record shop. In early 2007, Pudding Lane Records unfortunately became one of them.

Eric knew that part of the problem was age, the softening of edges and airbrushing of your generation's cultural past that inevitably comes with it. But he knew deep in his heart that it was more than that. He was living in an era unusually notable for its hollow sneer and corporate pandering. He felt cast out by it, by the way it kowtowed to The Man like none before it, the way it mistook ambition and imagination for pretension, ate shallow capitalist hogwash like it was a nutritious brunch. Owning a music outlet didn't put him at the epicentre of the bullshit storm but it made him aware of some aspects of it he might otherwise not have been. He was ready for a change and, when he closed the door of Pudding Lane for the final time, he did so not totally without the feeling of a man locking his own jail cell from the outside.

He decided he might quite like to build something. He was becoming increasingly interested in the philosophy of construction: the way that the structures which withstood the discerning critique of the decades were almost always the ones that had been built with most care and love and individuality. Houses. Cars. Boats. He also saw it in records: those he'd liked forty years ago but, somewhere in the interim, while his back had been turned, had, miraculously, without their creators having to lift a finger, mutated into masterpieces. They were pieces of architecture, too. So many things you didn't initially think *were* architecture were. When he thought about it, a desire spread through him to hatch and shape something all of his own. But what would his meagre bank balance permit it to be? One idea did occur. It probably wasn't one with much future in it. But perhaps now was the time to fuck the future, just as the future had frequently demonstrated no compunction in fucking him.

Since Carl's arrival in his life, Eric had been prone to neither loneliness nor debilitating bouts of dissatisfaction regarding his social life, but he had been a little sad the previous year when, shortly after making a new friend in town – a fellow toiler at the independent retail outlet coalface, by the name of Dimitri – that friend had decided to relocate ninety miles north east, and re-establish his small bookshop in an unassuming street on the fringe of the popular fossil town, Lyme Regis. Nevertheless, the two men had kept in touch, meeting for pub lunches a couple of times in the interim, and when, the week following Pudding Lane's dissolution, Dimitri asked Eric if he and Carl might be available to housesit for him in Sidmouth while he spent a long weekend in Brittany, Eric didn't have to pause for thought before taking up the offer. Carl was on cloud nine rooting through the house's multifarious library and lounging on the sofa as Dimitri's cat, Archimedes, nuzzled purringly into his stomach. Eric renewed his love of car boot sales, first ignited three decades ago by his magpieish aunt Joan, and on the final day the two of them hiked east and swam at a shingle cove where heavy overnight rain had stirred up the copper sea to such an extent that it felt like they were bobbing around in the planet's lifeblood. On the way home they reminisced about the day that Carl had spoken his first words.

'The thing was, I *had* recently had an accident at work, so it freaked me out even more,' said Eric. 'Although that accident definitely had been my fault, and I was working for myself, so I doubt I'd have been due any compensation.'

'I didn't really know what was going to come out until it did come out, to be honest,' said Carl. 'It could just as easily have been the Autoglass Repair theme tune. It was all driving me nuts even though I didn't yet quite understand what it meant, and why it had to be coming out of a metal box. Hence me changing the station, as soon as I worked out how. I'm not honestly sure what was worse: that or the cursed bell.'

'I was just trying to make sure you weren't lonely.'

'Is this definitely the way home?' Carl asked, noticing Eric had taken a turn off the new dual carriageway.

'You'll find out.'

Life isn't a delusional, doting admirer. It doesn't sit around on its backside, waiting for you to change your mind or come to your senses. It ploughs relentlessly on, ripping up the playing field as it does, dragging the goalposts along with it. Few were more aware of this than Eric, so when, after parking, passing between the grey stone bowling-ball gateposts and wandering along the permissive footpath that formed part of the driveway, he saw the woman in the light-blue sun hat, pruning the same pink rhododendrons she'd been pruning ten months earlier, he let out an involuntary guffaw. Startled, the woman looked up from her pruning. He could see that she did not recognise him. Perhaps he'd just been one of many marginally outdoorsy-looking men in their fifties whom she'd spontaneously offered gardening work to in the last few years. But after a little clarification from Eric, during which she politely pretended to suddenly recall their earlier encounter, she informed him that the position she had mentioned last summer was, indeed, still open. She said he'd been fortunate in his timing: she spent less and less time here now, devoting the rest to her flat in Kensington and business trips abroad. She'd even been thinking, in recent weeks, of putting the place on the market, as it was getting a bit much for her.

Her name, she said, was Mathilda Flockhausen. She was Eric's age, almost precisely, but still had something about her of the flighty art student she had once been, and showed Eric and Carl around the garden in the manner of a person freshly bewildered by adult existence and all of its trappings. 'It's a little silly but I only found this bit of the garden about a month ago,' she said, with a shrug and a lopsided smile, leading them through an overgrown arch behind a Victorian sundial. In the early eighties, she'd worked in set design: theatre, then a few films. But it was short-lived. Family life came along, then, after the death of her father, the responsibility of overseeing a millinery business stretching back two centuries, which, to this day, in its hugely reduced state, she still took care of, when she couldn't find any clever method to avoid doing so. 'Of course, nothing's ever been the same anyway in the hat business since the 1940s and 50s, when people started buying more cars,' she said. 'Fewer people at bus stops needing to keep their head warm, you see!' There was a daughter, too, from a long-dead marriage, but she'd recently moved to Edinburgh to 'live out some of the theatrical dreams that I never could' and there was a man on the scene, sometimes. 'I *believe* we are still together in an official sense,' she said. 'But I haven't seen or heard from him in two months. Cloud is his name and he floats like one. Somewhere out in Nebraska, apparently. The random disappearances have become something of a pattern. You might seem him, at some point, but I would approach with caution, if you do. He's not the most sociable creature and doesn't like loud noises, unless they're the kind made by the true love of his life, which I am sad to admit is not me but his 1964 Harley Davidson Panhead.' As it transpired, in the ten months that Eric was in the employment of Mathilda Flockhausen, Eric and Carl saw Cloud just once, and even then only as a silhouette, pulling a wheelie on a distant clifftop in the half-light.

So that was what Eric built: not a house, not a record, not even a shed, but a garden. Someone else's garden, at that. There was no interview. He was coerced into no conversation that would have revealed his lack of horticultural experience. He merely turned up, accompanied by Carl, and began to dig, prune, hoe, lop, chop, sow, mow, rake, brush, propagate, aerate, water and saw. All of it was easier, and more satisfying, than he could have imagined. He had never been averse to covering himself in muck, and the gardening gene, it appeared, was another he had inherited from his aunt Joan. Much of it was just common sense and instinct: you dug holes, you kept breathing space in mind, you remembered you were dealing with living things with their own particular needs and didn't try to force the issue, you saw what didn't work and learned from it, you thought about your colour scheme. Of course, it helped to no small extent that, during their period as Dimitri's housesitters, Carl had polished off Vita Sackville-West's early 1950s books *In Your Garden* and *In Your Garden Again*. ('What's the next in the series called, *No Longer in Your Garden Since You Took Out That Restraining Order on Me*?' asked Eric. 'No, it's called *More for Your Garden*,' said Carl. 'It was published in hardback in 1955 by Michael Joseph.') That Mathilda was rarely around offered a huge advantage in terms of productivity, with Carl's knowledge and superior strength, in his preferred bipedal form, being fully utilised. 'Vita is of the opinion that when you're pruning roses you should snub them no less harshly than Victorian parents snubbed their children,' he would say, as Eric hovered timidly over a woody tangle. He talked about Irish cottage gardener William Robinson's emphasis on not merely copying ideas from elsewhere but thinking primarily in terms of the specific ground you were working with, and Robinson's railing against artifice. 'Kind of like making music,' said Eric. 'You don't want to just brainlessly trot out some of the same shit that some other Herbert's doing.' 'Sort of,' said Carl. He was vehemently anti-lawn – 'numb monotonous symbols of wealth' – and pro-wildness. Of Astroturf he would not even speak, aside from his one sorrowful dismissal of it as 'another small nail in the planet's coffin'. He painstakingly laid on half-acre wildflower banquets for butterflies, rescued caterpillars from puddles, fetched refreshments for buff-tailed bumble bees. He planted and sculpted with a more ambitious version of the same instinct as Eric, plus the know-how he was gaining from recent library trips, but there seemed to be more past toils to the inspiration plus perspiration equation that made up his talent: a sense that, at some point, he had done this before. When she returned from London and Bali and Istanbul and San Diego and Amsterdam and Tokyo and Tasmania and Cirencester and the Algarve, Mathilda surveyed their work with delight, less like an employer and more like some ethereal queen or duchess from a nineteenth-century folk tale who had come back home to find that, out of the pure goodness of their hearts, a family of fairies from some nearby enchanted woodland had popped over to do some decorating on her behalf.

'I bet *you've* been working hard too, boy,' she said to Carl, stroking him inexpertly behind his ears. 'Yes you *have*, haven't you? Yes you *have*, haven't you?'

'I fucking have,' he thought, in an uncharacteristically profane moment. 'I'm absolutely cream-crackered and I could completely destroy that giant bag of Bombay mix I saw you bringing in from the car earlier.'

'*What* a clever Longtail Cast-On you are! *What* a clever Longtail Cast-On!'

The term was one Carl had learned early in his days as a fibre arts hobbyist. It described a sturdy way of using a long piece of yarn to establish the stitches you knitted from, a swifter method than casting on with a more traditional loop. Eric's idea of inventing a canine of the same name was, Carl believed, one his most seminal brainwaves, and had saved him from innumerable awkward conversations in the last few years. If he said it with enough conviction and attributed its origins to one of the less publicised Eastern European nations, even if he was talking to a somewhat doggy person such as Mathilda, who had spent time in several less publicised Eastern European nations, they generally just made a somewhat interested sound out of a closed mouth and stopped asking questions. Carl had heard it so many times now he had, to some extent, absorbed it into his being, grown comfortable with its connotations. 'I'm the sturdy initial loop people knit from!' he sometimes found himself thinking. 'That doesn't seem like the worst thing someone can be.'

By now they were temporarily living in the one-storey annexe at the back of Mathilda's place: a damp, unheated afterthought to the main building that had little in common with it. She'd told them they were welcome to use the space until they found another house to rent. 'Nobody's lived in here for decades,' she said. 'Apart from Cloud when he's been having one of his spells after going a little too avidly at his funny cigarettes.' The walls were dripping to the touch, spiders rampaged and bred with Catholic abandon, the 1970s hobs and oven's primary skill was making food a bit warmer and a lot soggier than it had been before it was cooked, Eric had been required to put his records and most of his furniture in storage, and the space was horribly cold in winter. At one end of the annexe, which was more of a lean-to in appearance, was an attractive double-panelled hexagonal window, through which they could see the dining room of the main house. There was something uncomfortable about looking into this large pristine space, unlived in for 75 per cent of the year, from their somewhat squalid, cramped full-time one. But rent-free lodgings in tandem with a not ungenerous hourly wage was not to be sniffed at, and one of its rewards was Eric was able to accrue some savings to put towards a more comfortable living space. When he wasn't gardening he sold a few records and trinkets on eBay and at the Friday market, seventy minutes' drive away, in Causley Mopchurch, and, during the clement months, trod the dew at as many early-morning boot sales as was feasible.

He remembered some bit of poetry Carl had once quoted, something about life being essentially made up of the ways we miss life. He'd known a feeling not unlike that: in the early part of his twenties, a little, perhaps, and certainly during his time as an out-of-place public relations officer failing to find warmth in a city not shaped for him. Strangers were quickly impressed by Eric back then, usually because of some famous person or other he'd met, or because the strangers, picking up on something about his aura, suspected he'd been in a band and asked him about it. Those days were long gone and he did not miss them. Nobody you'd just met was going to be knee-jerk impressed because you hung out backstage with a lily of the valley or just last Thursday had collaborated artistically with a deciduous magnolia, but once you chatted to them a bit about it, it might assist a deeper bonding process. Life, though not going anywhere that anyone who took it upon themselves to imperiously decree specialness would have categorised as 'special', was attaining colour and stretching out its roots. Living it did not feel like missing it.

'I do hope you're not working too hard,' said Mathilda. 'Do you ever take a walk over to the cliffs? There's the sweetest little writer's hut up there and some most intriguing lichens. If you're going right up to the top, though, don't take your credit card. I took mine once and it blew clean out of my hand into the sea. I expect it's washed up somewhere around Perros-Guirec or Saint-Malo by now.'

They were only a month or so before the end of their tenure by then and had moved out of the annexe into a place near the market. Mathilda's eighty-eight-year-old mother and fourteen-year-old nephew were visiting and sun-scorched wind kept whipping down from the coast, tearing around the garden and shaking all the shrubs and trees, as if determined to free them of coins and pens before it washed and dried them. Eric and Carl sipped cold drinks – Eric from a glass, Carl from a bowl – and watched the nephew destroy Carl's cherished moss garden with his 5-iron, intermittently almost braining his sleeping grandmother with low-flying Titleists.

'I should have worn a hat,' said Eric, loud enough for Carl, but nobody else, to hear him. 'I think I'm going bald. I've got a big patch of sunburn on the top of my head.'

Carl's brain went straight to his favourite hat fact: the one about the impact automobile sales had on the decline of the millinery industry. Being a little too close to other humans for safety, he was frustrated not to be able to say it. But then he remembered that Eric knew it already, and they'd learned it together, right here.

'That soddin' gargoyle up there is freaking me out,' continued Eric, pointing to an agonised face above them, just below the gutter.

'How many times have I got to tell you?' thought Carl, who had been enjoying the low-budget laptop Eric had bought him as an early sixth birthday present and his accompanying discovery of the rapidly growing website Wikipedia. 'Gargoyles are the ones that have a spout. Grotesques are the ones that haven't. Both are frequently carved in the form of lions, dragons or half-dog-half-man creatures and were initially used by the church during the twelfth and thirteenth centuries to scare people in the direction of religious obedience. *This one* is a grotesque.'

Mathilda always appeared thoroughly pleased with their work, in an absent-headed sort of way. When prospective buyers started arriving to view the house, they unfailingly reserved their most gushing compliments for the garden, with liberal use of phrases such as 'tremendous biodiversity', 'abundant pixie wonderland', 'al fresco room dividers', 'viridescent resource' and the question 'How could anyone bear to leave here?' It had not precisely been a wilderness when they'd arrived but it had become, since then, a completely repainted canvas. And now they would leave.

What had it all been for? A person might as well ask 'What is anything for?' There was something seductive to Eric about the idea of leaving the world a handmade present and moving on; doing the precise opposite of saying 'Here I am, and here is what I do, please show your appreciation for me lavishly because I'm not going anywhere.' That was what so many of the people who'd made his favourite records had done; especially the records initially thought lost in the dustbin of culture who, while the world turned, had been crawling slowly up the bin's sides and back out into the light of their ultimate day. But of course that potential eventuality wasn't the *why* of his recent project. He hoped Mathilda enjoyed wherever she lived next. He hoped her successors didn't concrete or turf the whole space over. Ultimately, though, he had to accept it wasn't any of his business. At least he, with immense help of Carl, had made an attempt to pass something special into fresh hands. And perhaps, ultimately, it was here, rather than as an architect of anything, where his true talent lay.

He continued passing records into fresh hands, too; more of them than he had done for some time. He was noticing something beginning to change in that area: a re-evaluation of the odd and scarce, a growing hunger for the physical in a metaphysical culture. His stall at Causley Mopchurch market had become busier of late, younger faces crowding around it. He replaced the headshell on a 1973 Pioneer turntable he'd picked up at a car boot sale and sold it for a £150 profit, with no fear that anyone had been ripped off. Every week, he effortlessly shifted old Pudding Lane stock that not much more than a couple of years ago had sat gathering dust in the shop, unloved and unbrowsed, even when halved in price. His placid, mellow dog only drew more people in. The goalposts were being dragged along by the plough again. Was it possible that, against everything he'd assumed, he could once again make a full-time respectable living at this business?

Their new place near the market hadn't been convenient for the final few months of the gardening job but Eric's definition of the word convenient was one that had stretched since he had been living in the West Country: a country, though nobody ever quite admitted it, all of its own. The house was a 1950s one, formerly council-owned, on the edge of a village a couple of miles outside the cheaper side of town. Gas central heating, twelve-month contract, two bedrooms, decent-size patio garden, no cats, dogs by negotiation. The negotiations had played out as follows:

ERIC: 'I *do* have a dog. Will that be a problem?'
LANDLORD: 'What breed is he or she? And how old?'
ERIC: 'He's a Longtail Cast-On. And he'll be seven in October. He's extremely clean and well-behaved.'
CARL (from the far side of the room): 'I really am!'
LANDLORD: 'What was that?'
ERIC: 'Oh, nothing. I just sat down on the sofa. It's a leather one, quite squeaky.'
LANDLORD: 'Ok, I'm sure it will be fine, as long as he doesn't eat any of the walls.'

It was a pleasant and, by Devon standards, fairly diverse neighbourhood: mostly a combination of pensioners, the scattered offspring of old farming families who no longer farmed, the odd bohemian or two, and that group of people that estate agents lazily and snobbishly describe as 'young professionals'. 'Ok but what about us old amateurs?' asked Eric. They fitted in just fine. In fact, the only neighbours Eric clashed with were the couple who lived directly behind his and Carl's new garden, in the most polite and chocolate-box building on the road, a pink seventeenth-century thatched cottage whose interior the couple had chosen to decorate solely with a framed three feet by four feet photograph of themselves. Local rumour had it that the prominence afforded to the framed photograph was down to its rarity, since it documented the only time that either party featured in it had ever smiled. Their van, by contrast, was brimful of humour, featuring such stickers as 'SHITBOX', 'NO FUCKS GIVEN', 'IT'S ALWAYS BEER O'CLOCK' and a ticklist of all the creatures it had 'run over' so far, including a cat, a rabbit, a badger and the silhouette of a person in a wheelchair. 'How could anybody find that funny?' asked Carl. 'I think it's a matter of stepping out of yourself for a while,' said Eric. 'You have to do that and put yourself in the brain of some early part-developed form of *Homo sapiens* life who got trapped in the twenty-first century, then maybe there's a way to understand.' To be fair to Toni and Guy – these really were their names, and Toni in fact was a hairdresser, though not that one – Eric and Carl didn't witness them run anything over, aside from one of Eric and Carl's tomato plants. This hurtful – especially to Carl – crime Toni and Guy denied, along with their responsibility for being liable for half of the emptying fee for the septic tank that the two houses shared. 'I'm afraid it's not quite that easy, when you're a single mum,' said Toni. 'Four is a lot of legs for a single mum: I've never seen one with that many before,' Eric almost replied. He also felt tempted to ask where the child was, since he'd never seen one. Instead, he just paid the bill. 'Everyone is paying for their shit anyway, so I might as well join in,' he told Carl. But what really upset Carl was Toni and Guy's dogs who, locked up for hours on end and unconditionally yelled at for much of the remainder of the time, barked angrily from behind the living-room window every time he and Eric passed the house. 'I just want to look after them, take them on walks and give them some love,' said Carl. 'I wouldn't be so hasty about that,' said Eric. 'Given half a chance you can guarantee those two would be gnashing their teeth around your bollocks, and I'll bet neither of them has read Emily Dickinson.'

Town was different: aesthetically debonair, unabashedly organic, cleverly stuffed into a steep river valley, a place with a striking amount of higgle to its piggle. Everything thoroughly pleasant about it – its arty pubs, its ethically orientated independent shops, community litter picks and nature trails – was counterbalanced by something equivalently sanctimonious and grating. To the outsider it resembled a promise. To those who'd wriggled inside that promise, it could soon feel more like a smug echo chamber, with its surfeit of trust-fund artists, phoney culture warriors and skewed lifestyle evangelists. You were either with the programme, or you weren't, and, despite its groovy outerwear, the programme was surprisingly unforgiving of those who didn't conform to its rules. Also the programme was fucking expensive. Jill Monk would later describe it to Eric as 'the kind of place where a white baronet with dreadlocks will tell you off for abandoning your punk roots and shopping at Sainsbury's'. People who'd visited for the weekend talked about how much they'd like to move there, while people on the adjacent pub table tried to find spiritually framed positive comments to make about people in their experimental yoga group who were getting thoroughly on their tits, and complained in a scrupulously peaceful fashion about the ways in which they felt the town had gone downhill, such as the influx of new residents who they felt at heart were a *different* kind of people to them but had the same footwear and had read the same trendy *Guardian* newspaper-sanctioned book that year and had similarly wealthy parents paying a similar monthly stipend into their bank accounts. Everyone was in agreement, however, that it had an extremely nice river.

Eric found the place alternately enlightening and suffocating and energising and infuriating and kind and mean and couldn't get enough of its organic cheese. He was additionally aware that, right now, in 2010, it would have been quite a shrewd place to open a record shop. But he wasn't sure if he was ready to go down that road again and, besides, it already had one, down at the bottom of the hill, beside the bridge over the river, next door to a lovely community-orientated bookshop that would close in a few years to make way for a less community-orientated seller of electronic cigarettes. He knew this because one day the record-shop owner had come to say hello to him on his market stall.

'Some super-nice vinyls you've got here, man,' the record-shop owner had said to Eric. 'I heard you've been undercutting me. Naughty naughty.' Stubble. Hair in a little bun. Received Pronunciation running from his lips like clotted cream. Eric put him at thirty-fiveish.

'Ah, I wouldn't know about that, pal,' said Eric. 'I just do what I do and try to give people a fair deal.'

'It's all cool, brother. Doesn't bother me. *Different clientele* and all that. Different requirements and aspirations. Listen, I'm organising a little get-together in the town hall next month. A few DJs. You should come. Play some tunes. Good old-fashioned rock 'n' roll, maybe.'

Good-old fashioned rock 'n' roll. Just what era did this guy think Eric was born in? The Great Depression? They shook hands. Or rather the record-shop owner presented Eric with a small complicated fist and Eric made a tentative attempt to do something with it, in the way a person might if they had been unexpectedly handed the tiny offspring of an unlovely animal whose existence they had been previously unaware of.

'Ah, Everett Mockridge, you want to give that guy a wide berth,' advised Reg Monk's son, Julian. 'Essentially, his retired admiral of a granddad bought him a hipster record shop for Christmas. He's got what they call a "radar for favour". Born networker. Always looking for someone influential he can coax something out of. And I have it on good authority he paid a seventy-eight-year-old woman £50 for her late husband's collection of rare psych LPs. Must have been worth three grand, minimum.' Nonetheless, Eric kept an open mind. Selected some records. Put some thought into it. Gave consideration to tempo and narrative. Turned up. A band – a heavy one – was sound-checking. Nobody could hear a note of anything Eric was spinning. Or they wouldn't have been able to, if anyone had been there. 'Have I definitely got the right time and place?' Eric asked the sound engineer, gesturing to the empty hall. 'Yep,' said the sound engineer. 'All good. Everett told us you were coming.'

'I suppose it could have been a genuine mistake,' Eric said to Carl that evening.

'Hmmm,' said Carl. 'I applaud a mindset that gives people the benefit of the doubt but in this case I'm not so sure. I think he might be one of those people you talk about sometimes. I forget what they're called now. Oh yes, that's it. A binhead.'

It was confusing for Eric sometimes, landing in this place where people who clearly thought you were a massive worthless twat went out of their way to say polite and positive stuff to you, as a person who had been brought up in places where people with the most genuine fondness for you more often than not went out of their way to speak to you like they thought you were a massive worthless twat. Some of his encounters also reminded him of his old life in the capital, a 'get back in your corner, pleb' aspect of his conversations with entitled people who'd never spent a day in their life worrying about money.

'I've read a considerable amount about the British class system now, but I'm still not sure I entirely understand it,' said Carl. 'Although I know a lot of it is William of Normandy's fault. Not that I'm blaming Normandy itself. I gather it's ever so pretty.'

'Well, my furry highbrow friend, it's not easy to boil it down,' said Eric. 'But one way of putting it would be to say that people who've been born with nothing work really hard and finally have something but then when they do people who've been born with everything who are pretending to have been born with nothing tell the people who have been born with nothing that they're not allowed to have nice things and should remain in their lane.'

But Eric sold small slices of history to plenty of nice people – people who cared about the environment and art and people from non-privileged backgrounds and people from privileged backgrounds who were well aware of that background and had turned out just fine and had chosen not to employ the skillset learned within the halls of that background to belittle anyone – and nerded over music more pleasurably than he had done for years. He met people who knew people getting rid of record collections, some of which hadn't already been nabbed by Everett Mockridge for a contemptuous price. Reg Monk, currently taking it easy in the hills just east of Axminster after heart surgery, passed on some contacts, collections he didn't currently have the time or energy to root through. As a thank-you Carl knitted Reg a scarf which Eric pretended to have found in a posh shop in Frome. Carl alerted Eric to the existence of the rapidly expanding record-selling website Discogs. Post offices became a more important part of life. Eric's favourite, in a village near Okehampton, was owned by a man called Sanjay who had won awards for being in charge of a post office. Eric denied Carl's charge that the reason for his loyalty to it was because he liked it when Sanjay called him 'Mr Eric'.

As the second decade of their friendship progressed, they yo-yoed over the border, as both renters and hunter-gatherers. Devon was a warm comforting coat, with secret fake pockets. Cornwall was a stark, haunted picture in a pretty frame: something that told him truths that Devon didn't, something that, for some reason, he couldn't quite get out of his system. Somerset was 'basically London', hence visited only for important work purposes (e.g. Reg had heard a rumour that there was a passable first pressing of a Nick Drake album in the St Margaret's Hospice Shop in Wincanton). Dorset remained as yet mostly unexplored, hastily dismissed, despite Reg and Jill Monk's continuing enticements and Dimitri's proximity to it. As for the remainder of the United Kingdom: it may as well have been Norway.

They were a team, always. They were They. People, even though they had no idea of the reality of it, talked about them as if they were a TV duo: Carl and Eric, Eric and Carl. It was more true than they could ever have guessed. Carl at home, doing the books, writing the envelopes, sending the invoices. Eric doing the chat, the negotiating, driving them to the next location. They bought records off people who were or had been miners and plumbers and roofers and lecturers and sound recordists and microbiologists and bistro owners and zoologists and builders and people who were sixty-one and fifty-four and seventy-three and still figuring out what to do with their life and people who had never worked a day in their life and didn't look likely to any time soon. They went to happy homes where people had made little floral curtains to hide records from the glare of the sun, and unhappy homes where furious relatives had written 'YOU ARE RUINING THIS FAMILY WITH YOUR RECORD BUYING!' and 'PLEASE STOP OR IT WILL BE THE END OF US ALL 4EVER!' on boxes containing records belonging to people who had finally stopped buying records because they were now dead. They began to see everything through the prism of records even more than they already had, which was a lot. They weighed strangers up in parks and dental waiting rooms and on trains and hilltop picnic spots, wondering if the strangers owned any records, and tried to guess what those records might be. They saw the initials 'VG' next to a meal on a takeaway menu and, even though they knew what it stood for, took it as meaning 'Very Good' and didn't order the meal because what they were ultimately looking for was a meal that was 'VG+' or 'M-' or even 'M': a meal that had been played few times by its previous owners and didn't have any scratches on it that would affect the sound quality during the meal's playback.

Heading south east on the way home after buying a small collection of 1990s jungle in Tiverton, one day in late 2013, Eric looked up at an electronic road sign and chuckled.

'What's funny?' asked Carl.

'Ah, just that sign, saying that it's sixty-one miles to Bodmin. It reminded me of something.'

'What, you mean when we used to live there? It already seems a long time ago, doesn't it?'

'Well, yeah that, but also I used to have a cat named after it too. I don't think I ever told you. Me and this woman I used to go out with had a joke about him. Her name was Rebecca. I would talk about something to do with Bodmin the town and she would pretend that I was talking about Bodmin the cat. For example, I'd say, 'Bodmin was a bit grim today in the rain,' and she'd say, 'Take that back this instant! He's a beautiful boy and always looks nice and bright and orange.' Or I'd say, 'I went swimming in Bodmin this morning. He didn't seem to mind, and I got a good number of lengths in, considering his size, but the pool was a bit dirty and busy,' and she'd say, 'That's not Bodmin's fault. He's just trying to survive, as a large ginger cat, running a leisure centre inside himself near a dual carriageway on the edge of a small town.' So now when I see that sign telling me how many miles it is to him I picture him down there over the ridge behind the last bit of the moor that's also named after him, somewhere near Asda, with a dim look on his face. He would be thirty-one next week, if he was still alive.'

'Thirty-one! I can't even imagine what it would be like to be that old.'

'Hey, watch out, you cheeky fucker.'

'Rebecca sounds like she had a lovely sense of humour. How come you've never talked to me about her before?'

'Ancient history now, intit? Buried deep. No point going over it with a rake. Everything bustles on.'

In the van they listened to acid country and agricultural funk and uneasy listening and slightlydelic pop and floral hip-hop and gangster folk and eighties pop and – until Carl complained – proto metal and face-melting stoner rock. When the road around them was clear, Carl danced as well as his seatbelt would allow to 'Push It' by Salt'n'Pepa and Gustav Holst's *The Planets*. They rebranded boring journeys along irritable tarmac arteries and fraught potholed inclines as 'road trips' in order to perceive them as adventures, which they often turned out to be, in at least some minor way. They drove to car boot sales in Marshfield St Peter and Buckland Monachorum and Lympstone Commando and Lanrocket and Treknobble and Cat & Fiddle, which wasn't a place at all, just a pub, with a field, and no cat, or fiddle, although Eric did purchase a rusty-stringed 1940s Russian balalaika there for a tenner. They drove to a car boot sale where a man walked around with a live chicken in his coat pocket, asking people if they had any mirrors. They drove to a boot sale where Eric bought a fascinating, possibly Victorian woven object of obscure origin which Jill Monk later informed him was a dog's chew toy. They drove to a car boot sale where a man selling duvets off the back of a lorry shouted, 'I'm not posh. I don't have a bidet. I stand upside down in the shower.' They drove to a car boot sale where a man called Trevor asked a man called Kev if he'd like a pineapple for 80p and the man called Kev told the man called Trevor that he would give it a miss because he'd just had breakfast. They drove to a car boot sale where there was no escape from a man attempting to seduce crowds with polythene bags of refrigerated bone and flesh, a bizarre DJ of Death who left Eric and other attendees under the impression that they had wandered by mistake into some nightmarish 1980s BBC Radio Roadshow where lamb cutlets had taken the place of Rick Astley and Bananarama. They drove to a car boot sale where a man selling a small, quite ordinary cabinet said, 'What the fuck are you doing?' when Eric took a photo of the small, quite ordinary cabinet the man was selling and, when Eric told him he was taking a photo of the small, quite ordinary cabinet, the man said, 'Well, fucking don't. I didn't give you permission,' which led Eric to wonder if the small, quite ordinary cabinet had experienced trouble with the paparazzi in the past, and to picture the man and the small, quite ordinary cabinet attending various high-profile events in Paris and New York and London, the man indiscriminately swinging at photographers who got too close to the small, quite ordinary cabinet as the pair entered the VIP area, and to picture the photos that would appear on the front pages of the tabloids the following day of the small, quite ordinary cabinet and the man's violent face, mid-punch, which would only exacerbate the problem, leading to more photographers hustling to get shots of the small, quite ordinary cabinet at future VIP events in major cities.

Granny Kettlebridge

'Any gossip, m'dear?' Granny Kettlebridge asks me. What she means by this is, 'Have you bonked anyone new and interesting lately?' There is a crow at the window and we are in her kitchen, the kitchen that has been her kitchen for 79.8 years and was her own granny's kitchen before that, and which back then probably smelled of the exact same odour of vinegar and tea and chair dust and potatoes and turned salty earth blowing through the always-open window as it does today. You can't see the sea like Granny Kettlebridge used to be able to because the trees and vines and ferns out there have grown back up since her childhood when the land last lost its grip and devoured itself and because winter's rot has not quite yet set in, but I know the sea is there, growling behind the drapery. There is never a moment when you don't know it's there. Granny Kettlebridge said that when she was a girl there were more people living around here: pig herds, cottagers, dairy farmers. But one night late in 1926 people heard tree roots snapping and saw plaster falling off the walls of their houses and panicked and feared it might be like December 1839 – which a few of them still remembered firsthand – when as a special Christmas present the Undercliff gave most of itself to the sea, so the people gradually moved away or died and their empty former homes slowly crumbled and now it is just Granny Kettlebridge and her house, hanging on to the last sheer edge of everything. 'They would have burned me at the stake in any other century,' Granny Kettlebridge has told me lots of times, and I have to admit that her house is just the kind that you can imagine a witch living in, with its resident crow, and Granny Kettlebridge has the fingernails you might expect a witch to have – long thin pointy ones, fingernails almost half as long as the fingers they defend, fingernails that play their part in her immense skill at hanging onto the sheer edge of everything. Their length and pointiness used to scare me when I was small, but doesn't any more, and I don't think Granny Kettlebridge is a witch, or at least not one of the cartoonishly evil ones that the film industry likes to foment in the minds of children. Granny Kettlebridge is the one who knows me best, the one person I can tell anything to, and I am the one person Granny Kettlebridge can tell anything to, although I doubt I am the one who knows Granny Kettlebridge best; I come fourth in that regard, after the sea and the wind and the hungry dripping shrubs of the undercliff, and did come fifth, until recently.

Granny Kettlebridge loves hearing about what she calls my 'conquests' and I know that there is a vicarious pleasure in that for her. Not that Granny Kettlebridge has been a stranger to casual sex in her life but I know that her existence could not have been more different to mine when she was my age, apart from the fact it took place on the Dorset-Devon border. 'Try before you buy,' she tells me. 'Give them an inch when you've known them a year and not an hour before.' When she says these things I know she is talking not just about me but about her own life with my Granddad Kettlebridge, who I was not born in time to meet, though from what Granny Kettlebridge has told me about him, that absence does not make me as sad as it otherwise might have. When Granddad Kettlebridge died by falling off the cliff above Chippel Bay in 1953 everyone who knew Granny Kettlebridge – which, outside her immediate family, was probably about three people – thought she would be lonely and unhappy but that didn't happen. Granny Kettlebridge filled the cottage with cushions and cats and – even though she wasn't the biggest lover of dogs – one dog, who wasn't like other dogs, and filled the cottage's steep garden with hens and began to write romantic novels for a popular romantic-novel publisher. Sometimes, she found forlorn-looking solitary men in the Undercliff and took them home and, while the sea made the consciousness-expanding music of a sheet of giant wobbled cardboard, found out aspects of herself that Granddad Kettlebridge had never empowered her to discover. She claims one of the forlorn-looking solitary men might have been the novelist John Fowles, while he was out brooding on the cliffs and imagining the events that would form his 1969 novel *The French Lieutenant's Woman*, but having checked the timeline as best I could, I am not convinced it tracks. Whatever the case, when I took Granny Kettlebridge to see the adaptation of the book last year at the Regent cinema in Lyme Regis, we both agreed that the focal character Sarah Woodruff was not without Kettlebridgian qualities and Meryl Streep wore some excellent blouses and cardigans.

In 1969, when I was twelve and her dog Cowper was eight and the nameless crow in her garden was an indeterminate age and my sister Beth was seventeen and off living it up with her friends at some hippie commune over in Devon, something upsetting happened to Granny Kettlebridge: the romantic-novel publisher told her that they didn't want her to write novels for them any more. When Granny Kettlebridge asked them to explain why not, they told her that the world she and they were living in was a brave new one, and the romance-writing marketing had to do its best to catch up with that world's braver, racier needs. When Granny Kettlebridge responded that braver and racier was absolutely no problem where she was concerned and she'd in fact been holding back in her books up until now, especially in 1964's *Hasty Engagement* and 1967's *The Pirates of Seaton Bay*, the romance-novel publisher said that, be that as it may, some midlist trimming needed to be done, and those authors who had never progressed to the higher echelons of sales potential were to unfortunately be a casualty of that trimming, at least for now, although they would be sure to be in touch if that position changed. Granny Kettlebridge, who had written all of her thirty-two novels under the pen name Violet Axminster, was not left even with a reputation as a published author of fiction to show for her work. She was just an old lady, who a few unkind people suggested might have pushed her husband to his violent craggy death sixteen years earlier, living on the damp brink of the known world with seven cats, a weird overattached waxy crow, fifteen hens and a startlingly attractive dog.

There was an argument that Granny Kettlebridge could have left it at that: she was sixty-five, with no mortgage, and enough savings to see her out to the end of her days, even if those days lasted until the end of the century (which she was doubtful about, considering the history of heart disease on both her mother and father's sides of the family). She derived plenty of joy from witnessing her two granddaughters growing up, especially me, who she already saw a lot of herself in. But that winter Granny Kettlebridge proved everyone wrong: she wrote, every day, thousands of words; wrote out on the cliffs, wrote while making tea, wrote with such absorption that even the whistle on the kettle was an intrusion, wrote with a lack of inhibition she'd never previously channelled, wrote in a way that made her feel like a human battery, constantly in use, except in the four hours at night when she was recharging. When, the next March, she finally looked up from her writing and properly remembered the planet she lived on was earth and it was still there beyond the cottage walls, turning, she was pleased to discover that in front of her on her kitchen table were the typewritten pages of two complete, albeit unedited, books: both different to anything she'd written before, both no less different from one another, both the work of fictional women, one familiar, one new.

Thus Violet Axminster had her sweet and salty revenge: her epic saga *The Shagserpent of Branscombe Mouth* became one of the biggest selling titles of 1971 for the erotic imprint Stiff Books, with *The Cerne Abbas Giant's Naughty Weekend* and *The Loch Ness Bonkster* following swiftly and no less successfully in its wake. Meanwhile, as the less libidinous, more experimental Penelope Chalkridge she was able to unleash the other previously locked and chained side of her creativity, publishing a series of Dorset-inspired historical poetry via a small private press based in Swanage. So it could be said that, out of the dry husks of disappointment, Granny Kettlebridge found the seeds of a fulfilling life: two steady income strands, outlets for her dreams, both light and dark, and the blissful bucolic anonymity that many other writers experiencing a similarly steady level of artistic success are not granted access to. And when I speak to her now, as an adult who knows the full story, it is with the awareness that I am not just speaking to a granny but to a stealth icon of twentieth-century life. And when that same granny/icon makes me blush by asking such ungranny questions as 'Was it hefty in a wide way or in a long way and if we are talking about the latter did it have any bend to it as long ones often do?' and 'Before you got it out of his trousers did he walk around like he knew what he'd got or was he was one of the rarer ones who prefer to lower your expectations then surprise you with it?' I try my best to forgive her immodesty by remembering the laws of relativity and that, to her, who has undoubtedly spent much of the week in front of the typewriter grappling with octodicks and brontococks vis-à-vis their intentions as regards spreading around their essential liquid, it probably doesn't seem so immodest.

'Another musician, was it?' she asks now.

'Yeah,' I tell her. 'I quite liked this one. He talked a lot but I think he was quite shy. Sticky hands and chin. He wasn't awkward, though. Northern boy. From Leeds or somewhere. I forget now. After the second time we'd done it, he talked so much he sent me to sleep. He doesn't live around here, though. They almost never do.'

'That's my girl,' she says. 'You keep those musician boys on their toes, have your fun. There's plenty of time left for the rest of it.'

There's a big empty space in her cottage today. It's not so much like a sofa has been moved, more like someone took away a source of heat that you'd always deeply valued but come to incipiently take for granted purely due to the progression of the days around it. I can feel the space but I'm sure I can't feel it to anything like the extent that Granny Kettlebridge can. I am relieved to see that, if she does appear sad, it's in a philosophical way that is wholly Granny Kettlebridge. It is only two weeks since Cowper left her and she must miss him an immeasurable amount: his beautiful fur, his natural empathetic awareness of the times she had slid into the doldrums, his needlecraft skills, exemplary grammar, instinct for propagation and infinite erudition in the area of British history, especially its maritime strand. Regretfully I was not there at the end but she tells me it was curiously beautiful and that he is in the waves now, which she knows is the place he wanted to be. He was twenty-one. 'A good age', as they say. I can confirm it was one that I found thoroughly enjoyable.

If I say that I believe, in some ways, that Cowper was the remaking of Granny Kettlebridge, that is no denigration of the spirit and drive and iconoclasm of Granny Kettlebridge, merely a statement about the loveliness and genius of Cowper, which was staggering in its breadth: he always put others before himself, and was never judgemental, even when confronted with subjects that were not to his personal taste, such as, for example, the proofreading of a fictional scene involving the copulation of two mersluts with an aquatic version of King Kong. I will never forget the way when, as a ten-year-old, I ran fast, overreached the capability of my small legs and slipped down a bank in the undergrowth east of the Cobb in Lyme Regis, he selflessly carried me the two miles back to the cottage on his delicate back, reciting as he did so a selection of the passages of *Wolf Solent* that he had learned by heart.

A talking intellectual dog. Who would believe it today, in 1982? Not anyone sane, not unless they had, like Granny Kettlebridge and me, witnessed it firsthand, and then realised that what they were looking at was not a dog at all, but something far more precious. And surely any rumour of such a phenomenon would do nothing positive for the reputation of a long-fingernailed, eruptively haired solitary woman, a writer of strange secret books, a friend of few, living in an allegedly haunted cottage, chewed on by ivy, with no near neighbours, where scrawny hens often wandered at will into an outmoded pantry. So Granny Kettlebridge and I mention it to nobody: not my parents, not Beth. These many years it has been our secret, the one that, alongside so many other matters, has bound us ever closer, the one that has become strangely effortless for us to accept, quotidian but never banal. And now his decline and departure have coincided with the last blinkers of youth falling from my eyes and a wider curiosity blossoming in me, I find I want to know more, so much more than the considerable amount I already know and have found it so oddly easy to accept. Agonisingly, it is too late. But also perhaps it's not, because, although Cowper is no longer here, Granny Kettlebridge is, and I suspect she knows everything there is, or was, to know about Cowper. And as she interrogates me about my healthy commitment-free young sex life, I find that it is not that, but him, that I want to talk about.

I listen to the drapery flap – the outdoor version and the indoor version that he painstakingly hemmed and embroidered – and the storied growl of the sea coming through its gaps, and I feel sure that, despite all I have been told, South West England is not yet deprived of him.

Mel Is Other People

After Mel's first stand-up gig, her bookings began to dribble steadily in, the flow ratcheting up a notch by the end of August, aided by the new business cards Penny had made for her, plus Eric's indiscriminate distribution of them and the hyperbole with which he touted Mel's performances to anyone who would listen and many who wouldn't. In a review of Mel's fourth gig, the *Dorchester Echo* newspaper had described her as 'like a more energetic Jo Brand made in a lab to soothe the complex and impossible world we live in today', although when Mel and Penny ran into the reviewer in front of a batch of striking multicoloured carrots at Causley Mopchurch Farmer's Market the reviewer explained that what the review had originally said, before the cautious censorship of the editing process, was 'like a methamphetamine-fuelled triple-brained Jo Brand made in a lab to soothe the complex and impossible world we live in today' so that was the version Penny got printed on the cards. Mel had originally thought of calling her touring routine 'How I Know My Imaginary Boyfriend Is Drunk' or 'What Have You Got to

Tell Me' but finally, at the urging of Penny – a big Sartre fan – settled on 'Mel Is Other People'. Reliably well-received material included a section about Bathsheba's tragic addiction to ear wax and the takeaway Mel procured for her from the ear doctor, exaggerated with poetic licence to include an epilogue where the ear doctor becomes an unofficial 'dealer' for Bathsheba and the stray cats who pass through Mel's garden.

Keeping in mind the 'tragedy plus time' equation and deciding the time part was still a bit on the short side, she decided to omit the incident where Cliff Falls pretended to be a predatory jizz leopard, but did include a recounting of a few other, more historically distant episodes from her dating life. The most popular of these was unfailingly the story of Mel's mum's catchphrase 'What have you got to tell me?' – a question she had, for many years, put to Mel and her sister Fiona every time they arrived home or spoke to her on the telephone – and Mel's difficulties later when she realised that it was her fifth boyfriend's unshakeable habit to put the same question to her at the apex of sexual intercourse, albeit in a deeply contrasting tone. Having heard rumblings of all these themes, Eric had travelled east over the border to Causley Mopchurch for Mel's debut with trepidation, and not just for the usual reasons he approached the town – which in one of his more darkly generalising moods he had once described as 'a comprehensive wankland of smug fakery' – with mixed feelings.

'So is there going to be anything about me in this?' he asked Mel, collaring her by the bar ten minutes before curtain call.

'Nothing much. Just the bit about the Parma Violet. But I've called you Derek, not Eric.'

'What Parma Violet?'

'The first time we met you had a Parma Violet stuck to your arm. I had a bet with myself on how long it would stay there. I decided four hours, but it was longer. When you went home, it was still there, but the next time I saw you, which was four days later, it had gone.'

'I don't remember that at all.'

'Well, I suppose you wouldn't. You never seemed to realise it was stuck to your arm, and I never told you, and I suppose in the end it just fell off without you noticing.'

From that point on, he became her biggest supporter: not just the one he had already been but of the exaggerated professional her, the Mel who weaved gold from her life's misfortunes and pratfalls. He spoke to a re-upholsterer of lampshades who owed him a favour and was able to get a 50 per cent off deal on the printing of 300 white t-shirts with 'MEL IS OTHER PEOPLE' emblazoned across the front in Blackletter font. He drew on public relations skills unused for almost three decades. He gushed about fundraisers, spontaneous guerrilla gigs in community woodland. Recognising Primal Scream's lead singer Bobby Gillespie outside The Alleys antique centre in Bridport, he thrust thirteen business cards into his hand with the wink of the pedlar of a rare elixir, the holder of secrets, then, before Gillespie had chance to open his mouth in protest, was gone. Eric and Roy from Clocktower Records made plans for a gig in the shop. On Burton Bradstock beach Eric managed to offload four t-shirts onto the circle of shingle being temporarily occupied by one of the stars of a locally shot ITV drama and her family, even managing to elicit a vague promise from her, through a mouthful of sausage roll, that she would wear it for her upcoming appearance on a reality TV cooking show. He postered walls, flyered cafés and bookshops, stirred and simmered schemes, planted himself in the front row of Mel's gigs the way the managers of the pop bands he'd loved as a kid would plant teenage girls in record shops to scream hysterically about newly released songs.

All the while, nobody noticed summer quietly unbolting the back door and slipping away. Its wonderful reds and yellows and greens and oranges and purples fostered complacency. Families on their way to pick strawberries for £6.99 per kilogram admired the dahlias growing in front of a gatehouse haunted by the restless spirit of a persecuted apothecary who'd administered her own seventeenth-century death by swallowing hemlock and mandrake and thought, 'Naturally nothing bad can or ever has happened in this place of sun and imminent fruit.' Eric, while on a verdant plateau discussing the merits of Freda Payne's *Band of Gold* LP with Carl, became the fourth person in the area that day to spot a stalking creature, coloured like fox, shaped like badger, then shrug it off and rationalise it. 'Well, cats *can* be massive sometimes,' he reasoned to Carl. 'Especially the ginger ones. I should know, having had one myself.'

The words rang empty to Carl, seemed like the self-convincings of a man drugged by cosmic rays. The two of them were high above Minterne Magna at the time, in the bright fields which form the upper part of the panelled living room of Dorset's most famous chalk hill figure, the Cerne Abbas Giant. Their destination was a small festival, a folkloric celebration of Dorset amongst the grassy dumbles between the Giant's feet and the north end of Cerne Abbas village, where a group of astoundingly well-preserved medieval buildings offered an impression of an alternative Britain, unannihilated by Henry VIII, undissoluted. There was a village stocks, where during their last visit here, in a brief triangular glimpse back to 1451, Carl had seen an unruly artisan smashed in the face by a rotten goose egg while a drunken crowd mobbed and tore out the hair of a shoemaking rapist in the thoroughfare behind him. Normally, he'd have been all excited chatter, telling Eric about the forming of the nearby St Augustine's Well by the magic beer-giving staff of St Augustine; the alleged Roman roots of the Giant – which he'd in fact confirmed in April last year, by way of one of his visions; and the story about his eleven-metre hard-on actually being the result of the merging of a smaller penis with his former navel. But he was feeling muted and unwell. He'd noticed via some posters for the festival that the Dorset Ooser – a man-bull visage which Carl had never liked – would be in attendance, his chest felt like a small weakened coffin of air, and he was tired from a morning spent clearing up the mess Eric, in his current promotional frenzy, had made in the living room. His personal feeling was that, as great as it was that Eric was getting fully behind Mel's new career, he was overexerting himself, forgetting, once again, that he wasn't twenty-six – or even fifty-six, for that matter – and heading for a crash.

It turned out to be a strange and regrettable afternoon, full of all of August's hot, raggedly overpopulated confusion. Eric, who had got them to the start of their walk in a taxi and was relying on the Meat Tree for their lift home, immediately went at the scrumpy a bit hard and was swept off in a huddle of dancers made up of a key cutter from Glastonbury, a pub landlady from Child Okeford, her Suffolk-based visiting daughter and this year's designated Ooser, a towering folly of a man called Michael who was currently in the process of expanding what he later described to Eric as his 'personal drainage business' from North Devon across the border into the Somerset part of the Quantock Hills.

Carl was left in the company of the Meat Tree and two of his friends from the bookselling universe: a man Eric called Long Arm Jeff, who never appeared to listen to anything anyone said to him and was always going up to animals he'd never met, and some he had, and saying '*Settle!*' to them, and Jeff's partner Judy Nettles, who everyone agreed was wonderful aside from her fervid habit of buying terrible and inappropriately bulky Christmas and birthday presents for people she barely knew. Jeff, whose arms really were extremely long, and had been known to each carry as many as sixteen semi-rare vintage paperbacks at once, was talking about the ulterior motives of hornets, how vigilant you had to be for them nowadays, and what the best methods were of keeping a house hornet-free. Carl, who'd had plenty of experience with hornets, thought that the best way to deal with hornets was probably just to get out of their way and let them carry on being hornets. '*Settle!*' said Jeff to Carl, who was settled, at least in a superficially visible sense. The Meat Tree told Jeff that in his bathroom last month he'd seen the biggest hornet of his life and that it had stayed there for almost two whole weeks. 'You should have called me,' said Jeff. 'And if he had, what would you have done?' thought Carl. 'Told it to settle?'

At this point Judy got up and announced she was going to get a 99 Flake from the ice-cream van. 'They do still do them, don't they?' she asked. Jeff didn't appear to be listening but the Meat Tree said he thought they did but that they probably didn't cost 99 any more, unless it was pounds, not pence. A moment after that, Carl realised he was alone, there beside the wall at the far side of the festival, near the cemetery. He tried to look on the bright side: at least he was in the shade. He wasn't feeling well at all.

The 7.4 per cent fermented Wessex apples had hit Eric, who rarely imbibed alcohol at all these days, hard. 'If you want to get drunk quickly and inexpensively, I highly recommend being quite old,' he thought. He moved through the crowd, away from the flute-driven folk music he'd been twirling with part co-ordination to, but when he reached the place where he'd left his friends, he found all of them, including Carl, gone. Queasy for at least two reasons, he moved over to the grounds of the Benedictine Abbey, aware of Carl's enthusiasm for it, and began searching for him inside one of the two adjacent monastic buildings that were unlocked. As he did so, he noticed a tall but stooped man of at least eighty hopping towards him, flailing his arms in a state of some agitation. The nine-year-old urban trespassing part of himself that Eric always carried with him was instantly activated. 'What's this old whopper want to tell me off for?' he thought, and almost began to sprint away as the man, quite gently, but in a state of obvious alarm, inquired if Eric had any knowledge pertaining to the switching of an unfamiliar television from standard TV mode to DVD mode.

His name, he said, was Roger Buzzard and he'd been drawing Romans, studying Roman history, dressing up in Roman costumes, since he was six years old. When TV companies wanted someone to tell them what Romans wore, what Romans might have said, what a Roman villa might have had in it, they still often called him, as they had been doing for decades. Roger and his West Virginian wife Barbara said they were here because they were intrigued by the arguable Roman connections of the chalk figure on the hill above the self-catering cottage they'd hired. 'I know just the person you should be talking to,' thought Eric. 'But unfortunately I can't locate him right now. Also you might find him a little different to most amateur historians you've encountered.' As Barbara fed a cherry tomato tart to the small dog sitting on her lap and Eric rummaged for the missing HDMI cable behind the back of the cottage's TV, she told Eric that she wrote books, including one about stress that had 'caused some harsh ripples in the stress industry'.

'Ah, now there's an industry I know well,' said Eric, fighting to identify cables and beginning to lose hope.

Nonetheless, he emerged victorious. 'Our hero!' said Barbara, applauding fanatically.

'What on earth would we have done, sitting here twiddling our thumbs, with no director's cut of *Spartacus* to watch?' said Roger. 'It doesn't bear thinking about.'

Eric was momentarily back at that house in Broomhill in 1970s Sheffield, bashing out the chords to 'Strange Brew', as Alun Bannister emerged, impressed, from his mum and dad's bog.

'Does this go on forever?' he wondered. 'Is there always someone a bit older than you there, somewhere, to make you feel young and impressive, no matter how old you become?'

But Eric was *not* impressed with himself. Not at all. Even less so when, thankfully not many minutes later, he located Carl in a dip at the back edge of the Commonwealth War Graveyard, half submerged in St Augustine's Well. His eyes had a sideways-slanting, pinched look to them that Eric had not seen for several years. There was nobody around but, upon seeing Eric's approach, he didn't even speak, just sort of rocked, there in the water.

'I am *so* sorry, pal,' said Eric. 'Time ran away from me. How are you feeling?'

'Mmmnnn,' mumbled Carl.

'Was it the Ooser?' asked Eric. 'I know it sends you a bit funny. I should have thought of that. I should never have brought us. It was a mistake.'

He didn't even bother to try to find the Meat Tree. Instead, as soon as he could locate a spot of the cemetery with decent reception, he called a taxi company, Joe's Cabs, up the road in Sherborne. It was a Sunday: Joe wouldn't be too busy. Eric could rely on Joe, whom he'd sold a WWII motorbike helmet and a set of rockabilly albums to a few years ago. Everything was going to be ok. He was almost sure of it.

And it sort of was, by the time another month's worth of weekends had passed, bringing the last Saturday of hot itinerant fog, of coatless laxity, the detained final Saturday of what was still summer in all but name; the Saturday of the three-act show, with Mel at the top of the bill, that Eric and Roy from Clocktower Records had organised in the shop. Carl, after being extensively lavished with curries and trips to some of his favourite swimming coves, appeared back to his normal self: serene in public, inquisitive and conscientious in private. But, as Eric greeted the gig's attendees, he kept Carl close, declining all offers of alcoholic drinks and never prioritising social butterflying over his all-important duties as a friend and guardian. He quipped and promoted and complimented, all the time aware of a nagging question inside him and lightly subdued in his interactions by it. The question was not entirely new to him but was one he hadn't had to confront for several years and, though his fear of it stopped him from fully articulating the question to himself, it could be summed up loosely as, 'What do you do when you need something that is probably somewhere between a vet and a doctor but doesn't exist?'

When he contemplated the question what often popped into his mind was a sign on a road not far from the Meat Tree's house that he had seen and sometimes joked about. 'JURASSIC VETS,' said the sign. 'Now I know where to go if my Stegosaurus gets the flu,' he'd said to Carl a couple of times, as they passed the sign, and then, later, a third time, but not a fourth time because Carl said it had stopped being funny by then. Now Eric felt bad for ever making the joke at all. He hoped Carl had never thought that, by talking about a Stegosaurus, he was making an allusion to Carl himself. Carl was not a dinosaur, not any other primitive creature, and Eric had never seen him as one. Eric had always seen Carl as Carl.

'Did you know that the gap between the Stegosaurus and the Tyrannosaurus Rex was longer than the gap between the Tyrannosaurus Rex and us, here, right now?' Carl had asked Eric, the first time Eric had made the Stegosaurus joke. And Eric *hadn't* known but then he did, and had filed it away with all the other facts he knew because of Carl and his wonderful brain which, like his, was a brain only interested in everything, only more so.

If one of the two of them was feeling a little out of sorts tonight, it was Eric. What his brain was mostly interested in was sleep. Yesterday, as part of his continued pampering of his housemate, he'd cleaned the cottage from top to bottom, in precisely the way Carl liked it, and found the process dumbfoundingly exhausting. His neck buckled obstinately in place like the lock on a steering wheel when he tried to turn it too far to the left and there was a pain in the lower part of his back that gave him the periodic urge to check to make sure nobody had attached some abstruse rusty piece of industrial machinery to it while he had been otherwise detained. A sore little ball bearing darted and rattled around behind his eyes as he watched the support acts, neither of which connected with any of the more erogenous parts of his musical imagination. The first, a band from Bournemouth called The World and His Wife, whose heavily tattooed lead singer took the stage with the words 'Hello, I am your Wife . . . and this is the World', gesturing at the three near-identical-looking, bearded, baseball-booted men behind her, trudged through seven songs which probably would have sounded invigorating if you'd only heard four or five records in the preceding part of your life. The second, a white punk rapper called Tommy Hill Figure, whose lyrics largely concerned themselves with the legends of the nearby countryside, was novel and amusing for the first six and a half minutes of his set.

But Mel was, once again, on form, testing out some material about the removal of appendixes which revolved around the preparations for a trip to Antarctica of her 'nature-writing friend Bobby' and a story she'd read about Eddie Fisher, fourth husband of the film star Elizabeth Taylor, checking himself into hospital to have his unobtrusive and perfectly healthy appendix removed just so he could have a few days' break from Taylor, who was in an especially high-maintenance frame of mind in the troubled early stages of the filming of Joseph L. Mankiewicz's ostentatious *Cleopatra*. At the point where Mel had confessed, 'It seems extreme, I suppose, but we've all done it: I think immediately of the time Bathsheba was protesting about the food I was feeding her and I asked a back street surgeon to remove my gall bladder just so I could have a little quiet time away from the house,' her 'nature-writing friend Bobby', in his thinly altered real-world guise on the front row, laughed so hard that he triggered some severe acid reflux and was, as a result, remanded in the toilet at the gig's climax. This immediately presented Eric with two epiphanies, the first being its clue as to why the night's supply of Aldi's least expensive sauvignon blanc had depleted so rapidly, the second a nudge to play the punters out with one of the better tracks from Acid Reflux's *Bilious Attack* LP: an album he'd been intending to critically reappraise since finding a 1971 first pressing of it amongst Penny's uncle's possessions at Batbridge Manor.

As the night simmered down, Eric took over from Penny on the merch stall, Carl dozing at his feet with his chin on a large hideous cushion emblazoned with a Siamese cat's face that had been purchased for Mel for her recent birthday, to the puzzlement of Mel, by Judy Nettles. In the alley outside, Carl could hear Long Arm Jeff and the Meat Tree catching up on small talk with the owner of an equine laundry business who had caused quite a stir by travelling to the gig from Powerstock on her Clydesdale, Warren, Long Arm Jeff periodically interrupting the catch-up to instruct Warren to '*Settle!*' Eric introduced himself to Natalie, the young lady Billy had brought along to the gig, possibly as a date but possibly as just someone called Natalie, and who was, to Eric's knowledge, yet to glance away from the screen of her phone since first stepping across the threshold of the venue two hours earlier.

'So how do you and the lad Billy know each other?' asked Eric.

'Oh, *online*,' said Natalie. 'You know how it is, these days.'

She paused, apparently to look up some clarifying addition to this information on her phone, but nothing was forthcoming.

'Can I interest you in anything from our exquisite array of merchandise?' asked Eric, gesturing at the sixteen CDs and five t-shirts on the table in front of him.

'No, you're ok, cheers, I need to be in Haselbury Plucknett tomorrow,' Natalie replied, confusingly.

Natalie and her social media accounts moved on, making way for the next customer: a strong-nosed analytically faced woman Eric put as mid-to-late thirties, wearing bright red lipstick and a jet-black batwing sweater. It was a coincidence that Mel had been talking about the actress Elizabeth Taylor earlier since it was she, more than anyone, that the woman reminded him of, perhaps around the era Taylor had starred in *The Sandpiper*. But there was more to her familiarity than that. Eric asked her if she'd like a t-shirt for 50 per cent of the advertised price and, as he did, it dawned on him that she was the woman he'd seen in the small car, waiting on the dirt lane outside Billy's party, back in spring.

'They're very nice,' she said. 'And I might well pick one up later. But it's actually you I'm here to see.'

'Ooh, I'm honoured,' said Eric. 'Not many people come here to see me. So what's the reason for the visit?'

'Well, I think the short way of putting it would be that once, a long time ago, you shagged my mum.'

'Oh amazing,' said Mel, arriving from the nearby toilet. 'You finally found each other!'

All the Heavy Unlikeliness of an Intricately Frosted Potato

On the way back from a boot sale near Polperro in 2015, where Eric had been pleased to pick up a metal owl, a job lot of 1960s brocade fabric, a Lloyd loom chair, thirty 1950s knitting magazines for Carl, a Timothy Leary spoken-word album and four copies of Kate Bush's *Hounds of Love* for no more than a quid each, Carl gazed across at the greenish sea on the horizon, and asked, 'Did you know how people first discovered how to pickle vegetables?'

'No,' said Eric. 'I've got to say I haven't a clue. But I do like my pickles, as you well know.'

'Well, nobody can confirm it, because it happened in Mesopotamia in about 2400 BCE, but there is a theory that somebody left some vegetables in some sea water by mistake.'

'That's a bit good, isn't it,' said Eric. 'You don't really get door-to-door encyclopaedia salesmen these days but if one ever rings our bell I'll know what to say. I'll tell them I don't need any because I've already got one and that it's got four legs and hangs out in my living room, amongst a load of loose yarn and wool.'

'Er, *two* legs *and* two arms, if you don't mind,' said Carl. 'But it got me wondering, the pickle stuff. Maybe that's what happened to me, before I first met you. I got pickled in some way, by the sea, and was waiting for you to unpickle me.'

Carl had been hoping that the conversation might lead further but at this exact moment the shuffle function on Spotify threw up the opening chords of 'Keep Your Mind Open' by Kaleidoscope from their 1967 *Side Trips* debut album.

'Sodding 'ell, I had forgotten how incredible this is,' shouted Eric, cranking up the volume. 'I know three bands called Kaleidoscope and they're all brilliant. I reckon if you call your band Kaleidoscope you can't go wrong.'

They continued to move.

They moved to a road called The Burrows where there were no longer any burrows and where they lived in a house that felt as redoubtable as a piece of planned obsolescence self-assembly furniture. They moved for a year to a house that was cheap to rent because it stuck out awkwardly into a junction of roads and people kept crashing their cars into it every three or four years, and thanked their lucky stars that this was not one of those years. They moved to the part of Whipley Crenshaw which a lot of people persisted in saying was in Bisley Winchhole. They moved for five months to the smallest darkest wing of a manor house owned by an alcoholic surfing atheist vicar where the workings of the kitchen radiator sounded like a robot doing something to a goblin that was still illegal in some more God-fearing countries and American states. They moved to a house in Bumley Crumpton because they couldn't get the house they really wanted in Crapstone, but never considered living in Shitterton, partly because it was in Dorset, but mostly because they didn't yet know it existed. They moved to a small shy house they completely forgot as soon as they left it. They moved because they were renters and because landlords didn't want tenants with pets and because a lot of rental contracts were temporary even though when people said 'Ooh you do move a lot, don't you?' to people who moved that was a fact they never kept in mind. They moved because they didn't go on holiday and moving felt a bit like going on holiday, in a way. They moved because of Mary Woodcock's restless Gaelic ancestors and because of Mary's ghost, who was still out there, somewhere, moving her stuff to new cities, hoping to meet a man who was less of a deceptive cunt but no less handsome or tall than Prestwich Harry Inskip. They moved because of Mike's ghost, for reasons that were harder to unpick. They moved because the ghosts of Pauline and Theresa and Joan pressed themselves into a moving shield around them and helped them through the emotional aspects of moving, just as they once had for Mary. They moved because their brains had a clever knack of blotting out the memory of the stress of the last time they moved. They moved because they looked at 3,000 albums and 2,000 singles and 31 CDs on some shelves and thought, incorrectly, 'This will be easy and won't leave any long-term repercussions on our physical or mental health!' They moved because they had become chronically addicted to moving. They moved because moving always brought hope, even when it didn't. They moved because they remembered what the hope felt like but forgot the rule about moving that they relearned every time they moved, which is that when you move you always think about the positive aspects of where you're moving to and wrongly picture them as an addition to the positive aspects of where you already live, which you have somehow been lulled into believing you will be taking with you.

 Autumn 2016 found Eric and Carl in the picturesque Cornish village of Lerryn, a couple of miles from the River Fowey, closing in on the deadline of a twelve-month contract living above a creek that never showed any great hurry in making its way to the sea and was all the more phantasmagorical for it. Within a fortnight of moving there, they'd made their biggest vinyl score of all time: a surprise stash of near-pristine albums, all released between 1966 and 1971, in the windfucked summer cottage of a deceased ex-record label exec down in one of the lonely declivities behind the humourless rock formations of Dodman Point, south west of Gorran Haven. At the end of a dark day, it had felt like a gift out of nowhere from a guilt-stricken god. Dodman Point was in fact a bowdlerisation: there had probably never been any Dodman or, if there had, this was no place with any time for the civilised points he might have wanted to make. The name for this headland, back in the eighteenth and nineteenth centuries, when its cliffs used to snack on ships like mid-morning pasties, had been Deadman's Point, and that was patently the name it still thought of itself by. A perfectly apt dead person's place to walk through beneath a funeral sky at a dead time of year before visiting a dead person's house.

They had almost not gone to the cottage at all. On the walk Carl had been bitten by an Alsatian, and while Eric rummaged inside the house, he waited in the van, half-reading an Anita Brookner novel with some antiseptic-soaked gauze pressed to the wound. Eric had offered to rush him straight home but Carl, who always recovered with preternatural speed from cuts and bruises, would not hear any of it. Eric, carrying nothing but worries and low expectations, hurried through uncherished rooms, scratching at parts of himself that did not itch, stalked without interest by the exec's pasty son and his patisserie hair: a forty-something accountant who moved across the surface of the Earth with all the heavy unlikeliness of an intricately frosted potato. Then there they were on a forgotten shelf in a study where, with the possible exception of the distant grey waves, nothing had ever been studied: precisely the kind of records that Eric was always most keenly hoping to find but almost never did. The ones that had been crawling up the walls of that cultural bin all these years, towards the light. 'AND I AM THE LIGHT,' thought Eric, then had a word with himself. 'Calm down, pal, don't get too cocky. It never ends well. Retain an attitude of respect.' Yes, the doings of the music industry's money men had ruined many promising young careers, callously pressed the buttons to open the black tunnels leading to suicide and drug abuse, but – who knew – perhaps this one had been one of the good guys.

With courtesy, Eric named his price. He made sure, as always, that it was a fair one. The price was accepted without cogitation. And, later, when Carl, scarred but otherwise completely recovered from his flank wound, began to spreadsheet the profits that had resulted from the trip – more profits than either of them had ever known or expected; not *quite* enough profits to provide a reasonable deposit for a house or prompt them to bounce on a waterbed throwing fifty-pound notes at each other, but enough profits to alter their outlook, forever – Eric forgave himself for not feeling quite the guilt he might have done if the profits had come from records that appeared to have been played and enjoyed and had *not* been the possessions of someone who had owned four cars worth over £50,000 each, three homes, and had (source: Carl, and an in-depth Google search) in an interview in the issue of the *Financial Times*' 'How To Spend It' supplement dated 23 September 2014, listed his greatest buzzes in life as 'the Boxing Day hunt, and a good day playing the stocks'. After all, it was not as if Eric had begged or hustled to be there. The bereaved son – acting on a tip-off from an acquaintance of an acquaintance of a friend – had called him. The son neither desired nor understood the records. He merely desired simplicity, materialistic closure, and an empty house.

So much of it was about finding ways to not be a vulture, or at the very least finding ways of not feeling like one. Of course, a lot of the time you just *were* a vulture, and there was no pretending otherwise, but at most of those times you were a vulture that people were moderately glad to see, a vulture that the people standing solemnly around the carcass had purposely beckoned down from the air with a resigned pragmatic smoke signal or whistle. At times it was too much. Eric would never forget the wretched and unheated flat on the west edge of Plymouth where, as a grieving mother hovered nearby, he knelt in the gap between a long-unwashed bed and a gothic double wardrobe, and, with a touch so light as to barely be a touch at all, he went through the records, books and guitars of a young musician who had, days before, taken his own life. The whole time, Eric had been no less aware of the foetally curled human-shaped depression in the bedclothes beside him than he would have been if it had been the musician's ghost itself, whispering desolate home truths in his ear. He prayed he would never be in such a situation again and was glad Carl and his gossamer emotional exoskeleton had not been present. It had been over a year before he could bring himself to price up what he bought that evening, let alone sell it.

Empathetic and gentle Eric might have always been, but tact and sensitivity to the hardships of others had not, earlier in life, always been notable strengths of his. Now that had changed. It couldn't not. Tact and sensitivity to the hardships of others were as crucial to his trade as a driving licence and a working computer, more crucial than the ability to distinguish a 1960s Beatles pressing from a 2000s one or know that Buffalo Springfield was a band and not, in fact, the brother of Dusty Springfield. His embracing of the importance of them was one of the ways he softened in these allegedly concrete years of late middle age.

Was he imagining it, or had the requirements of the job led him to walk through the hallways of death just a little more often, since he and Carl had moved to Lerryn? Even when music-hunting didn't take him to a bereaved household, its venues frequently had a touch of the sepulchral about them. After an enquiry about a rumoured relatively inexpensive original UK mono pressing of *The Kinks Are the Village Green Preservation Society*, the most sought-after of all Kinks LPs, he found himself trapped in a crypt beneath an antique shop in Liskeard listening to two men competitively compare their knowledge of vintage shotguns. He found no hint of the original UK mono and took almost forty-five minutes to finally locate an entry into the men's accelerated dialogue – which in character was far more machine gun than vintage shotgun – that allowed him to ask the crypt owner to unlock the exit, at one point even beginning to put his hand up, as an eight-year-old suddenly, painfully desperate for the toilet might in order to gain the attention of a teacher.

Back out in the light, he breathed the fresh manure and quad-bike fumes of the mid-Cornish air and drove to a small village post office where nobody called him Mr Eric and the debating topic of the day was the preferred way to slaughter a fox. On the plus side, somebody had moved the huge dead badger off the whiplash lane down to Carl and Eric's bungalow. Or perhaps some fast-working crows had already necked the whole corpse, bristles and all. Or a vulture. Anything seemed possible, here. Especially in the night or, as they used to call it, before November kicked in, 'the afternoon'. It all added to his sense of Cornwall as, beyond its fetching jewelled encasement, resolutely a landscape of winter, a landscape of ghosts. Winter of isolation. Winter of 'Oh shit all our friends live eighty or more miles away, there are no trains or buses nearby, the one good café within walking distance closed down and the van's still in the garage in Lostwithiel being repaired after we crashed into a hunk of laneside granite while trying to avoid that VW camper skidding down the hill towards us on black ice.' Winter of seeing a sign which says 'Dewspring

Tearoom' and instinctively misreading it as 'Despairing Tea Room'. Winter of empty second homes. Winter of mass unemployment, especially amongst the area's eighteen-to-thirty age group. Winter of deep southern lands doing northern gloom more uncannily well than northern gloom itself does. Ghosts of wild animals who, during their short lives, were viewed as no more than interference to agricultural imperatives or fodder for stubborn adherence to outmoded pastimes. Ghosts of lost brothers. Ghosts of scrapped trains that chugged and rattled past Par Down and St Pinnock Viaduct East and and Burngullow Junction a long long time ago. Ghosts of the arsenic earth. Ghosts that nobody remembers except the ghosts themselves because few people are remembered beyond the lives of their own grandchildren and not even that long if they don't have grandchildren and let's not even talk about people without children. Ghosts that Carl claimed he saw in the ruins of the 1920s pleasure garden down in the woods where the residential buildings peter out and the creek starts to make its snaking journey towards what might be Middle Earth or Toad Hall but will, if you keep following it to the main river, turn out to be the old china clay works and a startlingly good pizza restaurant with a waterside view, which is just around the corner from Shrew Books, run by a nice lady called Kate and her cat Bea, where Eric had bought Carl the 1995 Virago paperback edition of Sylvia Townsend Warner's diaries.

'I can't believe it!' shouted Carl, from the living room to Eric, who was in the kitchen, making two crisp sandwiches, one of which he intended to offer to Carl. Carl's laptop – the original cheap one, still going strong – sat open in front of him.

'Can't believe what?' said Eric, arriving in the living-room doorway.

'I found some photos of just what I saw, in the woods, in the pleasure garden. You know last week, when you went off to look for wild garlic,' said Carl.

'Oh yeah, blummin' 'eck so you have,' said Eric, bending to look at the laptop screen.

'Can you see? It was built by Frank Parkyn, a clay magnate, in 1920. There were ornamental arches and fountains and even a swimming pool. People came from miles around for a regatta and a running race through the woods and King Edward stopped by in the midst of a Cornish break during which he also "besported himself with young ladies". Look at these photos here. It's all just as I saw it, as it was, probably in about 1928.'

'It's amazing what rich people would spend their money on in those days.'

'I feel like you don't believe me. About what I saw.'

'I believe you believed you saw it. And I believe old buildings have a powerful atmosphere. And I believe you have the most top-class imagination of anyone I know, and you were quite tired that day.'

Below them, through the big window, a skein of Canada Geese followed the curve of the creek, against a horizon like freshly applied blusher.

'I can't quite get my brain around the fact that we live here sometimes,' said Carl.

'Me neither,' said Eric. 'When you were making that wonton soup last night and I went out for a walk and came back along the creek and saw light bulbs clicking on in the houses on the banks I thought, "Bloody hell, I would love to live in a place like this; wouldn't that be great?" and then I realised . . . I do, at least for now!'

Carl had never felt so intoxicatingly encircled by wildlife. He loved getting up at the moment that birdsong first sweetened the air and observing the garden mooching of a small fox. The animal had a wounded flank, possibly from a gunshot wound, which gave Carl a greater affinity with it. It seemed to be getting on ok despite its injury and was being fed twice daily by their neighbour, Philippa. She put on rubber gloves and hauled roadkill off the lanes for it, went to the village shop and bought it chicken that had been loosely earmarked for magazine families in nearby Airbnbs. Philippa always stared in a particularly curious way at Carl and threw toys and dog chews over the fence to him, which he pretended to sniff then later carefully carried up to the house, rinsed and handed to Eric to donate to the local animal rescue centre. She was often near the fence where the two gardens met, and something told Carl to be extra careful in making his choices about when and where to go bipedal, which meant that his plant care and herb garden took a back seat.

'What would she do with me if she discovered what I truly am?' Carl wondered. The answer to that question eluded him but he suspected it might involve worming tablets and an unnecessary number of thermal blankets.

But Philippa was a kind soul, someone Carl suspected would view virtually no sacrifice as beyond the line of duty when it came to the welfare of an animal. As well as the fox, she fed the local hedgehogs and swans and a huge black stray cat which she perplexingly misgendered as female on the basis that it had 'quite a high-pitched meow'. She and her husband Gordon generously took Eric and Carl out for rides on their boat and were a rich source of local knowledge, some verifiable, some dubious. It was Philippa and Gordon who first told Eric that Kenneth Grahame had written his book *The Wind in the Willows* as a direct result of inspiration found on creekside walks here when Grahame had been holidaying in Fowey, and about the Giant's Hedge, a tribal Saxon boundary running through the village and diagonally down to the coast to the strangely rowdy caravan town of Looe. Carl was already aware of both of these facts, thanks to his extensive online research about the village, which had also led him to discover that the kazoo player from Mungo Jerry, composers of the noxious 1970 drunk-driver anthem 'In the Summertime', had been involved in a highly publicised altercation in the village's pub after the kazoo player's former girlfriend moved in with the landlord. Later Gordon and Philippa told their version of the Mungo Jerry story, in which Mungo Jerry, who they clearly believed to be not a band but one pre-eminently sideburned human man, ran off with the landlord's daughter.

In other words, Lerryn was like a lot of West Country villages: a place in a constant slow spin cycle of chatter, where facts got mushed and shredded and some people shot foxes and other people protected them, where it was nothing unusual to find a man in wellies standing in the door of the village shop announcing 'I won't come all the way in because I smell of horse' or a woman nailing a sign to a post advising people to drive considerately, for the sake of hedgehogs.

The way Lerryn was *not* like many West Country villages was that creek, flouncing into the chimerical distance, through dense grandstands of trees: the Wild Wood, as depicted by Grahame in *The Wind in the Willows*, where you could forget the Wide World beyond. Up there on the hill overlooking that view, Carl and Eric experienced the VIP privileges of being part of an ever-evolving sky. Carl stared over the valley and dreamed himself into 1908, the year of *The Wind in the Willows*'s publication, the year that Great Western Railway ambitiously promoted the great similarity between Cornwall and Italy in 'shape, climate and natural beauties'. Sending himself tumbling into an abstract dreamland where rugged landscape intersected with engineering brilliance, he imagined himself as a painter of vorticist train poster art inspired by Kernow's unique light, who in his later more established days would be invited to the Lerryn Regatta as a special guest of a Cornish gardener-sculptor, where the pair would sit by one of the ornamental fountains and discuss the pros and cons of the Danish concept of the pleasure garden.

Eric looked at the same view and the way the falling sun hit the manor house on the hill across the valley, as it always did with such uncanny specificity, and tried unsuccessfully to place himself in the minds of upper-class people building a home in the 1700s. 'Whatever you think of the fancy tosspots, you have to give them credit for knowing what they were doing,' he thought. 'They didn't just plonk the foundations down anywhere that happened to be going spare and wasn't too close to the communal village bog or a major road.'

The last blushing clouds fell below the hill and owls came out in force, stronger than before. One sounded like it was in the bathroom. 'Is there an owl in the bathroom?' Eric asked Carl. 'No, it's just me,' Carl replied. Eric opened the back door, and the owl in question, clearly an experienced and comfortable ventriloquist, flew from the branch of a dead tree over his head. He was a male. Eric could tell from the deepness of his voice. His flight was almost groovy, a dance, like some dude in a hip club in sixties San Francisco, sidling up, checking you out, taking his time, getting plenty of evidence before making his move, which he would somehow shape into something that didn't resemble a move at all. Eric watched the owl and felt privileged to share its valley but also wondered if he would at some point, while living in a house, feel less like someone on a break between removal vans and correspondence with the Deposit Protection Scheme. He was sixty-one and a half years old.

The following September the Cornish tide intensified its relationship with the moon, the lows lower, the highs higher. If you'd seen what was going on between them you would have wondered why nobody was tipping off the newspapers or writing a biopic about the tide and the moon for Hallmark. A person couldn't help feeling caught up in their business. Carl watched it all compulsively, like the lead-up to an election. One evening during this period of volatile gravitational relations, not long before Eric and Carl moved east for what they hoped would be the last time, the creek sloshed over its banks and spilled far into the village. In the little car park near the pub, a swan sailed serenely past a marooned car and the advancing magenta dusk, reflected in all this water, made onlookers feel like they were existing inside a shrinking bubble of air between all the beauty that might soon drown them. Eric and Carl drove to their favourite cove to catch the last of the light and the water stood taller than they'd ever seen it. There was nobody else around and Carl wore his snorkel, the one Eric had found for him that, although not quite comfortable, was marginally more forgiving to the jut of his snout than most other kinds on the market. As they swam they looked down in wonder at pugnacious high rocks they'd once climbed which were now fifteen feet below them. Fish from all around the world had apparently heard the news and timed their arrival impeccably. Eric had never seen so many while swimming in the sea in the UK. One especially plump one looked him curiously in the face with a big sad Disney eye and a thousand of its tiny contemporaries turned themselves into a giant predator and encircled him and Carl with their curving body. 'We got water-strangled by a fake shark!' shouted Eric when they returned to dry land. He had some seaweed hanging off his head but, in his elation, didn't appear to have noticed.

'That seaweed looks a bit like a sideburn,' said Carl.

'Maybe I'll keep it,' said Eric. 'It'll give me a Mungo Jerry look. That fella had some huge sideburns. I hear it's what made so many landlords' daughters run off with him.'

Standing there on the empty beach Carl wondered if he was being treated to a glimpse of the boy Eric once had been. He was so glad to see it, after what had, for Eric, been a couple of curiously low-spirited weeks. Carl wasn't 100 per cent sure what had caused the low-spiritedness. He assumed, as Eric had hinted, that it was about missing friends and facing the ordeal of moving again, wondering how many more times they could physically and mentally cope with it and whether the answer was even as high as 'one'. But Carl also couldn't help coming back to an incident just prior to the low-spiritedness kicking in when, from his seat on a bench in the garden of the village pub, he had seen Eric engaged in a conversation with a man propping up the bar. The man wore a heavy green coat, a fisherman's hat, and was probably a decade or so older than Eric. Later at home Carl had quizzed Eric about the identity of the stranger. 'Ah, nobody interesting,' said Eric. 'Just a fella I met a couple of times in the eighties. I don't know how he recognised me.'

'You talked to him for a long time!' said Carl.

'Ah yeah, he just wanted to go over old times,' said Eric. 'He was quite trolleyed, I think.'

Although there had not appeared to be anything rancorous about the conversation, Eric had seemed distracted that evening: pensive, somehow cut-off, uninterested in the facts Carl read to him off the internet. But now that day felt like a turned page long in the past and Eric was back to himself and magic was diffusing the coastlands with its earthy pigments.

Magic, which had been undervalued in the early part of the century, had lately become a precious asset. The internet was where people generally looked for it, or for details and co-ordinates of its location, because the internet was overflowing with promises about magic and attractive photographs of magic. The paradox, of course, was that the biggest obstacle to the magic thriving and breeding was the internet itself. Out in the three-dimensional world people found the magic and, in their spontaneous rapture at seeing the magic, or their generous instinct to spread the love, or their atavistic need to show off and be perceived as cool, shared it on the internet, which sent other people looking for the magic with drooling tongues but also meant that when they arrived at its location the magic was often gone. People with the brain to step back for a moment became aware of this damaging cycle – which felt like part of a bigger cycle, a cycle of ecological ruination which, over the past decade, the population had become wiser to – but that didn't stop them often being lulled into believing that the magic might be lurking just over the next hill on the internet. On the plus side, rebel factions sprang up: people determined to make their own magic, outside of the digital realm, including some of the kinds of magic that in the collective mind-warp of those very early years of the century people had written off as pretentious but now came to their senses and realised was pioneering and imaginative and unique. But even when those rebel factions making their own magic – whether it was in the form of an off-grid community or a self-released vinyl record or a rewilded orchard or a no-dig allotment or an old-fashioned hand-printed journal or a sisterhood of rescue sheep providing the wool for a charitable independent knitwear company – found it hard to resist the internet's potential for helping to fund that magic, and those of them who fantasised about a completely internet-free life were thwarted by the increasingly clever methods corporations found to keep them glued to their devices.

Even people whose outlook was anti-nostalgia, people who were accepting of life's plough and the changing playing field beneath it, started to look back with affection at the period not so long ago before magic was being sucked ravenously from everything. How could they not? The sucking was evident in so many areas. Maybe people had felt comparably, in the early days of science, as their folksy belief systems and old wives' tales and appealing darkwood regional ghouls were trounced, one by one. But the additional feature of this twenty-first-century sucking was that it made what had not been sucked that much more prized. It amped up competition and the competitiveness reshaped human communication: it was one of the chief ways, along with the rewiring of people's brains by technology, that people were changing. Nobody was in the dark any more about what anything had been decreed to be worth.

Eric saw it during the weekend mornings when he trod the dew at the car boots. People who not much more than a decade ago might have written off a 1960s G Plan Astro coffee table they saw at a boot fair for £20 as 'something silly your gran once owned' now happily paid more than four times as much for it then posted it on their Instagram account where, as a result of people swooning over it, it gained a tiny bit more value. The value of records – especially the ones that had magic trapped in their grooves, but also some that didn't – was escalating via a similar process. Everyone knew the value because they just unlocked their phone, logged into a site called Discogs and looked it up. That was good and bad for Eric. People could see he was charging a little under market value for his stock and he benefited from the fact that more people wanted records. But some of the mysterious witchy spots in Record Collector Forest had been sucked away and that was something to lament. It also meant that the records with the magic, and where the magic had been teased out by time, were still more prized. Which, in a roundabout way, explained why, within six and a half minutes of his Discogs listing of it going up, Eric had sold the pristine disc and sleeve of Cornubian Batholith's 1970 LP *Rock Music for Granite People* that he'd found in the deceased exec's home near Deadman's Point to the owner of a Tokyo-based graphic design company at a £2,255 mark-up.

More significantly, houses – the primary protective shell people needed from weather and the amorphous monster outside the door that is ultimately coming for us all – were being sucked, too; not just in the sense that their uneven distribution amidst society meant it felt there like there weren't enough of them to go around but in the sense that they'd all been siphoned into the same digital ice rink, a slippery place where they could be easily gazed at by anyone but not so easily purchased or rented. While looking for yet another place to live, Eric fantasised about the days when you could drive down a no-through road on the edge of a village and see a 'TO LET' sign on a house and, because nobody else looking for a house to rent had driven down that lane at the same fortuitous time period, qualify, without fuss, to rent that house. He fantasised about a time before credit checks and waiting lists and screening processes and estate agents who when you told them you had a dog looked at you like you had just announced that you were the legal guardian of a griffin with big plans who'd just reached drinking age. ('Legless Griffin?' thought Eric. 'Do I own an album by them?') As he and Carl passed empty buildings on their walks, he hallucinated availability: a parallel dimension where any number of tranquilly situated bothies and barns and pig sheds and electricity substations were crying out for two respectful tenants to turn them into a home.

They viewed a house for let in Wiggaton and a house for let in Broadbury Steepleton and a house for let in Woodbury Salterton and a house for let in Devlin St Peter and a house for let in Otterton and a house for let in the worst corner of Upottery which lost some of the little charm it had when they realised Upottery was pronounced 'Up Ottery' and not 'Youpottery'. They viewed a narrow house for let with a walled garden that they loved and were told by a junior estate agent who held two thumbs aloft, 'Don't worry – you'll get it!' but they didn't. They viewed a house for let with no kitchen where a senior estate agent described the lack of kitchen as a 'minor drawback'. They viewed a house for let that looked like a crestfallen robot and a house for let whose front looked like the back of other houses and a house for let that Douglas Adams had probably once seen but not thought much about while writing *The Hitchhikers' Guide to the Galaxy* and a house for let that looked like someone's mum Eric used to know and a house for let that looked like a house but was thirty yards down the hill from a church that looked like an owl. They viewed a house for let in Morton Fussbridge and a house for let in Ryme Intrinseca and a house for let in Odcombe but not a house for let in Evencombe because the demarcating feature of combes was arguably their unevenness so nobody had ever called a village Evencombe and a house for let in Broadclyst Dog Village but not a house for let in Tedburn St Mary Pathfinder Village because it was just for retired people and Eric wasn't retired and neither was Carl and also the word 'pathfinder', and its connotations of a soft and easeful tunnel leading to death, made Eric want to puke. They met estate agents who appeared to quietly sneer at their coats – 'It's not as if I have a choice in the matter!' thought Carl – and estate agents who told them it was a renter's market and estate agents who told them it was a landlord's market and estate agents who implied Eric was violently wrong in his mild opinions about cupboards and estate agents who hurried them through houses like the estate agents were nannies and Carl and Eric were children who should have been in bed an hour ago, and just as they were passing into the far stages of estate agent fatigue at the end of a long day they went to a passable but damp house on a passable but damp street and met a pleasant estate agent who seemed instantly familiar and not like an estate agent at all.

'Eric Inskip!' said the unestate-agentish estate agent. 'It actually is you, isn't it. Mel Sherwood! What must it be? Thirty years? More? When I saw the name on the viewing list I did wonder but I thought no, it can't be. But then when you were late I wondered some more. Maybe you don't even remember. Maude. Sherbet lemons. I think I was still going by Melanie, mostly, at that point.'

It took him a moment. The big job to do was to unimagine the wide eruption of corkscrew hair. But as soon as he had, he remembered. Remembered hard. 'Well, knock me down with a sparrow's feather!' he said. 'What are you doing? What are you doing *here*?'

'I live here now.'

'What? Right here? Well, that's going to be a bit inconvenient, if I decide to rent the house, isn't it?'

'Ah-ha no, not here here. About twenty minutes away. Been down here, just over into Dorset I mean, for a decade now. Actually, I wouldn't live here, not in this village. It's kind of snobby. I've got a mate who used to rent a bungalow across the road and is still on the WhatsApp group. She shows it to me for a laugh sometimes. Accountants and retired judges and private-school headteachers going into communal meltdown every time some bloke turns up on their doorstep selling microfibre cloths, especially if he's got an accent that sounds like it originates north of Cheltenham. "What can we do to protect our precious precious cars?" and that sort of thing. You're not a lawyer or a retired judge are you? *Of course you're not.* Not unless you've had a personality transplant since we sold Opal Fruits together. But, no. Don't rent this house. Let me show you another. That is, if you like nice houses behind cliffs with no neighbours up in your business. Of course you do. You're human. I probably shouldn't because it's not officially on the market yet but I just happen to have the key down here somewhere in my bag. I hope I do, anyway. Give me a moment to check. You know what, I shouldn't be saying any of this. But what the hell. I'm changing jobs in a week. This one isn't me all. I mean, look at the state of me, in this suit. I'm not convincing anyone. You've got transport, haven't you? Of course you have. I just saw you pull up in your van. We can go in convoy. You need to stay close, though, because I drive quite fast and the last bit's steep and fiddly and the satnav tries to take you to a biscuit factory seven miles away instead, then after that, you need to tell me everything you've been up to since I last saw you, and I'll tell you about my new job. You won't believe it when you hear it. *OhmygodIjustloveyourdogsomuchwhatbreedisshe.*'

The pub down in the yawning mouth between the cliffs was full to bursting inside and the barman said the only food they could offer them was gazpacho, or maybe some chips, so they ordered both and sat on the drenched, forsaken terrace. Eric confessed he wasn't entirely sure what gazpacho was and was disappointed they had forgotten to heat it up but it hit the spot and complimented the chips surprisingly well. When the rain came back for the day's fifth round and began to refill their empty bowls they barely noticed and, as the gathering night entered a pact with the sea below them, were only ambiently aware of the primordial plotting sounds that transpired. After they'd each summarised more than three decades of personal history, Mel asked when Eric and his dog would be able to move into the off-white cottage behind the cliffs.

'We're pretty much ready to go now, to be honest. The last month's rent is paid. But we promised we'd stick around in Cornwall a while to worm a fox.'

'To what a fox?'

'Worm it. It lives between our garden and our neighbour's. She feeds it but she and her husband are going away for a fortnight and she's asked me if I can stay there for a bit and feed and worm it.'

'How exactly *do* you go about worming a fox?'

'I'm not really sure. I'm also not fully convinced a fox wants to be wormed. Put it this way: I'm not going to try and get it in a headlock and force the worming tablet down its throat or anything. But I'm someone who likes to keep a promise once I've made one. I suppose I'll just push the tablet inside a chicken breast and hope the fox eats it. If it does, it does. If it doesn't, I suppose it's not the end of the world. There are a lot of unwormed foxes out there and they seem to be doing ok for themselves.'

For the first time in over an hour, they paused and gave an opportunity for the autumn evening to get a word in, and looked out at the place where the sea was. All of Eric was chilly apart from his feet, which were being warmed by a contented sleeping Carl, who had found the day exhausting, especially in an emotional sense.

'So you never had kids, then?' Mel said.

'Nah, not my thing. Of course, I might be wrong. There might be a couple of hundred out there, from my rock-star days, doing their thing. You neither?'

'Let's just say the window of time seemed very small, and I filled it with too many plant pots.'

'I wonder what we'd both say, if we could go back to that sweet shop, and tell our old selves that we'd be here together, doing this, now,' said Eric.

'I don't know if they'd find it all that interesting,' said Mel. 'But they might find it a bit more interesting that in a week's time you'll be worming a fox and I'll be herding some swans.'

'I beg you a pudding.'

'Herding some swans. That's what my new job is: a swan-herd. At least, that's the hope, in the long term. At first I'll just be helping out. At the swannery. Over there.'

Eric turned his head urgently in the direction of Mel's gesturing hand but felt immediately a little silly for doing so. Even if there had been a swannery a few yards to their left, he wouldn't have been able to see it in the dark.

'They've had them for hundreds of years. Possibly thousands. Swanneries, and swanherds. Benedictine monks started this one in the 1300s when they realised swans liked to hang out there and started feeding them. I think it might be the only one in the world now. When I first heard about it, I was like, "Don't swans just do their own thing, in the place they want to?" And I suppose they do, but they also do it there. I was also a bit doubtful about whether swans could be herded but I guess they can or they would never have made up the word. The problem is when I tell people they always think I'm saying "swineherd" so people think I'm going to be a pig farmer. I'm so excited, though. All that fresh air, and so much better than lying to people about houses. You should come and have a look. It's over near Abbotsbury, behind Chesil Bank. I think there's something special about that bit of coast, something about the colour of the sky, especially at this time of year. It's like nothing else. Do you know it?'

On top of his warmed feet, he felt Carl stir. 'Yeah, I know the place you mean. I've been over that way a couple of times. But not for quite a while.'

Finally, Carl and Eric had found some stillness in their lives. But that did not mean they had reached a smooth plateau where everything was perfect forever. The years immediately following their move to Dorset and Eric's reunion with Mel contained plenty of troughs, wobbles and frights. In August 2018 on a visit to the Dorset Museum in Dorchester Carl saw a replica of the Dorset Ooser, with its frightening face and horns, fell into a state of agitation and suffered a week of nocturnal hallucinations of repurposed human teeth and hair and cattle hide and clanging hellish music and found it hard to tell if what he was experiencing was more visions or just generic nightmares. In September 2018 Eric crashed the van into a bollard in the car park of Axminster Tesco and lost the no-claims bonus on his insurance policy. In October 2018, due to an error in an understaffed kitchen, the vindaloo Eric had bought Carl for his fifteenth birthday turned out to contain lamb, not vegetables. In February 2019, their favourite hen, Janis, died, very suddenly, of unknown causes. In June 2019, during one of Carl's early-morning walks, a hectoring and intolerable professional dog groomer called Sylvia Monkhouse 'rescued' him off the coast path, dragged him back to her low-slung Audi using the belt off her protesting brother's trousers, drove Carl to her sterile greige house near Honiton and locked him in her conservatory. Fortunately, she left the key in the door, which allowed Carl to escape while she was in the living room calling a friend at a nearby vet's then run fourteen miles home through fields, woodland and a couple of gardens, worried all the time about aggressive territorial dogs, the potential of being rescued by another interfering nutter and what kind of panicked state Eric might have descended into at his absence. He was greatly relieved to arrive back at the cottage unscathed, although nonplussed to discover that Eric had slept through the entire saga and upset to go on the internet and discover that he hadn't been the one to first invent the disparaging interior decor term 'greige'.

'She sounds like a fucking headcase,' said Eric, when Carl had recounted his ordeal.

'I don't like to judge,' replied Carl, 'but I suspect she rubs a lot of people up the wrong way. I was shaken up and scared, obviously, but mostly I came out of it feeling sorry for the other animals in her care. I've never seen a group of poodles looking more depressed than the six I saw in her kitchen. She'd only abducted me five minutes before and already she was calling me Frankie. I don't think I look like a Frankie at all. Do you think I look like a Frankie?'

'No, you look like a Carl. I have always thought so, right from day one. Well, definitely day nine, at the very least.'

Then, in March 2020, just as people were starting to get used to the way their fellow humans had changed, the pandemic — terrifying, disorientating, liberating, divisive and finally platitudinous and a little tiresome — came along and changed them again. They hunkered down, waited it out, managed to avoid getting ill. Eric sold a lot of records through the mail but struggled with the new social limitations of his life. Carl, who was already well accustomed to social limitations, struggled a little with the grumpy moods Eric's cabin fever bred.

On the whole, though, Carl loved living in Dorset, which had from the first day felt, if not quite like putting down roots, certainly like a sort of alighting for the two of them after all their perambulatory years. Even though he couldn't talk to Eric's friends, he thought of them as his friends too and was glad to be closer to them, and be closer to the place where he and Eric met, and he began to realise how much and for how long – though he would have never been so demanding as to tell Eric – he'd wanted all this. And he had been rewarded with just a little bit more when, one night a couple of months after they'd moved, when he'd thought it was just him and Eric in the house and Mel, in her nightie, had wandered into the kitchen and found Carl standing upright, decanting some peppermint tea into a diffuser, life began to expand for him in an even richer way.

What does a person say in a situation like that? What Mel said was, 'Oh. No. Oh. But? Oh . . . *Oh.*'

'Yes, it's all quite embarrassing, really,' said Carl. He would have liked to come up with something a little more profound and pithy, something that immediately put her at ease, but he supposed that at least it was better than 'Have you been in an accident at work that wasn't your fault?'

'I mean, *how*?' said Mel.

'To be honest, I probably find it all just as baffling as you do.'

'I think I'm going to need some of that tea.'

After they'd got past the initial few seconds, where Carl was genuinely concerned she might be about to go into cardiac arrest, Mel would in fact be astoundingly calm and accepting of the situation and soon they would be chatting away about anything and everything as if one of them didn't have a tail or two dozen fur-enclosed fingers and it was all perfectly natural, which it was, or at least it felt that way to Carl, and he hoped it felt that way to Mel too. He would discover that she, like him, contrary to popular opinion, believed *The Lacuna* to be Barbara Kingsolver's best novel, and believed many other things that he believed too, but also was very much her own person, very much Mel: someone who, just by knowing her, could make you feel you were having energy and light gently filtered into your soul.

For now, though, they just stood in the kitchen together, she staring in silent wonder at his face as if seeing it for the first time, and he staring back into hers, sympathetically, with one strong arm across the small of her back, to prevent her from falling.

Carl (With Billy)

'I think you need to leave bigger gaps when you are planting your sweetcorn,' he told me. That's how he decided to show me he knew. He was obviously relishing surprising me so casually with his revelation. He was cold from the water and his nonchalance was undermined a little by the shivers shadowing every word. There had been something going on between us for a long time, some recognition in the eyes, of course, and I wasn't as surprised as I probably should have been.

He told me it was around two months ago when he finally saw proof. He had been walking off a hangover, a bit dazed, missed the footpath, and ended up in the field over the back: one of the ones where the Fentonbrooks sometimes put their deer but generally leave empty, and he'd seen me out on the veg patch, fully bipedal, planting the first of the year's savoy cabbage. He'd hidden himself well. I'd assumed I was alone that morning. Just me, the hens and Frank the crow, in the golden light.

'Yes, I was wondering if I'd made a mistake there,' I replied, throwing caution to the wind. 'I still have this habit of forgetting we've got space now. I'm still planting for the gardens we had before. There was one where I'd squeeze my tomato plants right up to the edge of the lane. Some idiot ran over one in his van. It wasn't Eric, if that's what you're wondering.'

'So you're actually a biped,' he said.

'Sort of. Kind of both. But I feel better when I'm upright. I move more easily.'

'It's funny. That's just reminded me of something. I sent a piece to a newspaper last week. It had a few typos in it and one was where I'd typed the word "mistyped" but mistakenly put a space in the middle of it. My editor wanted to know what a "misty ped" was.'

'Maybe that's what I am: a misty ped.'

'The legendary Misty Ped of West Dorset.'

'I've been enjoying your writing. I hope you'll have a whole new book for me to read soon.'

'I get blocked sometimes. It happens. Then it all floods out, in one exhausting rush. I think I need a new challenge, though. I just have to work out what it is. But enough about me. Tell me more about you.'

So I do. I say quite a lot, probably more than I've said before, more, in some ways, than I've said to Eric, or Mel. But we talk about him, too. We talk for over an hour. And then, the following morning, we talk even further. And I think, *hope*, even though I haven't told him yet, that Eric will be ok with it.

Penny (With Some Plants)

Hmmm. Two phormiums for £25. Not exactly a bargain, is it? Ok (*drunk Delia Smith voice*), come on then, let's be having you. In the trolley with both of you. I'm seeing it now: summer after next. Maybe a couple of those giant Indian pots I saw at the salvage yard Eric took us to. Think about the relationship of everything to everything else carefully. Just like painting. What are these? Plans? Those things I didn't think I made any more. Always surprisingly themselves, aren't they, humans? I suppose that's half the fun of being one. Setting the rules then breaking them. Ooh, a hosta! That might work nicely. Lots of space to fill. Last thing you want is just a big blank. One of those places that are all lawn. Ghastly. Lawns: the symbols of the blandest kind of wealth and status. Currently, and historically. Reminders to self: buy avocados, cut back lavender, start thinking about a birthday present for Eric. What do you get a person like that? You can't get him anything in one of his areas of interest because he knows too much about what he likes, too particular. Who am I to talk? 'I'm not going to buy you a piece of art,' said Mel. 'Your taste membrane is too fine and pedantic. It's a mistake to fuck about with something like that. Too many risks.' She's right. Love the challenge of buying a present, never too fussed about receiving one. What does one *need*, at this point? But here I am, filling an emptied-out life up to the brim again; with objects, people, flowers. Mistake? The people bit? No. What's the worst that can happen? We can't be islands, we can only be isles: you still need a little connection to the mainland. Isle of Portland, Isle of Purbeck. Magical places. Personalities of their own but still only half an hour to the nearest supermarket or garden centre. No rescue boat required. I think I'd like some poppies. That's not the way it works though is it? It's usually up to the poppies to decide if they like you. Do I remember Mel saying they make Carl sneeze, or did I imagine that? Geraniums. Bit late in the year to bother now? How did plants get so expensive? How did food get so expensive? How did being a person get so expensive? How did having emotions and a past get so expensive? But what are you supposed to do: wave a placard at a £40 papyrus and a £10 sandwich? Stage a protest concert about the messy impossible complexities of modern life? No. Not enough time. Strap yourself in and bloody get on with it. Embrace the chaos. Nobody grading you on neatness, when it's all over. Also, no right to complain, in my case. Not about the cost bit. The woman who dies rich is a failure. Who said that? Well, it was me, but someone else, too. Eric's daughter seems nice. Something a bit 1950s about her, in a way, until she speaks. Must attempt to engage her in a conversation about the Reformation. 'If she hurts him, I'll rip her apart with my bare hands,' said Mel. She was at least 97 per cent joking, I think. Told Mel about my dream last night. The one where we open the garden and I'm in the air, above the gateposts, welcoming everyone in. A lot of that business recently. A little annoying at times, but just little outbreaks. Normally just a minute or two, three or four inches off the ground, rarely in public. Microdosing, you might call it. Not that I have any choice in the matter. I skirted around the issue a little at first but she knows now what causes it. I tried to explain it as best I could. Excitement, but not just excitement: always something else at the centre of the excitement, a burst of hope for the future, but also sometimes panic, and, just possibly, love. The gerbera look very sorry for themselves but the crocosmia are hanging in there impressively. Let's have some of those too. It would be nice to reserve an area next year for everything to be orange. Nothing too showy. Just a little one.

People's Notebooks

MEL

Thank you for inviting me here tonight. It's extremely generous of you, especially considering that I'm a woman, and as we all know, women aren't funny. It's so great that opportunities like this are opening up for us now. Sometimes we can even get on a panel show where we can occasionally interject a joke or two amongst the better ones that men tell. Seriously, though, for anyone out there who is worried, I can assure you that, while I am a feminist, I am not one of the really frightening ones with no subtlety who shout all the time on the internet; I'm just one of the quite frightening ones who shout some of the time in the real world. I grasp nuance. I don't want to live in a world where people are afraid to create reprehensible female characters in books and films. I think women can be awful sometimes. I think men can be awful too, probably more awful overall, but I actually like men a lot. For example, all the seven I keep chained up in my cellar are extremely gentle and good-natured, especially since I've set up a more disciplined regime when it comes to their feeding and watering times.

BILLY
I thought I saw the light of a torch last night, around 3 a.m., out on the track leading up to the lane. What am I saying? I didn't think I saw it. I know what a torch looks like, when it is shone. Maybe it was just Brian Loosemore taking his sheep for a walk.

MEL
Everyone I know has been in a room with a celebrity at some point. It's no big deal, and it happens. I'll tell you what is rare nowadays: being in a room with a builder. It always feels so exclusive when it takes place and when it does I can't help feeling briefly like a very special and noteworthy person. We had a builder here yesterday, after months of whispers and rumours about him potentially being here then him not being here after all. At one point the builder's sleeve even brushed against mine. 'Can you believe he was really here, for almost an entire morning, in our actual house?' we asked each other, again and again, in the hours that followed. It is doubtful it will ever happen again but the important thing is that nobody will ever be able to take those memories away from us. 'This is the mug that the builder drank from,' we will say in years to come, sighing, as we boil the kettle in our otherwise ordinary kitchen.

HELEN
Interesting historical facts about fathers:

The amount of time fathers spend with their children has approximately tripled since 1965.

The word 'dad' was first recorded at the beginning of the sixteenth century but is believed to be much older, and derived from nonsensical baby talk.

In many hunter-gatherer tribes there was a strong tradition of both sexes foraging and hunting together and, alongside that, an even distribution of childcare duties.

It is thought that imperialism and the Industrial Revolution had a strong hand in the rise of the 'emotionally removed dad'. Men stayed away from home for longer periods, and came back from war in a silent and incommunicative state, including where their children were concerned.

The Sultan Ismail Ibn Sharif of Morocco was born in 1645 and died in 1727. During that period, he gathered a harem of over 500 women, who gave him more than 800 confirmed biological children. He is believed to be history's most prolific father.

The only male animal to become pregnant is the seahorse. Male seahorses accept between 50 and 1,500 eggs from female seahorses, fertilise them, then carry them through to maturity.

MEL
I totally cleaned up at my local record shop over the weekend. I didn't buy any records. I just noticed it hadn't been dusted or vacuumed since the 1980s so decided I'd help out.

ERIC
When my great-grandma Doris arrived on the boat in Liverpool from Ireland, it didn't take her long to get to work and pop out sixteen children. Or was it seventeen? Nobody around to check with now but I know it's one or the other. My nan, who was one of the youngest, decided that many kids was too many, so when her time came she stuck at just the three. To her mind, that way there'd be more love to spare for each of them. Sometimes I look at my record collection and it gives me an idea of where my nan was coming from. People who don't own a lot of records laugh at the filing systems of us lot who do, but, once you get to a

certain point, you need some kind of system, or you'd never find anything you wanted to find. But that filing always kills a bit of the magic: you're taking yourself further away from that boss feeling that comes from having a little pile of records you've just bought, spread across the floor, and getting to know them like they're new pals. You build that wall of music up for decades and stuff gets swallowed and forgotten. You sometimes end up neglecting albums you love, and putting others on mostly out of sympathy. 'Ah, sorry, mate. Are you lonely? Did I not make you feel special enough? You can have your go now.'

How did Doris file her grandchildren? My guess is it wasn't by genre.

Records never did a lot of what I thought they'd do for me. They didn't make me cooler or more handsome or help me solve the secret to the universe. But they helped get me through some hard times and taught me that magic is real.

It's getting late now. There's a lot in there that I'll never listen to again. I look at that wall of spines and it looks as smart and satisfying as it always did but it's become something else. What you realise, in the end, is you were just a custodian all along. But that's cool. If you want my opinion on the matter there are worse things a person can be.

MEL

I mistyped an email sign-off recently as 'all the bees' when I meant to say 'all the best'. I reckon I'm going to stick with it. I can't think of anything negative that can possibly come of wishing someone all the bees. Unless they have an allergy, that is.

BILLY

The shingle fades to damp compacted sand as you reach the shoreline and the dogprints are washed away. I am fascinated by that fading. Where is the line that separates faded from fading?

Where is the line that separates the lightest, most fragile shingle from sand?

MEL
I revile all sports involving guns, including the increasingly popular one where people shoot their own mouths off.

PENNY
<u>Grasshoppers: A Poem</u>
It's still light when you fall asleep
Your hair sprawls across your two pillows
The purpose-made one from a shop
And the other one that is me
And some might argue
No less purpose-made
I can hear the grasshoppers outside the window
A wise individual once told me
They first arrived on earth
250 million years ago
Whereas grass
Didn't arrive
Until 210 million years later
Imagine
All that time
Just hopping
Waiting for the grass
Before you fell asleep
You told me what you had been doing
But I didn't say
'What have you got to tell me?'
And I never will
Because you don't like that
And besides

I often don't need to ask you
Because I already know
And sometimes while you sleep
I pick things from your hair
Grass, usually
And straw
And once 1/4 of a receipt
For Carphone Warehouse
Where to my knowledge
You have never shopped
And another time a grasshopper
They are always more beautiful than I remember
More finely designed
I cupped it in my palms
Without waking you
And took it to the open window
Where it hopped away
And as it did
I remembered the time before all this
When I was just hopping

CARL

Walk number 637. The Ooser walk. We don't call it that, but that's what it is. Melbury Osmond: better known as the place where Thomas Hardy's parents were married, and the inspiration for Little Hintock in his sometimes surprisingly boring novel *The Woodlanders*. A thatched wonderland directly out of a calendar-maker's dream, these days: the kind of place that makes you feel like a sack of straw the second you step out of your car into one of its primped lanes. They used to store it in a malthouse here, the Ooser. Brought it out once a year, sometimes more, for public shaming: jeering, insults, rotten vegetables, clanging steel, cruelty – at times – to pets in the care of the shamed. Children would dare each other to look at the horned face where it rested, run away screaming and believe they'd seen the devil. There were others – one in every Dorset village at one time, it is said – but this was the one. Eventually it was sent to Crewkerne, got misplaced. Having been to Crewkerne – a town of many pockets – that somehow makes sense to me. How do I know all this? Was I there? Crewkerne? Melbury? I think I was.

I see the dark malthouse, as it was then. I hear somebody shouting insults at an old man's dog. The old man is being whipped with a belt, by the sounds of it, but the crowd stops me seeing him or his dog. The triangles are getting wider and clearer. Will I see myself, soon, in one of these visions? I somehow know I won't but the possibility feels closer. Eric is slow today. His body leaks a multifariousness of air as we ride the rhythm of the hills. But the walk is deeply pleasant. Chalky plateaus and quiet oaky country estates and little churches hidden in the navels of the land. You'll never get to know a person better than when you move your feet in tandem with them in the open air. They've always felt special, every one of these walks. Now, though, each one feels special in a different, extra way.

'I think the best approach would be to ask her if she fancies going for a walk,' I tell him.

BILLY

We are sticky orbs, rolling through the wet grass picking up debris, in a constant unavailing race to catch up with ourselves. We sometimes feel like we have got close but in the meantime some other part of us has disengaged to make way for the new debris that's attached itself to us. We set standards for ourselves and, as we finally approach them, we discover they are outdated, tailored to a version of us that has flaked away. We chastise ourselves sternly for choices we made long ago, not realising that in doing so we often might as well be criticising the ideological decision-making of an old fingernail or a clump of hair last intimately known to us a microsecond before it hit the floor of a long-defunct barber shop. The orb compacts and fools us into believing that compacting means hardening or freezing. Our pain numbs and is absorbed into a permanently sore and cracked whole, the same size as it ever was in theory, but bigger, too. 'Oh well,' we say. 'Here comes some more. But instead of being a mard-arse about it let's go out and see if the day has something positive to offer.' We rearrange, reassess, but we never stop coming away from ourselves. Because of our compacting we assume there is no more coming away to be done, no more debris to be added, but it keeps on coming, and we remain sticky, although some of us, undoubtedly, are stickier than others.

MEL

There's so much talk about 'unlocking your potential' from people trying to make money off others these days, just occasionally I feel like I'm going against the grain a little with my free fifteen-week online course all about the dangers of getting close to your potential, with a free three-week add-on course guiding clients through the best roadside verges and storage facilities where they can abandon their potential and never set eyes on it again.

BILLY

The personality of the trees beneath the trees. The furry branches you never see in the summer. The green mossy truth. There are no cars in the car park. Unhappy dogs bark from over the hill where the unhappy dogs live. The trousers you are wearing are inappropriate for the day's events. Well done. Another day has passed and you haven't died.

MEL
People continually ask me how I maintain the smooth angelic skin of a woman a third of my age as I progress towards my late fifties and I can now exclusively reveal it's because I permit young owls to fight on my face every night while I sleep.

We Are Not People Who Go into Rivers

Eric was dying. Since everyone was, to some extent, all the time, he decided it was no big deal. He'd probably get around to telling some of the individuals closest to him at some point. But first he decided he'd get the train to Belper.

'Can we make an attempt not to turn it into a last-minute panic on this occasion and arrive at the station in good time?' asked Carl.

'All right Longtail, calm your whittling,' said Eric. 'When have I ever let you down?'

'The man's lack of self-awareness in the area of timekeeping is quite remarkable,' thought Carl. He wondered, based on what he had read and heard about that industry, whether it was a vestigial music-biz thing, a conflation of lateness with easygoingness, but he suspected it was more ingrained than that, something in the genes, perhaps. When, during a brief and mostly regrettable period Eric had spent as a parish councillor in Causley Mopchurch, the council's chairperson Edwina Morrow had summoned Eric to a one-on-one meeting in one of the town's quieter coffee shops to discuss the problems and low morale being caused by his lack of punctuality. Eric, who defined any arrangement to get together with another person as an approximate half-hour window beginning at the time stated, had been baffled by the accusations levelled at him, especially as he'd made the effort to arrive at the café at 4.41 p.m. (Edwina had told him to meet her at half past four). Each time he showed up late for a meeting with a client or to one of Mel's gigs or a record fair or a doctor's appointment or a pub quiz he apologised in the manner of a man who had never been late before in his life and was mildly scandalised at this one-off blunder he had made. If he did sometimes show signs of an awareness of time he never appeared to recognise that his relationship with it was different to anyone else's.

But where Eric *did* have an awareness of his own tardiness was in a much larger, more existential sense. His self-perception was as someone who was always wandering into a personally or culturally important life event a little too late. He had begun to play psychedelic music well just when psychedelic music was becoming unfashionable. He had worked in one of his dream childhood jobs – as a seller of sweets – a little too long after childhood, and chased it up in his thirties with what was undoubtedly a career better suited to a twenty-something. He had become a person comfortably eligible for a 1995 mortgage only to be struck by the bombshell that it hadn't been 1995 for quite some time. He'd turned into an enthusiastic hiker just when his joints were starting to rasp and grind. And now, more frustratingly still, there was this whole lost-daughter business – the chance to catch up on years of a life he'd not known existed, to find out what the thing was that he'd missed that he didn't know he'd been missing – and his diagnosis with what looked, from all signs, to be a metastasised tumour in his spine.

Her name was Helen. His daughter's, that is, not the tumour's. He hadn't assigned a name to that yet, although he hadn't ruled it out. Helen had immediately made one thing clear: him, her, the two of them, right now, meeting up here, none of it was any big deal. Her mum had not been looking for a father for her child and, similarly, she was in no need of a dad, especially as she already had one of those, in all but the biological sense. There were no recriminations or obligations at play. Curiosity was the name of her business. As disorientated as he'd been by the explosive device she'd casually detonated in the foyer of Clocktower Records last autumn, the details had come to him and slotted into place instantly. 1982. The walk with Mike to Puncknowle, home of Puck, home of the first creature to walk Britain, the original forger of footpaths, long before deer and their contemporaries ripped his idea off and claimed it as their own. The paint-pot skies above them, crying out for a mix with a good brush. Eric's first true taste of Dorset. That lovely week, of whose loveliness sex – easy sex in which Eric had felt, more than any sex before or since it, like a not unuseful object carried under somebody's arm – had only been a minor part. The home studio in Uplyme. The little river just behind the walls, expertly judging the volume of its chatter like a courteous friend, making sure it was just loud enough to put a tactful muzzle over the sounds coming from the open bedroom window. The owner's daughter. He *did* remember her name. How could he not? 'Guess,' she'd said. 'Liz Taylor,' he'd said. 'You're actually half right,' she'd said. He had to virtually prise the other half out of her: Jenny. A muse? No. Not really the type. But he had been convinced his playing had been sharper and tighter, as a result of their two nights together. Not quite his bag, personally, the music, but the album, which was still waiting for its first reissue due to contractual tangles, regularly fetched well over £100 now. A spidery, minimalist new-waveish classic (even when Eric had played on a new wave record it had happened too late to be part of new wave) with echoes of late-sixties experimentalism that sartorially particular introverts born in the years directly after its creation somehow went nuts for. A guy from Bulgaria had even tracked Eric down through his guitarist credit on the album's Discogs page recently and asked him if he had any copies for sale (he didn't).

The internet was teeming with people like Eric now, dead and alive: mysterious former session musicians and garage rock also-rans of the twentieth century, rendered more occult and alluring by the pre-digital miasma hanging over the era they'd worked in and the stonewalling of their talent by the marketplace. Fans who now obsessed about the records they'd played on nosed their way down rabbit warrens to find what else they'd worked on, visited shoddy-looking half-finished 2005 websites, became even more obsessed because of all they failed to discover. But, at exactly the same time, each of these musicians continued to be viewed by the majority of the population – who, perplexingly to record collectors, had no interest in collecting records – in a thoroughly mundane light: they were 'just someone's relative who used to be in some band or other, years ago'. They were, if they *did* happen to still be living, usually living quietly, somewhere far from the action, gardening or cataloguing rare subspecies of damselfly or selling antique French breadboards and generally not perceiving themselves to be of much interest to anyone. To Helen, especially after she had followed that same Discogs listing and parted with most of a month's salary to purchase one of two available 45s of Witch Fuzz Magic's 'Jennifer's Orchard' and seen Eric, from a distance, going about his day-to-day business, this duality was more apparent and comic than most.

'Bloody hell,' said Eric, when she shyly showed him the single, the third time they met up. 'What do you want to own that for? They're making much better music these days. You want to hear this young Bruce Springsteen lad. They're saying he's the next Bob Dylan.' But he was secretly pleased. She asked him if he knew that – as she'd found out during her research – the 1960s music scholar Jon Savage had listed the song at number 28 in his 'The 30 Best British Psychedelic Classics You've Never Heard' list for the *Guardian* newspaper in 2017. Eric dismissively admitted that he had (Carl had shown it to him at the time), adding that he had met Savage at a gig by the space-rock band Loop in 1990 and that he seemed like a 'top bloke with a great record collection', although the topic of Witch Fuzz Magic, and Eric's stint in them, hadn't come up at the time, primarily because Eric had assumed it would be of no interest.

They were at a pub in North Dorset: quite a posh one that reliably made Eric feel like he was covered in soil every time he visited it. The bar hummed with the self-assured chat of catalogue thirty-something couples and their catalogue children. Even the formal little stream outside the front door gave the appearance of having chosen its trousers carefully, with no limitations on budget. Having failed to find a seat inside, Helen and Eric sat beside the water, shivering. Eric had fallen over en route while trying to find somewhere to piss at the side of a narrow lane near Sherbourne and now displayed a blood-soaked rip in his jeans: a beloved pair he'd bought on a trip back to Sheffield in 1988. Noticing it, Helen, who never travelled without first aid, offered him a choice from an extensive variety of plasters. Nearby, a couple of the catalogue children tried to sneak down into the water while their catalogue mums discussed the difference between house prices here and twenty miles north, in the Mendips.

'Absolutely not, Digby,' said one of the catalogue mums. 'We are not people who go into rivers.'

'I bet you used to meet loads of famous people when you worked for the record company,' said Helen.

'A few,' said Eric. 'A lot of it wasn't all that interesting. And a lot of the rest I can't remember. On the other hand I think I did piss Bobby Gillespie of Primal Scream off a bit a few weeks ago.'

'Oh no, what happened?'

'I was in Causley Mopchurch getting my turntable mended. He'd had an appointment to look at some vintage audio at the same time. I don't think he was too happy not to have had a private audience. He walked out straight away. I suppose it could have just been my aftershave.'

'So this is who I am directly descended from,' she thought, appraising him. 'Just one step further back down the ladder. He's funnier than my other dad, and seems younger in a way, but I am not sure about his clothes. He definitely doesn't seem horrific, though, or to hold any abhorrent opinions, and has a great relationship with his dog, which seems exceptionally well-trained.'

'Sodding hell,' thought Eric, appraising her in return. 'How on earth did my DNA co-manufacture something as artisan and refined as this?'

'When I first found the single I thought it was about my mum,' said Helen. 'Especially when I saw the name of the B-side was "She Brought Cake and Stories". That's her all over – well, it is nowadays, anyway. I was kind of disappointed when she told me it didn't have anything to do with her.'

'Yeah, you're a whole decade out. I don't think I'd ever even met anyone called Jenny when I wrote it. It just seemed a good name for that kind of song. But there was a Jenny's Orchard not far from where I lived in Sheffield. Me and my brother used to go scrumping there in our teens. Grotty place. Always broken glass and old jagged bits of car everywhere.'

She said she was forty-one, but of course, despite having failed his maths O level, he knew that already. She'd married young, too hastily, divorced too slowly. She supposed that coming to find him was not entirely unconnected to the reorientation that was part and parcel of the latter event but she assured him she didn't feel lost, wasn't attempting to assemble any redemptive spiritual jigsaw. In 2019, when the divorce had come through, instead of reverting to her maiden name, which had always bored her, she'd chosen the maiden name of her grandmother, the married name of her great-grandmother: Kettlebridge. She'd always liked the sound of it, its evocations and implications. The bridge that was better than the other bridges because, as well as spanning a physical obstacle, it provided the undeniable bonus of hot beverages. The pupils in the mid-Devon secondary school where she taught history did their best every year to reshape it into an insult, but a few months in would, invariably, throw the towel in. 'Mrs Kettlebum', it had been agreed, was downright uninspired, and 'Mrs Bridgekettle' hadn't stuck in the way that a few members of the class of 2023–24 had hoped.

She had those teacherly ways about her, shaped over the course of countless school trips and raucous assemblies, that all teachers have without realising it. She saw herself as a nervous person and was not entirely inaccurate in that assessment. She was always chewing on her bottom lip or a finger that she'd put somewhere near it. When faced with an awkward silence she ran her hands over masonry, picked at carpet threads, examined objects she had no interest in. But when she opened her mouth she had a way of bringing people to attention. Few were better at hustling the hungover dregs of a party out of the house and into the middle of the next day's itinerary. She was always making lists and brushing lint off the clothes of people she'd barely met. 'Right!' was her catchphrase. She said it directly prior to most events, big or small: the prepping of ingredients for a meal, the ordering of a pint of lager, the boarding of a plane, her own wedding ceremony, the loose planning of an afternoon on the sofa with the cat. She was springy, mildly elastic-looking. Her nose was the nose of a film star, but not, strangely enough, the film star she most resembled. She was commanding, not tall, but taller than she looked. It was one of the reasons another nickname the kids had given her hadn't worked. She was neither short nor stout, could not in any way be mistaken for a little teapot.

The nose had been one of the first things that had made Helen wonder about Clive, the man she'd formerly thought unreservedly of as 'Dad'. That, and his fine dirty-blonde hair. 'Dad,' she sometimes had an urge to say, as an adolescent. 'Do you ever think it's strange that I have thick dark hair and yours looks like some straw, and that my nose looks a bit like Leonard Cohen's, whereas yours looks like a radish that didn't quite grow properly?' Before she'd built up the courage to, the issue was settled. It had always been Clive and Jenny's intention to tell her the truth when she reached eighteen – though not, of course, on her birthday itself – and as time went on, and her pragmatic nature increasingly showed itself, they felt more confident about the wisdom of this decision. They'd instinctively felt she'd deal with it well, and she did. She kissed them both on their left cheeks. She made a pot of strong coffee. She travelled to Vienna by rail with her best friend Natasha and fucked a tour guide called Lukas, wrote to him twice, forgot him, spent three years at De Montfort University in Leicester, came out of it with an ineffectual fiancé and an only marginally more useful degree. Life did not change in any dramatic sense. Her respect and love for Clive as the squinting, kind, over-serious, catastrophising man who raised her did not alter. Her image of Jenny as a flailingly profane, fundamentally good-hearted intellectual gobshite remained, albeit underpinned with a flightier notion of her fancy-free past.

It was only much much later, when Helen's marriage began to unravel at its rashly weaved seams, and her decision to not have any kids of her own solidified, that the wondering began to creep in. For the first time, she pressed her mum for details, which Jenny gave up, with little resistance.

'Initially I just thought it might be nice to see a picture of you online,' Helen had told Eric, the first time they met up, after Mel's gig. Having realised they both liked walking, they'd decided the best way to chat would be on the move, up in the quiet hills behind Honiton, not far from her house. 'But then I followed the link to your website, realised just how close you were. I saw the bit about your stall at The Loft. Clive had a few records in the attic he'd been meaning to either sell or chuck for ages. Nothing special. His music taste never really progressed beyond Elton John and the *Phantom of the Opera* soundtrack. I thought I'd bring them in to sell, and that would be it. At least then I'd have been able to say I'd met you. But I waited, and I waited, and you never called me back. '*He* must be a bit of a shit record dealer!' I thought. 'Bet he never makes any money.' It sort of got my back up, made me want to give you a kick up the arse. The next bit I'm not proud of. Did you know your home address is on your Discogs page for everyone to see? You might want to change that. I was driving home one night from visiting some pals, feeling a bit light-headed. I wasn't over the limit or anything – I don't do that, unlike some people who live around here – just feeling a bit giddy from a small glass of wine and catching up with some friends I'd not seen for too long, and then I noticed that I was really near your house. But then I got a bit lost, on this rough muddy track, and found myself near this big farmhouse where there was a big party going on, and was just about to turn around, and then there you were, with your nice dog.'

'That was *you*?' said Eric. 'I thought you were one of Billy's stalkers.'

'Who's Billy? And why does he have stalkers?'

'You'll find out. Billy's one of my young, cool friends. The first time we met, two hours later we were in the hospital. It's all very rock and roll with us.'

'O-*kay*. Anyway, I'm not sure why, but when I saw you, I chickened out, felt a bit embarrassed about it all. Then I decided to leave it, as I'd done what I'd said I wanted to do and seen you in the flesh, then I decided not to leave it after all. Then just as I'd decided to not leave it, there you were, on the shingle, at Burton Bradstock, handing me a flyer for a comedy gig.'

'I don't remember that.'

'I doubt you would. You looked like you were totally in the zone, working the whole eighteen miles of Chesil Beach. I'm surprised they weren't turning people away at the door on the night. So I thought, "Come on, Hels, get your act together!" Also I liked the sound of a "methamphetamine-fuelled triple-brained Victoria Wood".'

'Jo Brand.'

'What about her?'

'It said "methamphetamine-fuelled triple-brained Jo Brand", not "methamphetamine-fuelled triple-brained Victoria Wood" on the flyer.'

'Well, even better, some might argue. And now here we are.'

'Have you told your mum?'

'I have. She says hello.'

'We never really got to know each other, at the time. I like to think that wasn't my fault.'

'No, I can imagine. She was what I believe is sometimes referred to as "a bit of a one" in those days. Her plan had been to bugger off around Europe on trains, meeting bohemians. But then Clive came along and put the kibosh on that, and then she discovered she was pregnant with me. Clive was cool with it, even though he knew it wasn't his own work. I'm told he was quite dashing in those days but I find it a little hard to believe.

That was back when he was just working on the first of his revolutionary latch designs.'

'Latch designs?'

'That's what he does. Designs latches. On gates. On public footpaths and bridleways. Ever heard of the Bagby Bolton latch? That's his.'

'Quite a jump, then for your mum. From hanging out in the studio with Richard Hell and the Voidoids to the Latch King of Lyme Regis.'

'Weymouth.'

'Ok then, not Richard Hell. Tina Weymouth. Same difference. Both total icons of the New York punk scene. What a fucking bassist. In fact, at a push, I actually prefer Talking Heads and Tom Tom Club to the Voidoids.'

'No, Weymouth. The town. That's where he's from, Clive. Not Lyme Regis. Lyme Regis is just where my mum's from. But I suppose she did get her European dream in the end. Just without the bohemians and with more Clive. The pair of them live in Gascony now. She sends me nude abstracts of her squatting form painted by local artists. He sends me news articles about tins of supermarket olives that have been recalled due to containing traces of glass.'

'Sounds like bliss.'

'It kind of is, to be honest. I do think they still genuinely love each other, despite being so different. I remember when I was eight, Clive got a potato, filled it with ketchup and dropped it off a wall at the end of our garden and told me, "And *that's* why you should never climb up anything tall." Meanwhile there'd be mum, in the kitchen, chainsmoking with the window open, yelling the word "cunt" at one of her editors or academic colleagues on the phone. But the point I wanted to make is that she's not angry at you. She could have told you if she wanted to involve you, and she didn't. Although I do think she was a bit freaked out that you didn't call her. I think everyone pretty much always did, afterwards.'

'Didn't I? Maybe I didn't. It's hard to remember but, whatever the case, I don't think I got much of a feeling she would have wanted me to.'

'No, I doubt you would have.'

They passed through a solid wooden gate from a rocky bridleway into a strip of woodland where the trees were decorated with the windblown remains of a fox-snaffled sheep. Helen let the gate slam heavily behind them. 'Hear that?' she said. 'So satisfying. That was a Morton Flickpot latch on that one. Not one of Clive's, but a really good, reliable latch.'

The woodland became quieter as they progressed through it, as if the trees were readying themselves for a performance arranged months previously, and they reached a fork in the path where it wasn't obvious which of the two scruffy prongs they should take. They paused and Eric leaned his aching hip against the stump of an oak that had been cut off at the knee.

'Right!' Helen said, grabbing her map, before he'd had chance to reach for his identical one.

But how could he stop his brain from asking itself what everything might have been like, if Jenny had found him, and told him? If some kind of union had come of that, and, against the odds, despite the tenuous initial threads of its beginning, blossomed? No lost years working in PR. No Leonora Arbuthnot and her chisel. No Wales. No difficult conversations with Rebecca about children. No Rebecca, full stop. No Pudding Lane Records. No reigniting of his friendship with Mel. No Carl. *No Carl*. He felt like he'd been chained by the ankle to a merry-go-round, just thinking about it all. Would he have been a good parent? Would he have been a worse person than he was now? Or a better one? Would he look like he did now, speak like he did now? Would he be in Gascony at this very moment, occupying the Latch King of Weymouth's studio while his wife sat on a chaise longue with her tits out in the next room, being painted by an insouciant Parisian? Who would have been there to meet Carl, when he walked out of the sea that day in 2003? *Who would have looked after Carl?*

He didn't let on to Helen, as he didn't feel they were familiar enough yet, and probably still wouldn't have even if they had been, but on their second walk together he had been in quite a staggering amount of pain, the stabbing in his lower back that had been bothering him for months now tracking down into his left hip and leg. If it had been anyone else he'd been with, he would probably have asked to cut the walk short. 'Please don't let me have to have a hip replacement,' he thought in the car on the way home. 'People die from hip replacements. I've heard about it. If I'm going to die, let me die in another way, not in a hospital ward with my hip hanging off.' As soon as he arrived home and found Carl, who'd decided to stick around the back of the cliffs that day and catch up on some pruning, he limped over to him and engulfed him in a hug.

'Well, this is all a bit unexpected. Are you ok?'

'I'm fine. I'm allowed to hug my friends, aren't I?'

'Absolutely. Except you're standing on my foot right now.'

'Oh, sorry, pal.'

'I suppose it must be quite an emotional time for you.'

'Yeah, I guess so. Plus . . . I'm really tired.'

'Why don't you invite her over for dinner some time?'

'I don't know. That sounds like a big step. I think she just wanted to find out who I was. I doubt it will lead to anything deeper than that. I'm just a boring old bloke. I'm sure she's got far better ways to spend her time.'

The following day, the day of his visit to the hospital in Exeter for two MRIs, the trip whose purpose he'd told Carl was to look a collection of old KPM and BBC library music in Shillingford Abbot, he found himself in the city centre, alone, eating the first of two pasties he'd bought. It was one of those days when the city was full of men who looked as if they'd been idly rolled around between the molars at the back of a giant mouth, and he wondered if he was one them. The street spat 3 a.m. energy from a lunchtime face. Outside the Little Valley Animal Shelter charity shop a man outlined to a woman his intention to travel to Newcastle upon Tyne to avenge the theft of his bulldog. 'I'm not big into violence so I'm not going to hit him, but I am going to slap him, without stopping, for half an hour.' A little further up the street a slanging match was playing itself out in a language that, though ostensibly some form of English, gave bystanders no clue as to the disagreement's goals or causes. A man in a bright green hooded coat hustled away from the scene with his girlfriend, to whom he announced, 'You just don't get it, do you, Kelly? I don't *care*! I'll knock anyone out.'

Eric could not help but speculate about the man's method. Did he tend to use general anaesthetic, on the whole? Monitored sedation? Or perhaps some form of gas?

'There but for the grace of God go I,' thought Eric. His bright-side take on what the consultant had said to him earlier was this: at least I'm not out on the street, with no roof over my head, with the same diagnosis. One part of him said, 'That could never have happened. I could never have been homeless. I've always had too many of my wits about me.' Another part said: 'Shut up, you arrogant bastard. It could easily happen. To anyone. Any time.' He stopped outside the Co-op and handed the second pasty to a man in the doorway huddled under two sleeping bags.

'Ah, cheers, mate,' said the man, shivering. 'I was just thinking I really fancied a nice ice cream but this will do just fine until I find one.' Amongst Eric's thoughts of what it must feel like, to sleep outside, in the ferocious cold, what it must do to your body and brain, he allowed himself a thanks to whatever powers there were that this had not been the fate of Helen.

'Here are the facts,' he thought. 'I created a child. Since then, marginally over four decades have passed. During that period, due to circumstances beyond my control, I have had no input on what that child has become.' As it was, she'd grown up to be a schoolteacher: well-read, thoughtful, inspiring, funny, stylish, appreciative of quality music made by under-appreciated Northern mavericks. He could tell himself that this was part of a fabric of logic, stemming from the core of who he was, but in truth it had probably been no more unlikely or likely than anything else. His child could just as easily have been a man called Nigel who felt his friends' wives up at parties and had a lot of time for Jeremy Clarkson. Or a woman called Nicola who took solace in trolling celebrities online while being taken to court for her remorseless bullying of a co-worker and waiting for her house to be repossessed. Or someone with a kid called Digby who was being raised as a person who did not go into rivers. Or someone sleeping in a doorway, or hustling down a city street, high on sleep-deprivation and pills, on their way to commit GBH. As he crossed from Exeter St Thomas station back towards the van, he wasn't quite sure what was buffeting him: the strong wind coming off the Channel, a few miles away, or the dizzying gusts of his recent luck and non-luck.

A tumour on your spine is different in one significant way to tumours in most other places: it's generally a secondary tumour, something that's metastasised from elsewhere. It means things have already progressed past a certain point of rescueability. 'What we need to find out,' the consultant had told Eric, 'is where the other chap is. Then we'll have more information to work with.' More information, Eric assumed, like 'how long'. In nine months' time he'd be sixty-nine. In around a quarter of that time, Alun Bannister, as plump as a sixteenth-century king, and almost as rich, off his catalogue empire, would be seventy. He was having a party in Matlock to celebrate. Eric had received the invite in the post last week. Surely Eric, who ate four cucumbers a week and could still just about squeeze into a pair of ripped 32-inch waist jeans was destined to outlive Alun?

He gave Carl another big hug when he got home, wider and more devouring than yesterday's. As he did, he thought he could feel Carl's arm pressing on the tumour. If there was only one. They say dogs can smell them, tumours. But of course Carl wasn't a dog, and never had been. He was Carl.

'This is becoming quite a habit.'

'Shut your moaning, Longtail. You fucking love it.'

'I actually do. It's nice.'

'I was thinking maybe we could train it up to the Peak District in January, for Alun's do. It will probably be a flabby kind of get-together, in more ways than one, but it would be good to see the old git, and Noel's going, too. Thought we might do a walk or two while we're at it. Cromford Canal, maybe. Black Rocks and Wirksworth. And there's a record fair on in Belper that weekend.'

'Sounds nice to me. But has Alun still got that horrible Doberman? I might sit it out if he has.'

'No, it kept chewing catalogues, so he gave it to Sandy in human resources. Have you had any more visions today?'

Carl swallowed his surprise at the question. 'Not today. But yesterday I walked over to Morcombelake and saw a lonely housewife wanking off a member of the Home Guard behind a hedge. 1942, I'm guessing, from some of the other outward signs. It was quite boring, once you got over the initial shock of it.'

'Bloody hell, it wasn't Russell Loosemore, was it? I wouldn't want to bump into his nob on a country lane. Not now, and not then.'

'Nah, he'd only have been about six back then. Bit too early to be in the Home Guard, even as one of its younger members who was ineligible for proper service on medical grounds.'

'Good point. So listen, right, pal, I was thinking about my dad this morning. And I realised that it's finally hit me, after almost seven decades, that I'm not going to turn into him. I know it might sound like a weird thing to say but something I realised is that I've always expected that it might happen. I mean, I know I'm not like him, but I didn't ever want to get complacent about it, in case it was around the corner in my future, waiting to jump out at me and happen. I think it might explain quite a lot. Like why I haven't had kids. Or why I sometimes didn't go out with really lovely kind people who wanted to go out with me. Maybe there was always this part of me that thought I might turn into him, and do to them what he'd done to my mum, just bugger off forever without leaving any details. And that might also explain my other kind of buggering off, all over the place, like it was something expected of me, or something I expected of myself, although that doesn't explain all of it. I mean, I know I got married when I was about five, and walked out, but that was different: we were totally ill-suited, I'd kind of brought the whole thing on myself, nobody had it off with anyone else – at least I know I didn't, and I don't think she did – and I was doing everyone a favour by ending it. And just earlier, when I was in Exeter, I thought about that too: about the way she used to kick and punch me and stuff, and how it might have made me subconsciously look for someone who might not like me very much, because that's the way I thought it was supposed to be in relationships. And of course I got over that after a while, and then there was Rebecca, and that didn't work out, but it could have, and maybe it should have, and maybe I should have let it, but it's all right that it didn't, and I remember feeling happy just because she was happy, and had got what she wanted, even though I didn't even really know her by that point. It's like something Reg Monk once said to me: as soon as the part of your life has ended where the future is your opponent, your past steps into the role and takes its place. He was always bloody wise, Reg. Wise, like you. Wise enough to get out of the music industry at the right time. Wiser than me, that's for sure. What would I do without him? What would I do without you? Or Jill? Or Mel? I'm always telling myself I'm self-made, but I'm not, really. I'm Mary-made, Carl-made, Mel-made, Monk-made. That's me. But on a slightly separate but also slightly related topic I was also thinking about choice. What a brilliant choice people like Helen and Billy have these days. I mean, they're in their forties, which is the age when my mum was telling me, after the bloke from the carpet warehouse had dumped her, "Who'd have *me* now, at my age: I'm on the romantic scrapheap, la', and thas just the way it is," and when lots of people she knew were stuck in unhappy marriages and thinking, "Ok, I better stick it out until the grave now, because I doubt there's much better out there," but Billy and Helen, they could meet anyone, the world's their oyster, and they're not like people in their forties used to be. They look about sodding eighteen to me. I talk to Billy like he's some kid, just out of school, who I'm preparing for life – maybe a little too much like that, sometimes, like he's some kid I never had – but he's a middle-aged bloke who's won awards and reached the top of his field. Of course, part of that is me, just showing my age. But that choice. It's fucking wild, compared to when I met Maureen, and thought, "Here's one of maybe forty girls I can meet, maximum, that I might fancy," even in Nottingham, which had lots of pretty girls in it in those days, or at least that's what they said. Compare that to Billy, now, with his dates. Of course, he probably has too many options. It probably keeps him in limbo, always wondering if there's a better option, always being shown that there might be. And that could end up being the case for Helen, too, and I worry about that for her – not that I have a *right* to worry, or I'm in any position to tell her, or ever will be. And that choice is also just a kind of problem generally, like the way it makes us sit in front of Netflix for forty-five minutes trying to decide what to watch then just watching *Harold and Maude* on DVD again, and the way it keeps people in a sort of holding pattern in the crevices at the side of real life, and makes music less special because there's so much access to it, and means books don't get read properly, except by you, and a few other people, and everyone just skims across the surface of everything and before they know it they're dead and they've not properly engaged with anything. But at the same time the amount of choice is perhaps good because it means some people are making better, more widely informed decisions. Like about what romantic partner they choose – because, even if it takes a long time, it will probably be an educated choice. And perhaps that's even more the case with the people they spend time with socially. Because what's the point, if you don't enjoy it? It's like me, and you, and Mel, and now Penny and Billy too. Yeah, I maybe look at him like the son I never had, but I just enjoy spending time with him. We all get together because we like being with each other, not just because any of us just happens to be there. And that's why I'll know that if Helen decides to hang out with me more, it will mean something. Because she's not looking for a dad. She's said that. So she's not going to do it just because she feels pressured to, and I'm not either. We're going to do it, if we do it, because we like each other, because we're living in an age of infinite choice, where you don't have to waste time on people you don't like. Would you like a cup of tea?'

Carl didn't have a mobile phone. Fingerprint recognition didn't work for his particular, rarefied and delicate digits. All his online chat was done contentedly via his laptop (he was still only on his second one, after defying the odds and making the first last a full decade) and he wasn't too fond of phones in general. But that evening, while Eric had nipped out to the supermarket to buy Bombay mix and light bulbs, he called Mel via the landline.

'Is everything ok?' she asked, immediately. The last time he'd called her had been in December 2018, when the boiler had broken while Eric was having one of his big Saturday morning lie-ins.

'I think so. I don't know. Yes. No. Well, he's talking a lot. He always talks a lot, I know. But it's different this time. He's talking about emotional things, things he never talks about. I mean, it's *brilliant*: I've been wishing he'd talk like this for years, but I'm also a bit worried. It's all so sudden. And I'm not sure if I'm qualified to be a therapist. I think something might have happened. He even asked me about my visions. Like he was properly interested, and believed they were a real thing. Do you fancy popping over?'

So Mel came over. And she brought Penny, who brought a Chinese cabbage salad, which brought nothing, apart from itself. And still Eric continued to talk. And when Mel asked him if he was ok, and Penny asked him the same thing later, and Mel asked him the same thing again after that, he said he was fine. He said he was tired. He said it had been quite a couple of months. What he still did not say was that he was dying.

That winter, in the era of unprecedented choice, one aspect of life remained as choice-free as it ever had: the weather. Where the M5 motorway crossed the estuary of the River Exe, directly above the South West Water Scientific Services Laboratory, midday traffic came to a total standstill due to the diabolical force of the rain, which made visibility more difficult than it would have been in the heaviest fog, more futile than it would have been if somebody had dropped a gargantuan pan of leek and potato soup on the entire 'EX' postcode. Forty miles to the west, the rain pulled down little chunks of golden-brown mud off the cliffs' scapulas and idly flicked the chunks at Eric and Carl's cottage. Assaulted morning, noon and night by water from all sides, Frank the crow began to look less like himself and more like a drowned ghost of the sea, a beleaguered once-proud pirate captain from a crow shipwreck. He hit the back window with ever-decreasing velocity and enthusiasm, leaving forlorn smears on the glass, until he finally gave up and one day, at chicken-feeding time, in what gave the appearance of a gesture of misdirected truce, landed gently on Carl's shoulder. Undaunted by their lack of banks, the lanes in the valleys filled up and posed as grouchy canals. Depressed, Billy invited an inflammatory bowel disease administrator from Dorchester he'd met online over for a last-minute date but water thwarted her and she instead ended up in a whirlwind romance with one of the two farmer's sons who'd pushed her Peugeot out of the flood.

The rain began to feel like a punishment for a hot crime committed by society as a whole. People blamed themselves for it, made rash decisions based on it. They beat themselves up, looked for other causes of the misery, not quite believing it could be just the rain. They planned a change of career, mistaking it for the central problem of their life, when in actuality the problem was just the rain. Billy talked about quitting writing forever. Eric cancelled his stall at a record fair in Bridgwater at the eleventh hour and stayed at home and rewatched the whole of season six of *Lovejoy* on VHS instead. Carl found himself unable to settle. The rain created earworms as he did his chores. Inside its patter, as he wiped mirrors and shelves, he heard Ray Parker Jr's *Ghostbusters* theme tune. 'Dusting makes me *feel* good!' he sang.

'Did you know that Ray Parker Jr wrote that song without seeing the film?' Carl asked Eric. 'All he knew was that it was a film called *Ghostbusters*, which he assumed was about some ghostbusters, and he tried to do his best to work something around that.'

'Funnily enough, I did,' said Eric. 'It's not a bad song. I thought of it the other day when I was in Whitchurch Canonicorum and saw those goats: the ones that couple we met at Billy's party own. I started singing, "I ain't afraid of no goat." Because I'm not. And then that led me to think about the cover of *Pet Sounds* by the Beach Boys of course. I think that cover says a lot about the band's dynamic. You've got all the other Beach Boys there, happily feeding the goats. Then you've got Mike Love, hanging back. Mike Love is suspicious of the goats. Mike Love thinks he's better than them. Mike Love's got some treats in his pockets, which he could give the goats, but, because he's greedy and likes Mike Love far more than he could ever like goats, he's decided to keep the treats for himself.'

Just as she'd been booked for her first London gig, Mel announced that she was retiring from the stand-up comedy circuit. But that wasn't anything to do with the rain. That was just Mel, getting out while she was ahead again, defying expectation, being predictable only in the sense that this was exactly what someone like her would do, and she was, and always would be, defiantly someone like her.

'You're basically the Bobbie Gentry of the West Country comedy scene,' said Eric.

'How do you mean?' asked Mel.

'Well Bobbie Gentry made six great albums, seven if you include the one she did with Glen Campbell, then retired, on a high. No synth pop eighties comeback. No reunion tours. Nothing. Totally unblemished track record.'

'But I haven't made one album, let alone seven.'

'That's what you think. I've got the recordings. They're ready to go! It's just a matter of production and marketing now. You mark my words: *Live At Puddletown* is going to be referred to as a seminal work, in years to come, right up there with Mitch Hedberg's *Strategic Grill Locations*, Sarah Silverman's *Jesus Is Magic* and Richard Pryor's *Live on the Sunset Strip* . . . So what will you do now?'

'I'm thinking of going back to the swannery. I feel like I never gave it a proper chance, before. I always felt right at home there. They've not got any vacancies right now but said it will probably be different by spring. In the meantime, I've decided to do some volunteering for the RSPB. I've already got a couple of days under my belt. The first job they've given me is to hold geese for the ornithologists while they inspect and ring them. It's good fun, aside from the fact that a couple of them clamped their beaks to my ear while it was happening. You probably noticed the bruise when I walked in.'

'I didn't. Come to think of it, I don't think I've seen your ears since 1984.'

'Oh yes. I still forget I have hair, sometimes. Even after all these years.'

'I rang a goose once. It was one of the most irate and confusing phone conversations I've ever had. What does Penny think about all this?'

'She's all for it. Says I should go where my heart takes me. We talked about what might have happened next. There was the possibility of panel shows and stadiums, of course, but I'm not interested in that. Success is a trap. History's proved it. Who does their best work when they're massive and everyone's telling them how great they are? I'll tell you who: sunflowers. That's about it. But even they die shortly afterwards, and become scary zombies, wobbling in the wind. Penny has been umming and ahhing about opening up her new place as a creative retreat – kind of like what Charles did, all those years ago, but a bit less chaotic. Or we've talked about a garden centre. Only a tiny one. There are plans afoot. Lots of discussions going on, that's for sure.'

The rain marauded down steep bridleways, pooled in rotting unheated porches, jimmied open shed doors, sending spiders scurrying up the walls. It displaced moderately imposing garden statues, pushed its way into rooms it had never previously visited, slurped at manholes until they floated up out of their firm slots. Seeing the subject heading 'URGENT', Helen opened an email from Clive. 'DO NOT FORGET,' she read. 'Fifty-five per cent of the people who die in floods do so because they fall down open manholes they can't see. So watch your step.'

The rain stole bikes, pulled bits off extortionately priced cars, robbing them of parts of their dull mimicking identities. Over the course of December and January, thirteen new registration plates were added to the Registration Plate Oak in the village of Masterton St Peter, where it was a tradition amongst residents to head down to a sunken, oft-waterlogged lane, fish out the plates that the water had forcefully detached, and nail them to the trunk of one of the parish's proudest trees. Mel, who was already in the process of moving her stuff into Penny's new place, brought the move forward when she got home to find her kitchen dining chairs sloshing about in five inches of light brown water and Bathsheba quivering on top of the Welsh dresser. A neighbour was less fortunate, her own cat – a former stray, estimated to be somewhere between fourteen and seventeen years of age, blind in one eye and almost totally deaf – fleeing to higher ground when the flood entered her conservatory and only returning two months later, when the ground had dried and, after a reported sighting nearby, the neighbour ingeniously laid a 500-yard trail of vacuum cleaner dust back from the point of the sighting to the catflap.

Carl listened to the rain and heard more songs inside it. The most dominant was the one written and performed by the sea. It felt like it was coming in closer, serenading him. He heard other earworms as he crafted into the early hours. The early 1980s hits of Judas Priest were weirdly common, despite his general antipathy towards the metal and sub-metal genres. '*Kni-tting* after *midnight!*' he chorused. 'Mowing the lawn! Mowing the lawn!' he lightly sang to himself, looking out of the window the next morning and dreaming of May, dreaming of turf-sculpting, petal care, the coming season's smells and composts and mulches. But in the rain's beat what he mainly heard was the sea, coming for him, singing its sober song, telling him it was almost time for the thing he always had known it would one day be time for although not with the knowing he had now, the innate knowing which redoubled with every day.

Up the hill, the rain sounded sober to Billy too, and he counterweighed its sobriety with a syncopating patter of wine, lager and spirits. 'Just one dry day and I'll be able to write again,' he told himself. He approached his brain like his brain was a puppy he was attempting to train via the use of treats: cheese crackers, dry-roasted peanuts, but also more exciting treats that it would be unwise to give to a puppy. 'Ok, one more half-decent sentence and you are permitted a double gin with a slice of orange,' he told it. He hated the way the rain overpowered and swallowed the sparse wildlife soundtrack the winter had to offer, worried about how, similarly, it could easily asphyxiate the noise of someone smashing a window or breaking a lock. He looked at long-established shrubs with undisguised envy, the ones who shrugged sturdily at the rain's violence and nonchalantly said, 'Bring it, fuckwad.' He scalded himself for his constant fantasies of escape from this place he'd so recently escaped to.

The rain made people stay at home, but it also made people travel when they didn't need to. It made people search for the curtain at the end of the rain or just for something soft and bright and hopeful they couldn't quite pinpoint, but they found none of it, only more rain. When you had driven or walked into the worst of it, you emerged slightly surprised that it hadn't killed you, and, in the rain, in its distorting relentlessness, that surprise became the primary perk of your day. 'Ok, get back up on your feet,' it said, just as you'd lost all hope, just as it had seen it had brought you to your knees. 'That's enough for today. Go home.'

In early January 2024, Eric, driving through the rain's thumping, slandering epicentre to a hospital appointment, planning the minutiae of his own death, was surprised to return, two hours later, with a 1971 pressing of Julie Covington's *The Beautiful Changes* LP and the feeling of a man who had witnessed a cowled stranger come out of nowhere on horseback and cut the rope a millisecond after the executioner had kicked the stool away.

'Hemangiomas?' said Carl, when Eric returned home. 'Yes, I think I've read about them. Am I right in saying they're benign vascular tumours? They're made up of blood vessels, aren't they? A little different to other tumours.'

'Yeah, so it explains the pain. And in a way they're eating away at my spine and replacing it with . . . blood. Which doesn't sound like quite the kind of massage I'm in the market for. But also, they're not malignant. What the consultant essentially said is that they are killing me, but a lot more slowly than I thought, and maybe not massively differently to the way that lots of other things are killing all of us, all of the time. So what do you reckon to this?'

'I reckon I'm upset and hurt that you didn't tell me immediately, back when you thought it was more serious. But I also reckon I'm extremely relieved.'

'No, I mean the record. Julie Covington. It's quite different to what she did later in her career. That last track, "My Silks and

Fine Array", is from some other planet, right? I mean . . . wow. But the rest of it's sort of . . . fine. I'm in two minds about whether to keep it. One great track probably isn't enough to justify it but . . . it's quite a rare and special artefact. The last one that was on Discogs sold for £250. God knows what this copy was doing in Cancer Research. They're normally quite on it, with their pricing. A bit *too* sodding on it, if you ask me. There's a scratched-up Bonnie Dobson LP with a sticker-damaged sleeve that's been sitting in there with a £45 price tag on it for two years now. No mug's going to buy that, no matter how hard they're rooting for a cure for cancer.'

'Did you know that they say dogs can smell cancer?'

'Yeah, I actually thought about that the other day.'

'I'm glad *I* can't. I imagine it would be ever so harrowing. I'd be constantly walking around worrying about animals and humans. I mean to say: even more than I already do. I was thinking this afternoon that I like the way Helen smells. There's something familiar and comforting about it. Maybe it's just because the two of you are related.'

The following Saturday, as an informal celebration, they invited everyone over for a madras: Mel, Penny, Billy, Reg, Jill and Helen. Eric insisted on making the madras himself, which Carl had mixed feelings about, since he had long been keen to test the true limits of Reg's legendary spice tolerance. There weren't enough dining chairs to go around so Eric brought in one of the armchairs from the living room, a taller than average footstool from the bedroom, and an old rattan peacock chair that had once belonged to his aunt Joan. Even then, there was still the problem that the dining table wasn't big enough to accommodate everyone so he and Mel had to eat awkwardly behind the main conversation, with their meals on their laps, after failing to find room for their plates, cutlery and elbows on a G Plan writing bureau.

Billy hit the 7.8 per cent Belgian beer hard from the word go. It was the first time Helen had met him and her initial impression was that he was a self-important prick, talking about his awards and his fan letters and responding in a patronising manner when she talked about her ambitions to one day write historical romantic fiction, sneering and warning her about the 'overcrowded marketplace'. The fact that he was sitting on a footstool, ten inches lower than the lowest of his dining companions, did nothing to detract from her sense of him as some weird precocious upper-class child who exuded needs, most of which were attention-related, and none of which were the damn good slap that might turn him in a better direction. Carl found it highly frustrating to witness, especially as he felt, if he'd been able to act as his full self, and insert a placatory comment or quirky fact into the conversation, it might have altered the course of the conversation for the better. He had an especially apt fact for a cramped social situation about the way the fashion for crinoline in the 1850s had increased women's girth to such an extent that it meant parties and the audience at plays had to be reduced in number, in order for everyone to fit in the venues. Mel and Penny, who might normally have stepped in to provide a pacifying element, were busy debating no-dig allotments with Reg and Jill: a conversation Carl wished he was in on for entirely different reasons. Eric just looked a bit stoned and dreamy as Helen continued to talk about books and the Kettlebridge tradition of writing them, whether it was her mum's psychology textbooks or the West Country-based romantic novels that her great-grandma had written early in the second half of the twentieth century.

'It's quite funny: Great-granny also had a second career after that, writing, well, what you might call a *different* kind of romantic book. Really quite racy stuff, especially for a lady in her sixties and seventies who'd been born in the Edwardian era. The titles were hilarious. *The Loch Ness Bonkster*, and *Grab the Bull by the Horn*. Things like that.'

'Ooh, Cliff Falls had that on the shelf under his glass coffee table,' said Mel, half-turning around.

'Who's Cliff Falls?' asked Helen.

'You don't know who Cliff Falls is?' said Eric, appearing to wake up. 'You obviously still haven't spent enough time in Dorset. Everyone in Dorset knows about Cliff Falls.'

'He was a guy I went on a date with,' said Mel. 'A bit weird, to be honest. Fond of big cats. He had it in his house, that book. *Grab the Bull by the Horn*. At the time I did wonder if it was a bit sexy. It's got a picture of the Dorset Ooser on it, hasn't it? I might be wrong but I got the impression he might have left it out for my benefit.'

'That's the one. She wrote it under a pseudonym. She had a few, I think. But the one she used for those books was Violet Axminster. Her real surname was Kettlebridge, like me.'

'I do love that name,' said Penny. 'So richly evocative. Funnily enough I have a friend with it, too, Elizabeth. I imagine there can't be many Kettlebridges in the world. She lives in Australia, but she did live in Dorset, too, many years ago.'

'The lady who made your nice bag!' said Mel. 'Ah, yes.'

'What does she do, and which part of Australia?' said Helen.

'The Gold Coast,' said Penny. 'She was a therapist. She's retired now.'

'Yeah,' said Helen. 'So that's my aunt. My mum's older sister. She did what I did: took my great-granny's surname, instead of her mum and dad's. That was kind of where I got the idea, to be honest. Oh my god. This is all so weird.'

'Well I never! You know, now I come to think of it, I believe I might have visited the house where those books were written. Very cut-off sort of place, in the Undercliff? Elizabeth took me there, when she was staying at my uncle's house. She did say her grandmother was some kind of writer, as I remember. We hitched in a gravel truck. I was rather excited because I'd just read *The French Lieutenant's Woman*, and a few other books about Dorset, including the novels of the Powys brothers. The driver made a pass at Elizabeth and she told him to piss off to hell, so he kicked us out at Seaton and we had to walk the last few miles. Oh gosh, and her dog! It's amazing what these little shards of memory trigger. Probably the most beautiful dog I've seen, apart from Carl. So much like Carl, in fact, in so many ways. Maybe he was a Longtail Cast-On too? I expect you wouldn't know, as it was all long before your time. Such a sweet sweet house, though, and a sweet sweet lady. Magnificent scones!'

Everyone looked around to try to locate Carl, but he was already on the stairs, making his way to a place of quiet. He felt like his head was exploding. Billy did too, although not for the same reason. In another half an hour they were both asleep. But when they woke up the next morning, in the places where they'd dropped, they were both struck instantly by decisive thoughts. Carl's was, 'I need to walk ten miles west, along the coast, alone, at the earliest viable opportunity.' Billy's was, 'I have finally met the woman I want to marry.'

There would be no Witch Fuzz Magic reunion in Matlock this time. 'My blummin' hands have gone and I can't even grip a drumstick any more, let alone use one,' said Noel. Alun said that just the thought of an hour on stage simultaneously moving his body parts and trying to remember words written more than half a century ago made him tired; he didn't have the foggiest idea how Mick Jagger still managed it. The carousel had somehow flicked onto the next image since Eric had last visited this part of the country and its replacement seemed somehow washed out, diminished. There was a lot of talk about doctor's appointments and angioplasty and scans and sleep monitors and cataracts and the brittle state of the NHS. Strangely, the aggregate effect was to make Eric feel younger than he had in months, more conscious of the relatively nimble way he still moved and talked, his life's playfulness and scope. He would have liked to have been able to discuss it all with Carl upon retiring to his room in the vast guest wing of Alun's 1980s McMansion but Carl had, close to the last minute, opted to stay in Dorset with Mel and Penny at their lovely new flat-roofed house behind the Undercliff. Eric found himself wanting to be in that house too, wanting to be amongst its thoughtfully designed paths of light and kentia palms and monsteras and woodsy fixtures. 'Does that make me a class traitor?' he wondered. 'Or just somebody who likes nice buildings?' Someone in Causley Mopchurch would surely have had something to say about it. But he was enjoying the record fair, enjoying its familiarity and unfamiliarity, enjoying the rare opportunity it presented him to be deep in his element, incognito.

He'd frequently pondered the meaning of his record collection during the weeks he'd spent preparing for his imminent death. Actually, he always frequently pondered the meaning of his record collection. 'Am I a record collector, or just a person stockpiling assets for a registered charity in preparation for my demise?' he would sometimes ask himself. His record collection was an unending story, full of edits and rash mistakes, and even when it did end, he liked the idea of it becoming lots of other starting points to other people's stories. And now, of course, there was another possibility he'd never previously considered: that of it staying in the family. And if it didn't, if it was instead used to financially springboard something else – the beginning of Helen's career writing those historical romances she'd mentioned, perhaps – then that was just fine.

He was well aware that, in the end, it was just all *stuff*. In his time, he'd watched people take that stuff far too seriously for their own good, pour their unaddressed problems and mental illnesses into the pursuit and acquisition of it. 'I'm having a cull right now – I've decided to cut everything down to 20,000 LPs, keep things really tight,' was the kind of statement it was not at all uncommon to overhear at a fair like today's, or a record shop. Where was the line separating archivism from affliction? The 3,000 records Eric still had at home had provided a magical escape from reality on so many occasions but they were also a neglecting of reality, a denial of the number of hours in a day, the number of days in a week, the number of weeks in a year, the number of years in a life: a wilful ignoring of time's cold facts, especially when you were almost sixty-nine. ('Ooh, that reminds me,' thought Eric. 'I must listen to Rodriguez's 1970 debut LP *Cold Fact*. It's been far too long.') Eric, just like so many others in his genre of music-obsessed people, was fully aware of that, but that awareness did little to halt the obsession's accumulation, its insane, illogical squirrelling. People still turned up at the fairs with the belief that records could change their life, spoke about what they had found or might still find 'in the wild' as if it were a rare flower or tree or lizard and not a mixture of grooved polyvinyl chloride and polyvinyl acetate.

These people could be annoying. They'd haggle over pennies or thoughtlessly dogear your original poster for the Action's gig at The Marquee in '66 as they bored you with the pedagogical self-absorbed telling of a story you already knew. They'd hover over your stall, pawing your stock, testing your patience by belching out blindingly obvious statements loosely connected to it – 'Ooh, old Rod Stewart – *liked his blondes*, didn't he' – then walk away without buying anything. As Prince sang about partying like it was 1999 from a small mobile speaker, the speaker's owner would vinylsplain like it was 1969 to any woman who happened to have mistakenly stepped onto the sales floor. Sometimes – and this was why the fair in Belper, with its new faces and stock, was refreshing for Eric, even though it featured belching dullards too, the belchers of Belper – it felt like you yourself were trapped in the damaged groove of a giant record, as you saw the same dozen or so blokes buying and selling and rebuying and reselling the same few albums, over and over again. But even when Eric was at his most cynical, he never stopped seeing hope in records, never stopped being seduced by their promise. And what exactly was that promise? It was usually a seed of mystery, planted many years ago by somebody who cared deeply about what they were doing and were determined to stubbornly follow their vision. That promise survived. The way it survived, considering the delicacy of its early axillary buds and stems, was a miracle. It was like the campanula and hellebores that Penny had originally taken from her uncle's garden in the late sixties that were still with her, even now, and would soon flourish in another new place. It was something from a past you could almost touch which kept offering hope for the future, when hopes were low. It was a bulwark against everything deadened and stifled and homogenous that you saw on the horizon, advancing towards you. And god knew those bulwarks were needed more than ever right now.

Out of what they had learned from records, from studying the careers of people who made records, an archetypal idea of a glorified life in music emerged: the one often lived by the people most responsible for the promise that lived on in records, those painfully sensitive gardeners of magic. The life usually didn't last long. There were no photographs of it with a paunch and some mottled skin where its long soft hair used to sprout. There was no footage of it chatting genially on *The One Show* about its fifty-year anniversary comeback album. It sacrificed everything for its art, lived it to the full. Then when critical and commercial justice was not done, and its art was not appreciated in the way it should have been, it made some more, even better art, pouring every drop of the pain of that into it. It got progressively more depressed and messed up, and congruently more brilliant for every bit more depressed and messed up it became. Only when it was no longer a life, only when all that was left of it was some cool photos and a few grainy bits of concert footage recorded on a Super 8 camera, only when it had been silenced in every other way apart from the songs it had recorded, did the slow process of artistic justice begin. Only then did people start – including, sometimes, some of the people who would have dismissed the work of the life with the comment 'Well, *I* 'aven't heard of it' – to gradually listen. Of course, nobody of Eric's ilk – none of these record collectors past a certain age, none of these lumbering men in love with their edited ideas of the past, and, come on, let's not hide from it, they nearly always *were* men – came out and said, 'I wish I'd been one of the ones to do all my living at once in a hurry, the ones to make the transcendental timeless music and leave an attractive corpse, rather than who I am right now,' but it was implied, again and again, by a lot of the other things they said, a lot of what they loved and venerated.

But what precisely was so fucking great about being dead? Especially if you didn't get to see people finally giving the music you'd made its dues? And what was left in death's and art's wake? What were the costs that fanned out from it into the lives of others, unglamorously but painfully?

In early 1970, as a sixteen-year-old, Mike had hitch-hiked down to London's Queen Elizabeth Hall to see a shy, strange singer he'd been raving about called Nick Drake. Eric, fourteen at the time, had nagged Mike to take him along and almost succeeded when their mother found out and put a firm lid on the idea. He wasn't quite on board with Drake's music – although, like millions of others, he certainly would be later – but he ached to see the husband-wife folk duo Drake was opening for that night, John and Beverley Martyn, partly because he had fallen in love with Beverley via the angelic photo of her on the cover of their just-released *Stormbringer!* album. When Mike returned to Sheffield the following afternoon, Eric made him describe every moment of the gig, including the bit where John, frustrated at what he viewed as the inferior playing of the musicians surrounding him, angrily hit his guitar while Beverley sang 'Sweet Honesty'. The incident confirmed what Eric had already intuited, during his many hours staring at the photo of the couple on the back of the album: that there was something demoniacal and untrustworthy behind John's innocent looks and Beverley should, if she knew what was best for her, get herself up to Crookesmoor as soon as humanly possible and start going out with Eric instead. Of the people involved in that weekend's real and imaginary events, just two remained alive: Eric, and Beverley. When, a couple of years ago, he and Mel had chatted about the subject of time-travel spouses, he'd put Beverley top of his list (for Mel it had been a tie between Harrison Ford and Madeline Smith from *The Vampire Lovers*). Few people had heard of Beverley now but even fewer people who liked the music of ethereal singer-songwriters had not now heard of Nick Drake and John Martyn. Drake's small, introspective music was regularly to be heard back-to-back in chain cafés with music made by people not fit to shine his chunky Cornish-pasty shoes.

Martyn's star, meanwhile, had been rising ever since his own death in 2009. Eric had sold seven original pressings of his 1973 album *Solid Air* in the past year, all at £50 plus. It was without doubt a unique and special record – who knows, maybe the sort of thing Eric might have made, if, after his dismissal from Witch Fuzz Magic, he'd seen that letter Duff Pickering had sent him. By the time of its release, Beverley had been elbowed into the shadows by John's egotism, was no longer making music of her own, and was instead left at home for much of the remainder of the 1970s at the couple's house in Hastings, with their young children, while John toured and descended further into alcoholism. Eric had met him once, on a hot day in the early 1990s, when he was looking after a newspaper art-section photographer who had been greeted by Martyn with the words 'You're a cunt, aren't you? I can tell' in the West London pub where they'd arranged to meet, then proceeded to wander down the street, walking into the houses of random strangers as Eric and the photographer remonstrated with him. A decade or so later Eric had watched a BBC documentary about Martyn: one of the first things he and Carl had watched together on TV. Beverley, who Eric thought was still looking super-hot, was also featured. 'Oh, he seems awful,' Carl had said. 'But I like her a lot.' The documentary had been a remarkable insight into Martyn's life and work and much of it had stayed with Eric: the detail of Martyn continuing to drink, even after his pancreas exploded in 1996, for example, and of him ploughing into a cow, while driving without headlights in an attempt to avoid the police after losing his licence, and breaking his neck. But what stuck with him most of all was a quote from Beverley: 'It doesn't matter if you are a great artist and play the blues and make people cry; it's what you do as a human being that counts at the end of the day.'

At Derby Midland station, the train filled up with people and their bags and their elbows and their legs and their bleeping, quacking, barking devices. Eric had only been on it for eleven minutes but he was already aching to get home to Dorset and see Carl, Helen, Mel, Penny and Billy. Every time he'd left this part of the country in the last couple of decades it had come with an odd feeling that he couldn't quite summarise: a feeling of emptiness, which also felt like he had forgotten to say goodbye to someone but couldn't quite remember who they were. Even though they couldn't have chatted here, and Carl wouldn't have enjoyed these travelling conditions, Eric missed his presence and felt a little envious of him for being the first guest to enjoy

Penny and Mel's new abode. They would have a good long chat when he got home, Eric decided, about all sorts of things, even some that they had never talked about before. He counted off the stations as they went by, ever more desperate for, and appreciative of, home, and all it contained.

Carl, meanwhile, back in the green Devon and Dorset borderlands, had been having the most excellent of days. As the rain hammered down, he, Mel and Penny had spent that Sunday afternoon watching a double bill of Powell and Pressburger films: *The Red Shoes* and *Black Narcissus*. He loved the depth and softness of their new sofa, the oaky smells of their new house, and now, left alone, the rain had stopped with uncanny timing and his plan was progressing more smoothly than he could have hoped. He unlocked the door, hopped the stone wall at the back of the garden and began to progress stealthily through the deepening woodland. He saw nobody but did not permit himself to become complacent because of that. He jinked left upon reaching the Rousdon Estate, under a line of beeches. After this, for the final half-mile, instinct took over. It didn't matter that it was almost dark. He could feel his way there. It was just like going to the kitchen in the middle of the night in a power cut. Not easy but if you trusted what you knew you could do it without bumping into anything.

'I never realised it, but I am so lucky,' thought Eric at Birmingham New Street.

'So this is it,' thought Carl, amongst the trees and vines and salted weeds. 'This is where I used to live.'

'I'm going to get Carl something properly good for his birthday this year,' thought Eric, at Cheltenham Spa. 'I know it's not for ages, but that's fine. It means I can give it plenty of thought, really look out for stuff on my travels. Because that's when you find the best presents, isn't it. Never at the last minute when you're really trying to rack your brain thinking what to get someone.'

'Maybe I will just go inside, for a while,' thought Carl.

'In fact, I'm really going to town for everyone's birthday this year,' thought Eric, at Bristol Temple Meads. 'I'm going to sell that Hetty Pegler's Tump album and use the proceeds. I know it's a masterpiece and all but I never seem to want to listen to it and there's no point it just sitting on the shelf. Better to get it into the hands of somebody who'd fully appreciate it.'

'Oh gosh, I feel quite nauseous,' thought Carl, stepping through the remains of a doorway.

After Bristol, the fields became lakes again and the train began to slow. A voice over the loudspeaker instructed Eric to report anything he'd seen that 'doesn't look right' to the transport police and he passed the time making a list of everything which fit the description. This included:

1. The train's upholstery
2. Much of the more recent architecture dominating central Derby
3. The pitiless thrust of the nearby motorway through formerly bucolic scenes
4. A dog in the seat directly across the aisle from him which looked too tiny to be a dog

He'd been surprised and pleased to see, when he embarked, that the train was a Class 43 – probably made in the late seventies. Mike, who was far less keen on the design that came after, would have appreciated that. Like cars, trains had angrier faces than they used to have. Was that true of people too? No. It wasn't. People just had different faces than the ones they used to have. Faces that had seen more other faces – perhaps too many of them. He looked around at a few now. Then he looked out the window into the dark and tried to sense the train's location: a little north of Cullompton, he estimated, maybe a few miles south of the Wellington Monument. He thought of the people in the houses beyond the darkness who might be hearing his train pass. He missed that sound: the smooth comforting one of strangers being carried home. He had no complaints about where he now lived but he did sometimes wish he still lived in a house near a railway line. There'd been one he and Carl had lived in near the old steam line, the one that had been reinstated purely for holidaymakers and heritage buffs. He'd liked that. Those sharp clear winter days when the steam would slice through the icy air like the breath of a jogging dragon. Days with none of the soggy abuse that had dominated this winter.

In the Undercliff, the rain had started again. It teased familiar smells out of the topsy-turvy earth, adding to Carl's nausea. He remembered Helen talking about the house's history: the people who'd bought it in the mid-eighties after her great-grandma had died. Then the property crash. Foreclosure. Neglect. And now what was really only a shell. But, as he and Eric had learned on so many walks, a shell was never just a shell. There was so much in these remaining bricks. He breathed it in, through his nausea. He heard the sea, through the green drapes. A familiar sound. Wobbled cardboard and intent.

About fifteen miles north of Exeter, by Eric's estimation, the train hit a fallen tree. Because he was in the front carriage, he felt the impact more keenly and the crunchy wrenching sound it made reminded him of when he'd heard a couple of old oaks come down in the gales of 1987 during a holiday in the New Forest with Leonora. The train dragged to a halt, the conductor announcing that they'd 'been involved in an incident', and he prepared himself for a long wait, relieved to still be on a railed vehicle and not upside down in the luggage compartment with a broken collar bone. About thirty minutes later he heard one of the train crew speaking to an elderly lady in the seat behind him who seemed very confused and was expressing worry she wouldn't make her connection to Redruth. The lady from the train crew reassured her everything possible would be done to get her to her destination, then said, 'Do you want to know what's happened? Ok. We hit a person.'

Carl was amazed that he'd never seen the house before on a walk with Eric or Billy, and was surprised how easy he'd found it to get there. Eric's trip north, and Mel's offer to look after him at her and Penny's new place, and then Mel and Penny's trip out to the pub quiz – everything had slotted into place. It could have been so much trickier. He had been feeling tired recently and it was a bit too far to walk from his and Eric's cottage and back in one evening. He might have had to go to all sorts of hassle, waiting until Eric was out, possibly having to sneak onto the back of a truck heading east. 'Ok,' Mel had whispered to him just before they left, while Penny was in the bathroom. 'Have a nice time. Chill out. Crochet. Knit. Sew. Watch the telly. But DON'T start doing any cleaning. Or I'll be angry.'

'Why is she telling the old lady this?' Eric thought. 'It's upsetting, and it's a lie. What the train hit was a fallen tree, brought down by the high winds. Everyone in this carriage, and probably in this entire train, knows this.' As the news spread, a couple of people reacted like it was nothing but an inconvenience specifically aimed at them. Passengers who'd been coughing started to cough more violently and frequently and wetly. Through the windows, police shining high-powered torches could be seen walking alongside the train. Mostly the people sitting close to Eric just seemed baffled, emotionally stranded in an oddly blank way that life until now had not prepared them for.

A train driver in the UK receives quite a handsome salary. He remembered Mike telling him that, years ago. Mike had added that one of the reasons for that pay grade is an acknowledgement of an unavoidable truth: that if you do it for long enough, it is highly likely that you are at some point going to see a human body explode in front of your eyes. He could still remember exactly which night it was when Mike told him. They'd been watching *The Red Shoes*. They'd both agreed it was a brilliant film. 'But *that*,' Mike had said, when the ballet dancer had jumped onto the train track, and the people had gathered around her lightly bloodied but still very much intact body, 'that's utter bollocks. It's not what happens.'

What he would keep remembering about today's incident was the noise. It had a shape in his mind which seemed born directly of the immense darkness of January: a shape that could never be a tree, because trees never terrified him, not properly, not even in the heart of winter when they revealed their spookier more intricate selves. Somebody had taken their own life. He knew that. Quite possibly a man – he'd heard that when men kill themselves they were statistically less likely to worry about the impact the act had on other people, especially strangers – but perhaps not. Yet simultaneously, despite knowing all this, a different, more dominant part of his mind remained adamant that what the train had hit was a tree, continued to work hard to protect and prevent itself from going to another place.

Forty miles south another unforgettable noise rang out into the night: the one that came from deep inside Carl on the Undercliff as he stood on its furthest frontier, above the sea – as shocking to Carl himself as it would have been to anybody else who heard it, if they had, which they hadn't. It was a noise, completely out of his control, that made him feel like he contained the whole sea. And as he made it, a crow flew overhead, and a triangle opened up in front of him. Inside the triangle was an intact building. Inside the building he saw things he knew from another life: hens, a clock. And then they were gone, and it was just him, shivering in the night. But he was back on Mel and Penny's soft deep sofa in good time, showered and dried off, placing his bets on who would arrive first: Eric, from the station, or Mel and Penny from the quiz. It was all as if nothing had happened, and, had you seen and heard the trains early the following morning, you might have said the same thing. They yawned through the half-awake valleys, the noise of their wheels on the tracks as undemonstrative and reassuring as ever. On either side of them, the water rested, calm and high; so much water, water where it had no legal right to be. It had now been there for so long that it began to feel like it had been forever, although it hadn't been, and wouldn't be, until one day it was. The trains floated serenely over it, grieving nothing. Eric imagined their progress being witnessed by dead people who had returned from multifarious points in history. It would seem to those people a miracle, probably, just as it did to him.

Excerpt from the Diaries of William James Stackpole
(*International Folklore Society Journal*, Autumn 2108)

EDITOR'S NOTE

In eight years as editor of the *International Folklore Society Journal*, there have been many highs and a few lows. Some of these highs and lows have arrived with a curious synchronicity: a high, one might decide, coming directly *out* of a low, existing only because of it. There are many joys that come with the job but I can say with total frankness that some of the greatest for me are when, by the very act of publishing a story, another story is unearthed, shedding more light on our world's rich and mysterious folkloric past. I don't think there are many more archetypal instances of both of the above phenomena than the document I am about to reveal below. But first, an apology, and a little background.

In her piece from the spring issue of this quarterly, 'Mermaids, Merpersons and Other Unexplained Creatures of the Jurassic

Coast', Colette Dobson referred to the bestselling twenty-first-century nature writer William James Stackpole as 'a volatile and unreliable juice-head . . . given to outlandish claims'. Miss Dobson – who, it should be added, is no longer an employee of this magazine – had, it transpires, little to no evidence to back up her summary of Stackpole's character in his declining years and it was an oversight by the editorial team to publish them. The *International Folklore Society Journal* would like to state that it retracts Miss Dobson's words and regrets any pain it might have caused Mr Stackpole's relatives.

Around a week after the publication of Miss Dobson's piece, a letter, with an East Devon postmark, arrived at our offices. Accompanying it were five sheets of lined paper, giving the appearance of having been torn from an old notebook. The pages were filled with dialogue, written in black biro, now somewhat faded. At first, the letter, from a Mrs Jennifer Kettlebridge of Causley Mopchurch, Devon, gave no clue to the provenance of the sheets of dialogue. Mrs Kettlebridge – who has requested that we not print the letter in full, but has given us kind permission to print the accompanying document – explained that she had only known her grandfather, William James Stackpole, for the first nine years of her life, but remembered those years with 'great fondness', and felt hurt by Miss Dobson's description of him and saw nothing recognisable in it. She added:

'I believe people are never one thing. William was undoubtedly a troubled man but, in the later part of his life, he was a contented one too. He remained deeply in love with my grandmother right up to his final breath. I clearly remember my grandma telling me the story of their inauspicious meeting – a rather awkward encounter, especially for my grandmother, which soon blossomed into an unlikely romance – and my visits to their farmhouse formed a strong template for me, vis-à-vis my ideas of what profound companionship could be. Each day, my grandparents would rise at 6 a.m., eat one banana spread across two slices of toast and share a pot of coffee, then retire to their adjoining studies to write, reconvening at lunch to compare their findings and frustrations. These meals were usually taken in the summer house that my grandfather, with the help of his neighbours Brian and Eric, had built at the furthest point of the garden, using some of the remains of a Second World War radar station. This tradition continued for the remainder of their life, including the period when reaching the small building necessitated my grandmother driving them down there on the 2020s quad bike that she was so fond of. "Right!" my grandmother would say. "Where have we got to." And while my grandmother's reports invariably charted more productivity, my grandfather never displayed any jealousy or bitterness regarding her greater output or earning power. It might be said, in fact, that the same workaholic drive he'd poured into his years of early celebrity he later poured into his support of her books and the writing of them.

'As far as the "extended periods of writer's block" Miss Dobson refers to in her piece, it cannot be denied that these took place. I believe their cause was not unrelated to incidents involving two of my grandfather's early readers who developed parasocial relationships with him and an obsession with his terrier, Ossenfeffer, who often featured in his books and died in 2019. These two individuals – who were not friends – believed that Ossenfeffer was in some way "theirs", and expressed anger towards my grandfather when, after Ossenfeffer's death, his books no longer featured a canine companion. I was too young, of course, when I knew my grandfather, for him to confide in me about these incidents, but I know from my father that they led to my grandfather questioning the merits of the fame he had once courted in a happy-go-lucky manner – especially after a break-in at his flat in Chiswick in 2021.'

As to the enclosed, handwritten document, Mrs Kettlebridge said only the following: 'No full notebook of my grandfather's survived his death. I believe he burned most of their contents during one of his more existential, inward phases. But, after my father's death, two years ago, a box file containing a few scattered pages from them came into my possession. The enclosed are an example. I believe they are a transcript of a conversation he had with someone – or something – during spring 2024. Like most of my grandfather's remaining notes, they lack context, and appear to be part of a larger chunk of text. Why he kept them, and not the accompanying parts, is unclear, possibly even insignificant and entirely random. However, in relation to his brief reference in his autobiography to his acquaintance with a "semi-aquatic speaking dog" – as mentioned by your Miss Dobson in her otherwise benighted piece – I believe they might be pertinent.'

The document is printed in full below, and all of us here at the *IFSJ* would like to express our gratitude to Mrs Kettlebridge for her kindness and clemency in allowing that.

Patricia Tongue, Editor

RUINED CHAPEL, 4.5.2024

ME: 'Beautiful morning.'

C: 'It is. I feel like I'm floating around inside liquid gold. I always find it painful, this time of year. The brevity and magnificence of it. Especially this year. For obvious reasons.'

ME: 'I might steal a couple of those lines for a book. If I ever write another.'

C: 'Be my guest. Just remember to credit me in the acknowledgements.'

ME: 'So ... coming back to what we were talking about, the times when you — for want of a better description — go out there and *make your return*. Do you ever remember anything about that part? Or is it just the parts before it you get flashbacks to?'

C: 'No. That's become no clearer. I just know that I don't fear it, even though I perhaps did, a few years ago. I sometimes see things in my dreams that seem to come from it: the place I go to, out there, whatever it is. In one I saw a seahorse, except it was as big as a proper land horse. That felt extremely real. So maybe I did see one, once.'

ME: 'But no mermaids?'

C: 'Only one I can think of right now. But she had Mel's face and hair. There was all sorts of stuff stuck in the hair: shells and confused fish and bits of frayed trawler rope and netting and even a small fishing boat. I think that was just the nonsense bit of dreams. The bit that really doesn't mean anything.'

ME: 'The dream I had last night wasn't such a good one. It was about Marge. I was at a book talk. The one I met her at. She always used to wait for me at the end of them, until I was done talking to everyone else, like she wouldn't stoop to competing with other people for my attention and wanted me all to herself. I know in the end she wasn't the one who went totally nuts, at least not as nuts as Gary, anyway, but she scared me more. There was something monolithic about her. I mean, she wasn't massively overweight or anything, but her presence was frighteningly big and solid, something you wouldn't have been able to budge. At this talk, the one in the dream, she had her face but her body was one of the sofas in the bookshop. The sofa was pushed hard up against the door, meaning I couldn't get out of the shop. I kept looking for other exits, behind bookshelves and the till and some of the bigger hardbacks. But there were none. And then Gary came out of the toilet at the back. "I've just done a wee all over Ossenfeffer," he told me. "But I think he'll be fine. And if not I'll buy you another one." Fuck knows what it was all about.'

C: 'I suppose it must be nice that when you wake up from something like that you've got someone to cuddle now, and tell you everything's ok.'

ME: 'Yeah, it makes a big difference. Bigger than I would have ever suspected. I feel calm and nice this morning, considering. Come to think of it, you seem very mellow today, too.'

C: 'How can I not be, in weather like this? Winter and early spring was so relentlessly miserable. But you only need a few good days and it's amazing how quickly the memory of it gets vanquished. But at the same time, I can feel something on the edge of the calmness. It's really big. There's so much I'm keeping in my head. Sometimes I think that's what it is, the reason I have to leave. Because it all gets too big, what I'm carrying, and what I'm seeing, through the triangles, and there's too much, too much history, and I suppose in a way it's another version of what you go through now, with technology, and why it might be better if one day it all exploded, but then I think of Eric and'

DOCUMENT ENDS

Old-Fashioned Letters

Dear Carl,
My brother Mike worked on the railways. I am pretty sure I told you that. He died a long time ago. I told you that too. But I never told you about how he died, or properly talked to you about it. I'm guessing you think I've been avoidant about it, just like some other things I've been avoidant about, and if you do think that you'd not be wrong. So I'll tell you now: Mike was hit by a train.

Mike had broken up with his girlfriend not long before it happened but we – me and my mum and her sisters, that is – always assumed it had been an accident, since that was the coroner's verdict. But I was never fully sure. Mike was different to me, a born risk-taker, a bit of a daredevil. He was brainier, too, thought about everything in a deeper way, and was prone to depression.

Do you remember that Daphne du Maurier book you gave me to read, *The House on the Strand*? I told you I was enjoying it but I never finished it and I never told you why. If you looked at the place where I left the page turned down as a marker – I know you hate it when I do that, sorry – you'd have seen that it was at the exact point where Magnus, the best friend of Dick, the main character, gets killed by a train near Tywardreath. Also, do you remember that one night while we were living in Lerryn, when you were outside on the bench, in the pub garden, and I got talking to a bloke at the bar, an older fella? You wanted to know who he was. I said it wasn't important, but that wasn't true. His name was Jack Thomas and he used to be a colleague of Mike's on the railways, a fellow track engineer. They drank and played cards together. I'd not seen Jack since the funeral and we got talking about our lives, in that way you do, just idly scratching the surface out of politeness. What brings you to these parts, that sort of stuff. But naturally the topic of Mike came up, Jack telling me what a 'good old boy' he'd been, how he always knew where he stood with Mike, and as the conversation progressed I learned something I'd never realised, which was that Mike had quit his job on the railways almost a fortnight before he died. You probably remember that I was quiet that evening. For once.

I suppose it doesn't matter now. It's all ancient history and the end result is the same, which is that he's not here.

But you are. Not that I've ever viewed you as a brother. Those bromance films have never been your bag – nor mine, to be honest. Not a patch on Harold and Maude or The Go-Between. I view you as a best friend, my closest companion, the person who truly gets me, my Maude or Harold (I've never quite been sure which of us is which). But what I mostly view you as is a Carl. And by that I don't mean like other Carls. Sometimes I'll overhear somebody in a pub or a shop calling someone 'Carl' and I'll look around and discover it's just some bloke that they're talking to. 'What a fucking joke,' I'll think. 'That's not a Carl!'

I'm sorry I have kept things from you and sometimes change the subject when you want to talk. I know what you think it is: you think 'It's just Eric, it's just fellas born in the fifties and the way they are.' But it's more than that. People talk about their problems and worries a lot more openly nowadays than they used to, and that's good. I mean, who knows? If it had been that way when Mike was young, perhaps he'd still be here now. But on the other side of that, I think you can talk about stuff that scares you or worries you too much. Sometimes, when you talk about something scary, you are giving it sustenance. It's a bit like what Billy said, about when he used to be on the internet and he'd get strangers sending him hateful messages: he learned that the important rule is that you don't feed your trolls. A lot frightens me and sometimes it's easier to get by if I push it away. Also I think people get themselves into too much of a state of self-examination nowadays and, while they're doing it, they forget to actually live. Something is telling them they have to iron out all the kinks, smooth out all their faults, and that's just not going to happen. It's not how life works. Life is short and I want to be fully in it while I can. Because living has been a special pleasure for me, particularly for the last twenty and a bit years.

The card game Mike was most fond of was pontoon, which as I'm sure you'll be aware in other countries can be known as blackjack, or twenty-one, or vingt-un. I was never any good at it, because I never wanted to stick, was always too keen to get as close to twenty-one as possible. And of course then I'd go bust and there was no coming back. I couldn't wait to get to twenty-one because I thought that would be the point when my life would be all sorted and I'd have everything I ever wanted. The times I was living in, the people I looked up to . . . that played a part too. Those pro footballers who were half-bald veterans by the time they were twenty-six. The pop stars who owned Rolls-Royces and houses in St John's Wood at twenty-three. The singer-songwriters who, when you listened to their songs, somehow seemed to have the wisdom of an old mossy boulder, even though they'd only been old enough to vote for three or four years. But me, pal? I had nothing sorted at twenty-one. Nor at thirty-one. Not even at forty-one, really. Fifty-one, though? That was different. I had help by then. And everyone can benefit from help. Even if they've learned to be fine on their own.

Something Penny once told me sticks with me. I probably can't remember it word for word, because she's much smarter than me and uses *bigger better words, but I can remember the gist. She said we're conditioned to believe that it's the time when we're young and pretty that matters most and part of that is because it seems most poetic and attractive and part of it is because when we are young and pretty and years seem so long we refuse, out of obstinacy, to give space to the possibility that the time that matters most is something we'll have to wait patiently for. Then because of that conditioning, when we haven't made the time when we're young and pretty matter most, we beat ourselves up for it and sometimes, because we're so busy doing that, we miss the time that does matter most. And countering that you've got this other conditioning, which comes from mortgages and the structure of the working world, especially in this country, which tell you everything is a campaign to protect a distant, future version of yourself, who you haven't even met, and who has entirely different cells to you, and you might not even like. And how is anybody expected to live in the present with all that going on? I'm with Penny: I've decided this is the time that matters most, out of all of my life. The best time. And if it isn't, and if that time is already long gone, does it even matter, if I can't remember it properly?*

If you'd told me some facts about friendships I know now back when I was young it would have absolutely melted my mind: that somebody you told everything to, somebody who was the first person you called when anything significant happened to you, could end up being someone you didn't even say hello to if you saw them on the street, and not because you'd fallen out, just because life had ever so slowly pulled you so far apart you finally couldn't reach each other any more. The thing about common ground is that it's situated on tectonic plates: it shifts, without you noticing. I don't have many friends left from my youth but I've got a few. Men are bad at keeping in touch, once they get past a certain age, nowhere near as good as women. I don't care if some idiot thinks that's sexist. It's a fact. Just like the fact that women – with exceptions – are better at touching a piece of washing on a line and gauging whether it's dry. And no, that doesn't mean I think women should do the washing and men shouldn't. It just means women have generally got better fingertips than men.

It's taken me a while to work out what good people are – what my definition of them is, anyway. I couldn't sum it up in words but I know it when I see it and, more importantly, when I feel it. Trial and error inevitably becomes a part of it. I used to think I knew what good people were but as it turns out I just hadn't met enough people. There were better ones out there: not ones that were better for everyone, but ones that were better for me. Of course, the problem now, for young folk, is that they can meet as many people as they want to. I hear that one result of that is that a lot of them are isolating themselves, retreating into their devices, behind closed doors. Maybe they're getting too critical of the people around them. What was it Helen called it? 'Cutting toxic people out of your life.' I don't know. I'm just an old bloke. But I know one thing: being surrounded by a lovely group of people, just a nice manageable number of them, not too big or overwhelming, at a time in your life when you properly know yourself is a rare and special gift.

You're always nagging me to let my sentimental side come out, so there it is.

You've been trying to tell me for a long time that you have to leave. I know it's true. I reckon, from what you've told me, that it's probably going to be in October. I suppose it makes sense: the season of mists and mellow fruitfulness. Perfect for someone as misty and fruity as you. The season when I first met you. You might remember that I said I lived with a cat before that. When he died, it almost broke me. Coincidentally, he was twenty-one. That's a great age for a cat. They are finally eligible to vote, for a start. But seriously. Twenty-one: I keep thinking about that number, the pontoon number. It's nowhere near high enough, if you ask me. But everything has to end at some point. Including me. Who are we to argue with what has been laid out for us? We're not members of the super-rich elite, conning ourselves into believing we're living gods, separated from reality by our billions, pouring them into research towards everlasting life or the creation of an intergalactic escape from this wheezing, desperate planet. We're just a couple of guys who sell old stuff and live in a cottage. We're here, with all the limitations that come from being mortal, and all the magic that results from that. Well, I am, anyway.

I always believed you. Right from that moment in Cornwall, in the woods by the creek, when you said you saw the pleasure garden. And then after we went to the manor, when you told me you knew you'd lived there before, I believed you more. I saw it in your eyes. You've never been the drama queen type, or one to make a mountain out of a molehill – or, as they say in those parts, 'mistake farting for sneezing'. If I acted like I didn't believe you it was because I didn't want to look it directly in the face, didn't want, again, to let it get in the way of life, of us, while we were both here. But I knew. And, if I say I don't believe, that it all sounds a bit farfetched, I can see what shaky ground I'm on there, as someone who lives with a hyper-intelligent, entirely fur-covered, twenty-four-fingered creature who speaks six languages and can knit a quality turtleneck in two days flat. I am not saying it's not going to be painful. But what I am saying is I'm sorry, for some other times, and let's make the most of the time we have. Summer never lasts quite long enough, does it, but that's what makes it special.

Fucking hell, this has been emotional. I'm not as good at writing as you are so I hope it makes sense. I'm going to go and listen to some obscure music now and look up some nerdy facts about the people who made it.

All the bees,
Eric (a fortunate man)

Dear Eric,
You asked me last night if I knew it was you I'd be meeting on the beach that day in 2003. I know more than I once did but I don't have access to that particular information. In some ways, when it happened, it felt right. Actually, in a lot of ways, it felt right. There is part of me

that has felt like we were always supposed to be friends, like it was preordained. Just for argument's sake, though, let's say it was a totally random occurrence. There I was, shrivelled, staggering about, unable to see. What if the first person I'd bumped into had been of a less forgiving disposition? I could have ended up in an animal rescue centre or, worse, a circus, or at the centre of a horrific media shitstorm. The person who found me could have screamed, or called the police, or the fire brigade, or their cousin Dennis on Exmoor who enjoyed shooting badgers and deer.

You did none of that. You took me home. You gave me my own bed and time to recover. You fed and watered me. You went to get me books so I could relearn your language from scratch and expand my knowledge of the world. You did your best to make my life fun and diverse, despite the limitations presented to you. You remembered my birthday every year and always put time and thought into my presents. If I was down, you bought me tasty takeaways, even when your bank account was already overdrawn. You always put my safety first, even though that was frequently highly inconvenient to you. Your devotion to my welfare has been impeccable. If they gave an award for stuff like that, you'd have won it years ago. In fact, it's an oversight of mine that I haven't made an award. Let's call it a cable-knit jumper. Have a jumper. No, have two. It's the least I can do.

I'm sorry I chatted to Billy without telling you. I'm sure you can understand. I love your company, and I love Mel's, but I think we all benefit from variety and colour and new perspectives in who we speak to, and I'd never chatted to an upper-middle-class person born in the southern half of Britain before. Often for me life feels like one long podcast: I'm listening to all these people talk about interesting stuff, and there I am, ready to respond, and then I realise I can't. Billy is a little insecure, but a good soul. I also think he's going through some positive changes. He told me a bit more about those two readers who used to follow him around, except he's not sure that they had ever properly read any of his books – not more than one of them, anyway – and were just obsessed with his life, or at least the surface of it, what they thought he was, and the dog he used to have. After the dog died he got home one day and found one of the two readers sitting in his living room with a dog that he said he'd bought Billy as 'a present'. A live dog. The same breed as Billy's that died. Can you believe it? He had to call the police. It got quite ugly. He made sure the dog was safe, though. That it found a good home. That was his priority. I saw him with Helen the other day, on the secret beach. I knew they'd been starting to spend more time together and Helen had softened towards him but it seems to be really moving on apace. I saw them whispering in one another's ears. Their fingers were lightly touching. It's a romantic beach, that one: lots of history. But that's another story. I was going to go over and sit with them but then they got a little more intimate so I decided it would be most tactful to leave it.

There is so much coming at me right now, I find it hard to get my thoughts in order. I don't know if it helps to put them down in a letter like this. I'll probably read it aloud to you, as you did with yours to me. But it doesn't make it all any less of a jumble: present and past — my past, and others — coming at me like an asteroid field in front of a spaceship's Plexiglas screen. Sometimes I wish I had some huge strong windshield wipers. But even if I did, I'd never manage to keep the spray refilled in the way I need to. After we were up on Lewesdon Hill last week and I saw that plane crash in the trees above us, I researched the details. I'm pretty sure it was the Spitfire flown by a Belgian pilot called Jean De Cloedt. It smashed into the hill on 15 March 1942, killing De Cloedt instantly. He'd been delivering the plane to the RAF base at Exeter when he got lost in one of those thick west Dorset fogs. The members of the Home Guard that day were two farmers called Jack Frampton and John Studley and a funeral director called Jack Wakely. Seems like everyone in the West Country was called Jack at one point, just as everyone in the North Midlands was called Ken. I thought the name Jack Frampton sounded familiar but it's probably nothing. Especially as I wouldn't have been there at that point; I would have been in, as you and Mel have started calling it, 'one of my aquatic phases'. You'll never believe this but *while you stopped for a piss in a lane last week I also saw Charles II briefly, finally, just for a moment, on the Monarch's Way, near Broadwindsor. He was looking for a place to stay for the night. Just my opinion, but I have to say: nowhere near as attractive as everyone claims. Bad skin. Dry hair. Also, did you know that the reason kidneys are called kidneys is that they're named after kidney beans, and not the other way around, and that when people talk about 'that baby's-head smell' and how lovely it is, what they are actually talking about is the smell of baby's brains, coming through their skulls?*

But I digress.

Mel says she's going to tell Penny about me. She thinks it's time, and I do too. Penny is one of the best and brightest and kindest people I know and I'd love to get to know her better. More to the point she's living with Mel now and hasn't seen any wool or yarn in the house and it's making her start to ask questions. I also think it's time you told Helen. She's family now – to me, as well as you. I'd love to talk to her more about her great-grandma and her mum. I remembered more about her great-grandma when I went over to her old house that night, including my old name, which was Cowper (I prefer Carl btw). I'm sorry I went there without telling anyone, but there was no real choice about it. I knew I had to do it. And I knew I needed to be alone. When I was on the cliffs, under all the vines, I felt like the sea was inside me, vibrating. And while it was inside me, it made this noise, which came out of my mouth, without me having any control over it. What I felt the noise was saying was, 'Soon but not yet.' I remembered a loud ticking clock, and some scrawny-looking hens. Then I saw them through a triangular space in front of me, even though all that's in the house now is dirt and broken bricks. I remembered the clock from before, the way I used to look at it, and the way I would know then, too, know I had been here before. I think you're right in saying the time will probably be October. Not just because there's a symmetry to it but because I feel it. I know everything that's going to happen in this odd way that seems to come from outside myself, like the way someone must have known what they were doing when they wrote the songs we really love: the ones that withstand everything and keep living on and improving.

So, if we are right, that gives us four months. By that time the dahlias out the back that I just deadheaded will be long gone. I thought of deadheading yesterday, when you asked me if I had any theories about why all this happens the way it happens: why I keep coming here, then going away for the exact same amount of time, then coming back. Maybe it's like deadheading? It's a way of promoting new growth by removing what's dead. Not that I'm dead. But I do feel overloaded, full of seeds, like I need to be snipped and renewed. But maybe that's nonsense. As I said, I don't know much. What I do know, however, are the following facts:

1. *I am extremely happy to still be here, in this special place, which is ours*
2. *I love you*
3. *You unpickled me, and for that I am forever grateful*

All the bees,
Carl

Dear Eric,
I regret to inform you that the time has arrived to terminate our long friendship. It was quite good, at times, while it lasted, but I feel we need to recognise that we have grown apart and I have moved onto better things. You are far too Liverpudlian for me and possess too many old trousers.

Not really. I was wondering if you, Carl, Billy and Helen would like to come to our belated housewarming party next month, which we are also – drum roll – quietly treating as an engagement party. 21 June. Midsummer's Day. Be there or be rectangular.

All the bees,
Mel

P.S. I was thinking about Cornwall yesterday, as I'm planning to go over there to do an archery course. Isn't that whole 'Tre' naming thing they have great? You just add 'Tre' to a word or phrase and it becomes a place. 'Trebadger', 'Trebigdickenergy', 'Trerentaghost', 'Treremovetoxicpeoplefromyourlife'. They absolutely rip up the naming rulebook. It's a totally open playing field.

P.P.S. Penny and I can't stop thinking about what you and Carl told us about him living at the manor, or the building that used to be there. That stuff he said about the monks that he saw moving through the garden in their long dark robes, with the scissors, clipping the blackberry bushes, it's really stuck with me. I'm not surprised he was a bit subdued that day! Bloody hell. I wish he knew when it was and there was some way he could find out. Penny can't stop talking about it. She's been on the phone to the Devon History Society and the parish council already. She's determined to do everything she can to research the place's history. It's got her wondering about that ghost her sister saw in the bathroom. Perhaps it was a wet monk?

P.P.P.S. Billy and Helen, eh? Exciting or what?

P.P.P.P.S. Re: 'all the bees' and the 'misty ped' typo Billy and Carl mentioned . . . and I made another one I liked the other day: 'sceptic tank'. The half-empty receptacle where the cynical fish hang out, seeking the bad side of everything and carping about society's ills.

The Untrue and Racist Thing That People Thought About Crows

That spring, summer and autumn – the spring, summer and autumn of 2024, the final spring, summer and autumn that Carl lived in the cottage behind the cliffs with Eric – a change could be observed in Frank the crow: a mellowing and chastening, what, at a stretch, might even have been called 'a gooey phase'. It was as if, having decided to finally stop being a twat, he had stepped over a line and there was no backtracking, only a future where decency, warmth and humour were to be embraced. In June, when Carl dropped some leftover tortilla chips from Mel and Penny's engagement party on the lawn for him, he delighted in holding them in his beak and prancing around on the wall, pretending to be a freakishly large male blackbird. Having finally let go of his bitterness regarding the death of his wife in a road accident on the A35 in 2020, he took a lover: a sadly nameless female crow from Wootton Fitzpaine who looked a lot like him, if you weren't a crow, and didn't if you were, whom

Frank had first met while squabbling over a discarded half-bag of chips near a bin on the slipway to Charmouth Beach. Observing that he was simultaneously larger and calmer than many of the other male crows she had met, she quickly marked him out as a solid candidate for life partnership, and when jealous rivals told her about his misspent cantankerous past, she paid no mind. That summer he became her idol and her rock, although he never quite appeared as solicitous of her attentions as he did of Carl's and Eric's. When he saw either of them working in the garden he was quick to swoop down onto a shoulder and, following rebukes and remonstrations, eventually learned to do so in a fashion that did not leave bruises or cuts. When Carl woke, at dawn, and padded out through the damp grass to inspect his vegetable patch, Frank was always there, waiting patiently for the previous night's scraps on a stone mermaid that Eric had bought for £11 in Exmouth in 2012, whose long curling flipper Frank had come to think of as his own personal settee. The smears he'd left on the window of the garden room by hurling himself at it were a distant memory. They had come to seem, to him, as well as to Eric and Carl, like the work of an entirely different crow.

But while Frank had learned restraint and decorum of late, he still prioritised fitness and took great enjoyment from the muscularity of his own body. While Eric and Carl were out on walks or buying trips or social calls, he spread his wings and took advantage of his full natural radius. Being – though he would sometimes humbly shrug off the title in public – one of West Dorset's strongest crows, and still just about clinging to his prime, this extended to an impressive fourteen miles in every direction. As he flew he would sometimes spot Eric's van below him. The untrue and racist thing that people thought about crows – that they all looked the same – was in fact true of cars and vans nowadays, but Frank often flew above Eric's van and, using his superior sight and hearing, could easily tell it apart from the other black ones on the road by the specific grumble-squeak from its engine and the light-blue smoke spilling from its exhaust pipe.

Frank flew west, over the hut that Billy had begun building in his garden from the remains of the old radar station, and over the new radar station, and over Charmouth. He flew over the spot where he met his new girlfriend, over the spot where the coast pivots for the Devon border, over Lyme Regis golf course, where Eric once mistook a dropped leather golf glove for a dead bat, over Greta Berlin's hauntingly brilliant statue of the teenage nineteenth-century palaeontologist Mary Anning determinedly carrying her hammer and her ichthyosaur skeleton through the dark woods, a statue that Carl had obsessed over like no other. He flew over Lyme – over its mollycoddled gulls and disquieting bookshop mannequins and faded mid-twentieth-century ideas of utopian single-storey riverside living – and into the Undercliff, over the ruined house he'd clandestinely watched Carl enter and poke around in back in winter. He flew over mess made by trees and rocks and animals and weather so much more attractively and successfully than humans could ever make a mess. He flew over Seaton and a veterinary surgery where an exhausted Mel had once taken Bathsheba for some blood tests and, while she waited, fallen asleep with her head on the vet's examining table, until she was woken by a man carrying a basket containing a frail and poorly goose. He flew over the paths and caves around Beer, where the Georgian smuggler and renowned crow-friend Jack Rattenbury stored his contraband. He flew over Branscombe, where the cliffs begin to redden, as if embarrassed by their own beauty. He saw the Weston Plats whose special microclimate allows the easy growing of flowers, strawberries and well-salted cliff vegetables. He saw the chalets there, established on the Plats in the 1950s and 60s. He saw the wooden steps that Eric had once been pointlessly told off for sitting on by a squat inheritor of one of the chalets, known to his two friends and numerous enemies as Stumpy Belltower. He saw the damage that winter and spring's rain had done, causing a landslip and annihilating and swallowing a couple of the chalets in this idyllic place where people came to escape when they felt the world was swallowing them. Frank flew no further than this, even though he sometimes yearned to, sometimes yearned to reach the Exe Estuary and the mysterious places that he didn't know were called Dawlish and Teignmouth and Torquay and Pain Town, but suspected – rightly – were places of funfairs, places of abundant litter, places of overflowing bins stuffed with tasty treats. It was a phenomenal achievement that he had flown as far as he had. No other crow who lived near the Golden Cap had ever flown further.

Frank flew south, over the sea. He picked at the parts of deceased fish that the mollycoddled gulls of the area had rejected: fins and half-eyeballs and spinal dorsals. And when he was tired of the sea and craved calmer, dryer air, he flew north, inland. He flew over the garage whose head mechanic, during an MOT for Eric's van in 2019, had found a rodent's nest living in its engine but reassured Eric that 'the rodent seems to have vacated the engine now so no work was necessary and you have not been charged for the clearing of the nest'. He flew over the tyre-fitters whose market research text message, on the first glorious day of this summer, Eric had mistakenly replied to with a photograph of himself wearing some seaweed as a hat, having believed he was sending it to Mel. He flew over the tips and farms, smelling the smell of things that shouldn't have been burned. He flew over the buttercup meadow where Billy and Helen would soon conceive their first and only child. He flew over Grape Lane – once known as Grope Lane and once, quite a long time before that, known as Gropecunt Lane – and over Grandfathers Knapp and Fishpond Bottom Road and Hell Lane and Puck's Lane. He flew over a lane where a man called Joe Bester with startlingly dark eye sockets had once, back in his youth when his eye sockets were less startlingly dark, taken a 'Police Aware' sticker that his friend Christ had stolen from a police station and placed it on a Ford Fiesta that had been neither crashed nor stolen and belonged to a lady he'd never met called Sylvia Monkhouse who was known amongst her peers to be a busybody, especially when it came to the topic of dogs. He flew over a calm, fully matured swan that once, way back when it was a rowdy juvenile delinquent, Long Arm Jeff had told to '*Settle!*' He flew over the warehouse where Joe Bester now repaired public-transport upholstery while waiting keenly for the end of each day so he could get back to the 'Extraterrestrial In Dorset' Facebook page he'd started in 2010 which continued to give Joe's life meaning and now contained over 200 doctored photographs of spaceships and mythical beasts, including one of a 'sea hound' he genuinely believed he'd seen, nearly twenty-one years ago, when he was, by his own admission, a bit of a young dickhead.

He flew east of Axminster, where on one of their favourite walks of the summer Eric and Carl had watched cocksure jersey bullocks being herded along a lane and trying their best to escape up drives and paths and into the homes of strangers, like a couple of dozen four-legged John Martyns. He flew over Bridport, where the Bridport Young Knitters group convened in the town's library and the knitters wondered, once again, why a member of their group called Carly, who was always so wonderfully positive in her comments about everyone's work on their Instagram page, and had a beautiful photo of her dog as her avatar, never showed her face or turned up at one of the meetings in person. He flew over the three-storey Victorian terrace of Eric and Mel's friend Marianne, who had recently cheated very publicly on her husband, and whom Eric and Mel now referred to as 'Marianne Unfaithful'. He flew a little north east of there, over the muscular and oddly astral Eggardon Hill, with its deep-time secrets, where he always became dizzied by ancestral memories and often saw the ghosts of hirsute dark-brown cattle. He scanned, with his superior vision, across from there, beyond the edge of his radius, towards the gorsey colosseums of land above the Cerne Abbas Giant, and to Dorchester, where Mel, upon waking from general anaesthetic in a community hospital, had intuitively punched a nurse called Darryl in the face, who had done arguably nothing to deserve such an attack.

Frank generally preferred to delay his flights east along the coast until autumn. There was something about that time of year that suited the shape of the land over there, something about the light in those parts that complimented the shortening days. In a sociable and curious mood, on one of his journeys over there in late October, he was pleased to hear a familiar sound below him and see a black van, moving parallel to the River Bride, through Burton Bradstock. He followed the van past Hive Beach and the entrance to the National Trust car park above Cogden Beach and the turn to Puncknowle – the turn to Puck's Knoll – then followed it on past St Catherine's Chapel, built by the swan-loving monks of the area in the 1300s, and down the hill towards Abbotsbury. The van turned sharp right here, and made its way down to a car park near the Subtropical Gardens, where, in spring, some of Dorset's most spectacular magnolias and camellias could be seen. Here – to Frank's relief, since this was the outer limit of his eastern radius – the van's driver and his five passengers got out and moved towards the beach. Between them, they carried two bags, out of the top of which Frank could see wine bottles and – excitingly – at least four generous grab-bags of salted snacks. The group was notably tactile, stopping every few yards to hug each other, and there was a general atmosphere of revelry amongst them. They moved down towards the beach, avoiding the main route and diverting slightly west along a footpath that Frank had felt greatly positive towards ever since the day in 2022 when, cruising low above its turf, he had chanced upon the corpses of two entirely intact freshly dead pheasants and the back half of a meaty hare.

It was a little before 5 p.m., chilly and crepuscular. Only the thinnest smattering of other people could be found on the beach, most of them making their way back to their cars and none of them within five or six pebble-throws of the party of friends. The sea was moderately calm and, with its tones, appeared to socially shun the sky above it, reflecting none of its grandiose purples and pinks. Frank found the ground uninteresting today and, preferring to stay as near to the complicated clouds as was practical, passed the time by grooming his feathers in the branches of a nearby ash tree. Everyone drank and ate and nothing much happened for the best part of half an hour but then, as if called by an unseen voice, one member of the party – Frank's favourite, if he was honest (and honesty was one of Frank's strong points) – made his way slowly into the sea, walking out farther and father, until completely devoured by the grey waves.

Frank did not fear death. Death was an important part of his business and business was never a thing to be feared. Death could be correct. But not always. When Frank's wife had been killed by a cement truck on the A35, for example: that was not correct. You couldn't argue with death, but that didn't mean death was always right. So when Frank watched Carl standing on his hind legs and striding into the water, striding so far out that he was no longer visible, he felt simultaneously sad – as sad, perhaps, as a crow could be – and at peace with events, but when, about a minute later, shortly after the last bit of wet brown fur could be seen above the foam and froth, he saw Eric, at a much speedier pace, following in pursuit, Frank felt less philosophical. Also, there was something more personal at stake here: a whole lifestyle. Frank had observed enough houses now – especially in this region, which was popular with people of retirement age – to know that when generous creators and distributors of leftovers who'd lived in them died there was no guarantee they'd be replaced by similarly generous creators and distributors of leftovers. Frank felt a bit selfish for dwelling on this – a bit less like his more recent, decent self – but in truth he *wasn't* just thinking about himself. He had a partner to support now. Kids had never been on his radar, but who could predict how his priorities might alter in years to come? Existence was change. Change was existence. As he knew only too well, from recent events. So, watching Eric's progress into the sea, hearing his uninhibited cries of sorrow and pain, Frank picked nervously at a claw with his beak. He stuck around. And when he watched the remaining four members of the party chase their friend into the surf and collectively drag him back to safety, it was with a level of relief that Frank had not known for many years.

He continued to watch, though, knowing he was not quite yet in the clear. As he landed – with the new gentleness that Carl had taught him – on the big hard pebbles, not ten yards away, none of the drenched humans noticed him. Not the supine Eric. Not Billy and Helen, crouched over Eric. Not Mel, beside them, who had not previously realised her own arms were that strong. And not Penny, hovering a few feet directly above them all. Why would they? Crows are not what humans notice at moments of intense personal crisis, although humans might be well-advised to change that. Frank moved in a little closer, heard a splutter, the sound of hard-worn fighting lungs.

'It's ok,' he heard his one remaining bankable food course announce. 'I'm still here.'

Then, having realised that everything was going to be fine, Frank flew home, taking the scenic route, through the most colourful part of the sky.

Acknowledgements

A special thank you to Elizabeth Garner, whose close reading and instinctive understanding of this novel in its earliest draft helped me turn it into a better one. And to Ellie McKechnie, who was by my side from beginning to end and helped me believe in it. And to all the readers who took the bold step of funding it when it was just a twinkle in my eye.

I also want to thank the following, for their vital contributions to *Everything Will Swallow You*'s existence and fine-tuning:

Editorial and beyond: Imogen Denny, Hayley Shepherd, all of the team at Swift Press and my heroic agent Ed Wilson.

Art: Joe McLaren, Jo Cox, Mark Ecob.

Conversations and inspiration: Michael Tanner, Roy Gregory, Jane Featonby, Ben Tallamy, Will Twynham, Andrew Male.